LAURA

The QUEEN of All that LIVES

Burning Ember Press

This is a work of fiction. References to real people, events, establishments, organizations, or locales are intended only to provide authenticity, and are used fictitiously. All other characters, and all incidents and dialogue, are drawn from the author's imagination and are not to be construed as real.

A Burning Ember Book
Published in the United States by Burning Ember Press, an imprint of Lavabrook Publishing Group.

GRANDMA HALL,

You're the woman I aspire to be. No dedication can do you justice. Thank you for being a beautiful human being.

Now, I am become Death, the destroyer of worlds.
—Robert Oppenheimer, quoting the Bhagavad Gita

PROLOGUE

WE FOUND HER.

Finally.

There had always been rumors that the undying king's queen lived. That she slept deep in the earth. That the king, mad with grief, put her there.

I step up to the golden sarcophagus, my men fanning out around it.

They weren't rumors.

The subterranean temple is just as the blueprint said it would be—same size, same location. Only, my information never told me it would look like this. I'm a hardened man, and even I have goosebumps being in this place. The gold, the marble, the shrine set in the middle of the room surrounded by a moat of water. All to encase a supposedly living woman. And not just any woman; we're retrieving a being this king and the rest of the world have all but worshiped for a hundred years.

"You're recording all this?" I say to one of my men, my voice echoing. They're the first words any one of us has breathed since entering the chamber.

He nods, the compact camera he holds focused on the coffin.

Styx would kill a hundred men to be here. Instead he's forced to watch from behind a screen.

I holster my gun and reach out, my hand trailing over the golden ivy that covers the sarcophagus. I find the lip of the lid, and my fingers curl over the edge. I'm almost afraid of what we'll find once we lift this sucker. I know what Serenity Lazuli looks like—everyone does—but the mythical woman has been gone for a century. For all I know, we're about to come face-to-face with her mummified remains.

"On the count of three," I say.

"One." *If the king finds us, we're all dead men.*

"Two." *If what lies inside this casket is everything we hoped for, the war might finally end.*

"Three."

My lips curl back as we push off the lid. Beneath it ...

"Holy shit," I breathe.

Inside rests a woman, her arms crossed over her chest, her eyes closed. I take in her long golden hair, the smooth, pale skin, the deep scar that mars an otherwise beautiful face.

They definitely weren't rumors, and these are definitely not Serenity Lazuli's mummified remains. As we watch, her eyes move beneath closed lids.

The queen lives.

CHAPTER 1

Serenity

I DRAW IN a breath of air.

Exhale.

I draw in another. And another.

The air tastes good. Is that even possible? To taste air? Because in this moment I swear I can. I take deeper and deeper lungfuls. Light filters in through my closed lids, beckoning like an eager lover.

"She's waking up!"

"I can see that, you wanker."

"Harvey, you capturing all this?"

"Styx is getting the livestream as we speak."

"Would you fuckers shut up? You're going to scare her."

My eyes flutter open. At first, I see nothing. The light is

too bright. But then my eyes adjust, slowly. Color bleeds in and my surroundings began to take shape.

I stare up at a metal roof. My brows furrow. The king's ceilings are either gilded molding or exposed wood. Not dented, rust-stained metal. And never so low.

That's when I notice the rocking. My body shakes from side to side. I'm inside a vehicle, I realize.

What the hell is going on?

I brace my hands against the edge of the bed I lay in, my pulse climbing.

Nothing about this is right. People don't wake up like this.

Where am I, and why can't I remember how I got here?

"I can't believe we did it."

I startle at the voice. I have an audience—of course I do. Situations like this don't just happen; people orchestrate them.

I begin to sit up.

"Whoa, whoa, my queen," a man to my right says, placing a hand on my chest, "easy."

I glance down at the hand touching my chest. I follow it back to its owner. A soldier in his late twenties stares back. He's not the king, and these are not the king's men. Which can only mean ...

I got fucking abducted.

Again.

"Who are you?" I ask, my voice hard.

I'm going to have to hurt more people, kill more people. That's the only way anyone's going to learn that I make a terrible captive.

The man dips his head. "Jace Bridges, Your Majesty. Former infantryman in the king's army. Current regional commander of the special ops unit, European division, of the First Free Men."

All I got from that was that this man is dangerous. That's helpful to know.

Five other men circle my bed. All soldiers by the looks of them, all equipped with weaponry, all standing between me and freedom. They stare a little too intensely, making me distinctly aware that for all my training, I am still just a woman lying in a bed in the back of some vehicle, surrounded by a bunch of men. There are too many of them and only one of me. I could easily be overpowered.

As my gaze sweeps over the soldiers, they dip their heads and murmur, "Your Majesty."

And all of them show me reverence. This is a first. I'm used to being hated. I don't know what to do with their respect.

One of them holds a camera, its lens trained on me. I frown, unsettled at the sight. If they're here to liberate me, why do I feel like an animal on exhibit?

The First Free Men. I've never heard of the organization, but I hope to God the king has, otherwise I'm going this one alone.

The king.

"Where is Montes?" I demand.

The six of them share a look.

"He's far away, Your Majesty," Jace says. The way he says the words, it's as though they're meant to reassure me.

Where *is* he? And why can't I remember?

"Is he dead?" I ask. And now I really have to control my voice. The thought of my brutal husband ceasing to exist is … unfathomable.

Another look passes between them.

"No, Your Majesty."

I release a shaky breath.

Alive.

I can work with alive.

"Why did you take me?" My eyes pass over the soldiers again.

They look at me wondrously, like I hold the answers to all their problems.

I'm in a car full of eager men. Not good.

Jace leans forward, resting his forearms on his thighs. "How much do you remember?"

Remember? My blood chills. If this is another one of the king's memory serums …

But that cannot be. I wouldn't remember him, I wouldn't remember myself—I wouldn't remember anything before this moment.

And I do. Don't I?

I eye the soldier warily. "Remember what?"

Jace sighs and rubs his face. "Does someone else want to take this on?"

"Shit no," one of the other soldiers says.

My heart is still pounding like mad, but now it has more to do with confusion than adrenaline.

"Your Majesty—"

"Stop calling me that," I interject. I hate the title, hate that the king made me what I am.

Jace inclines his head. "Mrs. Lazuli—"

Naturally, he chooses a name that's even worse.

"Serenity," I say.

"Serenity," he repeats. "My men and I were given the task of finding the lost queen."

I frown.

"We've been searching for you for decades."

I stop breathing.

What in God's name ... ?

I look over them again just to memorize their faces.

These men have lost their minds. People don't disappear for decades. *I* don't disappear for decades.

I went to bed last night, right after ... right after ...

"We found you buried beneath one of the king's palaces. He's kept you there for close to half a century, as far as we can tell."

Now we've gone from decades to fifty years? This is like one of those stories that gets bigger every time it's retold.

"What do you want?" I ask, sitting up a little straighter and eyeing the back doors of the vehicle.

"Jace, she needs proof," one of the other men says.

Jace squeezes the back of his neck. "I don't *have* proof."

"Wait," another soldier says. He reaches into the back pocket of his fatigues and pulls out a folded piece of paper. He tosses it onto my lap.

I raise an eyebrow as I stare down at it.

Nothing about the situation is going as it should. My kidnappers are not demanding things of me; they're beseeching me to understand what they're telling me. To be fair, what they are telling me is insane.

"A piece of paper is supposed to convince me I've been gone for fifty years?" I say.

"Not gone," Jace corrects. "*Asleep*. We found you in one of the king's fabled Sleepers."

My attention snaps to Jace. The Sleeper. I'd almost forgotten about the machine. The last time I had gotten in one of those was right after the king and I lost our child.

The memory has me tightening my lips and squeezing the sheets beneath my fingers. At least I can rule out memory suppressant. I remember that moment in vivid detail, and oh how I would like to forget.

"Open the paper, Serenity," Jace says.

I grab it, mostly because I'm curious. That, and I'm still unarmed and surrounded by six soldiers who have taken a keen interest in me.

I open the crumpled sheet.

Staring back at me … is me.

It's more of a sketch, really. My face is outlined in black and shaded in yellow and navy. The king's colors. I stare directly at the viewer, my face resolute.

I touch my scar as I notice the one on paper. It starts at the corner of my eye and drags down my cheek, making me look dangerous, wicked even. Beneath my image is the phrase, *Freedom or Death.*

I don't know what to make of this. Their proof hasn't convinced me of anything, except that maybe a few of my subjects don't hate me as much as I assumed they did.

"That poster has been in circulation for almost a century."

I fold the paper. "And now it's a century. By the time

we arrive to whatever destination you have in mind, you'll tell me I've been gone for a millennia."

"Jace, you're doing great man," one of the other soldiers says. It's a jibe, and it only confuses me more.

"If you want to fucking jump in, be my guest," Jace says.

He returns his attention to me. He rubs his cheek, studying my face. "How am I going to get you to believe me?"

"You're not," I say. I'm not a big fan of trusting strangers, especially ones that kidnap me.

And there it is again. These men *took* me. Perhaps if it had been the first time, or even the second that this had happened to me, I'd be more interested in escape than revenge. But it isn't. When I get the chance, and I will get the chance, I will mow these men down.

My eyes flick to Jace's gun.

His gaze follows mine to his weapon. He covers it with his hand. "My queen, I understand you are confused, but if you get violent, we will have to as well. And I really don't want that."

I meet his eyes, and the corner of my mouth curls slowly. I'm made of violence and pain. He might as well have welcomed me home.

The atmosphere in the vehicle changes subtly. The men are on guard.

"What do you want?" I say.

Jace looks at me square in the eye, and I notice that, just like his comrades, he stares at me like I'm the answer to his problems. "We want you to end the war."

CHAPTER 2

Serenity

THE LAST I remembered, the war was over.

No—war *had* broken out again. The king's council had turned on him. I had been working with the king to suppress the insurgents in South America.

"You do realize I have been doing exactly that since war broke out."

The soldiers exchange another look.

"Goddamnit," I say, "stop acting like I'm crazy."

The vehicle falls silent for several seconds, the only sound the jiggle of the bed's rickety frame and the men's weapons.

"No one believes you're crazy," Jace finally says.

He sounds so reasonable. That in and of itself is infuriating.

He leans forward. "Look at what you're wearing."

I narrow my eyes at him.

"This isn't a trick. Look at your outfit."

Hesitantly, I do.

I wear a fitted bodice of pale gold silk. A layer of delicate lace flowers overlays it.

I pull the blanket covering my legs aside. The material drips down my body, all the way to my feet. I hadn't noticed it earlier, but now that Jace has forced my eyes to take in my clothing, I realize how unusual my outfit is.

"Do you remember when you put that dress on?" he asks.

I run my fingers over the material. The honest truth is I've never seen this dress in my life.

"Do you?" Jace pushes.

I look up. All six of them are watching me with baited breath. They're waiting for ... something.

"No." Without meaning to, I've fisted the soft material.

Jace rubs his hands together. "What is the last thing you remember?"

It's a good question, one I hadn't seriously pondered since I woke up here.

My eyes lose focus as I retrace my final memories. The king and I had been working together to stop his traitorous advisors.

I remember him saying he loved me.

The revelation hits me all over again. It never should've happened, but in my world, a world filled with bloodly, broken bodies, love had grown in the most desolate of places.

I force myself to move past this memory, to the next one. Waking up, the blood-speckled sheets. I worried that the king had seen the evidence of my sickness. I reassured myself that he hadn't.

I searched for him, but I couldn't find him. I was sent to a room on the east wing and told he'd be there. But he wasn't.

It was a trap.

It was a *trap*.

I go cold all over.

The king had me cornered. I jumped three stories into the waiting arms of his guards.

And then ...

"This isn't forever," the king says.

The last thing I see is the king's face, and the last thing I hear is his voice. He leans over me, and I feel a hand stroke my face. "We'll only be apart for a short while. Once we cure your sickness, you'll be mine again."

I choke on a wrathful cry. He betrayed me. Drugged me, forced me to endure the Sleeper until he could cure me of my cancer.

I'd imagined months, years maybe, but decades?

I feel my nostrils flare as a tear drips down my cheek.

Not just decades.

A century, if what these men say is true. Locked away so that he wouldn't have to lose me.

It feels like someone has stacked stones on my chest. I can't seem to catch my breath.

Monsters will be monsters. Why I thought mine was

any different, I cannot say.

Perhaps because I am a foolish girl.

I can feel it, my anger, like a storm brewing on the horizon. Right now, my shock and pain are all I can focus on. But my fury is coming, and when it hits, no one is going to be adequately prepared for it.

My eyes return to the soldiers. They all wear looks of pity. They can keep their pity; I don't want it.

I'm no longer skeptical.

"Exactly how long have I been gone?" I ask Jace.

His eyes are sad when he says, "From our best estimates, one hundred and four years."

I AM 124 years old.

I stare at Jace, my nostrils flaring as I breathe through my nose.

One hundred and twenty-four years old.

My brain won't process that. It can't. No one lives that long.

The soldiers are quiet, and I hate that I have an audience. I'm so close to falling apart; I don't want these strangers to see me when that happens.

I turn my hands over in my lap. My skin has retained the smoothness of youth. I run my fingers over my flesh.

Over a century old. I wonder where the years are hidden. They must've left some mark. All things leave marks.

All things, save for the king's inventions. Those remove things—wounds, memories, ... *age.*

An entire century went by, and I saw none of it. The

king had kept me in a coffin, not dead but not alive.

I recognize the moment the truth settles on my shoulders.

Loss so big my body can't hold it is expanding, expanding. It tries to crawl up my throat.

Had I thought before I was the loneliest girl in the world? If what these men are telling me is true, and I'm beginning to believe it is, I have nothing left.

Nothing.

The world has passed me by, and the people and time I belong to are now long gone. I haven't seen anything beyond the metal walls of this car, but would I recognize the world outside? The people? A hundred years before I was put in the Sleeper, the world was a far different place from the one I lived in. I have every reason to believe that same logic applies to the future—*present.*

I rub my forehead agitatedly. Everything and everyone I've ever known is gone. Everyone except for the man I love, the man who did this to me.

My surroundings blur as my eyes water. But I will not shed another tear for that abomination. Not now, in front of these men, and not when I'm alone.

He deserves nothing but my wrath.

And what has he been doing this whole time while I rotted away?

I already know the answer.

He's been killing, screwing, ruling.

Betrayal is giving way to rage. Everything I have ever cherished the king has taken from me, either directly or indirectly. My family, my land, my freedom, my life. And I gave him everything. My body, my heart, my soul.

I'm taking them back. I hope he's enjoyed my stone cold heart for the century he's owned it. Next time I see him, I'm going to carve it right out of his chest.

I level my gaze on Jace. "You said you wanted me to end your war?"

He must see the mayhem in my eyes, because he hesitates. Then, slowly, he nods.

There is nowhere Montes can hide where I won't find him. And when I do find him—

"I'll end it."

The King

I SIT DOWN heavily on the edge of my bed and loosen my tie. The flight was long, the day even longer, but I can't go to bed. Not yet.

I shrug off my jacket and roll up my sleeves.

Someone knocks on my door.

"Tomorrow," I call. The world is going to have just as many problems then as it does now.

When the footsteps retreat, I move to the back of the room, right to the garish painting of Cupid and Psyche. I grab the edge of the frame and pull it away from the wall. It swings back with ease, and behind it is a door, barred to all, save for me.

I press my thumb into the scanner embedded next to it.

The light blinks green, and then the sealed off entrance hisses open.

I step into the narrow hallway sandwiched between the rooms of the palace, the cold air already settling into my bones. Above me the overhead lights flick on.

I used to believe that secret passageways were the things of spy novels, but during the course of my long reign, these hidden features have saved my life and land a time or two.

My shoes click against the stone floor, and I slide my hands into my pockets as I pass room after room on either side of the hall. One-way mirrors expertly camouflaged as decorations allow me to catch glimpses of my guests.

All those years ago, Serenity taught me a valuable lesson: trust will earn you a knife in the back and a shallow grave. This is my insurance policy against that.

Tonight, the rooms are all empty. I've been gone for a while.

Too long.

I'm drawn down the passageway like a moth to a flame. Even in sleep, Serenity calls to me.

The lights flicker on, one after another, as I gradually descend into the lowest levels of the palace.

It's when I get to the entrance of her mausoleum that I feel the first stirrings of unease. One of the doors hangs slightly open.

I stop, my eyes studying the inconsistency.

This has happened before. There have been times in the past when I've forgotten to close the door tightly. A bad habit borne from the fact that no one but me accesses this place.

I push it open, all senses on alert.

More than a hundred marble steps lie between me and

my wife. I take each one slowly, letting the peace of this place soothe my nerves.

The lights here are already on; they're always on. I can't bear the thought of Serenity laying here, alone in the darkness.

As I head down the stairs, the rest of the room unfolds before me. Grotesquely large marble columns hold up the cavernous ceiling, a domed roof at its pinnacle. Gold and indigo tiles are embedded into the walls of this place. And finally, the pool of water, the walkway, and Serenity's golden—

All my breath slips out of me when I catch sight of her sarcophagus.

The lid sits askew.

I can't move for a second; all I can do is stare. I've come here a thousand times, laid my eyes on that Sleeper a thousand more. Never once has the image changed.

I begin to move again. First I walk, then I run.

I reach her sarcophagus, her empty sarcophagus, and my worst fears are confirmed.

Serenity's gone.

CHAPTER 3

Serenity

"SO WHAT ARE you planning to do with me?" I say, assessing the six soldiers from my bed.

As far as I can tell, these men didn't wake me to let me go. The camera is proof of that, the weapons are proof of that. Hell, the way this situation is unfolding is proof of that. No one's treating me like I'm a victim. They're treating me like I'm an acquisition.

I give them hard looks. These men might be my rescuers, but they're also my captors, no matter how agreeable they've been.

Jace leans back against the metal wall of the vehicle. "Right now," he says, "We're trying to lose the king."

I lean back against the partition that separates the back

of the vehicle from the front, getting nice and cozy myself. "And once you lose the king?" I ask.

"We'll take you to our compound."

Just as the Resistance did when they captured me. Yes. This is all very familiar.

"And then?" I ask.

The car rumbles and shakes in the silence.

"And then, once you're ready, we'll hand you over to the West, where you belong."

"Where I belong," I muse.

It rubs me raw to hear these men talk like they have my best intentions in mind. They have no idea where I belong. *I* have no idea where I belong.

The only reason these men are even mentioning the West is because they've either been hired by them or they're going to get money from them when they hand me over.

I don't bother asking if I have any say in these plans. I already know I don't. Of course they didn't factor in the possibility that their slumbering queen might not agree with their schemes. That I might, in fact, violently oppose them. I'm sure they didn't consider that I might have an opinion at all.

But I do.

From the moment my father and I arrived in Geneva all that time ago, I've been passed around between men. The king, the Resistance, and now these men. How cruel must I become before people will begin to see me as a formidable opponent?

"One problem with your plans," I say.

Jace and his men wait for me to speak.

"Every time I've slipped from the king's clutches, he's retrieved me." I meet each soldier's eyes. "Every. Time."

Perhaps it's my imagination, but I swear the men shift a little uneasily in their seats.

"With all due respect, Serenity," Jace says, "we are good at what we do."

"I don't doubt that." The fact that they were able to retrieve me from the king's Sleeper is proof enough. I'm sure Montes hid me somewhere secure. "But the king I knew never did like it when people took away his toys." And I am his toy. I always have been.

"Maybe King Lazuli is not the same man you knew," Jace says.

That, I am certain of. A single year can change a person. A hundred is enough to evolve a man into whatever thing he wants to become. I can't even fathom the weight of all that time.

"Maybe," I agree.

It doesn't matter how much the king has changed; if he didn't care about losing me, these soldiers wouldn't be fleeing from him. They know that, I know that, and, unfortunately for them, the king knows that as well.

I fold my hands over my stomach and settle in. Hunting season has begun, and the only creatures that are sure to die are the six surrounding me.

THE CAR FALLS into silence after that. I have plenty of questions, but I want to sort them out before I voice them.

A hundred and four years went by, and during that time the world still warred, the king still ruled, and while I slept, some portion of the people turned me into a mascot, if the crumpled sheet of paper I saw was anything to go by.

Even now, after all these decades—decades I can't fully wrap my mind around—people know of me, which means the king has likely spoken about me.

No—more than just spoken. He's commodified me, turned me into someone larger than life. Someone people can rally behind.

This is pure conjecture, but I know enough about politics and the king to assume my theory is true.

God, when I see that man, I'm going to gut him, navel to collarbone.

"So the world's still at war?" I ask.

"Off and on for the last century," one of the other men says. "The West and the East make flimsy treaties every once in a while, but they usually disintegrate after several years. A bad bout of plague swept through both hemispheres at the turn-of-the-century—that also led to a temporary cease-fire."

War, plague, vigilante organizations—these are things I'm familiar with. Perhaps this world isn't as different as I assumed it would be. I find that possibility unsettling. I don't want to fit into this world if it means that everyone that lives here is suffering.

I run a hand through my hair. It might be slightly longer than I remembered, but it's by no means as long as it should be. Nor are my nails, now that I look at them.

I squeeze my hand into a fist. I've been groomed, my body meticulously taking care of. And now I have to wonder: is my cancer gone? After all this time, has the king not found a cure? Or has he abandoned the quest altogether? Have my muscles atrophied?

I don't feel weak; I feel strong and ruthless.

I won't get the answers, regardless. These men don't have them, and the man who does ... I don't want words with him.

Just revenge.

I'M GETTING RESTLESS.

Propped up in the hospital bed as I am, these men don't see me as a threat. Dangerous, yes, but not a threat.

That's good for me. It means that when I'm ready to act, I'll have an extra several seconds to catch them off guard.

Now I just have to wait, and I hate laying here like an invalid. My legs are getting jittery. I haven't walked in a hundred years. I need to feel the ground beneath my feet.

That's not even my biggest concern, though. My anger has come calling. It causes me to focus on the soldiers' guns and the knives a couple of them carry. It'll be easy enough to divest them of their weapons. They haven't locked me up, which was probably their biggest mistake. Once I make my move, I won't give them the same concessions they've given me.

I squeeze my hands together and rein my rage in. Long ago the king taught me something important about strategy: often not acting when you want to is more effective than the alternative. I'll wait for my opening, and then I'll strike.

There are still things I want to know, questions I won't dare ask these men.

What is the king like?

Does he have a new wife?

Children?

Is he still made of nightmares and lost dreams?

"How, exactly, did you want me to end this war?" I ask.

These men aren't going to let me go. That much is obvious.

"The people love you. All you have to do is convince them to get behind us."

These men think they can use me for their own selfish motives. They need me to win over people for them.

My earlier rage simmers.

"And I'm supposed to go along with this," I say.

They're not even asking for my permission.

You don't ask a prisoner for permission.

"It's what the people want," Jace says.

Spoken like a true conqueror. People who want power convince themselves of the most implausible things. I don't doubt the world wants an end to war, but I do doubt they see the First Free Men as the godsend Jace seems to think they are.

"And what happens when you and the West take over the world?" I ask.

"We intend to work together to rebuild it," Jace answers.

Surprise, surprise, the First Free Men don't want to abdicate the old rulers nearly so much as they want to become ones.

"And how do you intend to do that?" I ask. I work to control my voice.

"Serenity, I'm a soldier, not a politician," Jace says.

And therein lies the problem.

"So you want to use me to help the First Free Men and the WUN achieve world domination, even though you and I don't know what policies either will push once they take over?"

"They won't abuse it the way—"

"*Everyone* abuses power," I say.

I feel it again. That crushing weight on my chest. Greed and power, power and greed—they're the most constant of companions. Once you get a taste of one, you must have the other.

"I'll never do it." I stare him in the eye as I speak. I have been used by everyone—the WUN, the king, the Resistance. And I'm so damn tired of it.

I won't be anyone else's puppet.

I've been so deeply immersed in the conversation that only now do I notice the muffled sounds of chopper blades and engines.

"*Hold on boys, the king's found us,*" the driver shouts from the other side of the partition, the vehicle accelerating even as he speaks.

"You *will* do it," Jace says. "Our leaders will make sure of that."

I smile at him then. People keep making the mistake of

thinking that I'm someone they can control.

Before I can respond, a series of bullets spray against the side of the car. The vehicle swerves violently, its rear end fishtailing.

I'm thrown from my bed into the lap of several soldiers. All around me I hear grunts and curses from the other men, none so loud as the driver's. Even though the metal partition muffles his voice, we can still hear his words clearly.

"*They're coming in hot!*" he shouts.

As if that's not obvious.

I use the distraction to steal a gun from the soldier whose lap I've fallen into. He doesn't have time to react as I unholster and aim it. Just as the car corrects itself, I press the barrel into his chest and fire.

The sound of the shot is deafening.

Now the men are scrambling, some trying to stop me, some still confused.

I lift my torso, swivel, and shoot three more men, all while bullets continue to graze the outside of the vehicle.

In seconds the van is filled with blood. Spraying, misting, dripping down limbs, pooling around dying men.

"*What the fuck is happening back there!*" the driver shouts at the same time Jace bellows, "Serenity!" I can hear the fury in the latter's voice.

The car lurches again, and I'm thrown off the now wounded soldiers' laps. My body rolls under the bed.

Two men left, plus the driver.

A moment later, the mobile hospital bed is thrown aside.

I bring my gun up. I don't bother looking at Jace's face. I fire off a shot that buries itself in his stomach. He stumbles back, his hand going to his wound.

"*By order of the king, stop the car and come out with your hands raised.*" The intercommed voice drifts in from somewhere outside.

The king found me, just as I assumed he would. Adrenaline floods my system. I didn't enjoy killing these men, but I will enjoy killing *him*.

Rather than slowing, our vehicle accelerates.

I hear a familiar click. The sound of a gun being cocked. I look up at the final soldier standing. He has a gun trained on me.

"Don't fucking move. I swear I'll shoot," he says. His body is trembling.

Freedom or death—the poster got that much correct about me. I'm not letting these men take me hostage, even if it costs me my life.

Lord knows I hadn't expected to live this long.

The soldier doesn't shoot. I can tell he wants to look at his fallen comrades, the ones that are moaning and those that have gone still, but he's smart enough to know that the moment he takes his eyes off of me, he'll join their ranks.

"We freed you," he says.

"Swapping one prison for another is no freedom," I tell him.

He opens his mouth, but I don't give him time to respond. I turn my gun on him, and I shoot.

The bullet takes him between the eyes. He remains upright for a moment longer, then his legs fold and his body lands with a thump.

I take a moment to catch my breath. Blood is seeping onto my dress. I can feel the warmth of it against my thighs. It sticks to my back, staining the material crimson. The vehicle is a mess of dead men.

I can still hear two clinging to life, their breathing labored. When I catch sight of them, my stolen gun comes up and I pull the trigger twice. It's not just a mercy killing. Dying men have nothing to lose. Even though I'm some long dead queen, and even though they needed me alive, none of that matters much when you're bleeding out.

The vehicle is still canting from side to side, and I can hear the driver yelling, but I can't tell if his words are meant for me or for the men bearing down on us.

I lean my back against the wall. Until the driver is either killed or decides to stop the car, there's not much for me to do except muse over my dark thoughts.

I reach out and exchange my gun for another, wiping the bloodied metal off on my skirts, taking in my surroundings again as I do so. I expected the future to be clean and shiny like a new penny. But I'm not seeing clean and shiny. The interior of this vehicle is rusted and stained. The men's uniforms are faded. And the soldiers themselves had a sinewy, desperate look about them.

I don't believe I like this future very much at all.

Suddenly the car slams to stop. I hear the driver side door being thrown open, followed by the sound of pounding footsteps moving farther and farther away from the vehicle. More gunfire goes off outside.

Time for me to move.

I push my body off the ground, blood seeping between my toes. For the first time in over a century I stand on my own two feet. The gown I wear drapes off my shoulders, and my drenched skirts stick to my legs.

I am a thing made of lace and blood. Swathed in silk and dripping with the dark deeds of men. I suppose I'm finally clothed accordingly.

The adrenaline I felt earlier resurges through my veins, and I grip my gun tighter.

I'd like to say that I can feel all those years I lost, that they left some imprint on my body or my mind. But I can't. Other than my memories feeling a bit foggy, there's no indication that I'd been asleep for decades rather than hours.

That makes this all worse. Because it seems like only hours ago the king told me he loved me. The moment that love became inconvenient for him, that fucker let me waste away. My breathing is coming faster and faster.

My monster, my husband, my captor. Soon he will be my victim.

I always considered Montes the thing of my nightmares. Now I'll be his.

Yes, I think as I step up to the vehicle's rear doors, *I will enjoy killing him.*

CHAPTER 4

Serenity

"COME OUT WITH *your hands up!*"

Even the orders of the future remain the same. Has nothing changed at all?

Pressing my back against one of the vehicle's doors, I use my hand to throw open the other. Instead of the gunfire I expect, a dozen different soldiers yell orders to exit the car. Those orders die away when they catch sight of the bodies.

Finally, fearfully, one calls out, "Serenity?"

I close my eyes. "I'm here," I say.

"Is there anyone with you?"

"No one living."

There's a pause as the king's men process that. Whatever they were told about me, I'm guessing that it hasn't prepared them for who I really am.

"You can come out, Your Majesty. We won't shoot."

I open my eyes and push away from the wall and into the open doorway. Sunlight touches my skin for the first time in a very long time. I soak it in. The day is full of firsts.

I step down from the car and onto the dirt road.

A hush falls over my audience as they catch sight of me. Then slowly, one by one, they kneel.

I stop and take them in. I had prepared for their horror, dressed in blood as I am, not their veneration.

There are dozens of soldiers circled around the car I exited. Behind their ranks, several armored vehicles are parked, lights flashing. Above us, a chopper circles.

It's all the same. The machinery might look slightly different, but it doesn't appear to have advanced in all this time. Prosperity breeds progress, and this, this isn't progress.

I fear for the world I have woken to.

Beyond the cars, scraggly rolling hills stretch out as far as the eye can see. I can feel the solitude of this place. The whistle of the wind seems to exacerbate it.

I haven't dropped my gun, but the soldiers don't seem to mind. As soon as they rise, I catch sight of their expressions.

I'm a ghost. A myth. That's the only explanation for the spooked ardor in their eyes.

All the while, rivulets of blood snake down my calves. They're right to be spooked of me.

I scour their ranks, looking for Montes. My eyes pass over dozens of men and a few women. I look them over once, twice. I didn't realize I held onto some sick hope until I feel it vanish.

The king isn't among these soldiers.

Even in the middle of my bloodlust, my heart aches. Last time I was captured, he was there to retrieve me.

A hundred years to change into whatever he wanted to become. A hundred years to fall out of love. A hundred years to forget about the broken, deadly girl he forced into marriage.

The king that rules these people isn't the same king I knew. All my anger and pain are wasted on a man who, in all probability, no longer cares for me. The world's still at war, after all. If I can really end it, the king should have taken me out of the Sleeper long ago.

Reflexively, my hand tightens on my gun.

Behind me is open road, in front of me is vengeance. My twisted heart is breaking, but I'm tempted to leave my heartbreak and revenge to the past and walk away from it all.

I take a step back. The soldiers tense.

"Your Majesty," one of them says, "we're the king's royal guard. You can trust us."

Normally, when people tell you that you can trust them, it means exactly the opposite.

I look around; the soldiers encircle me completely. If I ran, how far would I get before they caught me? How many more men would I have to kill? I don't want to spill more blood. And even if I did, I couldn't possibly take them all out before the king's guard immobilized me. I'd lose whatever precious power I had to wield.

I'm still not free.

"I need your word," I say to the man who spoke.

He pauses. "Anything, Your Majesty."

"Don't let the king put me back in the Sleeper." My voice breaks as I speak. "Kill me first."

"I'll vow to you anything but that."

"Then I can't go with you," I say.

"Your Majesty," he says, all but pleading with me, "what you're asking of me is treason. The king would—"

I press the barrel of the gun to my temple. The soldiers tense once more.

"I need your word," I say. "I need *everyone's* word, or I will pull the trigger," I say.

I hear murmuring from all around me. It takes a minute to make out what they're saying, but eventually I do.

"*Freedom or death.*"

Even out here in the midday heat, my skin prickles.

What have you made of me, Montes?

As my gaze sweeps over all of them, I begin to see them nod. Then, one by one, they take a knee and put their fists over their hearts.

"You have my word," the first soldier says.

"And mine," someone says from behind me.

"And mine."

"And mine."

This lonely space fills with the sound of dozens of oaths.

Slowly, I lower my gun. They don't know me, but now they show me allegiance.

I slip my weapon into the bodice of my dress and approach the king's guards, leaving bloody footprints in my wake.

Time to meet the man of my nightmares.

THE FUTURE IS no place for civilization.

I stare out the window of the chopper that circled high above me only hours ago. Even this far away from the surface of the earth I can see the destruction.

What does a century and a half of war look like? It looks like ghost towns, like rust and wreckage.

Here and there I see evidence of small towns where people must live. Nothing about these settlements follow any sort of city planning. There are no straight lines, and they have none of the symmetry I recall from the time before the war.

The king appears to have left more than just me to rot.

Over the course of the flight, I notice the settlements change. They get bigger, nicer, and they seem to have some of the symmetry that the other ones lacked. Perhaps not everyone is suffering in this new world.

Once we begin to descend, I have an idea of where we're headed. A swath of deep blue ocean stretches below me, broken up by islands every so often.

The king rebuilt his Mediterranean palace.

An unnatural dread settles into my bones. It's going to feel like nothing's changed. I just know it.

As soon as we land, I stand, and the king's guards step into formation.

Dried blood flakes off me. I suppress a grimace. I'm a mess.

The back of the chopper opens, and I follow the soldiers out, the metal floor cool against my bare feet. My hair kicks up around me as I exit the aircraft.

No cameramen wait for me, nor any eager civilians. Instead, an armored car idles off to the side of the runway, and other than the few soldiers that stand in front of it, we are alone.

Still no king.

And now my mind skips back to the first time the king retrieved me, back when I thought he ordered my father to be killed. Even knowing that he was last person I wanted to see, he'd come for me.

Perhaps that's why he didn't show up today.

Because it if there is one person I do want to see, it's Montes.

I WAS RIGHT.

The king's world is all so eerily familiar.

The palace is just as abominably beautiful as his palaces have always been. Just as big, just as grand, just as oppressive. I stare up at it as the armored car I ride in comes to a stop. Exotic, flowering vines grow up the sides of its walls. Beyond the walls, the ocean stretches on and on.

Just as before, no one waits for us.

I slide out of the vehicle before anyone can try to help me out.

My entourage of guards fans out around me.

I can't look away from those tall walls.

"The king's inside?" I ask.

"He is," one of the men says. "He's ordered us to take you to your chambers, where you're to shower and dress."

I feel my upper lip curl. Of course he would want me to wash away all my sins like they never happened.

I follow the soldiers up the marble steps. Before I can cross the threshold, one of the men guarding the door clears his throat. "Your Majesty, your gun."

The cold metal rests between my breasts. "What about it?" I ask.

"You can't bring it inside."

"Says who?" I ask.

"It's the king's policy."

Reluctantly, I reach down my bodice and hand the gun over. I stole that one; I can always steal another.

Walking into the king's palaces always felt like entering someone else's dream. But now, more than ever, it feels surreal as I pass the colossal columns that line the great entryway. I'm in a time and a place that I don't belong. There is a bone deep wrongness to the situation, and I can do nothing about it.

So I settle for getting perverse pleasure dragging my bloodied skirts and dirty feet across the king's pristine floors.

As we wind our way through the halls of this place, I keep my muscles tense. The guards may have promised to keep me safe from the Sleeper, but their allegiance ultimately belongs to the king.

Our footsteps echo through the lonely, abandoned

halls. When I was newly married to the king, his corridors bustled with politicians and aides, servants and guards. Now they're eerily empty, the artwork that lines them covered with drop cloths.

Has my terrible king grown eccentric in his old age?

The few posted guards I pass stand stoically. If they're shocked by my presence, they show no sign of it.

Eventually my retinue stops in front of a set of double doors.

"Your chambers, Your Majesty," one of the soldiers says. "Make yourself comfortable. We'll be right outside."

I nod to them and enter the room.

I could still be an emissary and this my suite for all the similarities I see.

My eyes move over a large, gilded mirror, a canopy bed, and elaborately carved table and chairs to match.

I run a hand over and intricately carved piece of furniture. This is too similar to the time I left. It's destabilizing. Confusing.

On the far side of the room, two French doors lead out to a balcony. They have already been thrown open, and a sea breeze rushes over me. I'm sure that if I walked out there right now, I'd see the ocean in all its glory.

Instead I pace.

I'm right back to where I started, here where the tragedies of the world can never touch me. Everything about this place mocks my existence.

He should've just left me to die.

I press my palms to my eyes.

I don't want any of this.

And then there's what I do want. Answers, revenge, repentance.

I have a sick feeling I won't get any of them.

CHAPTER 5

The King

SHE'S HERE, IN the palace. Awake.

Even if I didn't hear the cars pull up or receive updates from my soldiers, I would know it.

Every square inch my skin is buzzing in a way it hasn't done for decades. Not since those beautiful eyes of hers closed a hundred years ago. I'm mortified to admit that I've long since forgotten their exact color.

I can't escape her face. It's everywhere—printed onto posters, mounted on billboards, tagged across the sides of walls—but I can escape all those details about Serenity that used to haunt me. I've avoided the footage of her I'd once so liberally dispersed.

Up until now, my feelings for her had moved from a

fresh wound, to an old one, to a dull ache, to a fond memory. A perfect memory.

That all ends today.

From the reports coming in, my men say they found her covered in blood. That the vehicle she was pulled from was full of dead men.

I put a fist to my mouth.

My wife's awake.

Awake and on a warpath.

And I'm her target.

Serenity

ONCE I'M IN the shower, I begin to assess myself.

Other than a few absent freckles, my skin looks the same. And from the brief glimpse I caught of myself in the mirror, I still retain the scar on my face, as well as the thin white ones that crisscross my knuckles.

I might be heartsick, but physically, I feel great. If I'm still riddled with cancer, then my health will change soon enough. For now, I count my blessings. I have few enough of them.

It's only once I leave the shower that I encounter disappointment.

I frown at the lone gown and heels that sit inside the closet. It's the furthest thing to combat gear I can imagine. The lacy lingerie that accompanies them is little better.

It takes me almost five minutes to dress, due largely to the number of holes and straps the deep crimson gown has. I ignore the heels altogether.

A thud at my back has me spinning around. My eyes lock on the gilded mirror that takes up a good portion of one of the walls. The surface of it trembles ever so slightly.

I walk up to the mirror and press my palm against its surface. The tremors die down, and eventually vanish altogether.

This eerie place.

Someone raps on the door. "*Your Majesty*," they say, "*The king will see you now.*"

More cavernous halls, more empty corridors. Everything is pristine, but there are no signs of life.

For the first time since I woke, I feel the stirrings of trepidation. I've been angry at the man who put me in the Sleeper, not the one who refused to let me out.

I don't know *this* man.

The guards that surround me carry no weapons. I was so confident that I could steal one off of them, but there are none to steal.

They take me to a room I assume is used for extravagant parties, judging by how large the double doors are.

We stop in front of it, and one of my guards knocks.

No one answers the door and no one responds.

I cast a side glance at the soldiers. They don't appear surprised about this.

What is waiting for me on the other side?

They pause for several more seconds, then reach for the doors.

As soon as they swing open, my breath catches.

If parties were once held in this room, they are no longer. A world map covers the far wall. The same hated strings and blacked out faces are pinned to it. But the two adjacent walls, those are filled from floor to ceiling with photographs and reports.

Conquering has become Montes's obsession, though *obsession* is not nearly a strong enough word for this.

A century to transform a man into whatever thing he wishes to become ...

Right in the middle of the room, staring up at his enormous map, his hands clasped behind him, is the one man I hate more than any other.

My tormentor. My lover.

The king.

Tha-thump.

Tha-thump.

Tha-thump.

My pulse pounds in my ears as my eyes land on his back.

There is no word for what I feel. It's too big, the pain too acute. It burns up my throat and pricks my eyes.

In my mind, I held this man yesterday, felt him move inside me yesterday, heard him whisper that he loved me yesterday.

But my yesterday was 104 years ago.

"Your Majesty, the queen."

The king's body is just as still as ever; he gives no signs that he even heard the guard.

The moment stretches on.

Finally, "Leave us."

That same smooth as Scotch voice echoes through the room, and it sounds grander than I've ever heard it.

Now, *now* I feel the weight of all the lost years. It might've seemed as though I went to sleep yesterday, but my ears know they haven't heard that voice in an eternity.

Montes doesn't turn around as the guards retreat. The door closes with a resounding thud behind them, and then it's just me and the undying king.

I don't move. I barely even breathe.

I'm falling apart.

From hate to love to hate once more. My hardened heart was not made to withstand such vast and ever-changing emotions. It's cleaving me to pieces.

Why did he do this?

Why?

WHY?

"You *bastard*," I whisper.

The king's entire body flinches at the sound of my voice.

"Are you even going to face me?" *You fucking coward.*

I hear the scrape of his heel, and then he's turning.

I thought I'd be ready to face him, I thought that this pain-laced fury churning inside me would obliterate any other feelings the sight of him would bring.

God, was I wrong.

Our gazes lock, and it's all right there—the love, the hate, the sorrow and happiness we hold for one another. All that time can go by, yet everything between us is just as raw and intense as it's always been.

My monster. My husband. He's utterly unchanged. He still has the same olive skin, the same dark hair, the same seductive lips and dark, dying eyes. And judging by the way he stares at me, that obsessive love he once harbored might not be completely gone.

He takes a step forward and nearly goes down to one knee, his legs are so unstable. At first I think something's wrong with him. It takes a moment to realize it's the sight of me.

"Serenity," he says, straightening.

Tha-thump.

Tha-thump.

My chest rises and falls faster and faster.

He takes another step towards me. And then another. He doesn't tear his gaze away from me. Not for a second. His face is impassive—all but his eyes. Those depthless eyes that have witnessed so many of his terrible deeds, they devour me. They move over my outfit, and then my face.

Here they linger, touching each one of my features. But it's my scar they finally rest on.

I swore I wouldn't shed another tear for this man, and yet I feel one slip out anyway.

Damn my heart. Even after everything, I love him, and it's ripping me apart.

"You came here to kill me." There's such resignation his voice.

"You motherfucker," I say. "You left me to *rot*." My entire body trembles. Had I once thought I was the colder of the two of us? I've gotten no reaction out of him, and here I am breaking apart in his midst.

The king blinks several times, his eyes a bit too bright. "Your hate—I'd … forgotten."

He's still coming towards me, and I can tell he wants to touch me. I begin to move, one of my legs crossing behind the other as I circle the king.

"I was your wife," I accuse.

"You still are my wife." That voice of his—so sure, so commanding.

"No, Montes, you forfeited that right a long time ago."

Suddenly, he's no longer casually strolling. He strides forward. "You will *always* be mine, and you will never—"

As soon as he is within range, I cock my arm back and I slam my fist into his face.

He staggers, his hand reaching up to his cheekbone.

I stalk forward, and then I sock him again. And again. Pain radiates out from my knuckles, and I relish it.

Montes falls, and I follow him to the ground. My fists have a mind of their own. They land wherever they can, and the meaty slap of skin meeting skin echoes throughout the room. My tears fall along with them. I didn't realize I could feel like this—angry and desolate—all at once. And with every blow, I wait for that flood of relief to come. I'm meting out my revenge.

But this doesn't feel like revenge. The king keeps taking the hits, and he doesn't raise a hand against them, not even to protect himself.

"Fight back, you bastard," I growl.

He laughs, and those white, white teeth of his are now stained red with his blood.

My husband is insane.

We both are.

Finally, his arms come up, but only so they can encircle me. He pulls my body flush against his. “God, I fucking missed you, Serenity.”

And then he kisses me.

CHAPTER 6

Serenity

I TASTE HIS blood on my lips. This is not how the reunion is supposed to be going.

It was supposed to end swiftly with his death, but in an instant I've gone from killing the man who betrayed me to kissing him. Unwillingly.

One of his hands comes up and palms the back of my head, making it impossible for me to pull away.

I move my own hands to his neck, and I begin to squeeze.

He releases me, but he doesn't try to pull my hands away, just stares up at me with those too bright eyes as I choke the life out of him.

"Death in a dress." He barely gets the words out, but I

hear them all the same.

I close my eyes, feeling two more tears slip out, and squeeze tighter. I remember the exact moment he first said those words to me.

"Why do you think I wanted you in the first place? Death in a dress. That's what you were when you descended down those stairs in Geneva. I knew you'd either redeem me or you'd kill me."

With a sob, I let Montes go, casting myself away from him.

I cover my face with my bloody, shaking hands. I can't do it.

I can't do it.

I *love* him. To kill the thing I love ... that might just destroy the last bit of my conscience, and there is so little of it left.

I feel another tear drip down my cheek, and I taste it on my lips. Tears and bloodshed, that's all this relationship has given me. All that this life has given me, really.

His hand touches my cheek. "You didn't do it," he says.

I drop my palms away from my face and open my eyes.

He watches me, and there is no indifference in his gaze. Quite the opposite. Whatever he feels for me, the years haven't dulled it, though they might've transformed it into something else.

It's not anger that's riding me now. It's a hurt so vast I can't see any end to it. I could fit entire galaxies into the space it's carved out for itself inside me.

I stand. I look around me. The room had, in all likelihood, once been used for entertaining. But not anymore.

This man's vices are devouring him from the inside out. I'm nothing compared to them, just a desperate, angry girl who's been under someone else's thumb for far too long.

I can't be around this. I just ... want out.

I back up.

Montes leans back, his arms slung over his knees. If I didn't know him better, I'd say he was completely at ease. But he never did like me walking away from him, and I can see the controlled panic in his eyes.

"The queen I remember never leaves until she's made a threat," he says, watching me back away from him.

He remembers more than I thought he would.

And now, of all things, he wants me to threaten him. Because that's intrinsically something I would do.

I pause, only for a moment, and exhale, suddenly very weary.

"Not for lost causes," I say.

And then I leave him.

The King

I DON'T MOVE until the door closes behind her. But once it does, I can't seem to move quickly *enough.*

I pull my phone from my pocket and dial the head of security. "Serenity is not to leave the palace grounds under any circumstances."

My guard is quiet for a beat too long.

"Understood?" I say.

Finally, he says, "Understood, Your Majesty."

I click the phone off and bring it to my lips.

For the first time in a hundred years, my soul flares to life, my heart along with it. And it hurts so fucking bad.

No one's ever been in my situation, so I couldn't have foreseen that love doesn't function as other things do. It took decades for it to fade, and an instant for it to come roaring back.

As far as my heart is concerned, no time has passed.

And yet, Serenity was nothing like my memory. None of my imaginings could've made her so perfectly flawed.

I can now recall the exact color of her irises—somewhere between gunmetal gray and a frigid ice blue. And her anger—part of the reason I didn't stop her from laying into me was that I was mesmerized by that inner fire of hers. My beautiful storm.

I touch the side of my face tenderly. The skin's beginning to swell.

I breathe harshly through my nose to beat back a shout. I did leave her in a machine to rot. She couldn't protest, so I didn't listen. And now she's back with a vengeance.

The fool I was who first laid eyes on her all those years ago did one thing right—he saw redemption within his reach, and he snatched it up for himself.

And then he sabotaged it again, and again.

I'm still brooding when I hear a knock on my door twenty minutes later. I already know who's on the other side. I squeeze my phone tighter as a wave of anger washes over me.

I should've known.

He should've told me.

I pull myself together, breathing in and out through my nose to calm myself down.

I knew this was coming.

"Come in," I call.

This is something else I'll eventually have to explain to Serenity, something else she'll want to kill me for. And maybe this time she'll be successful.

I rub my face. Redemption has always been within my reach. I'm just too damn guilty to accept it.

Serenity

I THREAD MY hands behind my head and pace once more inside my room.

I've only ever had one job: to take out the king. I failed at that task time and time again.

I can kill easily enough. There are six dead men who can attest to that.

And no one is more deserving of death than the king. The man has done so many unconscionable things.

My stupid, idiotic feelings.

And what now?

A century ago, I had a purpose. Marriage for peace. A voice for my people and all those who were downtrodden. I might not have wanted the life I was forced into, I might've lamented it, but at least then I understood it.

I don't understand this.

The future, the lost, obsessive king and the war he still futilely fights. Why life has made a joke of my existence.

I take a deep breath.

I never had much time for pity. I still don't.

The king and his world have moved on. I'm no longer needed to hold together two hemispheres.

My gaze travels to the window.

I could leave.

I could *leave*. Not as someone else's prisoner, but on my own.

The thought is heady. Freedom has always been just beyond my reach. To finally have it ... It would almost make up for my tragic, broken heart.

But if I did leave, I would need boots, fatigues, weapons, food, water and a means to get more. That would take time to acquire, and there's always a possibility that outside these walls, I will be recognized and fought over as a pawn to be played in this war.

It would be a hard life. A life where I couldn't make much of a difference, a life where I was expendable.

A life without the king.

I walk onto the balcony and spread my arms over the marble railing. The ocean stretches out as far as the eye can see.

That life might be what I want, but my existence really was never about what I wanted. I was woken to save the world.

And the best way to do that would be to stay here and work with the very man who destroyed my heart.

I draw in a breath through my nose.

If that is what is needed of me, then that is precisely what I will do.

Even if it breaks me.

CHAPTER 7

Serenity

NOT TOO LONG after I come to my decision, there's a knock on the door. I cross the room, my skirts swishing around my ankles.

When I open the door, my hand tightens on the knob.

Montes stands on the other side, his hands in his pockets. The gesture is so reminiscent of how he's always been that my knees weaken.

It's too soon. It physically hurts staring at his face and feeling like things can never be the same between us.

I may have decided I can't kill Montes, and I may have decided to help fix all those things the king and his war have broken, but I'm not ready to be civil with him. Not yet.

He just stares at me for a long time, not saying anything. His face has already begun to swell, and that leaves me cold.

Fuck love.

I turn on my heel and head back to the desk I was working at. I've been jotting down notes on what I must learn to help the people I now live amongst.

I hear the sound of his footfalls behind me.

"Are you here to torment me?" I say over my shoulder.

"How did you know?" he says. "That's precisely what I had in mind."

"You haven't lost your silver tongue," I note.

"Serenity."

I glance up from my writing, and my gaze meets the king's. Had I noticed how tormented his eyes were? How weary they appeared? But even as I watch, that weariness dissipates. In its place I see a familiar spark in them.

"What you have done is unforgivable," I say.

He moves leisurely towards me, every step deliberate. It feels like the whole world extends outward from him, like the very universe shaped itself around this man. The king's always been larger than life, but now, if anything, he seems grander and more unnatural than he ever was.

He shakes his head. "No, Serenity. When it comes to us, nothing is beyond forgiveness."

I feel my nostrils flare. "You think this is still a game. The world, your power, my life."

He shakes his head again. "No." He keeps those tormented eyes of his trained on me. "I really don't." His voice carries weight. His years, I decide, are sometimes worn in his words.

"Are you planning on putting me back in there?" After the words leave my lips, I swear I don't breathe. It matters very much how he answers this.

Montes steps in close. "No," he says, searching my face.

I shouldn't believe him, he's deceptive to his core, but I feel the truth of his words.

He reaches up, as if to touch my face.

"Don't, Montes, unless you want to lose that hand."

His entire face comes alive at my words. "You haven't changed at all." He says this wondrously.

He always did like the broken things inside me.

His hand is still poised.

"Don't," I repeat, raising my eyebrows to emphasize my point.

"Can't I touch my wife?"

He said those words once before, and this time around they level my heart. Even after all these years, he remembers them.

"What are you doing, Montes?" I ask.

Is it not enough for him to destroy my life?

"Winning you back," he says.

And then, despite all my warnings, he lays his hand against my cheek.

The King

SHE SLAPS MY hand away. "I am not some prize to be won."

God, her anger. It makes the blood roar through my

veins.

I am *alive*. Alive in a way I haven't been in decades.

To think I lived without this for so long. Unfathomable.

I see hate burning in her eyes. Time has distorted most of my memories of her, but I'm almost positive I've never seen this particular brand of it. This fierce thing I've bound to my side is dying from the inside out.

That I can't take.

I don't give her time to protest before I place both hands on either side of her face.

Now that this fateful day has come, and I have to deal with the fallout of my choices, I find I'm eager for it. Desperate, even.

Serenity tries to pull away, but I won't release her.

I shake my head. "Fight all you want, my queen, you're not going to escape me."

"Fuck you, Montes. Let me go."

She's about to get violent. Even if I hadn't remembered other interactions that spiraled out of control like this, I would be able to sense it.

This terrible angel of mine. I welcome her vengeance.

I squeeze her face, just enough to get her attention. "Serenity, listen—"

She renews her struggles against me. "No," she says. "I know what you're going to say, and I don't want to hear about your suffering."

I nod. "I know," I say quietly. "But you will."

I can tell that this pisses her off, but when I fail to let her go, she stops fighting against me. I think, deep down, she wants to hear me out.

"There is nothing—nothing—I have ever treasured more than you. I let myself forget." I can feel my eyes begin to water, and any other time—*any* other time—I would fight back the reaction. But I won't with Serenity. Let her see her frightening king strip away his barriers for her.

"But you need to know that no one ever made me happy the way you did, and no one ever made me feel the burdens of my war the way losing you did."

Humans should not be able to feel what I have for this woman. Flesh isn't strong enough to house this much sadness. If I wasn't so afraid of death and the reckoning that waits for me on the other side, I'd have exited this world long ago.

She's blinking rapidly. Despite the firm set of her jaw, my bloodthirsty wife is just about as exposed as I've ever seen her.

Breathing quickly through her nose, she wraps her hands around my wrists and removes mine from her face.

"I listened," she says, "but now you need to listen to me: you never gave me a choice in any of this.

"I watched my mom die when I was ten after one of your bombs exploded outside our house. I became a killer when I was twelve because your war destabilized my country. I became a soldier when I was fifteen because my people were dying, and you were winning. I had to take on my father's job when I was sixteen because our government no longer had the ability to hold elections."

Her voice shakes; I can tell she's fighting tears.

"I was forced to seduce you," she continues, "the single man I most hated and feared in the world so that my country could know peace. I saw my father die protecting me from you, I held his murdered body in my arms. Even then, once I escaped you, you made me marry you. And then, when you realized I was dying of cancer, you forced me to sleep in that hellish machine of yours for a hundred years. A *hundred* years.

"So tell me again, Montes, what do you know of suffering?"

The room falls to silence as I take in her pain.

"I know that it makes you come alive, Serenity," I say softly.

She flinches at that.

"I know that loneliness its own kind of loss, and I have been lonely for a long time." I want to reach out and touch her skin again just to assure myself she's real. It's been so long since I've touched anyone. "I know that I want your suffering. I'll cherish it, just as I do everything else about you."

I can see her body trembling as she frowns at me.

The footfalls of several men interrupt us. A moment later, they pound their fists against Serenity's door. Of all times to be interrupted, now might be one of the worst.

I see Serenity's face shut down. All that anger, all that pain, all that vulnerability gets sealed off. Whatever moment the two of us had, it's now gone.

"Come in," I call, not glancing away from her.

Half a dozen soldiers crowd the doorway.

"Your Majesties," one says, bowing, "footage of the queen has been leaked."

MONTES AND I stand in front of a large screen in one of his conference rooms. I try not to think about how little has changed inside these walls. The king's conference rooms are virtually identical to the ones I remember.

And then there's the role I've slipped back into seamlessly. I didn't even realize when I strode down the hall next to Montes that my actions were out of place until I saw him cast me several glances.

He hadn't had a queen to co-rule with him in over a century. Of course the situation must be strange to him. But he didn't say anything, and I wasn't about to relinquish power when that was my reason for staying.

I run my tongue over my teeth now, my arms crossed, as I watch Jace and his team lift the golden lid of what appears to be a coffin.

The camera pans in.

Goosebumps break out along my arms.

There I am.

My body is still, my arms folded over my chest.

If I still had any doubts about what happened to me, I no longer do.

My eyes are closed, my skin startlingly pale against my golden hair. And my face is serene. It's an expression I rarely wear.

I'd been like that for a hundred years. Forced somewhere between death and life.

When Jace and his men lift me out, my head rolls listlessly against one of their shoulders.

I grimace at the sight. I was utterly helpless.

Next to me, the king begins to pace. This shouldn't be as terrible for him as it is for me, and yet I get the impression it is.

Another clip directly follows this one. In it, I'm still asleep. The camera focuses on my eyes. They move rapidly beneath my closed lids. That footage cuts out, replaced by a close up of my hand as my fingers begin to twitch. That, too, cuts away.

This time when the camera settles on me, I'm fully awake.

"Who are you?"

My voice doesn't sound nearly as confused as I know I was. These men were foolish to not have their guns out and pointed the entire time I was under their care.

"Where is Montes?"

I glance over at the king just as he bows his head and closes his eyes.

Remorse is a strange emotion on him, and I find it both angers and placates me. I want him to feel guilt, but then, what I really want, what I can never have, is for him to have made a different choice and us to not be where we are.

The video ends, and the room is left in silence.

"Take it down, along with any new instances that pop up," Montes finally says.

The soldier stationed near us bows and leaves. I watch him go, my eyes narrowed. Somewhere in the time that's lapsed, Montes has gotten rid of his aides and his advisors, along with the men and women of court. Now all that's left are military personnel.

I turn my attention back to the screen. "This situation is bad because ... ?"

"Before this, the world didn't know you still lived. They're have always been rumors, but not proof," Montes says. He nods to the screen. "Now there is."

The King

I KNEW THIS was inevitable, I had just hoped to put it off a little longer. All those years ago, when I'd made Serenity a martyr, I never imagined my actions would have such ripple effects. Not until the years melted away and I had to face the reality of waking my wife up.

The world will come for her. Everyone on this godforsaken earth wants to be saved. What that video shows is something just as unnatural as me. From miraculous beginnings come miraculous endings.

"Montes," Serenity says, "I saw one of the posters."

I mask my surprise. So she knows to some extent that she's famous. I barely have time to process that before she continues.

"What, exactly, do people expect of me?" she asks.

Serenity says this like she's actually considering doing something to meet their expectations.

I turn from the screen.

"They see you as a figure who fights for freedom," I say. "I imagine, if presented with the real woman, they'd expect you to do exactly that."

"They want me to end the war," she clarifies.

I hide my surprise once more. How much does Serenity know? And who told her? My men? Those on camera? The situation is already spiraling out of my control.

"I think that's safe to assume," I say carefully.

This is history repeating itself. The instant Serenity's back in the game, people want to play her.

My enemies will either try to capture her or kill her. They've obviously tried to do so already. And there are so many enemies.

The prospect leaves me short of breath. All those reasons I left Serenity deep in the ground come rising up. There she was safe. Awake, she has a target on her back.

"Well then," she says, breaking my reverie, "that makes this simple: you and I are going to end this war."

CHAPTER 8

Serenity

THE VEIN IN the king's temple begins to throb.

It's pretty blasé of me to just announce this like Montes hasn't been trying to do the very thing for the last century. I also don't mention that ending the war and winning it are two very different things.

The bastard obviously doesn't like my idea. But just when I think he's going to put up some sort of fight, he nods slowly.

Those dark eyes of his gleam, and I worry that whatever he's agreed to is somehow different from what I've proposed. That terrible mouth curls up into a terrible smile the longer we lock eyes, and that terrible face I feared for so long—I'm going to have to deal with it until this is finished.

I'm seriously concerned that I'm getting played at this very moment.

"Tomorrow, we'll begin," he says, picking his words carefully.

I stare at him a beat longer, then it's my turn to nod. "Alright."

The tension between us evaporates when Montes extends an elbow. "Dinner?"

I huff out a laugh and shake my head. I walk away from the king and his elbow. We are so far beyond chivalry.

In a few long strides he's caught up with me.

He places a hand on the small my back as we exit the room.

"You *will* lose that hand if you keep touching me," I say, not looking over at him.

"You've always liked my hands too much to do them any harm," he says, but drops his hold anyway.

"I don't like much of anything about you right now," I say.

As of today, I finally, *truly* begin to understand my father's lessons on diplomacy. Sometimes you have to ally with your enemies for a higher cause. That means not throttling Montes, despite the almost overwhelming urge to do so.

"We'll see how long you say that," he says.

You know what? Fuck diplomacy, and fuck this.

Even as I swivel towards Montes my arm snaps out. My knuckles slam into his jaw, and even though they're already ripped up and even though his face is already bruised and swollen, the hit is incredibly satisfying.

He stumbles back, clutching his jaw.

"You can wait another hundred and four years for me to like you, asshole. It still won't be long enough. Just be happy I didn't kill you when I had a chance."

That dangerous glint enters his eyes as he rubs his jaw. He closes the distance between us until chest brushes mine.

"Yes, about that," he says, his head dipping low. "You didn't kill me when you could've. I wonder why *that* is," he muses, his gaze searching mine.

"One massacre was enough for the day," I say.

He leans in even closer, bending his head so his lips brush my ear. "You can say it or not, but you and I both know the truth." He straightens enough to look me in the eye. "You can't kill me, even now, even though I deserve it—and I *do* deserve it."

I pull back enough to get a good look at him.

The king I knew took, and took, and took because he felt it was his right. And now, what he is essentially saying is that what he did wasn't his right.

I narrow my eyes at him. "Have you grown a conscience?" It's an almost preposterous thing to consider.

"Age gives you wisdom, not a conscience," he says as we wind our way through his halls.

"And where was that wisdom when it came to me?" I ask.

His eyes look anguished when he says, "It was wisdom that kept me from waking you, *nire bihotza*, not the other way around."

MONTES LEADS US outside, where a small table overlooking the sea waits for us. Oil lamps hang from poles around us, already giving the area a warm glow as the sun finishes setting.

I glance over at the king. This Montes ... he isn't exactly the same man I knew. And the change has me confused.

Confused and intrigued.

He pulls my chair out. I ignore the proffered seat and take the one across from it.

He smiles at the sight, though I swear his eyes carry a touch of sadness.

Someone's already set out a bottle of wine.

The setting, the table, the wine—it all harkens back to those instances when the king tried to seduce me and I was unwilling. Or maybe this is just how the king eats, beholding the sea and the sky and everything that he hasn't managed to ruin yet.

"Re-creating our previous dates will not win me back."

He grabs the wine bottle and begins to open it, appraising me as he does so. "So you admit that I can win you back?" The cork pops.

"That's not what I said."

He begins filling my glass with wine, his eyes pinched at the corners like he finds this whole thing very humorous. "It's what you don't say that interests me most."

I pick up my glass. "I'd prefer it if nothing about me interested you." God, it's such a lie.

Montes meets my eyes. "Serenity, the sun would sooner fall from the sky. Even when you slept, I couldn't stay away from you."

The ocean breeze stirs his hair, and I have to look away.

Montes has had a hundred years to perfect not only being the very thing I hate, but also the very thing I love.

I breathe in the briny air and take in the horizon. The sky is the very palest shades of orange and pink. Beneath it, the ocean looks almost metallic blue. It's beautiful. Peaceful. Paradisiacal.

"Is this the same island where we married?" I don't know why I ask. Why I feel nostalgic over a memory I never wanted.

When I face Montes again, I catch him studying me.

"It is," he says.

All those people I met, they're long dead by now. I should be too.

I take a long drink of wine. "Is this where you kept me when I slept?"

"It is."

"Did you ever regret what you did?" I ask, setting my glass down.

He settles into his seat, his frame dwarfing the chair. Even his build hasn't changed. I find myself looking at his deeply tanned forearms. It feels like only days ago I touched that skin like it was mine. I ache to do so again. Even though I can't, the urge won't disappear.

"Every day," he says.

My eyes move from his arms to his face. It's so unlike him to admit this—to feel this. I thought hearing that would make me feel better; it doesn't.

I let out a breath. "And yet you never changed your mind."

"I am over a hundred and fifty years old, Serenity. Much about me has changed, my mind most of all." He says this all slowly, each word weighed down by his long, long existence.

I swallow. My anger still simmers, but it has nothing on the terrible loneliness that crushes me. I am the relic of the forgotten past.

And I'm beginning to understand that I'm not the only one carrying a heavy burden. If the king's demons don't eat him up at night the way mine do, then they at least fall on those great shoulders of his throughout the day.

The waiters come then, bearing plates. I study the men. Their shoulders are wide, their faces hard. Soldiers dressed as servants. Montes no longer employs civilians it seems.

The food they place on the table isn't quite like what I'm used to with the king. It's simple—a cut of meat that rests on the bed of greens with a side of rice. The portion sizes are much smaller than what the king used to dole out.

I stare at it, not making a move for the utensils.

"The food is not going to bite you, Serenity," Montes says.

"How bad off is the world?" I ask.

If the king eats like this, if he's given himself a demotion, what must the common people's lives be like?

"What makes you think it's the world that's different, and not me?"

It's an echo of his previous statement. That he's a changed man.

My gaze flicks up to Montes. He takes a sip of wine,

watching me over the rim. He lounges back in his seat, slowly setting his glass down on the table. Everything about him is casual. Everything but his eyes.

I don't want to believe what he's suggesting. Not my narcissistic king, not the bastard who ruined my life and the lives of those I loved. He can't have changed his ways. Because if he truly has, all my righteousness will be for nothing.

I can't do this. My hate is all I have left; I don't want to know that the object of it is no longer worthy of my wrath. And, hypocrite that I am, I'm not ready to hear that leaving me inside the Sleeper was a personal sacrifice he made for the greater good.

The king is the selfish one. Not me.

Dear God, please not me.

"I think I'll eat alone." I grab a bread roll from the basket that rests between us and stand. "Enjoy dinner. I'll see you in the morning."

Montes catches my wrist as I pass him.

I look down my arm, at those long, tapered fingers that completely engulf my wrist. "Let go."

The vein in his temple throbs. "Sit. That's an order."

The king and his orders. He always did like to lord them over everyone. That hasn't changed.

I lean in, getting close to his face. "Fuck you and your orders."

I twist my wrist out of his hold and stride away.

"Serenity!" he calls after me.

But I don't stop walking, and I never look back.

CHAPTER 9

Serenity

SELF-DOUBT HAS NEVER been one of my character traits, but now as I pad through the empty halls of the king's castle, I can't help but feel it.

When it comes to the king, I have always assumed the worst. Perhaps my assumptions are no longer correct.

Perhaps he's no longer the most abominable person on the planet.

Nodding to the guards posted on either side of my door, I slip inside my bedroom. As soon as the door closes behind me, I lean against it, my head tilted towards the ceiling.

I must be the worst sort of person to be angry at this possibility. If my father were here, he would be shamed by my selfishness.

But my anger always did a great job of masking every other emotion I felt, and right now the main emotion that lurks just beneath it is worry.

How long did I hold out against the king when he was wholly wicked? What will I do now when the king's wicked side is tempered by something just, something good, something I might actually agree with? Believe in?

That is something I fear.

I DON'T WANT to fall asleep.

Despite the guards' promises, I'm still concerned that the king will change his mind and force me back into that Sleeper. I should be thankful for the leaked footage. Now that the world knows I'm alive, Montes can't easily hide his little secret once again.

But it's more than residual concern that keeps me awake. I don't want to go back to sleep after sleeping for a century.

My wants don't seem to matter; my eyes still begin to repeatedly drift close. I fight it until I can't any longer, and then I decide to change for bed. I pad towards the closet, my skirts swishing around my feet.

I stare into the empty closet.

The room I'm staying in still has no clothes.

I mutter an oath beneath my breath and begin unzipping my dress. Just or unjust, the king is still a wily fucker.

The gown slips off of me, sliding to the ground, and I'm left in the lacy lingerie the king provided me with earlier. I step out of the gown pooled at my feet and head for the enormous bed.

Halfway there, I hear a dull thump from the side of the room. I twist around, my body instinctively tensing. My eyes find the source of the noise, my body stiffens.

The surface of the mirror is vibrating once more. As I watch, the vibrations slow, then eventually vanish altogether.

I walk over to the mirror. It's unusually large, taking up a quarter of the wall. I wait for the noise to repeat itself, my eyes fixed on the smooth surface. When the seconds tick by and nothing happens, my exhaustion creeps back up on me.

Ghosts I'm not afraid of. Far too many already haunt my mind.

I pad over to the bed and slide in. It's only once I'm amongst all those sheets made of fine fabrics that I notice how empty the bed feels. It's about to swallow me up it's so large. I've gotten used to the king's body pressed against mine. I never realized that once something like that is gone, you feel its ache like a phantom limb.

I don't want to think about him deep in the night, or pine for his presence the way I'm sure many ladies of the court have.

Monsters like the king don't sleep in beds, they sleep under them. And I don't yearn; I exact vengeance.

I ENTER HER room late that evening, long after I know she's fallen asleep.

If I thought it would work, I'd wait for her to invite me herself. But I'm not a complete fool; another hundred years would go by before that would happen. Serenity is vindictive enough to deny both of us this for as long as she seeks to punish me.

I'm not a fool, and I'm not some chivalrous knight here to defend her honor.

I'm her morally depraved husband.

So I'm bending the rules of propriety.

I shrug off my button-down and slacks and round the bed.

Serenity stirs as I slip under the covers. The sheets are warm from her body heat. There were days long gone when I would've ruined entire cities for something as simple as this.

I'd gotten so used to her inhuman coldness as she slept in that sarcophagus. I'd nearly forgotten that Serenity has always been fire and heat and blood and ignited passions. My injuries are a testament to that. The excitement that thrums through my veins is a testament to that.

Those grave robbers resurrected more than an ancient queen when they took Serenity. My heart and my spirit slept with my wife, and those two have now woken. Just as I feared they would.

"Montes," she murmurs in her sleep.

I still at my name.

No time has gone by for her. She hasn't felt that century like I have. I forced myself to exist without her, the fates' punishment for all those years I took from everyone else. Maybe I finally paid my penance.

She rolls against me, her body nestling into my side, her arm wrapping around my torso.

I close my eyes and swallow down what feels like a shard of glass in my throat. Her skin is all over me. I rasp out a pained breath. Nothing has ever felt so good.

My arms come around her hesitantly. I'm never this tentative, but tonight my mythic queen is in my arms, and I haven't been a husband in a very long time.

I move my hand to her hair and stroke those golden locks. I have to breathe through my nose to control my emotions.

I'm not dreaming.

Nothing should feel this good.

I shouldn't be here. I did this to her, to me, to us. And it's not over. Even once she forgives me—and she will, that I'll make sure of—there are my enemies. We're back to square one, where she was my weakness. Only I, in my infinite stupidity, have made her more than my weakness. I have made her a vital player in this war.

My men have been alerted to look for and eliminate threats, and already they've taken care of dozens. But more will come, and I'm no longer smug enough to think I can neutralize all of them.

Even now with her cancer gone, death looms over Serenity. I've brought this upon her—just as I have every one of her other misfortunes.

"*Nire bihotza*, I'm sorry," I whisper, my lips brushing the crown of her head, my shaky fingers running down her arm. "I know you'll never believe it, but I'm so, so sorry."

Serenity

I STIR, MY body stretching out. The first rays of dawn slide through the windows. It's almost enough to rouse me.

Almost, but not quite.

Montes's arm tightens around my waist, and I settle back into him. For once my king isn't up earlier than me. My lips curl and I drift back asleep against him.

Sometime later, I wake again, my body stretched along Montes's. I blink, taking in the room.

The drapes are the wrong color. The room is the wrong shape and size.

I furrow my brows, confused. I begin to sit up, only to have my king groan and pull me back into him.

Right as I feel the firm press of his skin along mine, everything comes roaring back to me.

The king, that slippery bastard, snuck into my bed during the night. He's been holding me this entire time.

And while I slept, my body has been encouraging him along.

I try to move away, but his embrace only tightens.

I flip over to face him. His eyes open slowly, heavy with sleep, and his hair is ruffled. That ache that's taken up residence in my chest only increases at the sight.

"You have no right," I say, my irritation overriding that horrible burn that imperfect love produces.

He stares at me from across the pillow. I can see my bruises on him, and it shames me all over again that I put my mark on his skin. And then I am ashamed to be ashamed, for if anyone deserves to get roughened up, it's the king.

"You are my wife," he says. "Spouses share a bed."

"Get. Out." I'm beginning to shake as irritation gives way to anger.

Montes's thumb rubs little circles into my back. The man looks downright content. "My roof, my rules," he says. "We go to sleep and wake up together."

"Oh, do we now?" I say. "I wonder what happened to that rule when you put me in a box for a hundred years."

He searches my face. "I never did it to make you suffer."

No, he did it to save me from death.

"*Is* the cancer gone?"

I feel Montes's hand creep up my back and into my hair. He hesitates briefly, then nods. "Everything is gone. The cancer and all other ailments you might have suffered from."

The king made good on his word.

"How long did it take?"

"Three quarters of a century."

Seventy-five years. He waited over seven decades for me to heal.

Seven decades.

Most people I knew never lived to be half that age.

"And was it worth it?" I ask.

His eyes turn heated. Fervent. "*Nothing* has ever been more worth it."

"And yet you never woke me." I slept three extra decades, and I probably would've slept more if I'd never been captured.

Montes pulls me up and onto his chest.

"Yesterday I gave you my repentance," he says, his voice rough. "Today you'll get everything else."

"You going to have to do a little more than repent for a single day, considering you took thirty thousand of them away from me."

An amused smile curls the edges of his lips. I hadn't meant for that to be amusing.

"I'll give you thirty thousand more," he says.

"I don't want thirty thousand more. I want you to let me go." I push against him. That only serves to tighten his grip and rub our bodies together.

His jaw clenches, and his eyelids lower just a smidge. "If you keep doing that, you're going to be coming rather than going."

"I *will* hurt you," I threaten.

"But you won't kill me, and that really is what's important." His thumb skims under a bra strap. "I rather like this on you."

I grab his hand. We stare each other down.

"Montes, you don't get to do this with me," I say. "You gave that up a long time ago."

He leans in close enough that I can feel his breath tickle my skin. "I gave *nothing* up. Be upset at me for making you live when you wanted to die, but don't blame me for this."

He moves the hand I still hold captive to my face, touching my scar. "You fought for me, killed for me. You wore my crown and carried my child. Don't distort what you mean to me, what you've always meant to me.

"And I'm going to keep you in this bed until you understand something: I won't let you go. Everything you are is mine, and everything I am is yours."

"That is something I've always known," I say.

Ever since the day my father died I've understood. So long as the king lives, I will never be free of him.

CHAPTER 10

Serenity

"Do you have anything besides lace that I can wear?" I ask, sitting up and frowning at the empty closet across the room.

Montes gets out of bed. I try and fail to not stare at his backside as he strides away from me.

You know what? Screw it. The man has always taken liberties with me when he shouldn't. I can look at my husband all I want.

He grabs his button-down he's thrown over a side chair and tosses it to me.

I finger the material. "This isn't funny."

"My men have restocked my closet with clothes for you, but wearing them comes with a condition."

A century was not long enough to stamp out the conniving side of this man.

I raise an eyebrow.

"You wear the clothes I provide, you sleep in my bed. Willingly."

My hold tightens on his shirt, wrinkling the material.

Everything with this man comes down to strategy and what he can take. Fortunately for him, I've made a habit of sleeping with the king even when I didn't particularly like him. I have few qualms about repeating the process.

"Fine," I say. "But when you wake up and your balls are missing, just remember that you asked for this."

A slow, smoldering smile breaks out across his face. "And when you wake up with me between your thighs, just remember that you agreed to it."

"You really do have a death wish." The audacity of this man never fails to astound me.

I slide out of bed. Ignoring the shirt he offered me, I put yesterday's dress back on. I can feel his eyes on me as I slide it over my hips.

"What?" I say, pulling the straps up.

His eyes pinch at the corners again, like I amuse him.

Rather than answering me, he grabs his shirt from the bed and pulls it on. I bid goodbye to his abs as he buttons it up.

I find myself watching him just as acutely as he watched me.

He doesn't bother tucking in his shirt or slipping on socks and shoes before coming back to me and taking my hand.

Montes brings it to his lips, kissing the split knuckles that hit his flesh.

I take a deep breath. He's going to keep doing this, whether or not I fight him. So I bear it and try to ignore the brush of his lips.

When he's done, he tugs on my hands and leads me out of my room.

"I don't know anything about you," I say as we walk. "I don't know who you are."

"It doesn't matter," he says.

"It does," I counter. "Do you have a wife?"

He's quiet for a moment, and the only sound is the soft tread of our bare feet and the march of the soldiers that trail us. "She wants to know if I have a wife. I think she's more interested than she lets on."

All that time managed to go by, and yet he still remembers how much I hate it when he refers to me in the third person. "*Montes.*"

"No, my queen," he says, his voice somewhat offended, "there are no others, save for you. There never have been."

I am mortified at the relief I feel. Am I so ready to forgive this man who's betrayed me at every stage of our relationship?

"Kids?" I ask.

He flashes me a skeptical look.

"Oh, don't act like you're a saint."

That vein in his temple begins to pulse. "No wives. No children, Serenity."

I take that all in stride, perversely enjoying the fact that I have upset my king. He has a hard look about him, the expression he wears before he damns someone to death.

My attention diverts from the king when I catch sight of the palace walls. Some of the cloths that covered large frames have now vanished. Now I realize why they were hidden in the first place.

My face stares back at me from half a dozen different places, the grandest of them is the photo from our wedding that once rested in my office. It's an odd picture to be so grand; it's not stiff and formal. But the tenderness captured in that moment—albeit, tenderness I distinctly wasn't feeling at the time—is almost overwhelming on such a grand scale.

The other photos are an odd combination of shots I never saw.

"I couldn't look at them until now," the king admits next to me, noticing my interest.

"Why did you put them up in the first place?" I ask, distracted.

"I had hoped they would bring me happiness. But I was wrong."

My gaze sweeps over the walls again. Not all of the frames have been unveiled. It all seems so very deliberate.

"What about the ones that are still covered?" What else is the king hiding?

Montes peers down at me. "Those are a story for a different day."

A story I'm bound to not like, I think as I stare into his handsome face. The secrets the king keeps are both huge and terrible. At this point, however, I must be impervious to the king's terrors. There's not much more that can frighten me; I've already endured all my fears.

We stop outside a set of double doors. Montes opens one of them for me and we head inside.

His room.

I don't know what I was expecting, but I'm not sure it's this. His room looks essentially the same as the one I stayed in last night. Beautiful, but lacking personality.

This man keeps all those fathomless bits of himself locked tightly up. Not even in his room does he set his personality loose.

I shouldn't be concerning myself with Montes, who I feel at my back even now. I should concern myself with my own fate.

I'm to stay here, in this beautiful, empty palace, full of these opulent, meaningless rooms alongside my terrible, tortured husband.

When I turn, I see Montes standing on the threshold.

He jerks his head to the side of the room. "Your clothes are in the closet. I'll be in the shower. We're in a drought, so if you want to conserve water, I'll allow you to join me."

I narrow my eyes on him. "I'll pass."

His monstrous eyes twinkle as he backs away. My nightmare won't capture me today.

"Then get dressed," he says, unbuttoning his shirt. "We have a war council in an hour."

The King

THIS SHOWER MIGHT go on record as one of the fastest I've

ever taken. I soap myself up, my skin quickly getting slick with it.

Day two with the awakened queen.

My heart beats fast, and for the first time in decades, I feel young again. Uncertain again. Of my feelings, of hers, of the situation we've now found ourselves in.

She can't escape, I ensured that, but I still don't want her out of my sight. My paranoia is a beast that could swallow me whole if I let it. And I have ample reason to feel this way. I thought Serenity would be safe below my palace. She hadn't been.

And now she's in my room. *Our* room. Ready to gut me alive. Everything that's wicked in me thrills at her savage nature.

I rinse off the suds.

Life with Serenity begins again.

This time around, it will be different. I'm not a good man, and doing the right thing has never come naturally to me, especially when it concerns my wife, but I'm trying. That's why I've decided to keep including her in my official decisions. I want her involved in this war, not only because I have made her a key player in it, but also because my queen thrives best on the front lines.

I turn the spigot off and step out of the shower stall. Grabbing a towel, I wrap it around my waist.

I remember the call I got when they found her. All those dead men. She'd been untouched. That's what happens when you corner my wife. That's what happens when you throw her into the fray.

I'm an idiot for trying to protect her this whole time.

She was never the one who needed protecting.

Everyone else was.

CHAPTER 11

Serenity

MONTES AND I head back to the giant map room together. I cast him my fifth skeptical glance.

"What concerns my vicious little wife?" he asks. He looks down at me fondly. It's so strange, how kind this man can be when he's been so cruel.

"You're wearing fatigues. And combat boots."

Like me.

I found my own standard issue clothes in his room almost immediately. Granted, these are more fitted than the pairs I'm used to, but otherwise they're essentially the same.

That was my first shock—Montes stocking my dresser with fatigues.

The second and bigger shock was that he wore them himself.

"I am," he says.

"I've never seen you in uniform." Not like this. Outfitted like a soldier. He looks good in it.

He runs a hand down his shirt front. "Like I said, many things about me have changed."

I'm finally starting to understand that.

He peers down at me. "You like this." It's not a question.

My eyes drop to his clothes. "It depends."

"Depends?" He raises his eyebrows. "On what?"

"On whether or not it's all for show." Wearing military attire doesn't make you a soldier. Battle does.

"I like what you're wearing," Montes says by way of answer, nodding to my outfit. "It's a reminder that we will be sharing a bed tonight."

My face heats at that. "We shared a bed last night."

"Yes, but this time my willing queen will fall asleep in my arms. I wonder what else she will be willing to do ..."

"Just because I agreed to your terms doesn't mean I'm willing," I say.

Montes gives me a knowing look. "Let's save the lies for the politicians," he says.

I thin my gaze. "You better get some custom armor to wear below your belt, my *king*," I say. "You're going to need it."

That earns me a laugh. "I'll look into it, *nire bihotza*."

Inside the king's enormous map room, a series of long tables have been brought in and arranged in a U-shaped pattern. More startling than the addition of tables is the addition of people. Dozens upon dozens of military officers sit at the thick oak tables, most wearing uniforms and medallions.

Several screens have been pulled down from the ceiling, covering much of the maps. More military officers watch from the other side of those screens.

And amongst them all, I see many women.

My heart beats faster. This is not the same king I remember. Not even close.

When the officers notice me, the noise dies down until room becomes ominously silent. Then, one by one, they stand and salute.

I lean into Montes, looking out at them all. "Did you pay them to do that?"

He places a gentle hand on my back. "No, Serenity. Money can't buy you that kind of loyalty."

Nor can fear, not with these types of men and women. I stare out at their stoic faces. If they've lived through enough battles, things like death and pain don't scare them. That begs the question: how did Montes convince them to join his ranks?

I flash the king a questioning look. Rather than speaking, he urges me forward. I nod to the soldiers I make eye contact with, still confused by the man and situation I find myself in.

This is the first—being inside the king's palace, surrounded by people that look just like me. It's destabilizing.

Montes stops us in the middle of the room, where everyone can see us. "Please sit," he says. The acoustics of the room carry his voice to the far corners.

Dozens of chairs scrape as they do just that.

The king glances down at me. "I would like to introduce you all to my wife, Her Majesty Serenity Lazuli, Queen of the East."

The room is as silent as the dead. Most of the officers school their faces to look impassive. But their eyes say what their expressions don't.

I'm the apparition no one expected.

"She's well over a hundred years old," Montes continues, "but she has slept through most of them."

He lifts his gaze to the room. "I have lied to you all, to the entire world. Serenity never died of her cancer. I had her sedated until I could find a cure for her. By the time that came to pass, I hesitated to wake her for other reasons."

My entire body tightens. I want to devour the words that will fall from his lips, but I have to rein my own emotions in. Whatever he says now is likely some official explanation rather than the actual truth.

My husband is not exactly known for truth telling.

"I was afraid of what would happen to her and the world if she was brought to life. Martyrs don't last long in war."

It takes hearing Montes's explanation to realize I wanted something else, something that burned hot. A reason worthy of a century of sleep.

Not this anesthetized explanation.

"I'm sorry I lied to you all in the process." The king looks back down at me, and now I really don't want his eyes taking in whatever reaction I'm wearing. "She's my wife. I don't want anything to happen to her. I thought that keeping her asleep and safe under my protection would be enough. But the enemy came in here, they stole her from me, and they were going to use her in the way the West uses all their subjects."

Montes's jaw tightens. Now *there* are words to get behind. Now there is the king. Not the king I knew—that one was a man wearing a title.

This is a title wearing a man, power and purpose given flesh.

I can't help but stare in silence. When did the West become the great evil, and this man a fighter for freedom? When did leaving me to sleep become a mercy rather than a death sentence?

And how, exactly, does the West use their subjects?

I find I really don't want to know that answer.

Montes steps away from me. "They came for my wife, trespassed inside my house, and tried to use her against us," he says, pointing a finger to the ground. He pauses for effect. "They will try again. And again. And again. They will try to capture her until they succeed or we stop them."

He orates to the officers like they are clay to mold into whatever shape he desires. And he's good. Really good. His adoration seems genuine, his pain seems genuine, his anger seems genuine.

But is it?

"They give us only one option: we must stop them. And we will." Montes casts his gaze about the room. "This time when we make war with the enemy, we do it for good."

One of the officers stands, and he seems like the meanest of the bunch from the sharp set of his features. His eyes move from Montes to me. "What does Your Majesty, Serenity Lazuli say to this?"

Suddenly, dozens of eyes are on me.

And I realize I'm not just a woman wearing a title, either. Not to these people. I'm their hope given form.

I walk forward, passing the king, my boots echoing as they click against the floor. I cast a wondrous glance around the room. I throw a look over my shoulder.

The hairs on my arm rise as our gazes lock. Montes, in his infinite darkness, has done the most twisted thing of all: he's fashioned his evil into something good men can get behind.

I face forward once more. "I won't pretend to understand these times or your ways," I say. "But a hundred and fifty years is too long to be at war. I am prepared to do whatever is needed, whatever it is you ask of me, to end it, once and for all."

The officer who spoke stares at me for a long time. Then he brings his fist over his heart, and he thumps it against his chest. The action is savage. He pulls his fist away, then does it again. And then a third time.

A chair scrapes back and the man next to him stands. He too places a fist over his heart and begins to pound it just beneath his decorated breast pocket. Then a woman stands and does the same thing. Then several officers.

One by one, like a wave, they stand and thump their fists over their hearts until the entire room is echoing with the sound.

I feel the devil's breath against my ear. "There is no higher compliment, my queen, than for the officers to give you their honor."

That's what this is?

"What have you done?" I say, staring out at the sea of medaled men and women. I've already agreed to this, to be what the world needs me to be, but I'm still horrified by all that comes with it.

I'm nothing more than a story to these men and women, a face to their beliefs. And they are all but ready to set down their lives for me.

Those terrible eyes of his capture mine, but he doesn't respond.

It's hard to believe everything that led me here wasn't orchestrated by his hand. That my escape and the fallout from it wasn't planned. Montes seems more omnipotent than ever, and the superstitious part of me wants to believe that he can see some endgame the rest of us can't.

But he can't control me, I know that. His reluctance to wake me up has everything to do with that. And I won't bow to him, no matter how drastically he's changed his ways. A long time ago I forgot I slept in bed with the enemy. I paid a hundred years as penance.

I won't make the same mistake twice.

CHAPTER 12

Serenity

"SO LET ME get this straight, the Western United Nations is still called the Western United Nations, and it's run by a group of representatives, just as it always has been."

The officers around me are nodding.

After the meeting in the map room adjourned, Montes and I moved to a smaller conference room with a handful of the officers. All of them are helping me catch up on what I've missed.

It's an impossible task; it took me years to understand the intricacies of my time's politics when I was studying as an emissary. It will take me years more to understand all that's happened between then and now.

"Some of these representatives are Montes's old advisors." This comes from the stern-looking officer that was the first to show affiliation to me in the map room. Heinrich Weber is his name, Montes's grand marshal of arms.

I'm surprised by how quickly he's taken a shining to me, considering how much of a threat I am to the king.

Or maybe he just doesn't yet know my true relationship with Montes.

"I believe you've personally met them," Heinrich adds.

A chill races up my spine.

Wait, *those* old advisors?

Some of them are still alive?

I shoot a glance at Montes, who sits in the chair next to mine. He lounges back in his seat, his thumb running absently over his lower lip, those sinister eyes of his narrowed like he's trying to figure me out. It was never me that was the enigma.

"So there's more than just one of you now?" I ask.

More men that can't be killed, each one more rotten than the last. Of course it's the worst ones that have managed to cheat death.

The corner of Montes's mouth lifts up. "My queen, there has only ever been one of me."

"Thank God for that."

The officers in the room stiffen slightly. It's not like before, when Montes's subjects scuttled about, perpetually in fear of his wrath. However, the king still appears to command their respect, and I'm not very respectful.

Now the other corner of Montes's lips lifts as well. He always did enjoy my insults. And just as always, he seems more captivated by me than the matters at hand.

To be fair, everything I've been learning he's known about for decades. If roles were reversed, I can't say I wouldn't be sickly fascinated with him as well.

I return my attention to some of the papers spread out on the table and the men and women seated around me. "Just what kind of people are these representatives as a whole?"

"The worst kind," Montes says.

I raise my eyebrow and flash him a sardonic look. "Refresh me again on what the worst kind of leaders are."

Tell me how they are different from you, I challenge him with my eyes.

I swear the air thickens as we stare each other down.

"The representatives have a long history of neglecting their people. From our best estimates, there haven't been significant efforts to clean out the radiation from the ground, so radiation-related medical issues are a big problem in the West. It doesn't help that their hospitals are critically understaffed and understocked.

"Food and clean water are also serious issues for them. And I haven't even gotten into the ethics of their leadership."

The more he says, the deeper my frown becomes. I don't know who I'm angrier at—the representatives, who abuse their power more egregiously than even the king, or Montes, who forced me to lay in stasis right when I was on the cusp of helping my people.

"And what about you?" I ask.

"What about me, Serenity?" He lifts an eyebrow.

"How are you any better than the enemy across the sea?"

"Within the last century, over ninety percent of the radiation has been removed from the Eastern Empire," one of the officers says, coming to Montes's rescue.

"Radiation that the king put there," I respond.

"I'm sorry, Your Majesty, but that's just not true," the officer says.

I furrow my brows and tear my gaze away from Montes. "What do you mean?"

"The WUN has dropped several bombs since you last ruled."

Sickly sensation runs through my body. "They dropped ... more bombs?" When I worked with the WUN, that kind of warfare had always been off the table. When you start playing with nukes, you flirt with global extinction.

The officer nods. "They hit a few major city centers in the East."

This is my land all over again, only everything about this story is wrong. My former enemies are the victims, and my homeland is the great evil.

Shock and something like despair fill me. I can't catch my breath. Is there no one decent left? Haven't the innocent suffered enough?

"What did you do to retaliate?" I ask.

"A peace treaty was formed in light of the loss, so that we could redistribute our resources," the officer says.

A peace treaty?

When I meet Montes's eyes this time, I don't like what I see there. It's not haughty, or selfish, or wicked. Finally, finally I see what I'd always hoped to in those eyes of his—repentance, sorrow, loss—and I can't bear it. The years should've made Montes more apathetic, not less.

"Is that true?" I ask.

"I have changed," is all he says.

I wait for him to say more. I find I'm desperate to know the secret to climbing out of the abyss our souls have fallen into. I'm even more desperate to know whether this is what happened to the king. He's already admitted his wisdom grew, not his conscience.

But Montes doesn't speak, and I'm left with one horrible question.

"How many have died?" I ask.

No one in the room answers right away.

Eventually, someone clears their throat. "Since you've been gone, the war has claimed over a billion casualties from the East, and about three hundred million from the West."

It's all hitting me at once. Over a billion lives—parents, children, spouses, siblings. Friends, lovers, comrades. Over a billion of them cut down because bad men decided they wanted to have it all. When that many people are gone, what is the point?

I actually feel a tear roll down my cheek at that. I look over at Montes, and he must see my despair.

I can see wounds in those old eyes of his; my king's finally been touched by his war, and his ghosts are eating him alive.

"The enemy fights more ruthlessly than we do," someone says.

A day ago, I wouldn't have believed it. Now I do.

A billion people gone. You really do reap what you sow.

Montes has cultivated fields and fields of violence and watered them with bloodshed. These are his crops.

I draw in a ragged breath. I was never able to fulfill my promise of healing this broken world. Not until now, when so much has already been lost.

Not glancing away from me, Montes says, "Everyone, out. We'll reconvene tomorrow at eight a.m. in the Great Room. Bring with you a comprehensive plan for your respective departments."

The room clears in under a minute, but not before the officers bow and salute us. And even on their stoic faces, I swear I catch a glimpse of hope when their eyes meet mine.

Once they leave, I rotate to the king. "Why did you clear the room?" I ask.

He leans forward in his chair, his forearms going to his thighs. "You don't like having an audience when you feel weak."

My throat constricts at that. This man can be so cruel yet so considerate. And God, does he remember me well.

My gaze slides to the door. "They love you." It's both a statement and a question.

"Not as much as they love you."

It's easy to love a dream. It's much harder to love the reality. Once these people understand who I really am, I doubt they'll remain blindly loyal.

"I thought you believed all the good men were gone," I say. He told me this long ago.

"I was wrong about many things."

I peer at him closely. "Are you a good man?"

A devil-may-care smile flashes across his lips. He wants to touch me; I can feel his desire as though it's a physical thing.

"Does it matter?" he says. "I'm still the King of the East, you're still married to me, and the world's still at war. Good and evil have little to do with it."

Now I lean forward, until there are only inches between our faces. "They have everything to do with it. So which are you?"

He leans forward, closing the last of the distance between us, and just as his lips meet mine, he says, "Both."

The King

I AM MARRIED to a lioness. Some dangerous, beautiful creature that cannot be tamed, and she will eat me alive.

As my lips move against hers, and I take my conquered kiss, I expect those claws of hers to come out. She hates me, perhaps now more than ever.

Instead, she kisses me back. And now I'm not just reveling in the taste and the feel of her, but the memory of the time when she wanted this every bit as much as I did.

Eventually, she pushes me away, and the look on her face … horror and regret. "I'm not doing this with you again, Montes."

I lean forward, refusing to let her put distance between us. "Is this one of your famous facts?" I say.

"Do you really think I'm here sitting next to you because I believe we can resolve our issues?"

Oh, the fire that burns within her. I want to stoke it until I can feel nothing but her heat.

"You're sitting next to me because I didn't give you a choice," I say.

She gives me a hard look. "I'm here to fix what you've destroyed."

What she doesn't realize is that our relationship is one of those things.

I pull my chair as close to her as I can get, until our thighs are pressed against one another. "The terms are the same as they've always been, *nire bihotza*—if you want to fix the world, you'll do it at my side."

I think she understands this. I can see the concession in her eyes. I don't want to be her second priority, and I don't intend to remain one. However, if this gets her to give me another chance, I'll take it.

"What happened once I was gone?" she asks.

I pick up one of her hands. She tries to pull it away, and I flash her a look.

"If you want information from me, you play by my rules." It's as simple as that. "One of those rules is that while I answer your questions, I get to touch you."

She glowers at me, despite the fact that we began our relationship this way. She came to my land prepared to trade secrets for sex.

"Fine," she says. I don't know how she does it, but she manages to make the word sound like a curse.

Satisfaction spreads through me. "Good."

I turn over Serenity's hand, running my fingers across her soft skin. Time has long since wiped away the calluses she wore like jewelry. I find I miss them. I like it best when my savage queen displays her true nature. If I give her long enough in this world, she will wear those calluses once more.

"After you were placed back in the Sleeper, I continued to war with my advisors and some of the surviving regimes of South America," I say, beginning to answer her earlier question.

She listens avidly.

"The West never much liked me, and the Resistance and other militia groups got behind South America's fight. Within a year, what little gains I had made in the WUN were undone, and the political leaders who remained loyal to me were slaughtered."

It should please her that the Resistance pushed me out, but she doesn't look pleased. She looks worried. She must be thinking about the advisors who fled to South America. Those were not men anyone should get behind.

I run my thumb over the soft skin of her inner arm.

"My enemies banded together and retook the West. They called themselves representatives and established their leadership throughout the WUN. Despite the similarities in names, their government is nothing like the one they replaced. Ever since then, we've been at war."

To be honest, I'm more interested in the feel of my hand along her flesh than I am in retelling this bleak history. The world has been the way it is for the last hundred years, and I've had a century to come to terms with it. Meanwhile, I've only had a day to drink up my wife's essence.

"Montes."

I am the ancient one, and yet every time I meet her gaze I can't help but feel I'm looking at someone even older than me.

"How is it that after all this time, you haven't managed to defeat the West?" she asks.

It's the most laughable question. No one tries to lose a war.

"I know you have the resources," she says. "So why, Montes?"

"They fought dirtier than I did."

"No one fights dirtier than you."

I'm still holding one of her hands in my own. I tug on it, pulling her close. "That was true until I met you. They are your people, *nire bihotza*. You care for them, as I care for you. I tried to do right."

Her eyes widen almost imperceptibly. "What are you saying?"

I bring her hand to my mouth and kiss those soft, scarred knuckles of hers, but I don't respond. It should be obvious.

She and I are love and war. Peace and violence. I have taught her how to be a worse person, and she's taught me how to be a better one. I fuel her hate, and she fuels my love.

I've torn the world apart and now I need my queen to help me stitch humanity back together, and my heart along with it.

CHAPTER 13

Serenity

A SWIMSUIT WAITS for me when we return to our rooms.

"What's this?" I say, picking up the two dainty scraps of material.

The king comes striding in behind me. "I've decided I'm only going to answer your intelligent questions. The inane ones you'll just have to figure out for yourself."

I flash him an annoyed look.

He begins to change next to me, and I realize a swimsuit has been laid out for him as well.

When I don't follow his lead, he says, "You don't have to get in the ocean. You can stay inside the palace, just as you have for the last several decades."

This man knows how to play me even better now than

he did a hundred years ago.

"I need to work more, Montes. There's so much I have to catch up on." Of course in his world, the king has time for idle swims when there's work to be done.

"I will allow you to continue to ask me questions while we swim," he says, unzipping his pants. He steps out of his fatigues a moment later. Reflexively, I back up.

He's shirtless and clad only in a pair of boxer briefs, all of that toned, olive skin on display. I feel my body react to the sight of him before my mind can catch up.

The king notices, and his gaze heats. "Provided, of course, that the same rules apply."

"What rules?" I ask, pretending that I don't feel the heat crawling up my cheeks.

"That I get to touch you while I answer them."

I narrow my gaze, still not making a move to put on the suit.

As we stare each other down, he drops his boxer briefs, and I get an eyeful of a very aroused king. He's not embarrassed in the least.

I am. Even after all that we've done together I'm still somewhat modest.

Leisurely he grabs his suit, taking his time to pull it on just so that he can toy with me a little longer. And then he's done changing, and I still haven't moved.

Seeing that I won't be joining him, he heads to the door, but then pauses when he gets there. "Serenity?"

I glance over at him.

"I was lying. You don't get a choice. I'll give you five minutes to change, and then whatever state of dress you're in, my men will bring you to me."

He's so lucky I don't have a gun.

FROM THE MOMENT I leave the back doors of the palace, I can feel Montes's eyes on me.

I scowl first at him, then at the guards that flank me.

I did change into the swimsuit he left for me. I'll give the king that much. Then I went into our closet and put on the most expensive gown I could find. Seed pearls are sewn into intricate designs across the bodice and down the sleeves.

I intend to ruin it in the salty water ahead of me.

Like I told him when we first met, I'm a vindictive bitch.

Not to mention that dresses like this one belong leagues under the sea.

The breeze lifts my gauzy skirts, like the wind wants to rub its phantom fingers over the material. It *is* lovely. That won't stop me from destroying it.

The king is thigh deep in the water, looking like some strange sea god as the waves roll in around him. His hair is swept back from his forehead, and all those fine muscles of his glisten in the sun. Even this far away, I can see him assessing my clothing. Whatever he's thinking, it brings a grin to his face. If I had to guess, I'd say my defiance amuses him.

"You got all dressed up for me," he says when I'm within hearing range. "I'm so honored."

My bare feet sink into the warm sand as I approach him. I don't bother lifting my skirts as the granules tangle in them.

"I'm beginning to believe you are genuinely suicidal," I say.

"You know me better than that," Montes admonishes.

"Do I? The evil king who laid down his arms to heal his people—if that is the man you are, then I don't in fact know you."

But I want to.

The realization comes as a shock, and not a welcome one. The king's seduced me once into forgetting that he was the enemy. If I'm not careful, he'll do it once more. And, unfortunately, I'm even more vulnerable this time around because my feelings for Montes haven't vanished.

A wicked man with a decent heart. That is the worst sort of combo. I have no defense against it.

Seawater begins to climb up my dress as the dry sand gives way to wet.

"Then it's my job to see to it that you do come to know me. Intimately, my queen."

Intimacy. It always is his endgame with me. I won't be able to avoid it.

I walk up to him, the saltwater rising up and up until it's nearly at my waist. My dark king watches me. He's enjoying this—my anger, his control.

"And what do I get out of that situation?" I ask.

If Montes is going to make my ignorance of current events a situation he can take advantage of, then I will use his desire to my benefit.

A wave crashes against us, the surf wrapping my dress around me.

"What does my vicious little wife want?"

"I'm not going to tell you," I say. "Not yet. Give me whatever it is I wish, and I'll give you intimacy."

A tradeoff—one not so different from the one we made when I was just an emissary.

He stares at me for a long time as the waves roll in around him, crashing against his back. I can't read him or the machinations of his twisted mind, but he's entertaining the thought, and that, at least, is something. To even consider what I proposed—

"Agreed."

I can't hide my surprise. The king must want me more desperately than I can imagine.

"We begin now," he says.

My small victory is only just beginning to sink in when his words register.

He closes the last of the distance between us and wraps an arm around my waist. I put my hands on the shoulders reflexively, about to push him away.

"Ah-ah-ah," he says. "You agreed to intimacy. Fight me on this, and you can forget about your pretty little request."

"I didn't mean *now*," I say.

"You never specified that. As far as I'm concerned, intimacy will be on my terms. Or, you can forget about your secretive wish and I will seduce you the old-fashioned way." Which might just be worse because I know myself well enough to understand with perfect clarity that he will pull me under all over again.

He knows he has me when I glare at thin.

"Now," he says, "put your legs around me."

This is absurd.

With a very obvious reluctance, I do so, giving him a not-so-subtle glare the entire time. His other hand cups me from below. He moves us into deeper water.

His eyes drop to my mouth. "Now your lips," he says.

This man is insufferable. Of course he would take complete advantage of his end of the deal.

I will let him have his moment. I'll get mine later.

I lean into him, brushing my lips against his. I can taste the salty ocean on his skin.

I assume that he'll find the kiss wanting—I'm not trying very hard to make it enjoyable—but he's patient, his lips barely moving beneath mine. And then, at some point, he takes over. His grip on me tightens, and the kiss becomes impassioned. Montes's fingers dig into my skin.

I don't know what to do with this fever. A part of me wants to fall just as deeply into it as Montes is, but another part of me wants to fight back, even though I just made a promise otherwise.

The king doesn't give me much of a choice. The arm cradling my back slides up, delving into my hair. I feel his tongue part my lips and then I'm not just tasting water and sea salt; I'm tasting this man's desperation and his toxic, undying love. How terrible that I'm the focus of it.

Finally, he ends the kiss. Both of us are breathing heavy when he pulls away to look at me. His thumb strokes one of my cheekbones. "I intend to do more," he says.

"I know you do." It is just like my husband to take full advantage of the situation.

His eyes drop back to my lips, which already feel swollen. And I see in his gaze the same thing I've been seeing in everyone else's—hope.

But he doesn't say it. He makes no mention of the fact that I can feel his need vibrating through him. He and I both know it's a weakness, and the king hasn't gotten to where he is today by being weak.

"I see you took great pains to destroy this dress," Montes says, moving one of his hands along the collar, his fingers brushing a string of the seed pearls and the tops of my breasts.

"Are you going to put me down?" I ask. He's still holding me to him, and my legs are still idiotically wrapped around his waist.

"You should never make deals without stipulations," he says. "For I intend to be intimate with you until you freely give into it."

"That's not going to happen," I say, more to convince myself than to convince him.

"It already has once before," he says, gripping me tightly as the ocean swirls around us. "It will again, my lady of lies."

What I hate most about his words is that he very well could be right. I'm not nearly as underhanded as he is. I can't mask my emotions, not the way some people can.

"I'm not the only one who agreed to a deal without stipulations," I say.

Mirth reenters his eyes. "It is my deepest wish that you will use me as I will use you."

An unbidden shiver runs down my spine at the king's

plans for me—for us.

"Be careful what you wish for, Montes."

Because I will use him. Oh, how I will.

CHAPTER 14

Serenity

"I HAVE SOMETHING to show you," the king says that evening.

I'm not a particularly big fan of Montes's surprises.

He leads me through the palace, and I catch another glimpse of his covered pictures. Our footsteps echo, along with those of our guards. What sort of madness must've overtaken the king for him to sequester himself in this lonely place?

We enter what looks like a small library. Montes presses a button embedded in the wall to our right. At the far end of the room, a screen descends from the ceiling. My eyes flick to him, but he gives me no clue as to what's going on in his twisted mind.

Montes begins to roll up his shirtsleeves with those deft fingers of his. I feel my heart break a little more, watching the careless action. He still does it.

His eyes lift to mine, and whatever he sees makes him pause. His gaze moves to his hands, then up again.

"*Nire bihotza* ..."

Whatever he's about to say, I don't let him finish. I stride over to the screen, trying hard to ignore his presence.

It's impossible. It always has been. But it's worse now that the gulf between us is larger than it ever has been.

"You will want to sit for this," he says from behind me.

There's a couch at my back, but I make no move towards it.

"I'm fine."

I hear him cross the room. I badly want to swivel around and watch him, both because I don't trust him and because my eyes can't help but be pulled to every pleasing feature of his. But I keep my gaze steady on the screen.

A moment later, it flickers to life. It looks like a computer's home screen, though it's slightly different than what I'm used to. Montes flips through menu after menu until a photo fills the display.

The image has me sucking in a breath.

General Kline's hardened face stares back at me.

Only, it's *old*.

And now I do turn to face Montes. I can feel my eyes filling, filling. I don't want to cry.

"How?" The word is barely even a whisper.

"You'll see." He looks pointedly at the couch. "You really should sit."

He presses something, and I catch movement in the corner of my eye.

It's not a photo, I realize, dragging my attention away from the king and back to the screen as the image of the general comes to life.

It's a video.

All the air releases from my lungs.

The sight of it, and the realization that the general lived and died all while I slept, is enough to shake my resolve. Without thinking, I sink back into the couch.

I'm not sure I want to see this. Not sure I can bear it.

Behind me I hear the king's footfalls retreating, then the door opens and closes, and I'm alone with a ghost.

"Serenity—" The general rubs his face on the other side of the screen.

He's far away enough from the camera that I can see his leg jiggling. Decades may separate us in time, but I can tell I am not the only one nervous about this video.

He sighs, staring down at his thick, calloused hands. They've seen action. I can tell by how rough they are. Even as old as the general appears to be, he clearly hasn't stopped fighting, hasn't stopped living.

Good for him. I hope he fought death to the bitter end.

"I don't know where to start," he says, frowning. "This situation is all sorts of fucked-up. I don't know when—or if—you'll ever see this. I hope to God the bastard unplugs that damn machine and lets you live or die the way nature intended."

I smile sadly at that. And then his words register.

How did the general know I was in the Sleeper?

Why does Montes have this footage?

They're enemies. Bitter enemies.

"I am going to tell you a story, Serenity, and you're not going to like it." He sighs again, running his thumb over his knuckles. "Two years after you were last seen, I found out that you weren't dead. The official story had always been that you died of cancer."

The general clenches his jaw. "No one believed it, most assumed the king had killed you himself, though there were those who believed that it was a suicide or that you met a violent end at the hands of an enemy.

"There always had been conspiracy theories that you lived, but I never believed them. Not until he showed me ..." General Kline's voice is gravelly with age, but it's lost none of its strength, not even when he's grasping for words.

"I don't know how much you knew before you were ... put under. Right around that time, the Southern WUN rebelled, and the Resistance was a part of that rebellion."

I watch him in wonder. Nothing about this video makes much sense to me. Why he made it, why he's telling me this.

"I didn't make the call to rebel with the South Western territories, but I lived long enough to regret it anyway. The men who've secured control make Montes look like a decent guy, and you know how fucking hard that is to accomplish."

The general runs a hand over his thinning buzz-cut. "The king captured me a couple years after war re-broke out. I was sure I was going to be tortured. Not much love lost between the king and me. Instead he spins me this story about wanting my help, and he shows me something—something every bit as wrong as him."

General Kline grimaces and looks away. "You were so still." His voice lowers. "He had you in this capsule, what I later learned was a Sleeper. And you were alive—unconscious, but alive.

"I'll give the bastard this—he loves you. He's mad with it. Even now. Unfortunately for the rest of the world, I believe he's still willing to destroy anything and everything to get what he wants, and what he wants right now is a cure for that cancer of yours.

"He recruited me and the Resistance to work with him. And we have ever since."

I bring a fist to my mouth. I can't put my finger on what I'm feeling. Relief, definitely. Knowing that the Resistance eventually opposed the advisors that hijacked the WUN makes me feel less disoriented about my own allegiances. But I also feel something else, something that makes me mourn the general more than I already do.

Montes killed his son, and General Kline still found it within himself to work with the king because he knew it would help the greater good. When it came down to it, he was willing to make the same sacrifices he asked of me.

"The king is not a good man," the general continues, "but he's surrounded himself with good men, so there's that. And he's trying to do right. The fucker actually consults me for advice from time to time."

Kline leans forward. "Listen to me carefully, Serenity.

The king might win the war, but I don't see him ending it. There is a distinction. That's why the war still rages on. All he knows is violence. It's a good skill for defeating the enemy, but it's useless once the fighting's over. And, Serenity, he knows nothing of peace."

He pauses for a long moment.

"You do. That's all your dad taught you in the bunker. As your general, I'm giving you one final task."

My body tenses, my pulse hiking at Kline's words. I already know whatever he tasks me with, I'll follow the order.

"If the world you wake up to is the one I fear it will be, then you and I both know your duties aren't over."

I already figured this out, and yet coming from the general, the prospect has my stomach clenching.

"You need to help him. Believe me, I know how wrong it is to ask this of you."

I'm sucking in air fast. My veins thrum as they get battle ready.

I understand him. The general and I might be more similar to one another than anyone else. Even my father. Even Montes.

"That man," he continues, "will eventually reconquer the world, and he's primed to ruin it over and over again.

"Serenity—" He levels his gaze on the lens, and I swear even though time and space separate us, he sees me.

"Don't let him."

CHAPTER 15

Serenity

I SIT THERE long after the video ends.

The general sent me a message from beyond the grave. That's obviously what this is. The final meeting that we never had.

I rub my palms against my eyes, ignoring the wetness that seeps out from under them.

I can't even say what I'm sad about—that the general's gone, that I've been left behind, or that a burden the size of continents has fallen onto my shoulders.

When I exit the room, Montes waits for me.

It's almost implausible, that those two worked together.

The king gives away nothing as he takes me in. I'm sure my eyes are still red.

"Why did you show me that?" I ask, stepping into the hallway and closing the door behind me.

"Why wouldn't I?"

There are so many reasons. The general wasn't kind to the king in his video.

"You've watched it?"

Montes steps in close, that dark hair of his swept back from his face. His features look more regal than ever as he stares down at me.

"I have," the king says.

So he's heard the general's unflattering assessment of him, and he's also heard my final order. I'd be surprised that he showed me the video, except that it benefits Montes. The general essentially tasked me to remain close to the king.

"How long has he been dead?" I ask.

"Sixty, almost seventy years."

I reel from that information, but of course. The general was already old when I knew him. For him to live three extra decades is extraordinary.

"He cared for you," Montes says.

"I know that," I say quietly.

"Does the Resistance still exist?" I ask.

Montes studies me, then slowly shakes his head. "The group splintered into several other organizations about a decade after the general died."

And, given the king's timeline, that happened over half a century ago.

"So they no longer exist?"

"They no longer exist," he affirms.

Time is a spooky thing.

A world without the Resistance … it seems just as implausible as a world without the WUN or the king. They were once a great ally, and then a great enemy, but for them to no longer exist at all?

I've never considered the possibility.

Apparently, even deathless things can be killed.

THE KING LEADS me back down the hall.

"Where are we going?" I ask. My voice echoes in the cavernous space.

"Dinner."

I haven't thought about food in hours and hours, full as I was on this new world and all of its revelations.

I catch more glimpses of abandoned halls and closed doors as we wind our way through the palace. The door we eventually stop at looks like every other, but a faint smell of smoke clings to the area.

He opens it, and I catch a glimpse of the room beyond. A series of antlers decorate the walls. A billiard table sits in front of us, and farther into the room couches surround a grand fireplace. That same smoky smell lingers like a haze in the air.

"What is the name of this room?" I ask, taking it all in.

"The game room."

I smile at the name. "The king and his games," I muse, stepping inside. "I'm surprised the game room and the map room aren't the same." Lord knows the man finds war and strategy vastly entertaining.

Montes whispers in my hair, "Now's a good time to remember that you promised me intimacy. Keep talking as you are, and I will put that mouth to other uses."

Hand it to the king to think of the most creative way to shut me up.

"I see you're still fluent in threats," I say because I can't help myself.

"My queen," he says, stepping away, "it's only a threat if you don't want it to happen."

A part of me *does* in fact want it to happen. My heart's deepest wishes contradict all logic.

I move farther into the room. The space is an ode to highbrow masculinity.

"This place looks nothing like you," I say, taking in the antler chandelier high above us.

Montes heads towards a round table that looks like it was made for card games. He pulls out a chair and leans his hands heavily over the back of it. "I'm glad you think so," he says, his voice genuine. "It was made more for the men I host than for myself."

I run my hand over the green felt of the billiards table I pass as I drift towards him. "Why bring me here?"

"Why not?" he counters.

"I thought we were having dinner."

"We are." He indicates the seat he's pulled out. "Please."

Chivalry—it's just another one of the king's games.

I take a seat across from him because that's just what we do. Montes tries to seduce me with his usual bag of tricks, and I turn him down over and over again. The king's masochistic enough to enjoy the rejection, and I'm petty enough to enjoy dealing it out.

I look around me. This place might not be the worst room in the palace, but it leaves me feeling cold. I wonder what kind of man enjoys a room like this. I imagine he has thick fingers and a large gut. And he'd probably despise a woman like me.

The king takes the seat opposite me and leans back in it, taking in our surroundings just as I'm doing.

"My advisors used to love meeting in rooms like this," he says. "I believe all men want the best of both worlds—to be ruthless savages as well as cultivated thinkers. And that's what this room is, a place where those opposing desires meet."

My eyes move to the king. "Is that what you want?"

"*Nire bihotza*, that's what I *am*."

I suppress a shiver as I take in his dark beauty.

"And what do all women want?" I ask.

Montes appraises me from his seat. Abruptly, he stands and heads over to what looks like a wet bar. He extracts two tumblers and a bottle of amber liquid from beneath it, and sets them on the counter. Uncorking the lid, he begins to pour us drinks.

"It doesn't matter what all women want," he says, "because you are not all women."

"Then what am I?"

His eyes flick up to me. *Mine*, they seem to say.

He returns his attention to his work. "You're right," he says, moving the bottle of liquor from one glass to the other, "I do play games.

He corks the bottle. "That's all life really is—an elaborate game of luck and strategy."

This—*life*—doesn't feel like a game. This feels real and terrible.

He grabs the tumblers and bottle of spirits and heads back to our table. Coming to my side, he hands me one of the glasses.

I wrap my hand around it, feeling the warm brush of his fingers. He doesn't let go.

My gaze rises to meet his. I don't want to look at him, this man that takes up way too much space—in this room, in my head, in my heart.

Montes stares down at me like the universe begins and ends in my eyes.

Nothing can be simple with this man. Not even a drink. I feel that thick, cloying chemistry rise up out of the ether and wrap around us. It doesn't matter that the cancer is gone. With Montes it will always feel like my life has come right up to the edge of death.

He still hasn't given me the drink, and I look pointedly at it.

"You really have no idea what I'm capable of," he says.

The hairs on the nape of my neck stand. I would've said that if anyone knew what the king was capable of, it would be me. But I'm not going to contradict a bad man saying he's worse than I remember.

"And that has you worried," he continues. "It shouldn't. You know of my depravity, but I'm not talking about my evil side."

"Are you going to give me the drink?" I ask, exasperated.

"My lap," he says. He backs up, forcing me to release my hold on the tumbler. He settles back into his seat, his legs splayed out.

You've got to be kidding me.

I see the challenge twinkling in his eyes.

I get up and move over to him, positioning my legs on either side of his chair. Slowly I lower myself and straddle his lap. I take the tumbler out of his hand, and staring at him the entire time, I down its contents.

I hiss out a breath at the burn of it.

"You're wrong, you know," I say, taking the other glass from him and handing him my now empty one. I'm going to need the alcohol. This close to the king, I end up either wanting to fight him or fuck him.

He raises an eyebrow, setting the glass and the bottle of alcohol he holds on the table behind me.

"Your depravity is not what worries me." I've lived through that. That part of the king is predictable. "It's all the other parts of you that do."

That was, after all, what led me to sleep for a hundred years. That wicked soul of his still has a bit of goodness inside it, but when he applies it ... sometimes terrible things happen.

Montes brings his knuckles up and rubs them softly against my cheekbone. "That might be one of the nicest compliments you've given me."

I shake my head and take a sip of my stolen drink.

His fingers wrap around the tumbler and he pulls it from my lips. My hold on the glass is trapped beneath his as he brings it to his own lips, and together we tilt the alcohol into his mouth.

Heat burns low in my belly. I want to say it's from the alcohol, but I can't lie to myself. It's anticipation I feel.

A knock on the door interrupts the moment.

"Come in!" the king calls, not looking away from me.

The door to the room opens, and the king's soldiers come in with dinner.

I begin to get up.

The king's free hand clamps down on my hip. "Stay here."

"Every time you exert a little more intimacy, the interest on my end of the bargain goes up," I say.

"I don't care."

And here we are, locking horns once more.

Behind me I can hear the soldiers. They make quick work of setting out our dinner. I wait until their footsteps retreat. Until the door opens and then clicks shut behind them.

Until I'm alone with my monster once more.

I yank my captive hand out of his, along with the tumbler. I down the second glass's worth of alcohol, then set the empty cup on the table.

Readjusting my hips on the king's lap, I place my hands on his seatback, caging him in.

A very honest smile spreads across Montes's lips as I lean in, my hair dangling between us. "Is this what you want from me?" I ask. I'm tired of fighting every inch he takes, and I'm tired of him toying with me.

Now both of his hands grip my outer thighs, holding me in place. "No," he says.

He closes the last of the distance between our mouths and brushes his against mine. “I want everything you have to give,” he murmurs. “And everything you don’t.”

He’s taken my memories, my mortality, my freedom, even my death. I don’t know how much more there even is to give.

CHAPTER 16

Serenity

"YOU'RE DIFFERENT," I say.

I'm sprawled out on my stomach in front of the fireplace in the king's game room, a now half-empty bottle of what I learned is bourbon and two tumblers sitting in front of me.

We've long since finished eating dinner. I don't mention how odd it is to no longer feel nausea or pain when I eat and drink. I'd gotten so used to both that it's strange to not have to deal with them.

The king healed me.

Between the initial betrayal that landed me in the Sleeper and his more recent reluctance to wake me, I let myself forget that Montes spent the better part of a century curing me, far longer than most people even live.

I can't fathom that kind of perseverance. That kind of loyalty.

I watch him as he lights the fire. And I'm not liking where my eyes are landing. It starts with his hands. He has nice hands. Not too thick, not to boney, just ... deft. Capable.

My gaze moves up his forearms. Underneath his bronze skin, his muscles ripple.

It doesn't take long for my attention to move to other parts of him. His dark hair, which is just long enough to have fun with. His corded back, hidden beneath his shirt.

To my utter mortification, he turns then, catching me eyeing him like he was my dinner.

"I know," he says. "I've been telling you this."

I almost forget what I said in the first place.

That he's different.

That's why my emotions can't seem to land on anger. Every time they're about to, I learn something that shakes up my entire worldview.

"I don't trust your word, Montes," I say. "I trust your actions."

I watch as he finishes lighting the fire. Who would've known a man like the king could do anything so practical?

He straightens, dusting off the last of the bark from his hands and thighs. "And what do you think of my actions?"

My mouth tightens, and that's answer enough. I haven't seen him pull any of his usual, horrible stunts where people die and he gets everything he wants.

He heads back over to me and stretches himself at my

side. "You're at a loss for words. How unusual."

I peer over at him. "I notice you're still good with them," I say, ignoring how that intense gaze of his is focused entirely on me. I lounge back on my forearms. "If I didn't think you were the devil, I'd say you'd be able to seduce even him."

"You give the oddest compliments," he says, his eyes pinching happily.

He's happy. I'm making him happy. And, for that matter, I'm happy.

Oh God.

Of all ironies to exist, we are the worst one.

I grab the bourbon bottle then, fumbling with the cap.

Montes takes it from me and pours a minuscule amount of alcohol into my cup. Really just a sip.

"I see you're still a control freak," I say. And now I'm just recovering from the fact that this is happening all over again. I'm getting sucked under, lost in his dark eyes and black heart. It takes so little.

Montes laughs, oblivious to the fact that while he maintains control, I'm losing it. "It just so happens that I actually care about how you're going to feel tomorrow. Shocking, I know."

Out of all the thing's he's said, I don't know why that one slips through my defenses.

But it does.

I cover the king's hand with my own, my fingers skimming across his skin. I've wanted to do that little action for a while now. It feels just as good as I knew it would.

Montes stares at the hand touching his.

Slowly, his eyes rise to mine. I see lifetimes and lifetimes of desires in those eyes. They all begin and end with me.

He never stopped loving me. That much is obvious from his expression.

And yet, the same man who stares at me in apparent adoration also shut me away in some desolate corner of this palace for decades and decades.

"When did you forget your feelings for me?" I ask.

His brows pinch, and his eyes grow distant. "When you live without someone for as long I have, love becomes this abstract concept, something you attach to a memory. And when memories are that old, they feel like dreams, and you wonder if any of it was real, or if your mind created it all."

It hurts to hear what he has to say, and yet, I understand, and that's the worst of all.

"Why didn't you just let me die?" He hadn't woken me, after all.

"I am over a hundred and fifty years old, and in all that time only a single woman has been able to move me." He looks over at me then. "You are mine. I would *never* let you die."

I should be horrified by the statement. Instead I feel the tempest of this man's love for me. It survived a century apart, it survived Montes himself, a man who shouldn't even be capable of something like love.

The king lifts himself up from where he lays and he leans over me, forcing me to swivel to face him until I've rolled onto my back.

And then he's there, his presence enveloping me.

I can see his intent in every line of his body, the firelight dancing along his skin.

It's happening all over again. This. Us.

It feels old and new all at once. Montes's intensity will always make me feel like intimacy is something I'm experiencing for the first time, and yet my body now knows his, as does my heart.

He dips his head, his hair trickling my cheeks. The moment those lips touch mine will be the moment of no return.

If I do this, I have to accept that my heart's going to get broken all over again. Because I can't become the king's lover once more without handing him my heart. And this time when Montes shatters my trust, I will be the fool who let it happen.

I'm making peace with that. The world is bigger than me and my heart, it's bigger than my life and the king's. It always has been.

"I'm going to trust you," I say softly, his mouth a hairsbreadth away from mine. "Even though you don't deserve it."

His intense face stares down at me. He presses a hand to my cheek. And then he kisses me.

Ash and fire, blood and death—it's all wrapped up into a single stroke of his lips. Both of us are burning, burning. This is heaven and hell.

His body lowers until it's pressed flush against my own. All the while, his mouth moves against mine. He savors everything about me, every scar, every wicked deed, everything remotely good. And I do the same.

He's not wholly evil. I've always known this about him, and yet it's a sweet lullaby to believe that he is.

My breathing picks up as he begins to run his hands up and down my sides.

Montes begins to move against me. My fingers find the edges of his shirt, and I'm yanking it up even as we continue to kiss.

He helps me out of it, and then it's his turn. His hand moves between us, unbuttoning the top of my fatigues.

Our movements become rushed at that point, our old, tormented souls desperate for each other.

Once we are both free of clothing, Montes settles himself between my legs. He bends his head down and kisses the skin between my breasts.

All those years ago, had I ever imagined people could be this way? That men were good for more than just friendship and fighting?

Montes's fingers slide into my hair, and he tilts my head to gaze down at me.

My broken, broken monster. I run my fingers down his cheek. He's just as beautiful as ever, but beneath his skin are the horrors of a century and a half of life. And not just any life, a tyrant king's life.

He turns his head to kiss my palm.

I know all about broken things. I came from a broken house, and a broken land full of broken people. I have a broken soul and a broken heart. This man doesn't know it, but all his cracks align with mine.

Montes shifts his hips, and I angle mine to meet his, and then he's entering me.

Bliss. I begin to close my eyes at the sensation of it.

"Look at me," he says.

My eyelids open, and I gaze up at the king as the two of us come together for the first time in over a century. It feels like it's just been days to me. I'm sure, to Montes, it feels like lifetimes.

We stay joined, unmoving, for several long seconds. I can feel his heartbeat pounding against my skin, he's so close to me.

"I imagined this moment countless times," he admits. "Feeling you around me again." He slides out slowly, then thrusts back in. "It never did you justice."

His lips brush my cheekbone. "You are better than any dream I had of us."

And we are worse than any of our nightmares. This conundrum we have.

It should never have been this way. The two of us have done so many unforgivable things. But at the end of the day, we are two wrongs that, together, make something right.

CHAPTER 17

Serenity

I BLINK MY eyes open. Early morning sunlight streams in to the king's rooms.

I can't immediately figure out how I got here. Last night was a blur once we started drinking. I remember what I did with the king well enough for heat to spread to my cheeks. It's what happened after that's hard to remember.

At some point last night, after we'd dozed off, our bodies twined around each other, Montes had woken me up. After feeding me water and some nondescript pill, he led us back to our room.

I shift slightly, and the moment I do so, I feel coarse fabric rub against my skin. I finger the edge of the shirt I wear. It falls to my thighs.

Not mine.

I wear the king's shirt. I must've walked through the palace last night in it. I scrub a hand over my face and muffle a groan. That's not one of my prouder moments.

Whatever he gave me, it must've countered the alcohol because I feel decent. Not great, but decent.

I lay in bed staring out at the room, trying fruitlessly to fall back asleep.

Time and memory are a strange thing. The room I spent my wedding night in, as well as every piece of furniture inside it, are long gone. And yet, I swear it's as though no time has passed.

My head tilts to the side. It's not just the room that's the same. Déjà vu sweeps over me as I stare at the king's muscular back, not for the first time reveling in his masculine beauty.

A duplicate memory assaults my mind. That first morning I had looked over at the king, the light streaming in just like it is now.

It's all the same, and yet it's not.

I reach out and run my hand over his olive skin. That freckle of his is gone, the one I noticed the first time I woke up next to him. I wonder what injury got that one, that tiny freckle that brought me to this man at the beginning of it all. All signs of his mortality have been wiped away by the Sleeper.

He stirs beneath my hand.

I hadn't meant to wake him. I don't want him to wake. Not yet.

But what I want has little to do with the situation. He

rolls over.

His eyes meet mine, and a lazy smile spreads across his face as he draws me to him.

He nuzzles my nose. "I dreamed of you and then I woke, and I realized it wasn't a dream after all." His words are sleep-roughened.

His voice, his touch, his expression … I'm remembering last night vividly.

The king must be too, because I see a flare of heat enter his features, and then he rolls us so that I'm on my back and he's covering me.

Almost immediately, my breathing picks up. The girl in me is embarrassed by it. I try to sit up, but Montes's hand presses against my sternum, pushing me back down as he begins to kiss between my breasts.

It doesn't end there.

The kisses continue, and he's dipping down, down …

He spreads my thighs apart. I'm about to push him away, when his lips press against my core.

My breath escapes me all at once.

He groans. "*Nire bihotza*, you taste the same as I remember."

Suddenly, I'm not so keen on pushing him away. And my embarrassment … It's still there, but it's taken a backseat to the more immediate sensations.

Montes wraps his arms under the backs of my thighs, pulling me even closer. His mouth is everywhere, and he's still just as good at this as I remember.

A small cry slips from me. I feel the breath of his husky laughter.

I'm climbing, climbing—and then it halts.

Montes releases my thighs, his body moving up mine. I don't have time to be disappointed; I feel the press of him against me as he slides in.

We stare at each other, twin points in the universe. I think I mean more to him than even I realize. He won't speak his thoughts, not a man like this, one who rarely lets himself get vulnerable. But I see them nonetheless, gleaming in the back of his eyes.

He captures my mouth, and I taste myself on his lips. It's wrong and it's right, it's dirty, it's pure—the king makes all my carefully crafted dichotomies disappear.

He pulls my hips close, deepening each stroke—

Oh God.

I break off the kiss. "Birth control," I rasp.

Birth control.

We forgot last night.

The king freezes, though he's practically trembling in an effort to hold back. We both are.

Montes leans his head against mine. "I have none."

None.

I think about what that means, how that changes my own plans. It doesn't—not really.

But shit, to do this knowingly ...

"You are my wife," Montes says. "This is how it's meant to be—how it was always meant to be."

Neither of us has moved.

"I can't," I whisper quietly, divulging this weakness of mine. It might've been a century since he lost his child, but it's still fresh in my mind.

Montes searches my eyes, and something like realization, or wonder, subtly changes his expression. I can only imagine the strangeness of the situation from his perspective—his long lost wife's mind still lives in a past he's nearly forgotten.

"You don't want to carry our child, or you don't want to lose another one?" he asks.

My throat works. I look away.

I am no longer fearful of having the king's child.

I'm fearful for it.

Montes must see it in my expression, my mannerisms.

He lets go of one of my hips, relaxing his hold so that he can tilt my jaw until I meet his gaze.

"*Nire bihotza.*"

Those two words carry a world of meaning. It's a strange mixture of love, and hope, and all other sorts of beautifully heart-wrenching emotions. "This time would not be like the last," he says, and I can tell he means it.

"It can't be." My voice breaks as I speak.

It really can't be. I am becoming Montes, paranoid of losing everything that I love. Because I've lost so much.

His hand brushes my hair back. "It won't be."

I draw in a shuddering breath and shake off somberness that comes with remembering.

And then I'm the one that pulls him to me, pushing this forward.

I've always wanted my pound of flesh, and now I'm taking it.

CHAPTER 18

Serenity

WE'RE BACK IN the Great Room, the king's mad walls hidden once more by large screens. And once more the space is filled with military officers. I intend to get to know each one, eventually. For now I have to hope that Montes's subjects respect him a whole lot more than the ones that filled his conference room a century ago.

In addition to the U-shaped table that takes over much of the space, there's now a smaller one that faces it, where the king and I sit.

I spend the first several hours of the day listening to officers discuss updates on the war and strategies they're implementing.

This world is strange. The moment I believe it's identical to the one I left, some tidbit filters in that has me second-guessing everything.

Eventually, however, a picture begins to stitch itself together. The world's population has been decimated by war and sickness. Efforts to clean radiation from the water and soil are ongoing. Not as many people are suffering from famine, but that's only because there are so few people left. Even the small annual outputs in the farming industry can sustain them. Aside from outright killing, cancer is the leading cause of death, though every once in a while the plague sweeps through and takes its place.

From what I understand, there are cures for many of the world's health issues, but there isn't enough money to make these cures widespread. The end result is a huge economic gap between the haves and have-nots. People are discontent. They know nothing but war and living on the edge.

I drum my fingers on the table as we hear yet another report from some lieutenant of some battalion on the state of his troops and the intel they've gathered on the enemy. I don't pretend to be the authority on anything, but if I had to guess, I'd say that these officers have been running in circles for as long as anyone can remember, discussing the same strategies, the same concerns, and applying the same answers they always have. And this entire time no one's realized that they need to derail themselves.

I stand, my chair scraping back as I do so. The sound echoes throughout the room, interrupting the speaker. The officer's voice dies away as dozens upon dozens of gazes move to me.

"Is war all we plan on talking about?"

These people don't understand. I can see it in their confused gazes. In a war council you talk about war.

I make eye contact with many of them. "War doesn't end war," I say. "Peace does."

I'm sure they think me an idiot. I'm saying nothing they don't already understand. But knowing something and framing the world through that lens are two very different things.

"You won't win this war by plotting ways to destroy the enemy—necessary though that might be," I say. "You'll win it by forging peace."

Again, I'm saying nothing new.

"Your Majesty, how do you suggest we forge peace?" One of the female officers asks this.

I glance down at the king. "You promised to give me whatever I asked for," I breathe.

His face wipes clean of all expression. He knows he's been had before I speak.

"I will campaign for it and break bread with whomever I must," I say to the room, though my eyes stay trained on the king. "And I will end this, once and for all."

THIS IS WHAT intimacy cost the king.

Power. Control.

He might have allowed me onto his war council, but I know with certainty Montes was never going to place me in a position of true power. Not when I'm so iconic. Not when a position like this often means capture or death.

So I'm carving the position out for myself.

That vein begins to pound in the king's temple as I hijack the meeting. It's not just anger I see rising to the surface. It's panic. The man who controls nearly everything is realizing he just bargained away something he shouldn't have.

I tear my gaze away from Montes to look out at the room. I can feel that wildness stirring beneath my veins, the same excitement that comes before battle. Only this time, it's so much sweeter because I'm solving a problem, not exacerbating it.

"The king will still lead all the current war efforts, but we will be incorporating my strategy into it," I say to the room.

I am no fool. I need Montes's expertise and knowledge. I just want to build my tactics on the foundation he's laid.

"I don't know how much you all know about my past," I say, moving around the table. I can feel the king's eyes like a brand on my back. "But before I slept, before I even married the king, I was a soldier, just like many of you. I was a soldier—and an emissary."

The people sitting in on this meeting look alive and attentive, when only minutes ago many wore bored, listless expressions.

"I was taught to fight, but I was groomed to negotiate."

I throw a glance back at Montes. His eyes burn with his fury and with something brighter, something much more honorable.

"Long ago, I forged a peace treaty with a hostile nation. I will do so again, and I won't give the representatives of the West a choice."

"You still haven't answered how you propose to go about attaining this." Heinrich says this. The grand marshal looks skeptical, as do many of the other men and women gathered here.

The true brilliance of this plan, and the ultimate irony, is that Montes had handed me the answer on a silver platter.

"I appear to already be a symbol of freedom to the people." I pace as I speak. "We are going to encourage that belief, and we're going to win the common people over. I am going to fight for them and speak for them until I become synonymous with victory, regardless of what nation they belong to."

I watch the officers faces as they mull this possibility over. Many appear unsure, but more appear intrigued.

"Ideology will win us this war," I say.

The room is quiet. I don't dare look back at Montes. All I can think is that he is indeed a changed man to have not intervened thus far.

"Whoever is in charge of coordinating the king's political maneuvers," I say, "I want you to schedule a series of meetings." My footfalls echo as I move to the center of the room. "I want to meet with every regional leader—especially those who have a history of disliking the king. Even those that belong to the Western United Nations. And I want to meet with the leaders of every grassroots organization and vigilante group."

Some people are writing furiously. Others are staring at me with bright eyes, and still others look grim. But no one, no one appears unengaged. That, if nothing else, is one accomplishment of this meeting. This struggle needs to mean something to people. And I bet it hasn't in quite some time.

"I plan on creating alliances with each and every one of these leaders."

Someone interrupts. "But what you're saying—some of these men and women are terrorists, most no better than the leaders of West."

I seek out the voice. I smile a little when my eyes find the officer. "I don't plan on catering to their demands. I'm going to convince them to get behind mine."

This lesson I learned from the king. When to compromise, and when not to. For all of Montes's terrible decisions, he's great at getting people to do his bidding without conceding anything himself.

I pause, my gaze sweeping over the men and women in the room. "And finally," I say, "I want to meet with the WUN's representatives—either directly or over video."

CHAPTER 19

Serenity

"ARE YOU INSANE?"

I turn to face the king.

The last of the room's inhabitants have left, leaving me alone with Montes.

He leans against the double doors that lead out. Only a minute ago he'd been swapping some final comments with his officers. Now that everyone's gone, he's dropped any pretense that this was a joint decision. Though, technically, it was.

I walk over to him slowly. When I get close I say quite slowly, "Fuck. You." All my civility is gone.

He rears back just slightly, enough to let me know I surprised him.

Good. Finally I can let the full spectrum of my feelings show.

I'm one raw, savage girl, and he has *wronged* me.

"You selfish bastard," I continue. "You really thought I would just jump into bed with you without a damn good reason?"

His jaw tightens.

I've learned how to play the king's games, and now the player is getting played.

"You had something I wanted, and I had something you wanted." I am treading in very, very dangerous territory.

Montes hasn't spoken, but that vein in his temple throbs.

I move away from him. The screens have been rolled back up, and I can see all those conquered territories once more. The sight of them still disgusts me.

"You can have your intimacy and I can campaign for peace," I say, rotating to face him, "or it can all go away—the intimacy, the camaraderie—all of it. I will become the bane of your existence."

He doesn't react—not immediately. I feel something like energy gathering behind him.

When he finally begins to stalk towards me, I have to force myself to stay rooted where I am. There's a reason he's been the king for this long. His power moves with him, and right now it's intimidating the hell out of me.

He cocks his head, assessing me like a hunter does prey. "So my little wife decided to try her hand at strategy?" he says, his footsteps echoing through the room. "I am impressed."

I run my tongue over my teeth. Now it's my turn to stay quiet.

He squints at me. "What other schemes have you been up to?"

I look over at the bits and pieces of the maps that I can see. "You're not the one who should be worried about their spouse scheming."

He captures my jaw with his hand and peers into my eyes. I try to jerk away, but he won't release his hold.

His gaze searches mine. "You do have something else up your sleeve," he says.

I do.

I don't look away from him. I don't give him any sign at all on whether or not he's correct.

The air shifts, and I can't tell whether it's anger or passion that fills the room, only that I'm choking on it. Knowing us, it's probably both.

"If you're hiding something from me, I will find out." His voice is steady and quiet. Lethal. People die after hearing that tone.

"And if you're hiding something from me," I say, "then so will I."

His calculating eyes brighten, and a whisper of a smile crosses his face. He inclines his head.

He still grips my jaw. "So my vicious little wife plans on ending the war. And she wants power and autonomy along the way," he says, still studying me.

Yes. That's precisely what I want.

The king taps my jaw with his index finger. His vein is

still pounding, and his features are just as uncompromising as I've ever seen them.

He pulls my head in close. "I will keep my end of the bargain."

He kisses me then, a punishing, severe kiss that lets me know just how displeased he is. I revel in it.

As his mouth moves against mine, his fingers drop to the waistband of my pants. He flicks the top button open.

I pull away from the kiss with a gasp, grabbing his wrist.

In response, he presses me closer. "This is what I get for your little stunt. You promised me intimacy," he breathes against my cheek. "I want it."

Surprise and a deviant sort of satisfaction unfurl within me. I enjoy sex, and I enjoy an angry king.

I release his wrist and let his hand dip down into my pants. I gasp again as he begins to work me.

"My vicious little wife, you do me proud," he says. "I should've known." He dips his mouth close to my ear. "You've gotten a taste for playing games after all."

And so I have.

"I WANT TO see it," I say that evening.

The ocean breeze blows my hair. We're back outside, finishing dinner as the sun sets.

The scenery of this place always gets to me. Oranges and reds shimmer off the sea's surface. It's breathtaking, and looking at it, you would never know that across those waters people are suffering.

"See what?" Montes says, lounging back in his seat.

"The place where I slept," I say.

It might be my imagination, but out here in the fading light, the king looks distinctly uncomfortable. He appraises me from across the table.

I wish I could appear just as relaxed as the king, but nothing will loosen my limbs. The thought of seeing my resting place has me wound up.

"Alright, my queen," he finally says.

Just like that. No fighting, no wrangling, no demanding on his part. The fact that he doesn't try to get something from me in return makes me more nervous, not less.

His chair scrapes back and he stands.

Now. He's planning on showing me right now.

I hide my surprise. I hadn't imagined the gratification would be this immediate.

I rise to my feet, dropping my napkin on the table.

Montes comes to my side, and, placing a hand on the small of my back, he steers me forward. We cross the gardens and head back into the towering building.

So it's inside the very palace itself. Part of me had imagined that I would be sleeping in some sort of crypt on the palace grounds, far away from the living.

He leads me down several hallways, and with each turn the setting becomes increasingly familiar.

We end up right back in front of our bedroom.

I raise an eyebrow.

I can't tell whether this is a trick or not.

Montes smiles at my expression, his eyes gleaming. "You thought I'd keep you anywhere else?" he asks as he opens the door.

"You kept me in your room?"

For a second, I imagine myself laid out on the bed, stiff like the dead, before I remember that I was encased in the Sleeper.

"Not exactly." He leaves me at the threshold, and I watch him, puzzled, as he heads to a large framed painting.

A familiar unease washes through me, one that's reserved for unnatural things. There is something frightening about watching this beautiful man share his dark secret. Something *wrong.*

Montes turns back to look at me as he swings the frame back.

My lips part with realization. There's another room. A hidden one. Now that the painting is moved aside, I make out a door camouflaged with the rest of the wall. A discreet thumbprint scanner is embedded next to it.

The king presses his thumb against it, and a second later it blinks green. With a pressurized hiss, the door unlocks. He holds it open for me.

What lies beyond is cloaked in shadow. Suddenly I'm not so sure how much I want to see where I rested. What's to stop the king from forcing me back into the machine?

He notices my hesitation. "Serenity, you don't have to see this."

My paranoia dissipates. If he wanted to put me under, he'd need a doctor and a sedative, and I know he has neither.

I still don't trust him. Not with everything.

I brush past him as I step into the corridor. Around us,

dim lights flicker to life. I press my palm against one of the walls and turn my head, following the line of the surface until it disappears into darkness. I squint as my eyes make out ...

Windows. Windows that look into the palace's rooms.

"What is this place?" I ask.

Montes's voice comes from behind me. "A king always has secrets. Secrets and enemies. This is where I used come to be alone with you."

The hairs on the back of my neck rise.

"Come." He places a hand against my back and leads me once more.

As we walk, more lights flicker on.

"There's another entrance to this passageway through my office. We believe that's the one your abductors used."

I'm not paying much attention to him, too busy staring in horror at room after room that we pass. He spies on people.

"This is wrong," I murmur.

"It's saved my life several times."

I come to a stop as a thought hits me. "These are one-sided mirrors, aren't they?"

"They are."

There was a mirror in the room I stayed in. Twice I had heard a thump on the other side of it. Twice its surface vibrated.

"You watched me." Horror bleeds to anger.

He appears amused. "When I wanted to see you, I visited." The light glints off his dark eyes. "I did not watch you from behind glass."

I search his face, looking for the lie in his words. I see only honesty. I believe him, and yet ...

"Who else has access to these passageways?"

"No one. I alone come and go through them."

I try not to think about the fact that Montes was the only company I kept while I slept.

"Well," I say, "we know at least half a dozen other men know of this place."

"*Knew*," he corrects. "I believe you took care of that situation."

It's an unwelcome reminder. I now have their faces to add to the ghosts that haunt me.

"Someone else was back here. I heard them while I was in my room."

Montes glances down at me, his brows knitted. He searches my face. He must see that I'm not lying because a frown forms. "I will look into it."

I appreciate this about the king. He takes my concerns seriously.

We walk for a while, the passageway twisting every so often as it maneuvers around rooms. The corridor widens as we get to a set of thick double doors.

The king leans away from me to scan his thumb once more. I hear the latch click as it unlocks, and then Montes is opening one of the doors.

My earlier skittishness returns as I stare down at the massive marble staircase that descends away from me and the giant pylons that hold up the roof high above. I lived under the earth for years when the bunker was my home. I should have no qualms about entering this room. But my blood and my bones know this place and they recoil from it.

My curiosity overrides superstition. I take the steps one at a time. My gaze moves up to the domed ceiling that arcs high overhead. Embedded into it, seemingly at random are indigo and gold tiles. Our colors.

The pattern of tiles is not random, I realize after a moment. The fresco has been made to reflect the night sky, and each gold tile represents a star, every cluster a constellation.

The sight makes me press my lips together. He gave me the sky.

The columns that rise around me seem even larger the farther down I descend. They look luminescent under the dim glow of lights.

I can feel the king watching me, this man who attended to me while I was down here. Here he could control me, here he could have me to himself. Here I could be whatever he needed me to be, and I didn't have the agency to defy him.

I glance back up at him.

Those eyes of his are wary, like I am the dangerous one.

I return my attention to the room as I reach the bottom of the stairs. I take in more marble and tile features. A small pool captures my attention. It gleams under the light of this place.

And then my eyes fall on the Sleeper.

Only, it doesn't look like a Sleeper. It looks like a sarcophagus, something rich people used to be buried in long before my time or the king's. Sheathed in gold, intricate flowering designs cover it. A marble bench rests before it, presumably where the king sat when he visited.

I'm drawn towards it, both horrified and mesmerized.

The place is an ode to me, to us. Even the pool of water and the way it dances along the walls reminds me of the first time Montes held me in his arms.

Montes did this all for me. My gaze sweeps over our opulent surroundings.

No, not for me. All of this is much too grand. He did this for *himself.*

"It's a temple," I say. A temple made to honor me.

But this place does me no honor, and I deserve none. I'm a soldier, a killer, a captive queen. But not a god.

His shoes begin to click as he walks down the stairs, the noise echoing throughout the chamber.

"Are you frightened?" he asks.

I don't bother answering.

Instead I reach out a hand and run it along the surface of the Sleeper. This is where I stayed in a state of stasis for lifetime upon lifetime, years stacked one on top of the other. People were borne from the earth and drawn back into it, and still I remained.

Montes's footfalls draw closer, and I'm so very aware of him. My muscles tense when he stops only a handful of feet away.

"Tell me something that makes this better," I say.

"I love you."

Now I rotate to face him.

I regret it immediately.

Montes's eyes go soft.

Will I ever get used to that face wearing that expression when he looks at me? Your nightmares aren't supposed to make you feel cherished.

His eyes rise above me to the room beyond. "This is the evidence of my love. I know you find it terrible, possibly even unethical, but I never saw it that way."

What's worse than not understanding the king is understanding him. Every time I do, I forgive him a little more.

His eyes return to me. "We've been here long enough. Come, my vicious little wife, there's much to do."

And together we return to the land of the living.

CHAPTER 20

Serenity

THE NEXT MORNING I'm set up in an office, three of the king's officers surrounding me.

Montes left me at the room's entrance, giving the door a parting glance. "The people you need to speak to are inside," he said mysteriously. And then, without elaborating, he stalked away.

I stared at his retreating form, wondering if somehow this was a trick.

But now that I sit with the closest thing the king has to advisors on the dainty couches in the room, I get the impression that the only trick being played is on my archaic notions of the king.

Because by all appearances, he's fully equipped me to

see my war strategy through.

The three individuals that sit around me must've been soldiers at one point. That's the only thing that can account for the hard twinkle in their eyes and the strong set of their shoulders. And now they wait for me to make demands of them.

I sit forward on the couch, arms braced against my legs, hands clasped between them. "I need to devise a plan to meet with our enemies, our allies, and anyone else in between who you consider important enough to speak with." I say, getting right to business.

Across from me, one of the officers pulls a file from the briefcase she carries and drops it onto the coffee table resting between us. "We've already put together a list of leaders you'll want to speak with," she says, tapping on the folder. "We've also included a tentative schedule of meetings that can be immediately arranged with your approval.

"We can fly in some of these individuals as early as the end of the week, but there will be quite a few that you'll have to visit yourself."

I pick the folder up and begin thumbing through it. It's dizzying, the amount of information inside. Schedules, names, titles. Most of them mean nothing to me. I've had a hundred years to lose all frame of reference.

I set the file down at my side. In most ways, I am utterly inadequate for this position. I have a century's worth of complicated political history I need to catch up on, a century's worth of knowledge that my allies and my enemies already know about. Ignorance is a great tool to be exploited.

My jaw hardens. I've already been exploited quite enough for one lifetime.

So I begin to look for one of the few names I do know. When I've skimmed through the entire file and don't see it, I set the folder aside.

"What about the First Free Men?"

"What about them?" one of the male officers asks.

I meet his eyes. "Why are they not listed among the groups I'm to speak with?"

"With all due respect Your Majesty, this was the group that broke into this very palace and stole you. The king has issued a KOS—kill on sight—order for their leader."

Montes hasn't lost every last bit of his depravity after all.

I lean forward. "The First Free Men were powerful enough to find the resting place of a woman who was believed to be dead. And they were powerful enough to smuggle her out of the king's palace."

The three officers are quiet, and I'm sure they know what my intentions are.

"Set up a video call with their leader. I want to speak with him or her as soon as possible."

"Your Majesty, Styx Garcia is in hiding," the female officer says. "There's no guarantee we will be able to get communication through to him. And even if we do, there's no guarantee that he will agree to the call."

I am the hundred year old queen he almost captured, the woman that slaughtered six of his men.

I look her square in the eye. "He'll take the call."

It takes five hours for Styx to agree to the call.

At 2:00 a.m. this evening—*morning*, technically—I'll be on the phone with the man who failed to abduct me.

I considered telling the king about it as soon as the call was confirmed. Montes is perhaps the most ruthless strategist that I know, and I can't help but want to pick his brain for advice.

The petty part of me also wants him to know I've openly defied his orders by arranging this.

But, in the end, I decided against it.

Someone else will likely tell him, and soon, but it won't be me.

I lay in bed for a long time, my eyes peeled open. Montes's arm is wrapped around my midsection, my backside pressed tightly to his front. He holds me like nothing short of another apocalypse will tear us apart. It's both comforting and confusing. I don't know how to deal with all these conflicted emotions I feel.

I wait until his arm slips from around my waist and he flips over before I slip out of bed.

I dress quietly, and then, ever so softly, I head out of the room. Even doing this is a risk. Montes used to have a habit of waking up in the middle of the night. He might still.

I can only hope his sleeping habits have changed since we've been apart.

I make my way through the empty corridors of the palace, towards the office I was given.

I flick the lights on and sit down behind my desk. I begin to flip through some of the documents I requested on the First Free Men. There isn't much on them. It makes me think they're even more powerful than everyone believes.

Their leader is Styx Garcia, a thirty-six-year-old combat veteran who fought for the West before being honorably discharged. A photo of him is paper-clipped to the documents.

I pull it out and frown. He would be handsome except that his face is a patchwork of scars. They slice down his eyebrows and cheeks, drag across his nose, and claw upwards along the edge of his jaw.

The sight of all that mottled tissue has me touching my own scar.

And in the midst of it all, he's got a pair of dark, soulless eyes. Just like the king's.

I set the picture aside and read his biography in the file. Like me, he was born and raised in the northern territory of the Western United Nations. He spent over ten years on active duty; far, far longer than the amount of time I had.

At some point after that, though the document doesn't say exactly when, he established the First Free Men. He's been building it ever since.

I close the folder. By all indications, this man is just as power-hungry as all the other corrupt men I've met throughout this war. What I don't understand is why the West would work with him at all.

Somewhere inside the palace, a grandfather clock tolls twice, my cue to leave my office.

My footfalls echo throughout the cavernous halls. This

place rubs me the wrong way. There is a hollowness to the corridors that only exaggerates just how empty the place is, and yet I swear I can feel the weight of unseen eyes on me as I head to the king's study.

His room is one of the few in the palace that has absolute privacy—or so I was told. We'll see soon enough.

The king was right yesterday. I am keeping something else from him, something he would rebel against if he knew.

When I reach the door to his office, I press my thumb to the fingerprint scanner. It blinks green like I knew it would, then I'm inside.

I slide behind the king's desk and pull out the set of instructions on setting up a video call from one of the royal computers. It takes five minutes to execute, and then I dial the number Styx's men gave to me.

Almost immediately the call goes through.

The large monitor in front of me flickers, and then I'm staring at Styx Garcia in the flesh.

I appraise this man with narrowed eyes. He has even more scars than his photo let on, none quite so gruesome as the one that's split open one of his nostrils.

This is a very dangerous man. It makes my decision to escape his men that much wiser.

"Your Majesty," he says, dipping his head. "It's an honor."

I nod back to him. "Styx."

He peers up at me as he straightens. His fascination is plain. And on his face, it's an unsettling look.

"Your men woke me," I say. It's as good enough conversation starter as any.

He inclines his head.

My gaze moves behind him, to a stark, dimly-lit cement room. "How did you find me?" I ask.

His eyes are too bright. "With difficulty."

My lips thin. "It's two a.m. here. I want to go to bed. Please give me the straight answer."

He flashes me a distinctly unsettling smile. It has my trigger finger twitching.

"Perhaps if you visit me," he says, "I will tell you in person."

"Oh, for fuck's sake," I say.

This conversation won't get anywhere if he keeps answering like this.

"Are you aware that there's a bounty on my head?" he asks, straightening in his seat.

"I am."

"And still you called," he says.

"And you answered," I reply.

"Why wouldn't I?" He smiles pleasantly, the action contorting all his facial scars. "You're the supposedly dead queen that's come back to life. And you somehow managed to kill half a dozen of my best men when you escaped." His gaze shifts subtly. I can tell he's taking in the hair that spills over my shoulder. "I was very eager to speak with you.

"But," he continues, "that doesn't explain why *you're* calling *me*." He tilts his head, the gesture almost mocking. "Tell me, does the dear King of the East know you're talking to me?"

I tighten my jaw. Styx is just another man that likes to toy with people.

"Tell me about your connection to the West," I say instead.

Styx throws his hands out. "There it is," he says. "Oh, you *are* transparent. You want my connection to the West."

"I do." I don't bother denying it.

"Why?"

"I need to speak with the representatives," I say. "Privately."

Styx folds his hands over his chest. "You don't want your king to know." He says it with such satisfaction. "What makes you think I have the clearance to speak with the representatives?"

"You were going to hand me over to them. Your men said so themselves."

"Hmmm ..." He appraises me.

He sits forward suddenly. "You know, I always believed." He stares at my scar with fascination. When his eyes meet mine again, an unnatural amount of fervor has entered them. "A woman like you can't be killed so easily."

"You have no idea who I am," I say.

Even though a screen and countless miles separate us, my hand is itching for my gun. I don't like the way he looks at me.

To be fair, I don't like the way most people look at me, but the way Styx does it ... In another situation it would've earned him a bullet. It might still, depending on the way the future unfolds.

"I expected you to be violent, Serenity Freeman."

"*Lazuli,*" I correct.

"But to watch you gun my men down in seconds ..." He continues on as though I hadn't spoken. "That, that surprised me."

When I don't react, he raises his eyebrows. "You did realize there was someone watching on the other end of that camera, didn't you?"

He's asking the wrong questions and giving the wrong kind of answers to mine. I don't know what I was expecting from him, or what the correct response to my call would be, but this isn't it.

He wants to understand me, I can tell. Capturing me would've allowed him all the time in the world for that, but he's trying to make up for it now.

"I never planned on handing you over to them—the West." The look in his face as he says that ... this man better tread carefully, he's setting all sorts of violent tendencies in me.

He leans back in his seat, watching me, his eyes unblinking. "So, how are you faring?" he asks.

I have a sick, sick admirer in Garcia. I assumed he'd be angry that I killed off his men.

"I'm fine." That was my last attempt at being civil. Entertaining this man's version of small talk is almost more than I can bear.

"What does your husband think of your being awake?" A flash of something enters his eyes. I would say it was jealousy, but I've seen that emotion so rarely that I doubt my own intuition. Not to mention that I don't know this man. To be jealous of a stranger receiving attention from her husband ...

He makes Montes seem normal, and that is an impressive feat.

"We are not friends, Garcia," I say, my voice hard. "You are the leader of the terrorist group that attempted to capture me. Save the personal questions for men who must answer to you."

His jaw tightens, and his gaze flicks off screen. He's the only person I can see in the room, but I bet there are other people behind the camera, people that just overheard their leader get slighted by me.

"Do you know how much money and resources went into finding and retrieving you?" he hisses. This is the first glimpse I've gotten of the real Styx Garcia. "You wouldn't be awake to sit here and insult me if it weren't for me."

The last of my patience evaporates.

I lean forward. "You are a fool if you think you're going to get either my pity or my gratitude." I'm just about done with this man. "You kidnapped me, I killed your men. I don't regret it, and I imagine if our roles were reversed, a man like you would feel the same way." Someone who collects scars the way Styx does has a taste for violence.

"Now," I say, "we can continue with the slights, or we can discuss how we're going to end this war."

That has him straightening. I see the fist that he rests on his desk tighten and then release.

I take a deep breath. "I want to work with you, Garcia, but what I really need is someone who has an in with the West. Do you have that in?"

He folds his hands and taps his two pointer fingers

against his chin as he studies me.

"Yes," he finally says.

"I need to speak with them. Can you help me arrange that?"

Another pause. Then, "Yes—for a price."

CHAPTER 21

Serenity

WE TALK FOR an hour. Unfortunately even by the time I end the call, that sickening shine in Garcia's eyes still hasn't waned.

Working with him might be a mistake.

I shut everything down and return it where I found it.

I sit back in the king's chair and bring my folded hands to my lips, musing on the situation I'm creating for myself.

I run my hands through my hair. If the king finds out everything I intend ... he might very well change his mind and shove me back in that Sleeper. I don't fear that nearly as much as I fear my plan will fail and the world will bear the fallout from it.

I stand and push the chair in.

I'm halfway to the door when a thought catches me off guard. I pause mid-step.

Slowly, I turn. My eyes land on the large gilded frame that hangs on the back wall of the king's study. I remember something Montes told me, something about a second entrance to my crypt.

I might very well be staring at that second entrance right now.

Hesitantly, I head towards the back of the room and touch the expansive painting. My fingertips run over the brushstrokes before wrapping around the edges of the frame.

I give it a swift tug, but the added force isn't necessary. It swings open with ease.

Just like the other painting, a door and a thumbprint scanner rest behind this one.

This is the second entrance to my crypt, the one the First Free Men came through.

Out of curiosity, I press my thumb to the fingerprint scanner. It's worked once before. I wait an agonizing several seconds, and then ...

A green light blinks, and the door hisses as it unlocks, swinging inwards.

The king authorized me to enter his secret passages. It makes sense; if the palace is ever under fire, this might be our best chance at escape. The king and I have already lived through one instance where I was locked out from such a passage.

Still, to give me access to areas where I cannot be watched ... my obsessive husband has surprised me.

I step through, shutting the door behind me.

I look down the corridor. The hall stretches out on either side, descending into the darkness beyond the motion activated lights. I begin heading back towards our room.

My footsteps falter as I pass by the first one-way mirror. It's unnerving to think that the king could just stand here and watch someone go about their business without them knowing. I understand his motives, but it's eerie and invasive nonetheless.

I begin to move again, passing several more rooms, each one dark. Eventually, I pass a room whose lights are still on. Without meaning to, I pause and survey it. What I see has me stepping up to the window.

A gun rests on the bed. That alone is eye-catching enough for me to give this room a second look. If only there were a way in. I could use a gun. Any weapon, really. I don't trust Montes, or this place, or these people. It's nothing personal—well, excepting Montes, of course. I was raised to mistrust my surroundings.

I force myself to step away from the window and resume walking. I can't shake my unease. It's this place. The king's madness and depravity is all concentrated here. It's messing with my mind.

My eyes drift down the hall, towards the lights that continue on into the distance.

Lights in the distance ... that's not right. The only time they come on is when they're motion activated. And then it hits me.

Shit.

I'm not alone.

I HEAD TOWARDS the illumination. Even if I were the type to hide, it would be pointless. The lights are convenient breadcrumbs for either Montes or myself to follow.

Ahead of me, the hallway is abandoned. But it veers sharply to the right, where the light appears to continue on. That's where the king will be—if, of course, he's still in the passageway.

I pass the double doors that lead to the crypt I was kept in, and I have to steel myself against the warm burn of anger it evokes. My shoes click loudly against the stone. Montes must hear me.

Once I round the corner, I see a figure peering into one of the rooms, his back to me.

I halt in my tracks.

His hair's too short to be Montes.

The king was wrong. He's not the only one who can access these passageways. And now I'm facing a stranger unarmed.

Beyond the man, the overhead lights trail off into darkness.

"*Serenity.*"

A chill runs down my spine.

I know that voice. I'd know it from anywhere.

But ... it's impossible. The man last drew breath a hundred years ago.

The figure swivels around.

My eyes take in the slight build, the brown eyes, the

skin that's every bit as tan as Montes's. The dark hair that's shorter than I remember it. And finally, that face I hated so much.

My ears didn't deceive me.

Marco, the king's oldest friend and advisor, is alive.

CHAPTER 22

Serenity

THE KING BROUGHT him back to life while he let me waste away.

The anger churning through me sharpens.

My hands fist, and I begin stalking towards him.

Sensing my violent intentions, Marco puts a hand up. “Whoa, whoa, whoa.”

I don’t let that stop me. As soon as I’m within swinging range, I lunge for him.

He catches me around the midsection before I can land a blow, pinning my arms to my sides.

I thrash against him. “You fucking murderer! Why did he let you live?”

Gone is the composed leader I’ve been for the last hour. I’m back to being an angry, lost girl.

"Stop. Serenity," Marco says. "Please. Stop."

To hear that asshole's voice … I'm seeing red.

What I really need is a gun. Any gun—

Something about Marco's tone has me redirecting my thoughts. Something … not right.

I seek out his eyes. He's not looking at me the way he used to, like I was just a thorn in his side.

And the way he said my name a few seconds ago … it's too familiar.

"Let me go," I say.

"Not if you're going to hit me again."

I struggle futilely against him. He's still staring at me, and it's setting off all sorts of unwelcome reactions.

The worst thing the king could do was immortalize me. I'm quickly finding I don't react well to the attention and the adoration.

And that's what I see in Marco's eyes. Adoration.

It shouldn't be there. We hate each other, and unlike the king, there is nothing else to our relationship beyond that.

Marco adjusts his hold on me. He pulls me in close, until our chests are flush against each other.

I bring my knee up, and he only just manages to pivot out of the way. "Jesus. Stop." He shakes me a little. "Serenity, I am not going to hurt you."

It's almost laughable that he thinks I'm the one worried about getting hurt.

"You killed my father, you bastard." I'm shaking I'm so angry.

It had been justice enough to know that Marco had

taken his own life with the same hand and the same gun that killed my father.

But now that he's so obviously cheated death and lived while I slept … the anger resurges.

"I am not the same man," Marco says.

This again.

"Screw you and Montes and all of your fucking excuses!" I spit out, jerking against the hands hold me captive.

I'm tired of evil, immortal people telling me this. Like they're recovering psychopaths. Time can change a person, but it cannot erase their past.

"You will *always* be the person that took the first man I ever loved."

I swear in Marco's eyes I see some mixture of surprise and devastation. "Montes never told me Marco did that."

I rear back, some sick combination of confusion and disgust filling my veins.

He continues on before I can get a word in edgewise. "I'm sorry for you and your father, Serenity, but I am not that man.

"You see," he says carefully, "I am his clone."

THE REVELATION IS enough to make me pause.

"You're a … ?"

I can't even say it.

Back in the time I left, clones were the things of science fiction, along with flying cars and humanoid robots.

"I am a copy of him," Marco says. "Same DNA. It's no different than twins, except that we never shared a womb and we weren't born at the same time—obviously."

He says this all as if his existence is somehow normal.

"You're not Marco?" I say.

It's still not registering

"I *am* Marco," he says, "just not the one you knew. I was named after him."

Suddenly all the pieces come crashing together. No technology could revive the king's brain-dead friend. So instead Montes made a copy of Marco to keep him company through the years.

That is the saddest thing I might've heard yet.

Marco must sense that I'm no longer a threat. His hold loosens on me.

I stagger away from him.

A *clone*. I'm still wrapping my mind around it.

I look everywhere but Marco, and that's when I remember where exactly we are.

"You were the one watching me," I say as the realization dawns on me. The noises I heard. I'd been in lingerie one of those instances.

My hands clench. "You *saw* me," I accuse, my face flushing. I'm ready to throttle him, the pervert.

He doesn't bother denying it. "I wasn't *trying* to watch you undress."

I narrow my eyes at him.

That *voice*. I can't help but hate it. I recognize that this is not the same man who crossed me years ago. That doesn't change the fact that everything about him reminds me of the pain his twin put me through.

"I just wanted to see you, and the king forbid me from

meeting you until he'd broken the news. So I came here," he continues. "He doesn't know that I can access these passageways."

"Why did he hide you from me?" I ask. I'm still angry and more than a little spooked, but I also feel an unbidden wave of pity. Pity for this creature who will always live in his predecessor's shadow, and pity for a king who must create his own friends because no decent human would truly and willingly become that man's companion.

Marco glances at my hands, which are still balled into fists. "I imagine he was trying to prevent this from happening."

The strangeness of the situation is beginning to wear off. I glance beyond Marco's shoulder.

"The king's room is at the end of this hall," Marco says.

I return my attention to him.

"That's what you're looking for, right?" he adds. "You came from the king's study."

It's not good that he knows that. The whole point of being in Montes's office was to draw as few eyes as possible. And now Marco's dangling that piece of information in my face. And I don't know whether he intends to blackmail me with it, but I've had enough of men trying to play me.

I lean forward, momentarily setting aside my disgust for the face this man wears. "I don't know who you are, but I will tell you this: if you threaten me in any way, you will regret it."

I've scared a lot of people in my time. Marco does not appear to be one such person.

He inclines his head. "I won't tell the king you were in here if you don't tell him I was."

I stare at Marco for a long moment, then I turn on my heel and leave.

"I'll be seeing you around, Serenity," he calls to my back.

"For your sake," I say, not bothering to face him, "you better hope not."

CHAPTER 23

Serenity

I PUSH THE framed painting softly open. Beyond it, the king's bedroom is dark. As quietly as I can, I slip through the doorway and close the door and painting behind me. They shut silently.

I tiptoe across the room, removing my clothing as I go.

It's still odd, sleeping skin on skin with the king. I enjoy it, much to my shame. Too many years spent without touching of any kind has left me famished for it. And Montes is all too ready to provide the contact I desire.

I pull back the sheets and slide into bed.

Several seconds later, the king's arm drapes around my waist and he pulls my back to his front.

"I am king for a reason," he whispers into my hair.

Immediately, I stiffen in his arms. He doesn't sound sleepy. Not even a little bit.

He brushes my hair away from my ear, his touch proprietary. "I will let you have your secrets," he says, "so long as they serve me." His hand skims down my arm, then lays flat against my stomach. Idly, his thumb begins rubbing circles into my skin. "The moment they no longer do, my queen, bargain or no, I'll strip you of your power." His hand continues down my outer thigh. "And I will enjoy it."

"And how will you know when my secrets no longer serve you?" I ask.

He presses me even tighter into him, until his body feels like a cage and I am his prisoner.

He's quiet for several seconds, but not because he's at a loss for words. He's toying with me again. I can tell by the way he's still calmly stroking my skin, building up the tension between us.

"You are not the only one with secrets, my queen."

"Secrets like Marco?"

The king falls silent again, and now I do get the impression he's at a loss for words.

"You met Marco?" His tone changes from threatening to shocked.

"Unfortunately," I say.

He rolls me onto my back so that he can study me. The moon's bright enough to cast him in shades of blue.

"I was going to tell you," he says.

"Just as you were going to wake me from the Sleeper?" I say, the comment biting.

He moves a wisp of my hair from my face. "I felt it better to wait until you had adjusted. You hate me enough as it is. Marco was supposed to make himself scarce."

"Well, Marco has his own ideas."

Now that neither of us is pretending to be asleep, Montes strokes his finger down my nose and across my lips. "What, I wonder, did my vicious queen do to him?"

His hand finds my own and he rubs his thumb over my knuckles. Even in the dim light of the room I can see the smile he cracks when he feels the scabbed skin. "I'm disappointed, Serenity. Here I was hoping someone else might get a taste of your wrath for once."

"I thought you had brought him back to life," I whisper.

He stares at me for a long time. "You thought I had woken him and left you asleep," he clarifies.

It's times like this that I seriously question whether Montes was ever human. It's not just his lifespan that's unnatural. It's the way he sees right through people.

"And you thought I'd be mad when I found out," I say.

"You're not," he says it like a realization.

"I was. And then Marco explained it all to me." Now I'm just disturbed.

The king brushes a kiss along my knuckles. "Your reactions always were so refreshing. How I've forgotten." He presses my hand to his face. "How I wish to remember."

Now I look away. Even though fighting this magnetism we have is futile, I won't go quietly into it.

"Give me your eyes, Serenity." The pitch of his voice gets lower, more intimate.

Reluctantly, I do so.

His gaze holds a million things. He was never one to unburden himself with his feelings, but his eyes rarely lie.

Endless want. Hope. Grief. Love. Regret. Disbelief. I see it all.

I could resist him when he had no weaknesses, when I thought he was pure evil.

But this strange, time-wearied Montes who has lived a lonely existence for lifetimes and lifetimes, I can't fight him. I can't fight this. Us.

"I love you," he says.

"*Montes*," I say. It sounds more like a plea.

He lowers himself to his forearms, his bare skin meeting mine. "I love you," he repeats. "I know that makes you uncomfortable. It's made me uncomfortable for longer than I care to admit. But now I've gone a hundred years without saying those three words, and I've nearly lost the only person I want to say them to. So you're just going to have to listen to them."

He's now petting my hair, combing it back with his fingers. Now all I can see of his face are the sharp slashes of his jaw and the shadows that caress his high cheekbones.

He's terrible and magnificent. My monster. We are the two loneliest people in the universe, but we have each other.

"Tell me you love me," he whispers.

I shake my head. "Never."

"Liar," he says softly, a small smile playing on his lips.

"I told you a long time ago you'd never get all of me," I say.

He reaches over to the side of the bed and clicks on a

side lamp. "And I have always told you that you're mine," he says, returning his attention to me. "Every bit of you. Even your love."

He bends down, and I think he's going to kiss me. Instead, he murmurs, "We're going to play a little game.

His lips skim my jaw. "I'll ask you a question, and you'll either answer it honestly, or you'll touch me where I tell you to."

It's an iteration of the drinking game we used to play. Only this one has managed to incorporate our deal into the mix.

"I don't want to play any of your games."

He shifts against me, and I feel it all the way down to my core. The bastard knows what he's doing.

"Too bad," he says.

I exhale. "I really pissed you off today, didn't I?" I can't help the satisfaction unfurls at that thought.

"You caught me off guard," he corrects. "And I'm glad for it. My wife should be my equal. But now, you'll pay for it."

"The king and his games," I murmur.

"Do you love me?"

He wastes no time diving right in.

I lift my chin. "Pass."

He grins, his white, white teeth striking in the dim light. "Kiss me."

I stare at him for a beat, and then, gently, I pull his head down and brush my lips against his. It's over before it's even begun. Not that I'm trying to get out of anything. I know how this ends.

"When was the first time you felt something other than hate for me?" he asks.

It's my turn to play with his hair. I rub a stray lock between my fingers. Montes unconsciously leans into the touch.

"That evening you brought me to the pool house," I say.

"I remember that," he says, gazing down at me fondly.

His memory has aged a hundred years. Will that ever stop shocking me?

"You skipped my turn," I say.

"Tonight you don't get to ask questions," he says.

I frown, digging my hand deeper into his hair. "Is it wrong for me to want to know who you've become?" I ask.

I'm getting better at manipulating words to my will. It's what my father was so good at. What Montes is so good at. And it was almost inevitable that I would pick up this habit.

He's quiet. But then, "Forever is a long time to spend by yourself."

He's terrible and terrifying and monstrous and so ill deserving of any goodness, and yet—

And yet my broken heart bleeds for him. I have the strangest urge to run my hand down his back and comfort him as neither of us has been comforted in a long, long time.

"That's the last question you get to ask," he says quietly.

I don't fight him. His past sounds like a dark place, one he doesn't want to dwell on. I know all about terrible memories; I won't force him to divulge his.

"Do you love me?" he asks, drawing me back to the present.

My brows knit. "I already answered this question."

"And I am asking it again."

I really shouldn't feel bad for him. He's up to his usual tricks.

"Pass," I say.

Another triumphant smile. "Touch me."

I place my hand at the juncture between his jaw and his neck. My thumbs stroke the rough skin of his cheek.

"Lower," he says gruffly.

My touch moves down the column of his throat until it rests over his heart. *My* heart. The one he stole all those years ago and now holds captive. I can hear it beating. Long after I die, it will continue to beat in his chest.

His nostrils flare as some emotion overtakes him. "Lower."

I feel my cheeks heat. I know what he wants. I run my hand down his chest, over the ridges of his abs, and I wrap my hand around him.

This is so lewd.

"Happy?" I ask, raising my eyebrows.

"I will be," he says.

I release him. "Next question."

I can tell I'm amusing him. It's no one feature of his, but all of them—the wry twist of his lips, the shine of his eyes, the way his hands dig themselves deeper into my flesh.

"What is your favorite thing about me?"

I search his face. "It's always about you, isn't it?" I don't bother to add any sting to my words. I'm not trying to wound him. But I've taken it upon myself to dole out all the hard truths that Montes needs to hear.

"You follow through on most of your threats," I throw out.

He shakes his head, his eyes glimmering. "I know for a fact you like certain parts of my anatomy better than my follow through. But I'll let that one slide."

How magnanimous of him.

"Do you love me?" he asks.

I give him a hard look. "You're not going to wear me down on this one, Montes. Pass."

His hair tickles mine as his lips brush against the skin of my cheek. "Touch yourself."

"*Montes.*" It's one thing to be intimate with the king. Quite another to do this in front of him.

"We can stop," he says. "Tomorrow morning when we sit in on the meeting with my officers, you can inform them that you are no longer willing to follow through with your role in our war efforts. I will not stop you. I want my queen safe above all else."

He's goading me, but at this point I can't tell if he wants me to dissolve all my plans or to continue doing things for him that make me distinctly uncomfortable.

Knowing how twisted he is, I'd say he be happy with either outcome.

I glare at him and reach between us, placing my hand between my thighs.

He tears his gaze from me and his eyes dip down. I hear his breath hitch.

A moment later he extricates one of his hands from my hair and uses it to cover mine. Wrapping his fingers around mine, he begins to move my hand up and down, up and down.

Now it's my breath that's picking up; I'm inhaling and exhaling in stuttering gasps.

Montes watches the way he works me. The whole thing is embarrassing and exhilarating all at once. If only I could have one uncomplicated emotion towards this man. Everything he does, everything we do, is mired in complexities.

His gaze returns to mine. "Are you not having fun?"

"*Fun*," I say, my voice breathy, "is not a word I would use to describe your games."

He leans in close, dipping both his fingers and mine into my core. "Then you're not doing it right."

Montes adjusts himself, so that he's right at my entrance. "The game's over—for now."

He takes my lips then. The kiss is rough, almost abrasive. As he does so, he thrusts into me. I'm gasping into his mouth, arching into him.

Gone is the girl who hated the king. Gone is the man who took everything from her. When we are like this, we're just two lost souls coming together.

He moves against me and I stare up at him. I bring a hand up and caress his cheek, swallowing as I do so.

"We lost a child."

I don't know why I say it. Maybe I'm feeling oddly vulnerable with him. Despite everything he's done to me, this man has buried himself in the deepest recesses of my heart. And we've been through things together, things that pulled us close when they should've torn us apart.

Whatever mood rode us a minute ago, it's been replaced with something far heavier.

"We will make another," he says.

It's such an enchanting thought. To create rather than destroy. That even we are capable of it.

I pull him closer. He moves gently against me, his strokes slow and tender.

There is no question how he feels about me. I'm the one holding back, refusing to give in fully. And I don't want to. God, I don't.

After we finish, the king tucks me against him, our skin is damp with sweat. He places a soft kiss behind my ear. "Tonight, you win my queen."

I haven't won anything. I can see that even if I hold out, there is no way this ends well for me.

Montes shifts, clasping me in close. "Now," he says, "sleep."

And I do.

CHAPTER 24

Serenity

"YOUR ITINERARY IS complete." The officers I met with yesterday are now discussing the peace talks I will be having with the heads of several of the king's territories.

None of them have broached the subject of last night's call with Styx. I doubt they will either.

Montes sits next to me in the conference room, his presence dominating the space.

His leg and arm brush against mine as he settles in, and I can't help but think it's deliberate. That everything about him is deliberate. And these two casual touches serve to remind me that this monstrous man can make my heart flutter even when his attention is focused elsewhere.

The king doesn't need to be here, but of course he

wants to be. If he can micromanage every step of this process, he will.

I grab the document set out in front of me in an effort to refocus my energy and attention.

"The queen's tour of the East will begin next week," one of the officers says.

I lean back in my chair, flipping through the itinerary. We're starting my campaign for peace in the East. I have to win my own people over before I can consider swaying the people of the West.

Next to me, Montes reads through his copy, pinching his lower lip. One of his legs begins to jiggle. I take the subtle hints of his aggravation as a good sign.

"How did you pick these places?" I ask.

"Your Majesty, we followed your requests—these are the biggest cities or the ones that have the least loyalty to the East."

Most of the city names I recognize, but some are new. When I get the chance, I will discreetly find a map and plot these places out.

The king closes his copy and tosses it onto the table. "No."

We all look to him.

"Half of your scheduled visits are in wild country. We've long since established that we can't secure many of these locations."

"Yes," the female officers says slowly, "the lack of royal presence in those regions is partially responsible for their fractured loyalty."

"These are exactly the places I want to be," I say.

The king stands and shrugs off his jacket. "No," he repeats.

"Yes," I say just as forcefully.

The vein in his temple pounds. "Goddamnit, Serenity, don't test me."

I stand, my chair screeching as it slides back. "Or what?"

"Or I will lock you in a fucking room where no one can hurt you."

I take a step towards him. "Are you threatening to put me back in the Sleeper?" I ask, my voice low.

He flinches. So the bastard has some remorse after all.

"I'm not going back in there, Montes. Not ever."

"You've said that before, and then you went back into the Sleeper." He says it like I chose to return to the coffin. Like I wasn't forced into it by his own hand.

I step in close. "How *dare* you. Consider yourself lucky I'm unarmed."

Before the discussion can devolve any further, the door to the conference room opens, and Marco strides in.

Marco the clone. My skin still prickles at the thought.

It takes him only a handful of seconds to register that he came in at a bad time.

He puts his hands up. "By all means, don't stop on my account."

I turn back to the king. "So now that I know about Marco, he's allowed to join us?"

"He's my right-hand." To Marco, the king says, "Have you seen the itinerary?"

"I have," Marco says, taking a seat near us and kicking his heels up on the table.

That little gesture makes me like him just a smidgen more.

Montes folds his arms across his chest, widening his stance. "And?"

Marco drums his fingers against the armrests. "And I think it's a good idea."

I try not to smile. I fail.

The king throws me a lethal glare.

"It's not safe," he says, returning his attention to Marco.

"You act like you're not married to the most dangerous one of us," Marco says. He juts his chin towards me. "She woke up in a car full of armed men. When she was retrieved, they were all dead."

I appreciate Marco sticking up for me. He has no reason to. I haven't been kind to him.

The king frowns at his friend.

"Montes," I say, "let me do this."

He fully turns his body towards me, and his nostrils flare as he tries to tamp down his emotions. When I look into his eyes, all I see is agony. I'm someone he loves, someone he respects, someone he cannot bear to lose under any circumstances.

I take it all in, and then I do something uncharacteristic.

I place a hand against the side of his face, in full view of Marco and the officers.

"We need to end this war," I say. "I have a good chance of doing just that, but only if you let me try. I'm not going to hold our deal over your head, and I'm not going to force your hand."—*Yet.*—"I'm asking as your wife and your queen to allow this to happen."

He looks moved, but I'm not sure.

"It can be how it was before," I say quietly. "We rule well together. Let me do this. Nothing bad will happen."

Montes grimaces then closes his eyes. He places his hand over mine, trapping it against his cheek.

"I always knew you'd make a good queen," he murmurs.

He opens his eyes. "Fine. I'll agree to it, provided there's extra security."

I nod, my expression passive. But there's nothing passive about how I feel. The king doesn't readily make concessions, and I don't usually get my way without threatening someone.

The two of us are making progress.

"Serenity?" he says quietly. "You still need to work on your lies. You and I both know that with diplomacy, something bad always happens."

CHAPTER 25

Serenity

AFTER THE MEETING, the king takes me to the palace gardens.

Montes and his gardens.

The plants that grow here are far different than the ones in Geneva and his other palace in the United Kingdom. They're greener, brighter, more exotic.

"Do you still have your palace in England?" I ask.

Montes glances over me. "I do. Would you like to go back at some point?"

What an absurd question. That place was just another example of the king's decadence, another example that I was just a brightly colored bird in a gilded cage.

My retort is on the tip of my tongue. Only ... I find

I can't say the words. That terrible home of the king's might be one of the few things about this world that I remember. People need familiarity. I need to feel like I'm not swept out at sea.

"Maybe," I say.

I look over at Montes as he squints off at the sea.

His handsome face is made all the more so by how well I know it. His palaces are not the only thing I am familiar with.

I could reach out and touch his face. I want to. I want to run my finger down the delicate folds of skin that pinch when he squints. For the longest time I've held back my affection. I thought it important to punish the king for being the king and me for wanting him.

I reach out and ever so softly run two fingers along the skin near one of his eyes, smoothing out the crinkled skin.

He turns into my touch. I can tell without speaking that he's surprised and pleased. Both of us stop walking.

My fingers move to his mouth. I trace the edges of his lips. "What happened to all your wickedness?" Even that has changed. Oddly enough, I miss it.

He gives me a what-can-you-do-about-it look. "I got old."

"You don't look old," I say.

We haven't discussed it, but the king must still be taking his pills. He looks identical to how I've always remembered him.

And he hasn't tried to make me take any; it's just further proof that he's not nearly so wicked as he used to be.

Montes touches my temple. "I got old here." His fingers move to the skin over my heart. "And here."

I understand that. Age isn't just a number; it's also how you feel.

Montes takes my hand and tucks it into the crook of his arm. When I try to tug it away, he holds fast to it.

The age-old battle of chivalry versus my stubbornness.

He wins this round.

We resume walking.

"Marco likes you," he says, absently running his thumb over my knuckles.

I don't bother hiding a very real shiver. "That's regrettable."

"It is."

There's something about the way Montes says this that has me glancing over. I can't put my finger on it—

"What do you think of the future?" he asks, changing the course of my thoughts.

"It's disorienting," I say, "though not as different as I imagined it would be. The world does not appear to have made any progress."

"War does that," Montes says. "The only thing that ever gets more impressive are the new ways we find to kill each other."

That's more than a little disheartening to hear.

"In what ways has the weaponry gotten worse?" I ask.

"Mmm," he muses, staring out at the horizon, "I'll let you figure that one out on your own. It's probably in my best interest not to have you knowing about all the new and ingenious ways you can kill me."

I smile at that.

I'm so fucked-up. *We* are so fucked-up.

"So you still think I might kill you?" I ask.

The king stops again.

This moment is too much. The warm, bright sun, the sweet smelling flowers, the sound of the surf crashing. The way the king's staring at me. I am getting gluttonous off of it.

"That's the beauty of being with you," he says. "I never quite know."

A WEEK GOES by in a blur as I prepare for my tour of the East. A tour that begins tomorrow, when we leave for Giza, the first of nearly two dozen cities I'll be visiting.

Most of my time has been spent locked up in meetings. And when I'm not listening to other people discuss world affairs, I'm locking myself away to study them.

The king, being who he is, has decided to hole himself up along with me. He's fashioned himself into my personal mentor.

I pity the world; under his instructions, it will undoubtedly burn.

"So there are thirteen representatives," I say, leaning back in my office chair. Spread out in front of me are photos of a dozen men, each with their name neatly typed beneath.

"Correct," Montes says, "thirteen representatives, but we only know the identities of twelve."

Montes sits on the desk itself, his legs splayed wide, his shirt sleeves rolled up. After being here for over a week, I've noticed he alternates between fatigues and suits. Today is a suit day.

I pull my attention back to the matter at hand. Thirteen representatives, but only twelve identities. That's more than a little odd. "Why don't we know the identity of the thirteenth representative?"

Montes reaches forward and hooks his hand underneath my seat. With surprisingly little effort, he drags my chair forward until I'm sitting between those splayed legs of his.

My eyes are level with his crotch.

"Forcing me to look at your dick is not going to help me learn who the representatives are," I say.

"You could always sit on my lap," he offers.

"Pass," I say absently, my gaze drifting back to the photos. I stand to get a closer look at them.

As I do so, Montes's arms go around my waist. I'm now trapped in his embrace.

"Had I realized how fun diplomacy was," he says, his lips brushing against my hair, "I would've taken it up much sooner."

"No you wouldn't have," I murmur, my attention still locked on the photos. I move them around, reading the various names, and trying to memorize the faces that go with each. "You're an asshole, and assholes don't give a shit about peace."

One of his hands falls heavily over mine, trapping it to the desk.

"You think that what I've done is bad?" he says, his voice deadly quiet.

I don't have to look at him to know I've offended him.

"I will tell you a story about what I've seen in the West," he says. "Girls sold as slaves—some younger than ten. Those went for the highest price. Women taken from their families, raped and sold then raped some more."

Now he has my attention.

"Don't blame me for being hesitant to forge peace between my land and theirs," he finishes.

I feel a muscle jump in my cheek.

I search his eyes. "Is that true? What you just said?"

He frowns, his eyes dropping to my mouth. "It is."

Women and children enslaved? Raped? This is not the West I knew. This is every one of my nightmares made flesh.

"Why?" I know Montes can see the horror on my face.

"You've asked me the same thing," he says. "Power can twist people."

He wraps his hand around mine and begins moving my fingers over the photos. "Gregory Mercer, Ara Istanbulian, Alan Lee, Jeremy Mansfield, Tito Petros, ..." He lists off all twelve of them.

"Each has his own brand of evil. Alan—" Montes moves our hands over the photo of a man with dark hair and beady eyes, "coordinates disappearances. People of importance he doesn't want alive—sometimes he has them killed outright, sometimes he detains them for torture, and sometimes he sends them to state-funded concentration camps."

A lock of hair falls into his eyes as the king speaks.

"Jeremy—" Our hands travel to a photo of a man with pale, blotchy skin and a weak chin, "was the mind behind the development of these concentration camps. All that radiation has led to widespread disease and genetic mutations. He decided some WUN citizens were too sick or unsightly to be left amongst the regular population, so they were moved. It's a great place to send anyone who doesn't fall into line as they should. It also incentivizes violent individuals to join the West's military. If they're stationed at one of these camps, well, anything really goes."

I'm about to ask him why he hasn't taken action sooner. Why evil like this hasn't been stamped out. But before I can, he moves on.

"Tito." Our hands trail to a man I recognize, the Eastern politician who always reminded me of a walrus. He was one of the king's former advisors. "This man knew exactly where all my research laboratories were, as well as my military outposts and warehouses. The WUN had them bombed almost immediately after I placed you in the Sleeper. Then they hit the East's hospitals."

I can understand bombing military outposts and warehouses. I can even understand wiping out laboratories.

But hospitals?

The West has thrown any sort of code of ethics out the window if they're hitting hospitals.

"Ronaldo," the king continues, moving our hands again. "You remember him, don't you?"

God help me, I do.

Once upon a time I'd saved him from death only to find out he was the advisor who'd sanctioned the atomic bombs dropped on the WUN.

I nod.

"As soon as he traded alliances, he was back to his old tricks. He dropped a handful of bombs on the biggest, most successful cities in the East. The damage was so disastrous that many of the cities have not been rebuilt."

His hand moves on. "Gregory sanctioned human trafficking, and he personally has close to a hundred slaves—"

"*Enough*," I say, pulling my hand from the king's.

I'm going to be sick. How does evil get concentrated like this?

Bombed hospitals, slavery, concentration camps—this is ghastly even by my standards.

Beyond my horror is that roaring monster inside me. The one that loves the taste of blood and vengeance.

Already I can feel my hands aching for necks to squeeze and my knuckles for skin to split. I will get my day, I vow it to myself.

Montes turns me in his arms so that we're staring at each other. "You asked me why the thirteenth representative doesn't show himself. The truth is, I don't know. But if I had to guess, I'd say it's because he's either hiding from his enemies—or lying amongst them."

I take that in.

"How haven't you managed to kill them yet?" I ask. That's what the king was good at, after all. Slaughter. And he had so many decades to eliminate these men.

Montes absently plays with a strand of my hair. "You kill one, they elect another." He smooths my hair back in place. "This wouldn't be a problem if all thirteen representatives gathered together—I could wipe them out all at once. But they don't. And if you can't kill them simultaneously, it's not worth the effort."

I return my attention to the photos.

"What *would* cause them all to gather?" I muse aloud, my fingers tilting one of the images to better see the representative.

My hand stills as the answer comes to me.

Slowly my eyes return to the king.

He already knows, I can tell. I say it anyway.

"Victory."

CHAPTER 26

Serenity

THAT EVENING, THE officers gather in the large dining room for a goodbye dinner. The atmosphere feels celebratory, like they already know I'll accomplish what I set out to do.

I'm not so certain.

I lean back in my chair and finger the velvet tablecloth. It's worn. I don't know how long it takes to age material, but I would guess years, maybe decades if it's well cared for. It makes me wonder about that dress I wore when I so carelessly ran into the sea. It makes me wonder about every grand detail of the king's lifestyle.

I've made a lot of assumptions, about Montes and everyone else. In the past, they've been founded, but I no longer know whether they are or not.

My eyes move across the table I sit at. It's round, which means I get a good view of everyone. And they are all watching me, though some are more discrete than others. There's an energy to the room, and excitement, and I know I'm responsible for it. The dead queen's come back to end war once and for all.

They believe in me far more than I do.

There's no magic to this. In fact, chances are, someone will bury a knife in my back before I'm even halfway through visiting countries. That's what happens to powerful, dangerous people. They lead very short lives.

A heavy arm brushes my back. I glance first at the hand draped over my seatback, then its owner.

Montes is casually talking to Marco, who's seated on his other side.

The soft lighting gentles the king's features. I find my breath catches as I look at him.

He breaks conversation to turn to me. "My queen is quiet," he says softly so that only I hear. "Never a good thing."

"I have nothing to say."

Montes contemplates me. Beyond him I feel Marco's eyes on me as well.

The king stands, his chair scraping behind him. He reaches a hand to me.

I inhale sharply as I stare at Montes's hand.

I am a stranger to this world, this future I must live in. I don't know what to talk about, because I know nothing of this world. And I want to save it, I do, but I don't know how to be a part of it.

Montes figured that out all with a single look, and he's giving me an out.

The entire room's attention focuses on us.

I take the king's hand and I stand.

I can leave. Montes is willing to cut this dinner short. I can see as much in his expression. But I'm not going to run from these people just because I find these types of gatherings uncomfortable and I feel a little lost.

So instead I squeeze the king's hand and then turn to the officers seated around the table. "Tomorrow we begin what will hopefully be the end of this war." That earns a few claps and a couple of whoops from the dinner guests.

I can feel the king's assessing eyes on me; I sense his curiosity. He likes my spontaneity.

"Many of you are used to fighting," I say. "I know that I am."

The king squeezes the hand he still holds.

"But I don't want to spend the rest of my days watching young men die."

The evening's lightness dries up in the room.

"I want to see them grow old, and fat—I want to see men fat because there is so much food to go around."

Several officers nod at that. As I gaze out at their somber faces, I realize that these are my people. A hundred years ago I couldn't relate to the men and women the king surrounded himself with. These men and women I can.

Change is possible.

I pick up my wine glass. "A toast to peace."

I meet the king's mesmerized gaze. A small smile creeps along his face.

People raise their glasses. "To peace!"

AFTER DINNER, WHILE people are moving into the adjoining room to drink and chat, I slip away. I'm sure my exit gains some attention. Once I made my toast and sat back down, I had more interested guests eager to talk to me than I knew what to do with.

It's for that very reason that I take my leave early.

At the end of the day, I am a solitary thing. I'm not sure if this is the result of circumstance, or if I would've been this way had war never altered my life.

As soon as the dining room doors close behind me, the tinkling glasses and jovial conversations cut off.

I head through the cavernous palace, my steps echoing. I pass the massive entry hall, with its long entryway and towering columns, and keep going.

Down the corridors, all those sheets still cover most of the royal paintings. It's vaguely irritating. Why put a picture up at all if it's just going to get covered?

I don't know where I'm headed; I have no place in mind. I just want to keep moving. And the more I walk, the more I notice how much of the walls are covered up.

Whether it's curiosity or irritation that halts my steps, I can't be sure, but I stop in front of a section of wall partially covered by velvet drop cloths.

I reach out, towards the material.

It only seems like a bad idea at the very last second, when I've already bunched the velvet up into my fist. By then, gravity has taken over. The fabric slides off the frame.

A young Marco stares back at me from inside the frame. It's a formal photo, one where he's posed rigidly in a uniform. He can't be more than fourteen or fifteen years old. He has a wispy mustache boys at that age get.

I take a step back. It's hard to look at Marco as a boy. I don't associate his cruelty with this version of him.

I glance down the corridor, noticing over half a dozen similarly covered frames.

Surely they are not all photos of Marco? Not that I would put it past the king. He's obsessive with his affection.

I move to another covered frame and tug the cloth off of it. It's another of Marco, this one when he's older. In it, he and the king are clasping shoulders, laughing at something together.

I move on. My heels click against the floor as I stride down the hall.

This time when I pull down the velvet covering, I'm not prepared.

What lies beneath it has me recoiling.

The person I'm staring at is me.

Only, it's *not*.

It can't be. For one thing, I'm posing in a huge fucker of a dress. I'd knock someone out sooner than I would put that thing on. And I would've remembered it if I'd worn it. I mean, the thing's practically as big as a tank.

For another thing, my scar is gone.

I walk several paces down the hall and pull off another sheet of material.

There I am again, this time as a young teenager. I can't be older than thirteen or fourteen.

And I'm not alone in the photo either.

My arm is slung around the neck of an equally young boy.

But not just any boy. A cloned one.

Marco.

CHAPTER 27

Serenity

I TAKE A shaky step back.

Oh God, what is this?

"Her name was Trinity."

I startle at the voice. When I swing around, Marco is watching me. His eyes drift to the wall.

My pulse is in my ears. I can hear my own blood whooshing through my veins.

I place a hand to my temple. "Are you saying–?"

"He couldn't bear waking you, so he cloned you," Marco finishes for me.

It takes several seconds to process his words.

"Montes cloned ... *me?*" The proof is hanging on the wall, but I don't want to believe it.

Marco steps up to the photo.

My chest is rising and falling faster and faster. "Why would he do that?" I ask.

"Marco. Serenity." That powerful, ageless voice. It's wiped out cities, ordered countless deaths, whispered sweet platitudes in my ear. It's fooled me into loving it.

I stiffen when I hear it.

He cloned me.

It doesn't take long for shock to slide to anger.

I spin to face the king. "You did this?"

The king strides towards us, his eyes taking in the framed photos.

The bastard wouldn't wake me up, but he'd make a copy of me.

I back up when I realize he wants to eliminate the distance between us. "Stay away from me," I warn.

"Marco, leave us," he says as he continues to stride forward.

Marco hesitates, earning an arched brow from Montes. With one last, long look at me, the king's right-hand turns on his heel and leaves.

Montes steps into my personal space, and even when I cock my arm, he doesn't stand down. Instead he lets me throw my punch, but only so that he can catch my fist.

I growl my frustration, trying to tug my hand out of his grasp. "Let me go, you bastard."

"Not until I explain."

I keep yanking on my arm. "I'm tired of your explanations," I say between gritted teeth.

What I don't say is that something in me is broken and

bleeding. Something that no Sleeper can heal. I force back a sob.

When he still doesn't let go, I bring my knee up to his crotch. He swivels out of the way.

Now he's mad, his features taut with his anger. He thrusts my body back up against the wall, the force of it making the frames shiver. His hand is at my throat. "Listen to me," he growls.

"Fuck. You." I don't want to listen. I want to bathe in the horror of this moment because this is the Montes that I remember.

"That was forty years ago," he says as though he can read my mind.

"And let me guess," I say. "You're a changed man."

His vein throbs.

Hit the nail right on the head with that one.

"Where is she now?" I ask.

The king's face closes down.

Dead.

I can read that much off of him. For however long she lived, she no longer does.

Goosebumps break out along my skin. It's equally disturbing to think that my clone both lived and died while I slept. And for all the king's unnatural technology, he wasn't able to save her.

"What did you do to her?" I say.

This psycho.

He grimaces. "I didn't *do* anything to her, Serenity. Or can you not tell that from the photos?"

I close my eyes because I can't bear to gaze into his dark,

anguished ones. I don't want to know if he loved her. Not on top of all the deception and pain he's given me.

"Why not just wake me up?" I ask. My heart is primed for breaking. I really know nothing but destructive love. So he can tell me whatever pretty words he thinks are going to soothe me, but I doubt there will be any to make this better.

He gives my neck a light squeeze. "*Nire bihotza*, look at me."

I open my eyes, not because I'm interested in following his demands, but because I've never hid from unpleasant truths, and I don't plan on starting now.

"Haven't we already established that I was a fool to not wake you up?"

"We can always establish that more," I say.

Montes cracks a smile, but it quickly disappears. "There was a while where I felt like I'd gone insane from loneliness. The Sleeper was still repairing your body at the time, though I will admit that by then I was afraid of seeing you again. But I was even more afraid of the possibility that you would never get out of the Sleeper, never be healed. So I cloned the two people I missed most."

"You depraved son of a bitch."

Montes played God, deciding who got to live and who didn't.

He frowns, his features hardening at my words, but he doesn't try to defend himself further.

"What happened to her?" I ask.

It's taking a lot not to lash out like a wild animal. My basest nature wants to. But at this point, throwing a fit like a child won't change the past.

I take a deep breath.

"She was killed," Montes says releasing me reluctantly.

"How?"

"She was captured much the same way you were. The West was planning on using her as their puppet.

"She was not like you—not at all." He says this last part quietly.

"We recaptured her." He looks away and rubs his eyes. "But the plane was shot down."

There's real emotion there. Real anguish.

He takes a deep breath. "They thought I'd cloned her to end the war." Montes shakes his head. "It's a good theory, but I had the real thing the entire time."

I search his face. "You cared for her." Just saying those words is a bullet to the gut.

His expression doesn't alter, but it does intensify. "I couldn't *stand* looking at her."

He reaches out and tries to touch my cheek. I step away before he can. His fingers curl into a fist.

"There was only ever one of you," he says. "I didn't want anything else—not in any sense. Once I realized that, I stayed as far away from her as I could. She suffered because of it. But I tried to care for her."

Some bitter combo of disgust and relief flow through me. I find I don't want to be replaceable, and it's a dagger through the heart to know that he must've created her with that in mind. And then there's the unbidden pain that comes when I think of this woman he created after me, created and then abandoned. All she got for it was death.

He must see me withdrawing because he seems desperate to close the space between us.

I back up, shaking my head. "You ruin everything, Montes. *Everything.*"

I turn my back to him and walk away.

I can't be sure, but I swear I hear him whisper, "That's all I know how to do."

CHAPTER 28

Serenity

LONDON'S GONE, AS is Paris, Cairo, Delhi, Beijing. On and on the list goes.

Today, in the hours before we leave, they show me the footage of it. What little there is left.

I stand in the middle of the Great Room, dozens of men and women as my witness. They didn't need to be here; it's all old news to them. But I think they want to remember, or to try to see it all with new eyes.

I watch the bomb that rips apart the Eiffel Tower. The steel beams that had held for over two centuries now buckle and collapse.

The footage cuts away, only to be replaced by the Burj Khalifa, the tallest building in the world. Or at least, it was.

I don't want to see this. I don't want to see man's greatest achievements blown away in an instant because someone somewhere thought it would be a good idea to destroy the world.

I force my feet to stay rooted to the floor. I owe it to both the people of the East and the West to watch.

"Do you see that glint?" One of the officers has a laser pointer that he aims around a section of the frame taken up by sky.

The bright concentrated section of light flashes in the middle of it. The camera catches similar flare-ups of light glimmering along the windows of the Burj Khalifa. But this one ... This one has no business being in the middle of open sky.

"This was one of the first instances where the West used retroreflective material to camouflage their weaponry," the officer says.

I don't get a chance to ask what retroreflective material is before the side of the skyscraper explodes into flame, rows of windows and debris scattered to the four winds. Plumes of dark smoke bloom almost immediately.

The footage is time lapsed, and the next frame shows the building still smoldering, a dark halo of ash and dust enveloping it. We watch this for about thirty seconds.

And then, somewhere in the middle of it, the building begins to fall.

I don't breathe as I watch the world's tallest building collapse onto itself. It happens in a matter of seconds, one story after the next swallowed up by gravity and rubble-filled smoke. Somewhere in the middle of it all, I feel a tear slip out of my eye. It's the atomic bomb all over again. Destruction so vast and so terrible that my very bones ache for humanity.

And then it's over, and I know that within those few seconds, thousands upon thousands of people died. I can hear the observers' screams through the speakers. And though their language is different, and though I've never set foot onto their land and never walked the earth during their lifetimes, I ache for them.

At some point, we are all the same.

"That's enough," Montes says.

The screen shuts off.

I feel my dark king at my back.

"Are you ready?" he asks me.

I turn and take him in. His eyes aren't giving away his mood. But he must feel it, this smoldering anger that burns at the sight of so much carnage.

Behind him the officers wear grim expressions.

I nod to all of them. "Let's end this."

THE PLANE WE board has all the accoutrements I remember. Plush central seating, a bedroom, and a conference table, each sectioned off into separate segments of the cabin.

A dozen men board along with us, one of them Marco. He catches my eye and gives me a tiny, playful wave.

I thin my eyes in response. Divine intervention better strike this plane. That's the only way Marco will leave it unscathed.

"Play nice," Montes whispers in my ear.

"I'm not nice, *my king*," I say disparagingly.

"Well, you're going to have to learn how to be. Marco is my right-hand."

"He can just get used to me." I am, after all, the queen. The title has got to be good for something.

Montes flashes the man in question a penetrating look. "I think he's all too ready to do that," he says, his lips thinning.

Before I'm able to respond, he begins to herd me to the back room. I catch sight of Marco once again, and he watches us, his eyes filled with some emotion I cannot place.

"What are you doing?" I say, reluctantly moving towards the small bedroom.

As soon as we both cross the threshold, Montes slams the door shut. "Getting you alone."

I bump into the bed, and now I think I have an idea of where the king's mind is at. I can still hear the muffled conversations of Montes's men as they get settled.

"If you think–"

He cuts me off with a kiss, holding my face hostage as he does so. It's long and drawn out, and I know he's making a point, especially when he backs us up until we both collapse onto the mattress, my body pinned beneath his.

Only then does he release my mouth. "That is not why I brought you in here, though I would enjoy fucking you senseless ..."

"*Montes*." I'm still so pissed off at him after last night. Kissing me only serves to make my anger burn hotter.

"Do you trust me?" he asks. He has me trapped beneath him.

How does he expect me to answer?

"No, not with most things."

"And should I trust you?" he asks, his face just inches from my own.

"Not with most things," I repeat softly.

"Can you trust that I want to keep you alive?" he asks.

If there is ever one thing I can be sure of, it's Montes's obsession with my life.

"Yes."

"Good," he says. "We're going to dangerous places, and there will be people who want you dead. So you understand my concern." He doesn't release me. Instead he threads his fingers through my own. "You are not going in there unarmed."

I raise my eyebrows. "You're giving me a gun?"

"Can I trust you not to shoot me with it?"

"No." I need some target practice anyway.

He sighs, but there's a twinkle in his eyes. "If you shoot me, there will be very severe repercussions."

"I'm quaking," I say, but I'm excited. I feel naked walking around without my weapons. Being raised on violence has taught me to always be prepared.

Montes releases me and pushes off the bed. He heads to an overhead compartment. Opening it, he pulls out a box. I hear something heavy slide inside it.

A gun.

I stand, my hands itching to touch the heavy metal.

He turns, cradling the box. "Don't make me regret this,

Serenity."

I meet his eyes. "You won't." *You will.*

When he hands me the flimsy packaging, I sit down on the edge of the mattress, opening the lid carefully.

Nestled inside is not one gun, but two, each tucked into a belted holster. I recognize one of them immediately.

"It's over a hundred years old, Serenity. The thing jams fairly often."

I run my fingers over my father's gun. So it's not reliable. But Montes would only know that if ...

When I look up at him questioningly, he watches me, arms folded.

"I fired it on many occasions," he explains.

When I wanted to be close to you.

The king omits much of what his heart wants to say, but I glean it off of him anyway. And it's twisted that this weapon, which has ended many lives, is a bridge between the king and me. But everything about our relationship is twisted, so it fits.

"The bullets are also long out of production."

I unholster the gun and run my hands over it. From the looks of the thing, it's aged about as well as I have. Which is to say, not at all.

But it's a relic, nonetheless.

Just like me.

"So you gave me another gun," I say, re-holstering my beloved weapon and reaching for the other.

"Everything about its design is essentially the same as the guns you're familiar with," the king says, crossing his legs at the ankles as he leans back against the wall. "And those bullets are the most common ones on the market."

So I can get my hands on more if we find ourselves in a tight situation.

I loop the belt and holsters around my pants. Once everything's secured, I glance up at Montes.

"Thank you," I say. I mean it, too.

I'm still upset and unnerved about my twin, but for once, I'm going to bury the past. I have bigger worries on the horizon.

The king levels a serious look at me. "Don't die on me."

"So many demands," I murmur. "You're setting yourself up for disappointment, Montes."

"I didn't marry you because you were a pretty thing. I married you because you were a wicked one."

Was that a compliment?

"You married me because you're a bastard."

"Yes," he grins, though it lacks any mirth, "that too."

IT TAKES ONLY a couple hours to fly from the king's seaside palace to Giza. Only a couple of hours' time, but there appears to be lifetimes of differences between the land we left and the one we arrive in.

Giza is only a handful of miles from Cairo, one of the cities that the West apparently destroyed. But as we descend and the buildings come into view, I realize just how war-torn and desolate Giza itself is. Half the buildings are in various states of disrepair.

When I step out of the plane, hot, dry desert air greets me, and the very feel of it is nothing like what I'm used to.

I squint as a hot gust of air blows my hair around.

The king steps up to me and presses a hand to my back. Several men wait to greet us on the ground. From what I've picked up, these men are the territory's dignitaries, and they will be our guides while we're here.

They take one look at me and begin to bow, their hands clasped together as they do so, like I'm some desperate, answered prayer of theirs.

Montes puts pressure on my lower back, urging me forward. I dig my heels in instead.

"They're acting like I'm a god," I say to him. I can't quite take my eyes off the people in front of us.

"You are a queen and a rebel fighter, and you've been dead a hundred years only to turn up alive. To them you might as well be.

"Now," he continues, putting more pressure on my back, "you need to meet them and act like it."

When I approach them, one by one they clasp my hands and kiss my knuckles.

"It is an honor to meet you." The man who speaks has a heavy accent, yet his English is crisp and sharp. The result is a lilting speech.

"I am honored to be here," I say honestly.

"Where is Akash?" Montes asks, glancing about the group.

From what I read, all of the king's lands have regional leaders. Giza and its surrounding land is managed by Akash Salem.

"Your Majesties," the man who first spoke now sobers, his easy smile disappearing. "On our way here, we received worrisome news concerning Akash and his family."

"What about them?" I ask.

No one seems to want to be the one to break the news. Eventually, however, one does.

He takes a deep breath. "They're missing."

CHAPTER 29

The King

"How could this have happened?" I pace up and down one of the rooms in the royal house we're staying at. We've been here mere hours and already I'm itching to drag my wife back onto our plane and return to my palace.

If my regional leaders can be taken, then so can Serenity.

"Akash's servants were found slaughtered and there were signs of forced entry," one of my men says.

My eyes cut to my queen.

She sits in an armchair, her expression stormy. She's been sitting there brooding since we entered the room.

"Serenity," I say, my voice softening.

Her gaze flicks to me, returning from wherever she wandered in her mind.

"Are they dead?" she asks.

One of the men behind me shakes his head. "We don't know, Your Majesty."

She looks to me because she knows I won't euphemize the situation.

"If it's the West,"—and it surely is—"they'll be tortured. All of them. Even the kids."

She flinches at that. Buried beneath all my queen's violence is something soft and righteous.

"How old?" she asks.

"Eight and five," one of the dignitaries says.

She gets up from the couch, and everything about her looks heavy. Evil does that; it weighs you down, makes you weary. I know all about it.

Serenity removes her father's gun from its holster, and everyone tenses just a fraction. She flips it over in her hand.

"How easy we kill," she murmurs. She sets the gun on the table in the center of the room. "It never solves our problems."

Something about her words and her voice has my hackles rising. Only recently Serenity discovered the art of scheming. It's a talent of mine, one I fear she's taken a liking to as well.

"We will get them back," she swears to the room.

"Serenity," I cut in.

There are some promises we cannot make, and that is one of them.

"We will get them back, Montes," she reiterates, her

eyes glinting.

I stare her down. We might get them back, yes. But they might not be alive by then.

"Leave us," I tell the men.

Once the room clears, I approach her. "You can't save everyone," I say.

She leans her knuckles against the tabletop and bows her head. "I know," she says softly. She lifts her head and I see resolve in her eyes. "But I owe your subjects, *our* subjects, safety for their allegiance."

It's almost too much, seeing her like this. She might be the best decision I've ever made.

"How did our plans get leaked?" she asks.

"You already know," I say.

Even surrounded by honest men, I have traitors in my midst.

She presses her lips together and swipes her gun off the table, holstering it at her side. She might've hesitated killing me, but she won't when it comes to our enemies.

"If this continues," I say. "I'm pulling the plug on this campaign."

Her eyes flash. "Montes—"

I stride towards her slowly, well aware that when I'm like this, I'm intimidating.

Even to her.

And that's the point. She will not question me on this.

"This is your chance at peace," she says.

I shake my head slowly. I've had a hundred years to devise ways to end the war. I know she feels there's some rush to save the world, but we've gotten by without that elusive peace for a century now.

"It's not worth your life," I say.

Just the thought has my knees weakening. At times like this, I feel regret that she's not still in the Sleeper where I can keep her safe. Losing her, *really* losing her, could very well be the end of me.

And then she says something that has my blood curdling.

"But it *is* worth my life, Montes." She looks out the far window. "It is."

Serenity

I'M ESSENTIALLY ON house arrest.

One little comment was all it took for Montes to double up the original number of guards, bar the doors of the mansion and secure the perimeter of the property.

All so that I never have the chance to put my life on the line. Already our itinerary is being changed to accommodate his paranoia. Less time in each location, extra security around each building we'll be meeting in. He's even pulled extra troops to guard the large stadiums I'll be speaking at.

I can barely piss without someone watching over my shoulder.

Anyone who thinks that with power comes freedom is wrong. I'm a prisoner to it, and it doesn't matter that I never wanted this for myself.

Morning sunlight streams into our bedroom, and I

swear it looks different here. A part of me yearns to linger in this place just see all the ways the sun shines differently.

But there are things to do—loyalties to sway.

I sit on an ornate couch in our room, my weaponry and ammunition spread out along the coffee table. Gun oil, cleaning rods, and rags are littered between them.

I'm sure I'm quite a sight, clad in the dress and heels I've been forced to wear, my face painted and my hair coiffed for today's speech.

Cleaning my weapons is my little act of rebellion.

The door to the room opens, and even though I don't look up from my work, I know it's the king that steps through. Perhaps it's the heavy sound of his footfalls, and perhaps it's the power of his presence alone.

I hear him pause. "Should I regret giving you those guns?" he asks.

I lift an eyebrow but otherwise ignore him.

The narcissistic king doesn't like that very much. He strides over and places a hand over mine and the gun that I hold.

"Look at me," he commands.

I lower the weapon and raise my eyes. "What?"

He narrows his. Before I can object he sweeps his hand across the coffee table, brushing aside all the items I have laid out.

I curse as they clatter to the ground, beginning to reach for them.

He catches my wrist. "No."

"In a hundred years you haven't managed to be less of a control freak," I bite out.

"Hazards of being king," he replies, his voice hard.

Only then do I notice he's wearing his crown. Just like the last time I saw him in it, he looks devastatingly deadly.

It's then that I notice he's holding another. And it's not just any crown. By the looks of it, it's *the* crown I wore when I was coronated.

"No," I say.

"Yes," Montes counters.

I stare at the crown in his hands.

"*No*," I repeat more vehemently.

I've already compromised enough with the day's attire. The deep blue gown I wear is far too tight along the bodice and the heels I'm forced to wear will break my ankles if I need to run. I allowed it all without complaint.

But a crown?

"You might find this hard to believe," he says, and now his voice gentles, "but people don't carry the same stigmas they did a hundred years ago. They're not going to see the crown as you see it."

I don't want to concede, I don't want to give this man anything. But the truth is, he might be right. I really don't know this world and the people in it. Perhaps a queen is what they want to see. Their lives and their pasts are so very different from mine. I can't presume to know their hearts.

While I hesitate, Montes places the crown on my head, his hands lingering.

"Does getting your way all the time really make you feel good?" I ask.

The corner of his mouth lifts. "Not nearly as much as

your charming personality does."

His hands drift down, towards the low neckline of my dress. Maybe I hear his breath catch, or maybe the action itself is enough.

Does this man's passion ever wane?

"I look forward to your speech," he says. "And I look forward to after."

CHAPTER 30

Serenity

I AM A fool.

That's all I can think as I climb the steps of the dilapidated stadium, the king at my side, his men fanned around us.

I am a soldier, not a public speaker. At times like these, I'd rather lay my life on the line than stand in front of an audience. And that's just what I will have to do.

Over two dozen times. A speech for every city I visit.

Like I said, I am a fool.

I can hear all those lines I memorized, each one jumbling with the next. The words lodge themselves in my throat.

As we near the top of the stairs, my gaze moves to the

horizon.

My heart pounds as I get my first glimpse of the pyramids of Giza.

Or what's left of them.

They're mostly rubble. The ancient blocks that were painstakingly placed one on top of the other thousands of years ago now look like anthills someone's kicked over.

I run my tongue over my teeth, remembering the footage I watched yesterday. And now a renewed sense of purpose drives away my anxiety.

As we summit the steps, the event's coordinators descend on us from all sides, boxing us and our guards in. Most wear headsets and carry fancy equipment.

"My king," one of the women says, "you will go up first, and my queen, he will introduce you shortly thereafter."

Our entire group is shuffled to a small waiting room, where couches and platters of food wait for us.

Montes takes a seat at one of the couches, lounging back against it, his legs splayed wide. He looks completely at ease.

Oh, how I envy him.

Relaxing is the last thing I'll be able to do. I'm already amped up; my body doesn't know the difference between this and going into battle.

We don't wait long. Not five minutes later a woman raps on the door, then opens it a crack. "Your Majesties," she says, "it's time."

WE HEAD OUT of the waiting room, towards the stage.

More technicians and event planners crowd our group. The farther we walk, the more king's men break away from our cluster.

I do a double take of the hallway wall when we pass a poster with my face on it. Without realizing it, I've stopped.

It's almost identical to the one the First Free Men showed me. The sight of it is a shock to my system.

I approach the faded image and touch the worn paper. I keep forgetting what I am to these people, perhaps to the entire world.

"Serenity." I feel the king's eyes on me.

"It's old." I state the obvious.

The colors are muted, the paper has yellowed; the poster has obviously been here for months at the very least.

"People have believed in you for a very long time," he says.

I drop my hand, and reluctantly I resume walking, keenly aware of the crown on my head. I can't even fathom how strange this must be for the rest of the world. To find out the woman who symbolized freedom was not just alive after all this time, but also unchanged.

We stop in the wings of the stage. All that's left of our group is now Montes, me, Marco, and two guards that stand some distance away from us.

There we wait, the noise of the crowd drifting in. It sounds big.

I crack my knuckles, then my neck, shaking them out.

Montes leans in, about to make a comment, when a man with an earpiece approaches us.

"Your Majesties," he says, bowing to each of us in turn. "They're ready for you."

The king bends down and brushes a lingering kiss across my lips. It's soft and gentle—sweet. These moments always come as a shock to me.

His crown catches the light as he straightens, and he gives Marco a penetrating look. "Keep her safe."

It's all I can do not throw up my hands. I'm not some simpering damsel needing saving.

As though he knows what I'm thinking, Montes winks at me, and then he's gone.

AFTER THE KING leaves, I'm left alone with Marco. The king's right-hand stands to my side, far too close for my comfort. Despite choosing to ignore him, I know he won't ignore me. He's taken a keen interest in me since we met in the palace's secret passageways.

I wait for him to break the silence, counting off the seconds.

"Nervous?" he asks, as soon as it stretches on for a smidgen too long.

I clench my jaw, but don't respond.

Beyond the stage, I hear the audience roar; it sounds like something infernal and ferocious.

"Why do you despise me?" This time, Marco doesn't pretend to be jovial. His voice sounds sad, dejected.

I close my eyes. I should be thinking about my speech, about an entire hemisphere whose needs I now must represent. Instead my own emotions bubble up.

I'm being unfair to him. And I'm being petty.

"I don't despise you," I sigh out. "I despise the man that came before you." I have to force my next words out. "It's not your fault, but every time I see you, I relive those final moments with my father." And out of all the memories I have of him, that's the one I want to dwell on the least.

One of those people wearing the fancy headsets cuts into our little heart-to-heart. "Serenity, you're on in thirty," he says, waving me forward and saving me from continuing the conversation.

I'm led to a door at the end of the hallway, where he explains down to every minute detail how my entrance and exit should be executed. Then he leaves and I wait once more.

A countdown begins, and my pulse speeds up. These final seconds seem the longest as my adrenaline mounts.

And then the door I stand in front of is thrown open. As I move away from the wings, towards the stage, Giza unfolds before my eyes. I almost stagger back from the number of people gathered. A sea of them stand in the field in front of me, and many more fill the rows upon rows of stadium seats that wrap around it.

And as soon as they see me, they go crazy.

The soldier in me tenses. I almost reach for my gun before logic overrides the reaction.

The king still stands at the podium, and now he turns away from the audience, his deep eyes trained on me.

I walk up to him, and his hand falls to the small of my back. He resumes talking to the crowd, but I'm not listening. The audience has me mesmerized.

This can't be my life.

I've somehow gone from a dying soldier living out her limited days in a bunker to a mythic queen.

It feels like such a farce. Like *I'm* a farce.

I feel the king's eyes on me. He laces his fingers through mine and brushes a kiss against my fingers. When he straightens, he gives me a slight nod then leaves the stage.

Now it's my turn.

I take a deep breath as my gaze travels over the countless faces.

"The last time my eyes took in the world, it was at war," I began. "That was over a century ago."

If the crowd was silent before, now it goes dead.

"I slept for a hundred years and woke only to find the world is still at war. That should not be the way of things."

I take a deep breath, feeling the cameras on me. I'm going to have to be vulnerable, something I'm bad at in the best of situations. And this is far from the best of situations.

"One hundred and twenty-four years ago, I was born in the Western United Nations ..."

I don't know how many minutes pass by the time I bring people up to the present. I'm not even sure what I've told them matters. I wanted them to understand me, to know that for all our differences we are very much the same, but my life story isn't terribly relatable. It's mostly just sad. These people don't want a sad story. They want something to drive away the nightmares, something to hold onto when life gets tough.

"The world can be at peace," I say. "It was, long ago,

and it will be again. I will make sure of it."

My gaze travels over them. "I was awoken for a reason. My sleep has ended because it is time to end the war. I can't do it alone. I need each and every one of you. War ends when *we* decide it does. So I ask you this: believe in me and believe in humanity. Fight alongside me when the East needs it, and lay down your arms when our land no longer requires it. If you can do this, then the world will know peace once more."

The crowd goes quiet.

I've been too vague. Too optimistic. Too fumbling with my words. I feel it all in the silence.

I'm about to bow my head and walk off stage when one person somewhere out in the crowd begins to pound their fist over their heart.

Another person joins in. And then another.

Soon people are joining in handfuls at a time, then dozens, until eventually, the entire audience is thundering with the sound.

They begin to shout, and I can't make out the words at first. Eventually, the voices align and I hear it.

"*Freedom or death! Freedom or death!*"

I stare out at them.

A hundred years of life to become whatever it is you want.

And a hundred years of death to become whatever it is they want.

CHAPTER 31

Serenity

I DRAW IN a shaky breath as soon as I leave the podium and retreat back to the wings of the stage. I see Marco first, watching me with too-bright eyes. He steps towards me, but I brush past him.

I don't want to be around him or anyone else for that matter. I'm not sure what I'm feeling, and I want to sort my emotions out alone. I see the king standing off to the side, engrossed in a conversation with several of his officers. His eyes catch mine as he speaks, following me as I walk down the hall.

Several guards fall into formation, two behind me, two in front.

I'm never alone. Never, never alone. And I really would

like to be.

I head back to that little room where I waited earlier with the king. Five minutes is all I need to decompress and deal with the fact that I am no longer some abstract concept on a poster, but now a living, breathing ideology that people can consume.

The corridor outside the room is abandoned. I should be relaxing at the sight; solitude is what I wanted. Instead I find myself tensing up.

Behind me I hear several slick sounds. Something warm and wet sprays across my arms and back.

A trap.

In the next instant I hear the wet gurgle of dying men gasping for breath.

I swivel just as my guards fall to their knees, one clutching her neck.

Beyond them, three men wait for me, two holding bloody knives, and one with his gun leveled on my chest.

He adjusts his aim, then he pulls the trigger.

I HEAR A grunt at my side as the guard next to me takes a bullet to the chest. He staggers in front of me, covering my body even as he chokes for breath. The shooter's gun goes off several more times, and the other soldier flanking me goes down.

In the distance I hear shouts, but they're too far away.

I reach for my gun as they come at me.

I unholster my weapon just as the three reach me. One of my attackers jerks my arm up. I use the motion to align the barrel with the bottom of his chin.

I fire.

The back of his head blows away. Whatever pretty beliefs he had, whatever life he'd made from himself, it's gone within an instant.

As quick as I am, I'm still outnumbered two to one. One of the men forces my hands behind my back while the other covers my mouth with a damp cloth.

Now I'm having flashbacks to when the king pulled the same stunt.

That will *never* happen again.

They are still grappling for my weapon, and now I begin firing, hoping that I can hit some piece of enemy flesh. Blood splatters on my hands and wrists. One of my abductors shouts, releasing me reflexively.

I don't hesitate. I raise my gun and shoot the man point-blank in the face.

The final man, who's still pressing the damp cloth against my face now slams me into the wall in an effort to dislodge my weapon, cursing under his breath as he does so. I can hear the panic began to enter his voice.

I'm likely putting up more of a struggle than they expected.

The drug I'm being forced to inhale starts to take effect. Colors are blurring and my movement is slowing.

I lift my gun wielding arm.

Suddenly, I'm yanked back from the wall. The hallway spins with the movement.

My body begins to sag, each muscle feeling increasingly heavy. I still hold my weapon, but it takes an increasing amount of focus to get my body to move.

"Don't shoot!" the man behind me says.

It takes a second for my eyes to focus.

When they do, I see what my attacker sees: over a dozen different guards and officers, most with their weapons drawn. And right in the middle of them, Montes.

Our eyes find each other. He doesn't show his fear or his anger, not like most men do. But they're both there, simmering just beneath the surface.

I know his men aren't going to shoot, not when my captor is using me as a human shield.

The edges of my vision are starting to darken when I feel the man at my back trying to pry my gun from my grip.

I'm not going out like this.

It takes the rest of my strength just to pull that tiny little trigger. The shot echoes down the hall and the man cries out. I'm not even sure whether or not the bullet hit him or he was just taken by surprise. Either way, it's enough.

I fall out of his hold, and a dozen other guns discharge. And then the last of my attackers meets his grisly end.

I SET MY bloody crown down on the airplane's conference table, the gleam of it somewhat dulled by the blood splatter.

It's been over an hour since the attack, though you wouldn't know it by looking at us all. I'm still coated in blood. Despite the fact that I have worn blood more often than makeup, it never gets less horrifying.

Heinrich Weber, the king's grand marshal, is the last to enter the cabin, the door to the aircraft closing behind him.

"Your Majesties," he bows to me and Montes, the latter who is stalking up the aisle from the back of the plane, a damp hand towel gripped tightly in his hand, "we found several dead employees in the stadium's storage closets," he reports. "From what the investigators have been able to piece together, it's believed that Serenity's attackers disposed of them then took their ID badges and gear."

"That was all it took?" the king says. He kneels in front of me. Placing a hand against my cheek, he begins to wipe down my face with the cloth. I'm so taken by the gesture that I let him tend to me.

"The queen of the entire eastern hemisphere goes to her first—*her first*—speech," he continues, "and all it takes for the enemy to infiltrate is a couple stolen badges?" His ministrations roughen with his anger.

As soon as the towel gets close to my lips, I take it from Montes. I don't want anyone else pressing a damp cloth near my mouth. Not even the king.

He stares into my eyes, one of his hands dropping to my thigh and squeezing it. When he removes his palm, I notice it's stained red from just touching the fabric I wear.

I'm a bloody, bloody mess.

He stares at his hand for a beat, then his fingers curl into a fist.

Someone's going to die. I can feel it. The king's anger has always needed an outlet.

He stands. "Did you discover who the men are affiliated with?"

I begin wiping my arms down. It's a hopeless task. The blood's everywhere.

The officer hesitates. "They're still not sure, but it appears that they were associated with the First Free Men."

I go still.

Styx Garcia.

The man tried to capture me again *after* the deal we made. The thought makes me seethe. Surely there's an explanation for it.

I remember the way Styx looked at me when we last spoke. He wants me for more than just power and political leverage. There is some personal aspect to this.

The king glances back at me, and for a split second I'm almost sure he knows of my talk with Styx. My heart pounds in my ears, but I stare at him unflinchingly.

"These sorts of things will continue to happen so long as the queen visits these places," Marco says, interrupting the moment. He sits on the far side of the room, his eyes on me.

"Then we will call this off," the king says.

A bit of the old tyrant ruler peeks out. I knew that bastard wasn't gone.

I stand, setting aside the now blood-drenched towel. "*Montes.*"

The king isn't the only one who can call the room to heel with his presence. It takes just a single word for all eyes to focus on me.

A century of sleep has given me a strange sort of power, one that I never had when I was just a young foreign queen.

"You think this is just going to go away if you lock me up in one of your palaces?" I say.

His head tilts just the slightest. "No, but it will keep you alive longer than this." He holds up his bloody palm. "I didn't hide you all this time just to watch you die."

Sometimes I get so swept up in his dominance plays that I forget he's just a broken man trying to save his broken woman.

My voice softens. "You've tried hiding me away. The world found me. Why don't we try a different tactic now?"

He holds my gaze.

Finally, he blows out a breath.

He gives a brief nod to the men that await his orders. They seem to relax at the gesture, many of them returning to whatever it was they were previously doing.

The king comes back to my side then. "I'm going to trust you. Don't make me regret it," he says softly, echoing the same words I said to him a week ago.

I had wondered once whether it was possible for people like us to redeem ourselves. Now as I stare at Montes, my conscience whispers, *perhaps.*

Perhaps.

CHAPTER 32

Serenity

OUR NEXT STOP is in Kabul, a city smack dab in the middle of the East's territories. It's a barren place bordered by huge, austere mountains.

We arrive early that evening, just as the sun is beginning to set.

Endless war has made this city even more desolate than Giza. Most of the dwellings are mudbrick, and the older ones seem to be crumbling where they stand. Then there are the buildings that came *before*. Steel and cement skeletons are all that remain of those.

Here it appears that the city is returning to the earth. We rose, we peaked, and now we fall.

I can't say it isn't beautiful, however. The rosy hue of

sunset makes the ruins look deliberate, like some city planner crafted the desolation into the architecture of this place.

As our car winds through the city, I catch glimpses of street art. On this street it's a spray-painted grenade. The artist went to the trouble of adding eyes to the explosive. Eyes and a single curving scar that looks like a teardrop. Beneath it a caption reads, *Freedom or Death.*

I see several more tagged iterations of this propaganda on our drive. Some with just a grenade, others with renditions of my face. In some, I can only tell it's me by the scar they include.

I touch my face. Perhaps I'm the wrong person to encourage peace. From everything I've seen, I'm a war cry. A liberator, but a violent one.

Marco was right—more attempts will be made to capture me or kill me.

I am, after all, a walking revolution.

I SIT OUT on the back patio of Montes's royal residency in Kabul. The mansion rests on the mountainside overlooking the city.

An evening breeze stirs my hair, and I pull the blanket around me closer.

"You know, there are other ways to stay warm." The voice at my back is like the richest honey.

My king has decided to join me.

"If I was trying to stay warm, I wouldn't be out here," I say over my shoulder before returning my gaze to the brutal landscape.

Montes comes to my side, placing two tumblers and a bottle of amber liquid on the table in front of me before pulling out the chair next to mine.

"I don't like it when you're alone," he admits.

I glance over at him, some of the hair that was tucked behind my ear now falling loose. "Why?"

He pours us each a glass and hands one to me. "Another way to keep warm," he explains. From the way he's gazing at me, his eyes will do more to heat me up than the drink will.

"I don't want you to ever feel like you're lost," he says, returning to the previous subject.

That's so oddly sweet of him.

"I've been alone enough for the both of us," he adds. He stares at his glass, as though he can divine his next words in the liquid.

After a moment, he brings it to his mouth and takes a sip. He hisses out a satisfied breath after he takes a swallow.

I follow his lead and take a healthy swig of the alcohol. I almost spit it back out. It scorches the inside of my mouth.

"*Mother*—" I curse. "That's *strong*."

Montes look like he's trying not to laugh. "I hope you never change, Serenity."

I glance over at him again. Between the light streaming out from inside and the lanterns scattered throughout the garden, Montes seems to glow.

Beautiful, haunted man. How is it that I'm only seeing how tragic he is now?

"I hope I do," I say softly.

I squint out at the small, flickering lights of Kabul. "Tell me how you've changed."

He sighs, like it's all too much. And what do I know? If I lived for a century and a half, life might overwhelm me as well.

He bows his head. "I've always felt such ... *discontent*. Even as a boy. It didn't matter what I achieved or what I was given. I wanted more. Always more," he murmurs, staring at his glass. "To hunger for success—that's a good trait to possess as a businessman and a conqueror, but it needs to be balanced with temperance, morality, and wisdom. I'm not sure how much I have of any of those. Even now."

His gaze moves up to the stars. "I can't tell you how many nights I wished upon your Pleiades. For you to heal. For you to live. Once you were gone, for the first time in my life, success was overridden by something else."

I feel a lump in my throat. I couldn't speak even if he asked me to.

Montes looks at me. "How have I changed? I fell in love. I needed you, and you were locked away in a Sleeper. And the only way you were getting out of that machine was if I found a cure for cancer. It changed my entire focus. I began to understand loss in a way I hadn't before—I began to feel the weight of your life and your suffering. Of everyone's suffering. I couldn't ignore it. God, did I try, too. But after a time ... well, even an old dog like me can form new habits. Better habits."

I'm gripping my glass so tightly I can feel the blood leaving my fingers.

He shakes his head. "You go so long without someone and fear can eat you up. The idea of you sustained me for decades but—and it's inexplicable—I felt that once you were healed I couldn't wake you. And I had all sorts of reasons for it—and so many of them are legitimate—but at the end of the day I don't know, I just couldn't make that one leap."

Montes is finally explaining his decision to me. *Really* explaining it.

I take another swallow of my drink, and this time I don't feel the burn, grappling with my thoughts as I am.

"You and I are the only people who know the world as it once was," he says.

I shiver. Right now I feel like Montes and I are the only two beings in the entire universe, tied together by love and hate, time and memory.

"Us—and your former advisors," I say.

"They aren't people," Montes says.

I take a deep breath. "Neither are we."

We are all just self-fashioned monsters posing as gods.

"You're wrong, Serenity. You and I cling to our humanity more fiercely than anyone else."

He has a point. We cling to it because we know just how close we are to losing it.

"*Your Majesties!*" Heinrich dashes out to the patio. The alarm in his voice has us both standing.

Almost reflexively, Montes steps in front of me.

I frown at his back. I never wanted the old Montes, but he became mine anyway. I want this newer version even less. This is a man whose evil deeds I can truly forget. And I don't want to forget. I want to remember to my last dying breath that even though the king might now be the solution, in the beginning he was the problem.

Just as soon as that thought comes, another follows in its wake.

No one is beyond forgiveness.

Both my parents used to say that, and *that* was something I had almost forgotten.

"We just got word from our men who were supposed to change guard for the regional leader of Kabul," Heinrich says. "They said the place is a bloodbath—our soldiers are dead and the family is gone."

CHAPTER 33

Serenity

"YOU'RE NOT GOING," the king says.

He and his men are equipping themselves in the living room.

A mercenary king. I hadn't expected that from Montes. I don't know whether I'm more surprised that he's joining the unit assigned to the task, or that his men seem unfazed by this.

After all these years, the king has finally come down from his ivory tower.

"I am if you are," I say, checking the magazine of my gun to make sure my weapons are fully loaded. My new gun isn't. I haven't had a chance to replace the spent bullets I fired off in Giza. I cross the room where box of communal ammunition rests. I pull out my own bullets and compare.

A match.

I begin to slide them into the magazine. The soldiers around me tense, their eyes darting between me and the king.

"Anyone have a spare magazine?" I say.

Just in case we run into any difficulties.

One of the soldiers lifts one sitting next to him and begins to hand it over.

Montes catches his wrist. "*Don't*," he says. "Serenity won't be joining us."

I finish loading my magazine and force it up into the chamber of the gun. "Who's going to stop me?" I ask.

Many of these men saw me kill today, which means they saw my lack of hesitation, and now they're seeing my lack of remorse.

Some of the soldiers look uncomfortable, but I also catch some suppressing grins.

Montes steps forward, crowding me. "Don't force my hand, Serenity." His voice has gone quiet.

"Then don't force mine."

We stare each other down. Us and our impasses. Montes knows just how easy it would be for me to lift my arm and point this gun at him, and I know how easy it would be for him to have his men detain me.

He knows I can hold my own if something bad should happen. I've proven that to him over and over.

"Let me into your world," I say softly. My plea cuts through the tension in a way that none of my previous words could.

Montes's nostrils flare and his lips press together. It used to be that the king couldn't resist me when I got physical. Now it's something else. Every time I tear down an emotional wall of ours, I make headway with him.

"If anything goes wrong—*anything*—I won't be repeating this, and nothing you say or do will stop me."

BY THE TIME we arrive at the home of the woman who ran Kabul's government, all that's left are bodies and blood.

I step over one of the king's fallen soldiers just inside the entrance of the home. His throat has been sliced open. I can still hear the slow drip of his blood as it leaves his body.

The king's men who were on the scene first have secured the perimeter of the house and the surrounding neighborhood, but aside from them, we'll be the first ones inside the home of Nadia and Malik Khan, the regional leader and her husband.

I have my gun out. Even though there are plenty of guards, some who were here before us and some who came with our brigade, it never hurts to be ready.

We move through the residence, our footsteps nearly silent. I take in the sparse furnishings. Even regional leaders live fairly humble lives, if this home is anything to go by. The furniture and decorations are faded, and the wooden tables have lost their polish.

Montes walks slightly ahead of me, his broad shoulders largely obscuring the hall ahead of us.

We head to the back of the house, where the bedrooms are.

More fallen soldiers lay outside the doors, their eyes glassy. These ones have gunshot wounds.

My eyes drift back to the door. Hesitantly, I step inside.

The reports never mentioned that Malik and Nadia had kids, but they very obviously do. Two beds rest against the far wall of the children's room, both empty. The sight of those ruffled sheets is harder to look at than the dead soldiers. I grip my gun tighter.

Someone will die for this.

Once we scan the room, our group moves back out into the hall. We make quick work of the other rooms, until there is just the master bedroom left.

I don't particularly want to go in there. For one thing, the closer I get the stronger the smell of raw meat and death is. The reason for that is obvious—four dead guards line the hall leading up to it.

But there's also the less obvious reason for my reluctance. My intuition is now kicking in. Maybe it's just the partially open door and the darkness beyond it, but my heart rate's picking up.

We enter, and my eyes land on the empty master bed. There are several drops of blood on the sheets, but I have no idea what sort of injury caused them.

My gaze doesn't linger on the bed for long, though.

Not when I catch sight of a crib.

My knees go weak.

Not a baby. Please, not that.

My chest tightens. I really don't want to get any closer.

But, in spite of myself, I creep towards the crib with the rest of the soldiers. There's a bitter, metallic taste in my mouth. The room is too silent.

In front of me, Montes stiffens. "*Nire bihotza*—"

He tries to block my view, but it's too late.

I catch sight of a tiny, unmoving body.

I barely have time to push away from my guards before I vomit.

I'm not the only one either. Grown men and women join me, people who I know have seen horrible things.

My stomach spasms over and over. I try to catch my breath, but I can't.

Montes was right. We might be monsters, but we're not evil.

Not like this.

MY CROWN SITS heavy on my head as I stare out at the crowds the next day.

The first day I wore a crown, my child died. And that's what it will always represent to me. Innocents dying for causes evil people uphold.

As heavy as my crown is, my heart is heavier.

"How badly do you want peace?" I open.

The people of Kabul roar in response.

This city has no official stadium, so I'm giving my speech on an open expanse of land, one where several old buildings once stood. Now all that remains are ruins.

There are cameramen both offstage and on, and I see them move closer as I began to speak. At my back I know there's a large screen magnifying me. I wonder just how much they can see of my expression.

"Good," I say, "because there are people out there that will make you fight for it. They will make you *die* for it."

My eyes flick only briefly to the side of the stage, where Montes watches me.

"What I'm about to tell you—I was advised not to say. But you have a right to know."

I see at least one officer begin to rub his temples.

"The leaders of each of the cities I've been visiting are being taken, one by one."

Already we've begun to notify the other cities and put their leaders on high alert that the West is targeting them. Many have pulled out of the tour altogether. Others have gone into hiding.

Murmurs run through the audience. Up until now, the king has kept quiet on this. His greatest fear was that the news would spark aimless violence among the citizens of the East.

And it might. They still have a right to know. And if I'm to be some great savior of theirs, then I should be the one to deliver the news.

"Someone doesn't want peace. Someone is afraid of what I am doing."

I turn my attention to the cameras because what I'm about to say is for the representatives. "To our enemies, listen carefully: Pray I don't find you. If I do, I will make you pay."

My gaze moves back to my audience; the crowd is roaring with outrage and excitement. "If you are angry, you have a right to be. No one should live in a world where they must fear for their life. But I will also tell you this: death cannot avenge death, and bloodshed cannot avenge bloodshed. Justice must be served, but it shouldn't turn good men into wicked ones."

I take off the crown. I flip it over in my hands. My audience has gone quiet.

"I've also been told that I should wear this. That this is what you want to see." I look up from the crown, towards the people watching me. "This," I hold up the headpiece, "means nothing. I am not above you. I am one of you.

"The world is interested in telling you all the ways we're different. You have the East and the West. Ruler and ruled. Rich and poor.

"But they lie."

I was never a very good orator. But this is different. The words are coming to me, born from a fire in my soul. I'm angry and excited and so very, very full of life.

"I killed many men during my time as a soldier," I say. In the past, admitting something like this would be a disaster. But these people already know I'm no idle ruler. "And I saw many men die. They all bled the same. *We* are all the same. And this," I hold up the crown. "This can go fuck itself." I fling the crown offstage, towards some of the king's soldiers. Much as I'd like to give it back to the people, I fear something as precious as gold would be enough to draw blood between civilians.

The audience bellows at the sight. This is fervor. This *is* revolution.

"We are all the same," I say. "Let's end this war together. As equals."

The crowd begins thumping their chests, the rhythm picking up pace until it's one continuous sound.

My eyes cut to the king, who stands just offstage. He rubs his chin, his eyes glinting as he watches me. When he notices me looking, he inclines his head, and the beginnings of a smile form along his lips.

Our enemies should be afraid.

I am a bomb, and they've just lit the fuse.

CHAPTER 34

Serenity

We leave Kabul shortly after the speech, our next stop, Shanghai. The pacing of our itinerary was brutal to begin with, but now that figureheads have been disappearing, we're moving through the tour at a breakneck speed.

I fall asleep fully clothed on the airplane's bed, my face smooshed against the sheets. I rouse only once, when a familiar someone covers me with a blanket.

Montes's fingers trail down my cheek. My eyes open just enough to see him staring intently at me.

"I–" I almost say it then. Those three dreaded words that I've kept from the king for so long. It's equally shocking how natural they come, and how badly they want to be let out.

The king's touch stills.

"I'm happy you're here," I murmur.

"Always," he says, his fingers moving once more.

I'm already falling back asleep, like I didn't almost just surrender the last bit of my heart.

I'm jerked awake when the plane dips sharply to the left. I grip the edges of the mattress to keep from rolling.

The door to the back cabin is closed but on the other side I hear raised voices, their tones laced with controlled panic.

Quickly, I get up, shaking off the last of my grogginess, and stumble to the door.

When I open it I see Montes on the other side, heading straight for my room, presumably to wake me.

"What's going on?" I ask.

"Three enemy aircraft share our airspace," he says, his expression grim.

I glance out the window but see nothing.

"Are they armed?" I ask. It's a ridiculous question. Of course they are.

"Undoubtedly," Montes echoes my thoughts, "but they haven't shot us down yet."

No sooner are the words out of his mouth than I hear a distant hiss.

I've missed out on a hundred years of civilization, and yet in all that time weaponry hasn't changed much. Not if the sound I'm hearing is a—

"Missile incoming," the pilot informs us over an intercom. "Engaging the ABM system."

It's a fancy way of saying we're going to blow that fucker

out of the sky. That is, if it doesn't hit us first.

The noise gets louder, and louder, and then—

BOOM!

The sky lights up as a fireball unfurls some distance away from us. A split second later the shock wave hits us, sending the plane canting, and throwing us idiots not belted in across the cabin.

I slam into the wall, my body dropping into the row of seats beneath it. When I look up, I see Montes on the floor nearby, crawling towards me.

"Are you okay?" he asks.

I nod. "You?"

"Yeah." He exhales the word out. He jerks his head towards the seats. "Strap in. It's going to get rough."

I right myself and begin to do just that. The plane starts losing altitude rapidly. I grab my stomach as we plummet. An alarm goes off and the overhead lights start to flash.

Montes makes it to the seat next to me and straps himself in.

"Has this happened to you before?" I ask.

He grabs my hand, his face stony. "Yes."

The king's men follow our lead, scrambling into seats and hastily buckling themselves in.

"And how did that end?" I ask. He obviously survived it.

"I was in the Sleeper for a month." He doesn't elaborate, which means it was likely worse than what I might imagine.

I hear another distant hiss start up as our plane continues to drop from the sky.

"ABM system reengaged," the pilot announces.

Another explosion follows the first, rocking the plane further. The people that still aren't buckled go tumbling across the cabin once more. One of them is Marco, and he falls close to my feet.

Fighting my baser impulses, I reach out a hand and drag him up to the seat next to me.

He nods his thanks, buckling his seatbelt right away. I feel the king's eyes on me, but I refuse to look over at him. I don't want to see his gratitude.

Shrapnel pings against the outside of the plane. But it's not until I hear the screeching sound of metal smashing into metal and the aircraft shudders that my eyes move to the window. Outside I see one of the engines catch fire.

How long does good fortune last for people like us? This is Russian roulette, and this might be the shot the kills us.

I squeeze the king's hand and take a calming breath. I don't fear the end. I haven't for a very long time. This isn't the way I'd choose to go, but there are worse ways to die than reclining in a plush chair, the world spread out beneath you.

The alarms are still blaring, the officers all have wide eyes. But no one screams. Montes brings my hand to his mouth and holds our entwined hands there.

I see his lips move. I can't hear his words, but I know what he's saying.

I love you.

I pinch my lips together. Only hours ago I almost said those very words right back to him.

His gaze meets mine. My mouth parts. I feel those words coming back, moving up my throat. They want out.

The plane hits some turbulence, breaking the spell. My gaze cuts away from him as my body's jerked about. The moment's gone, and if we die right now, we'll die with him never hearing those three words fall from my lips.

I can't tell if I feel relief or disappointment.

Both, I think.

Our seats begin to shake as our velocity increases. Above the shrill alarm I swear I hear the rumble of engines. Through the aircraft's tiny windows, I catch a glimpse of fighter jets. If they've come to end us, they got here too late.

But as I watch, they accelerate past us, presumably towards the enemy, who I still haven't seen.

The officers begin to clap and whoop at the sight, like we've been saved. All those jets managed to do was head off one enemy. But now gravity is our more obvious opponent.

Our aircraft continues to plunge straight towards the earth. I hate that I have enough time to feel my mortality slipping through my fingers.

I swear I feel the plane pull up, but I have no way of knowing whether that's just wishful thinking.

The ground is getting closer and closer. Our angle is still bad.

I look at Montes one more time. If I'm going to die, it will be staring into his eyes. We were bound to go down together.

When I meet his gaze, I can see relief, but I don't know

what put the expression there.

It turns out that, whatever the reason, he'll live to tell me about it.

The plane levels out at the very last minute.

My gaze is ripped away from him as we slam into the earth. I'm jerked violently against my seatbelt. Part of the ceiling pulls away from the metal frame on impact, cutting off my view of the front half of the cabin.

The world is consumed by an awful screeching noise as the plane slides across the ground. I hear plastic and metal ripping away from the underside of the plane. A few screams join the noise, some panicked, and some high-pitched cries that cut off sharply.

And then, miraculously, we grind to a stop.

For several seconds I do nothing but catch my breath.

I didn't die.

"*Nire bihotza*, my hand."

I hear Montes's voice, and my chest tightens almost painfully.

The king didn't die either.

A choked sound comes out of my mouth as I face him and see that he is, in fact, alive.

I release his hand, a hand I've been squeezing the life out of, and cup the side of his face. I can't put into words what I feel. But now the relief that was so blatant in his eyes earlier seems to be making a home for itself beneath my sternum.

I pull him to me and kiss him roughly. How horrifying that my heart has come to rely on this creature.

I feel his surprise—he still isn't used to my affection,

especially when I do it in public. But once his shock wears off, he kisses me back with a possessive intensity I've become familiar with.

Death will come for us both, sooner rather than later, but it won't happen today.

CHAPTER 35

Serenity

I WATCH THE unfamiliar scenery pass me by. Montes and I sit in the back of the armored vehicle that arrived on scene shortly after we crashed.

Two of the king's men didn't survive the crash landing. One's neck snapped and the other was crushed under the section of ceiling that ripped away from the airplane's frame.

I'm so numb. At some point, you see too many people die. It becomes just one more ache in your heart. Another person taken too soon.

It takes several hours to reach Shanghai. When we do, I can only stare. Many of the buildings are in ruins, but what remains is in use. And the structures are from *before*.

They've been kept up for over a century.

We eventually pull up to a high-rise that faces the East China Sea.

I should be taken with the sparkling ocean. I never imagined I'd see an ocean this far east. And it's beautiful. But I can't seem to tear my gaze away from the goliath we've stopped in front of.

We step out of the car, some combo of sewage and ocean air carried along the breeze.

"Have you ever been to the top of a skyscraper?" Montes asks, steering me towards it.

I shake my head. Montes had cornered me inside an abandoned skyscraper once, when I lost my memory, but I never made it close to the top.

"We're going to the top?"

Montes gives me just the barest hint of a smile. Some uncomfortable combination of excitement and trepidation fills me at the possibility, especially so soon after we were shot out of the sky.

The rest of our brigade exits their cars, and we all enter the lobby. The people inside stare and stare. It's probably a shock in itself to see the king of half the world. But their eyes linger the longest on me. And then out of the blue, one of them begins to thump their chest slowly.

Several more join in. Within seconds the whole room is doing it, the tempo increasing to a frantic pace.

This is becoming a habit, I notice.

I nod to them, and I'm sure I look more demure than I am. Montes waves, his other hand pressed against the small of my back.

"You were right," he says, his voice low. "This campaign will help end the war. Look at them. They will die for you."

"I don't want anyone to die for me," I whisper furiously back to him.

"That, my queen, is no longer for you to decide."

The King

THE SOUR TASTE at the back of my throat hasn't disappeared since my enemies tried to shoot us from the sky. It's been decades since the West has pulled such a risky maneuver.

They will pay for it.

Already I've ordered attacks on several Western outposts they thought I didn't know about. I feel the familiar blood hunger. I want the sort of intimate revenge I swore off a long time ago.

It was easy enough to swear it off back then. For a long time I was deadened to most things. And then Serenity woke, and my heart awoke with her. Now it doesn't know how to remove itself from cold strategy.

My eyes fall on my queen as she moves about our quarters, taking in each furnishing and every detail.

No, my heart is no longer cold.

Christ, I want to hide this woman.

If I thought she'd forgive me for it, I would lock her away someplace where my enemies could never find her. But I think that would just about push the last of my luck with Serenity, and I don't want to give her another reason to despise me. She has too many of those already.

She stops in front of one of the windows, placing her fingertips against it.

"I'm used to seeing these without the glass still intact," she says.

"War hasn't destroyed everything," I say.

"No," she agrees, dropping her hand. She casts me an enigmatic look. "Not everything."

She begins removing her weapons and setting them on the small nightstand next to our bed.

Savage woman.

I watch her as she peels off one soiled clothing item after the next, dropping them where she stands. It's obvious her mind is in other places; she's oblivious to my eyes on her.

There's a smudge of dirt just behind her ear—a place she'd never notice or think to clean. I have the oddest desire to wipe it away.

Instead my eyes travel from it to the delicate line of her neck, then down her back. Her body is so small for such a force of nature. Sometimes I forget that. She takes up such a big part of my world.

Bruises speckle her skin. I frown at the sight. She's received each one in the short time since she's woken.

She turns her head in my direction, doing a double take when she realizes I've been watching her. Belatedly she covers herself.

I begin to walk towards her, unbuttoning my shirt as I do so. I decide then and there that whatever she's planning on doing naked, I'll be joining her.

"Don't you think it's a little too late to be shy?" I say.

"Not with you, no."

I can tell she wants to back up as I close the space between us. But she won't. Her pride and her nerves will prevent her from showing weakness. I love this about her, and I take advantage of it, stepping up to her until my chest brushes against her arms.

I pull them away from her body, exposing her. "I'm your husband."

She lifts her chin, staring up at me defiantly. "You haven't been for the last hundred years."

I grab her jaw and tilt her head to the side, so that I see the back of her ear. With my other hand I rub away the smudge I saw earlier.

I turn her head back to face me. "Save your anger for our enemies."

Our gazes hold, and I think I've gotten through to her.

She pulls away, slipping through my fingers once more. She wanders to the bathroom, closing the door behind her—but not all the way. It hangs open several inches.

An invitation.

Several seconds after the faucet turns on, the shower door bangs closed and I hear her suck in a breath, presumably at the temperature.

"You know, you could wait a minute for it to warm," I say, removing the last of my clothes.

"That's a minute's worth of water wasted," she calls back to me.

I close my eyes and savor the moment. Everything's changed—everything except for her. It's almost unbearable. Like a memory come back to life.

With a shuddering exhale, I open my eyes and head into the bathroom.

Her back is to me. She doesn't turn, even when I open the shower door and step inside. I know she knows I'm there, but she doesn't object.

I don't think she hates me nearly as much she wants to.

I push her mane of hair over one of her shoulders and kiss the back of her neck. This is how it was always meant to be between us.

I run my hands over her bruises.

She leans her head back into me, and I wrap an arm around her torso, pulling her even closer. This is the woman I never deserved, and this is the life I always craved.

Letting my eyes drift shut, I brush my mouth against one of her shoulder blades, leaning my forehead against her neck.

I would inhale her in if I could.

"Montes—"

I squeeze her even tighter. Just my name on her lips undoes me.

"Why do you love me?" she asks.

My lungs still and my eyes open. Serenity has turned her head halfway towards me.

Back on the plane I sensed she came close to uttering those very words. And now she wants to explore my feelings for her.

Because she's trying to figure out her own.

My heart will burst, I'm sure of it.

But I let on none of this.

Instead I press a kiss to Serenity's cheek.

"Why does anything happen the way it does?" I ask, resting my chin just above her head. "I don't know. I don't know why that first night in Geneva, when you entered my ballroom with your father, I couldn't take my eyes off of you. Or why, in a hundred years I haven't been able to banish you from my mind." Now I turn her to face me. "Or why, even after all the ways I've changed, I can love you the same way I always have.

"But I do."

God, I do.

CHAPTER 36

The King

BECAUSE OF THE attacks, and our quick exits from each territory, we have an extra day built into our schedule and nothing planned to fill it.

If we weren't at war, and if my enemies weren't actively trying to attack us, I would show her all around Shanghai. One day, once this is all over, I will take her to every distant corner of our world and show her sights she's never seen.

But that won't be today.

I let her sleep until noon comes and goes. When she still doesn't wake, the old worries begin to fester. That the cancer has come back. That the Sleeper never fixed her. That her exhaustion comes from within.

So, only hours after I've dressed for the day, I undress and slip back under the covers. I settle between her thighs, my hands snaking around her legs. And then I wake her up with a kiss.

There is no slow rise to consciousness with my wife. One moment she's asleep, the next she's trying to jerk away. I hold her hips in place, enjoying her surprise.

"*Montes.*" She squirms under me.

My lips return to her. Almost unwillingly, she moves against me, like she can't help it.

I groan against her core. I'm not going to last much longer like this.

Before she has a chance to protest, I flip her onto her stomach and move up her torso, my chest pressed to her back.

"Mon–"

With one swift thrust, I'm inside her.

Whatever she was about to say turns into a breathy sigh.

"Morning, my queen," I say against her ear.

My earlier fears concerning her health vanish now that I'm near her.

She relaxes against me, her body pliant beneath mine.

I thread my fingers between hers.

"Say it," I whisper.

It's been a demon riding me, the need to hear those words. I sense she loves me, but I want to hear the words from her.

I *must* hear them from her.

She stiffens beneath me. "No."

I swear I hear true worry in her voice.

She's close to cracking.

I nip the shell of her ear.

I will get her to say it.

And soon.

Serenity

CREATURE COMFORTS STILL make me feel guilty. I'm not sure that part of me will ever go away. I spent all my formative years as one of the have-nots. I don't know what to do when everything I ever wished for is in the palm of my hand.

So I only reluctantly spend the day in bed with Montes, who appears to have no problem enjoying his creature comforts.

And oh, how he enjoys them. He hasn't even let me out to eat, instead bringing our meals to bed. And when we're not eating ...

Like I said, Montes enjoys his creature comforts.

It's only as the sun begins to set that he lets me slip from his arms.

He watches me as I dress. I feel those eyes, those thirsty, thirsty eyes drink me in.

When I go to grab a shirt, Montes says, "Ah, ah."

I give him a look over my shoulder. "Unless you'd chain me naked that bed, I'm going to have to dress at some point."

Give this man an inch, and he will take miles and miles.

He throws the covers off himself and leaves the bed to

stride towards me. "Much as that would please me," he takes the shirt out of my hands and tosses it aside, "I'll have to save the chains for later."

Montes heads to our closet and pulls out a dress with black and gold feathers along the shoulders and what looks like armored scales along the bodice. "We have dinner tonight."

Between the relentless traveling and the attacks, I'd almost forgotten about the hateful dinners sprinkled liberally throughout the tour. We canceled all of the previous ones because they'd been contingent upon the officials of each territory.

"Shanghai's leaders?" Now I feel doubly guilty for spending a day in bed.

"They're fine," Montes says.

My attention returns to the dress.

"What *is* that?" I say, eyeing the gown with equal bits curiosity and revulsion.

"Armor for a queen."

OUR DINNER IS being held in an extravagant building with architecture even older than the skyscrapers, the roofs slanted, the colors deep and vivid.

I walk into the enormous main hall on the king's arm. My dress shivers as I move, the result of all those metal scales rubbing against one another.

The walls around us are gilded in gold, and the columns bracing the ceiling are a vibrant red. It's beautiful and foreign, and it makes me feel like an interloper.

As soon as the two of us catch the attention of the guests already inside, they begin pounding their chests, just like the men and women earlier. I press my lips together.

I never meant to become some sort of celebrity, and I'm unused to the positive attention I've been receiving. In the past, a good portion of the king's subjects didn't like me. I find it's much easier to deal with hate than love.

I dip my head. Even that doesn't stop the strange salutes they're all giving me. Not for several minutes. And once they do stop, it's not over. Not really, because everyone there wants to talk to me.

A waiter passes by, carrying several glasses of wine. I snatch one up, earning me a raised eyebrow from Montes. But for perhaps the first time since we've been together, he doesn't actively try to prevent me from drinking.

An hour goes by like this. Drinking and talking. The king is by my side the entire time, smoothly managing the conversations without letting on that he's doing so.

At some point, we come across Shanghai's regional leader, Zhi Wei, his wife, and several dignitaries he works with. All of them look a little spooked.

They're smart to be afraid. We've marked them for death by coming to their land. I still can't think of that house in Kabul without feeling nauseous.

Zhi bows, his entourage following his lead.

"It's an honor to have you here," he says when he straightens.

It's a curse.

I swallow down the bad taste I have at the back of my throat. I'm cursing these people by coming here.

"Thank you for hosting us," I reply.

He gives a solemn nod.

"We are eager to end the war." Zhi glances briefly at his wife. "We've lost two sons to it."

This part hurts. It always hurts. I think most soldiers don't fear death nearly so much as they fear this—their family's grief. Soldiers know better than most the mind games the dead can play with you.

"I will do everything in my power to make that happen," I say.

We chat with Zhi and his wife a little longer, then we move on to greet more people. I drink and greet, drink and greet. On and on it goes until the alcohol makes my smiles a little more genuine and my body a little less stiff.

I don't notice I've drawn closer to Montes until he brushes a kiss on my temple, a kiss I lean into. I realize then how much of my side is pressed against his, and that my arm is wrapped just as tightly around his waist as his is mine.

A glass clinks at the far end of the room, and for one brief instant, I fear it's another one of those embarrassing kiss requests meant for me and the king.

Instead, the waiter holding the glass clears his throat. "I'd ask all the guests to move into the dining room." He gestures to a room to my left. "Dinner will commence shortly."

Guests begin to meander towards the room, many throwing eager glances in my direction. Each one makes my heart stutter a little. Surely there are types of people that would like this attention, I'm just not one of them.

The king sticks closely to my side. If I had to guess, I'd say that he doesn't like the attention on me any more than I do.

We enter a small, overly ornate room dominated by a large rectangular table and dozens of place settings. Just like the main room, the walls here are gold. It feels like something out of a dream, something I will wake up from.

I scan the room for our seats. It's then that the back of my neck prickles.

I stiffen.

Even with the alcohol dulling my senses, there are some things I can't shake. I've been a soldier too long. Self-preservation and paranoia are two sides of the same coin.

So I covertly place my foot in front of the king, and then I push him. I exert just enough force to have him stumble forward and trip over my leg. He begins to fall, and I go down with him.

The sound of the bullet is explosive. I hear a ping as it hits a silver serving bowl just to the left of Montes.

That's all the time it takes for me to realize—

"They're trying to kill the king!" I shout, grabbing Montes's shoulder and shoving him the rest of the way to the ground. He forces me down along with him.

Distantly, I'm aware of others diving to the ground, but at the moment my attention is limited to the king.

When I try to cover his body with my own, he simply gives me a look and flips us.

He's looking at me with wild eyes as more shots fill the air. It's apparent from the agonized screams that the king was not the only target.

Wood and plaster dance in the air as the bullets tear through walls and furniture. I hear glass shatter as one of the shots rips apart a window. From my vantage point beneath the table I see people tumble to the ground.

My hands slide between me and the king and I grab my gun from the inner thigh holster I wear. All the while the sound of bullets and screams is a dark cadence in my ears.

I try to get up, but Montes isn't budging. I can see the warning in his eyes. *Don't you dare.*

"We need to take out the shooters," I say. I can't hear my own voice above the noise, but Montes must because he gives a slow shake of his head.

"*Stay down.*" I read his lips.

The air is filled with a hazy red mist. I taste it on my lips, and I feel it brush against my face. This isn't a simple execution, this is a butchering.

Montes won't let me up, but I can still see legs beneath the table. I look for pairs that are stationary. Panicked people run or hide. Attackers don't.

I see three separate sets of legs. I'm pulling the trigger before I can think twice about it. They go down, one after the next. When I see their heads and chests come into my line of sight, I shoot those too.

For a moment, I'm not positive I hit the perpetrators. There's the terrible possibility that these were innocents I took out. But the shots cut off abruptly.

An eerie silence follows.

Dust, plaster, and misted blood hang heavy in the air. Around us, scattered bodies lay. The woman closest to me is missing an eye, and across from me the wife of Shanghai's regional leader slumps against the wall, clutching her heart, her blood seeping between her fingers. Her eyes meet mine, and I see her surprise as she gasps in a breath.

Zhi crawls towards her, his body trembling with the effort as he drags his limp lower body across the floor.

The king's face is awash with horror as he takes in the pair as well.

That could've been us. I can tell that thought is running on repeat in his head.

"Montes," I say, gently pushing at him. He still pins me down.

His nostrils flare when his attention returns to me. I push against him again, signaling that I want to get up. I think he's going to refuse, but then, reluctantly, he rolls off of me.

I rise to my feet, Montes joining me a moment later.

Most of our guards have sustained some sort of injury. Those that haven't now move over to our attackers. I begin to follow.

Montes catches my forearm.

"*Not yet*," he says. At least, that's what I think he says. My ears are still ringing.

I don't bother arguing with him, I simply yank my arm from his grasp and head towards the rest of the men.

I can feel the king at my back, bearing down on me, and I sense his frustration. He's having trouble controlling an uncontrollable thing.

I reach the king's soldiers just as they're checking the shooters' vitals. I kick away our attacker's weapons, though I'm almost positive all three are dead.

I study our attackers. Two men, one woman. All dressed as waiters. One of them was the very man that ushered us into the dining room.

He'd timed the attack.

As I stare down the three gunmen, I notice several strange lumps around the woman's midsection. Now I crouch down, my hand going to the edge of the woman's shirt. I untuck the fabric and peel it back.

Beneath ...

It's been a hundred years since I last saw an explosive, but unless this is an elaborate hoax, they haven't changed much.

"Bomb," I whisper.

"What was that?" Montes says from behind me.

I stand and began to back away, one of my hands aimlessly groping for the king's.

"Bomb," I say much louder. "The woman is rigged."

The king's guards peer beneath the shirts of the other two shooters. I don't have the same view that they do, but I still see enough. And when their grim gazes meet my own, I have all the confirmation I need.

My eyes move across the room where half a dozen of the survivors stare at me with frightened eyes. Several more moan from the ground. "Everyone needs to evacuate," I say. "*Now.*"

CHAPTER 37

The King

I'M TIRED OF this, tired of death always following my queen. We barely escaped with our lives. *Again.*

Immediately after Serenity discovered the bombs, we were evacuated, along with the rest of the surviving guests, leaving only the dead behind.

I lean back in my seat, ignoring the view of Shanghai as it begins to blur past us. If I look back now, I'd still be able to see the tiled roof of the shikumen-style building we were in not five minutes ago.

But I don't glance back; I look at Serenity, really look at her.

Her jaw's tight as she stares out the window. She looks tired, angry—desolate. I can hardly bear it.

I reach out, my thumb rubbing against her cheekbone. She leans into the touch, closing her eyes briefly. There are smears of blood and dust all over her.

I'm so tired of seeing her wear this war paint.

I have only myself to blame. She's a monster I created long before I had her in my clutches. This is the karmic reckoning I've put off for so long.

I want her eyes on me, her eyes and her bloodied, bruised skin.

Without a second's more thought, I drag her onto my lap, refusing to fight the impulse.

"Montes, stop." She pushes halfheartedly against my chest as I reel her in. I'm surprised she's still going through the motions of keeping me away. We both know she no longer wants to. "Let me go."

"*No*," I whisper harshly.

And then, all at once, Serenity gives in. Her body sags into mine, and she leans her forehead into my chest. I feel her body quake, and automatically I begin to stroke her back, like I'm some caring, good guy and not a heartless son of a bitch. And Serenity clutches me tighter, like she's a fragile, docile thing and not the killing machine *she* is.

She breathes in a ragged gasp, pulling herself together. Slowly she draws her head away from my chest. The look she gives me ... men have lived and died and never seen that look.

BOOM–BOOM-BOOM!

The explosions go off at our backs, one right after another. Serenity's eyes widen.

A second later the car skids from the force of the shockwave.

Shit.

The two of us are thrown forward, and I hear our driver curse.

Out the back windows a fireball lights up the night.

The undying king and his mythical queen were nearly killed as they ate dinner from dainty china. The West would've loved that story.

Next to me, Serenity is transfixed by the explosions, and her expression makes my blood run cold.

Whatever soft emotions overtook her a moment ago, they're gone.

I wish she feared more and lived through less because right now, I don't see desolation—or even anger—on her pretty face.

Just ruthless resolve.

Serenity

TONIGHT WE SLEEP inside one of the king's garrisons, located just outside Shanghai proper.

Montes is taking no risks.

The two of us lie together in a windowless cement block that's buried dozens of feet below the earth.

Once again, I'm back in the fucking ground.

The subterranean structure is the closest I've ever felt to my bunker. And I hate it. I hate the very thing that's made me *me*. I can't decide whether the king's lavish lifestyle has rubbed off on me, or whether it's simply the knowledge that I've spent lifetimes belowground—it doesn't honestly matter. I'm devastated anyway.

First to find the king is no longer evil, then to find I can no longer passively endure what I once readily accepted.

Who am I?

"A queen."

I startle at the king's voice. Only then do I realize I spoke out loud.

"My wife," he continues. "The woman that's going to change the world—the woman that already has."

I roll over in bed and gaze at Montes.

He brushes my hair off my face, his fingers lingering. When did he get so achingly sweet?

He must sense my inner turmoil because he says, "This is right. What you're doing is right."

Color me shocked. I assumed the king was only going along with my peace campaign because of our deal. But to hear him admit that he essentially believes in me and my cause ... it's doing strange things to my heart.

His eyes move above us, around the room. "Was this what it was like, living in that bunker?"

I nod, not bothering to look away from him.

His gaze returns to mine. "I should hate this," he says, "but I would take a lifetime of living underground if it meant you'd be by my side."

I swallow.

I don't want to hear this. I don't want to *feel* this. But only because I do—I really, really do, and I can't fathom this vision breaking my heart. Montes, in his infinite cruelty, did this very thing to me a hundred years ago. He convinced me of all the ways he couldn't live without me. And I fell for him, even if I never admitted it, and I paid for that terrible love with my life.

Now, this wise, *decent* Montes is demanding more than just my body all over again.

I knew this would happen, but oh, how I'm—

"You're *afraid.*" The mind reader says this like it's some great revelation.

I open my mouth, fully prepared to lie. "I'm not—"

"Oh," he interrupts, tilting my chin up, "but you are."

My nostril flare as our gazes hold. And hold. And hold.

And then he sees something he shouldn't.

"*My God,*" he utters. His chest expands as he takes in air. And then his mouth descends on mine.

And now I have to deal with the very real possibility that I lost my last bit of power, because the king, I think he *knows.*

He knows that I love him.

I WAKE IN the middle of the night to an empty bed. I lay there for several seconds staring up at the cement ceiling before I realize what woke me.

Light.

Just like the bunker I spent many years in, there is no natural light in this subterranean fortress. When the lights are out, you can literally see nothing. But I can see the cement ceiling dimly.

I sit up and search for the source of the light. It comes from the edges of the door, which isn't fully closed. I can hear voices in the distance.

What's happened now? And why wasn't I woken?

Getting out of bed, I hastily pull on a pair of fatigues, wincing when my feet touch the chilly cement floor. I shove on my boots, then leave our room.

Out in the hall, a single sentry stands guard. I nod to him, then head down the corridor toward the sound of voices.

Ahead of me, the hallway bends sharply to the right. I'm almost around the corner when I make out who's speaking.

"How could you not tell me?" I hear the king hiss.

"They never told *me*," Marco replies.

I hadn't seen or heard from the king's right-hand since before we left for the dinner.

"Do you realize how badly that could've gone?"

"How could I not? You forget that I care for her too," Marco says, his voice heated.

"No," Montes's voice is low and lethal, "let's be clear about this: she is not Trinity. She is not yours. Serenity is mine."

I lean my head back against the wall and close my eyes. I've already heard too much. Before either man knows I'm there, I return to our room and slip back in bed.

If I had heard that all correctly, then Marco had loved my clone.

Can this world get any more fucked-up?

Turns out, it can.

CHAPTER 38

Serenity

SEOUL. OUR NEXT stop.

This is no longer the same tour we started the trip believing it was. The meetings with regional leaders have been cut out completely, our stay in each local has been drastically shortened to just the speeches, and our immediate surroundings are now safe rather than luxurious.

The military aircraft we sit in is a far cry from the king's royal plane. I can see the structure's exposed metal framework as well as the insulated wires that run along the walls and ceiling, and we sway in our seats with every subtle movement the aircraft makes.

This new king. I assess him while he's not watching me. His head dips towards the sheet of papers he reads, one of his legs jiggling like he can't possibly sit still.

He's still a workaholic. Still vain. Still controlling. Still scarily powerful.

Montes glances up, and his eyes heat instantly.

Still in love with me.

"What is my vicious little queen thinking about?" he asks over the drone of the engines.

A hundred years for a man to become whatever it is he wants.

I cock my head. "I think you're afraid of getting everything you ever wanted," I say. "I think you know that once you do, you'll be forced to realize how empty it all was in the end."

He lowers the papers in his hands. I have his full attention now. His eyes are alight with an emotion I can't quite put my finger on. I don't know if it's just his usual intensity or something else.

"My queen came back to me a psychoanalyst."

"You wanted to know my thoughts," I counter.

He watches me for a beat longer, then unbuckles his harness.

"Your Majesty," one of his guards is quick to intervene, "you need to—"

The king raises a hand and quiets his officer. Now we do have some attention drawn our way. And among those eyes are Marco's. I meet his gaze briefly, just long enough for him to look away. And then my attention returns to the king.

Montes crosses over to my seat and kneels before me, his hands resting on my thighs. The gesture is casual, but like anything that has to do with Montes, my mind moves to more intimate things. Stripping off clothes, hot breath against my skin, and more caresses from those hands.

"I don't know," he says softly.

I furrow my brows. "You don't know what?"

His thumb absently strokes my leg. "Whether you are right or not. I've wondered the same thing myself. Whether I could've stopped the war from being drawn out this long."

I search his face.

"But I'm not sure I could have," he adds, "not without staying the same man I was."

It's still there; I see a flash in the back of his eyes even now. The urge to be cruel.

Montes leans forward, and I get to see that face of his up close and personal. If I thought he was intense far away, it's nothing to this—having this man's complete and utter attention.

And then he kisses me, his captive queen.

The entire production draws out. Montes won't release my lips, not even when I try to move away. We have an audience, after all, an audience that only moments ago I was all too willing to entertain. The king has manipulated me yet again.

It's only once he feels me give into the kiss that it sweetens. Eventually I manage to rip my face away from his.

I'm breathing heavily. This man that lays waste to all sorts of things, his head is still close to mine. At some point during our kiss, his hold on my legs tightened. It's almost bruising, but I only now notice it.

My voice is low when I speak. "It doesn't matter what you say, or what you do now, Montes. You're still always going to be the man that ruined the world in the first place."

He draws away, his eyes lingering on my mouth. "I am. And if it meant getting more time with you, I would've ruined it sooner."

As soon as we arrive in Seoul, I sense it. The day feels ominous, like a storm about to break.

My new gun is holstered at my hip. No one's asked me to remove it, but I wouldn't anyway. The West's violence has only increased throughout this trip.

We're taken straight from the airfield to the stadium where I'll be giving my speech. By the end of the day I will be back on that aircraft, heading towards the next location. Trying to stay one move ahead of the West.

Like the other cities I visited, Seoul show signs of the toils of war. Half the buildings are nothing more than rubble. And on many of them I see more posters and wall art depicting my image with the words *Freedom or Death* scrawled beneath. In one instance, I even see two assault rifles crossed beneath my image, like a skull and cross bones.

I've become a freedom fighter.

As our vehicle pulls up to our destination, I catch sight of the stage I'll be speaking from. It's nothing more than a temporary construction set up at the end of one of Seoul's city streets. Some stadium seating appears to have been brought in, but other than that, the people use the topography itself to get a view of the stage.

And the people! I expected a low turnout. We had to change the time of the speech to fit into our rushed itinerary. But, if anything, the place looks overcrowded.

The street in front of the stage is packed with hundreds, if not thousands of bodies. Large skyscrapers border the road on either side, and judging from the people camped out just inside the broken windows of many of them, I can tell that this is the city's improvised seating plan.

The armored vehicle comes to a stop at the fenced-off back of the stage.

"Are you sure you want to do this?" Montes asks, casting a speculative look at our surroundings. He doesn't let on, but I know he's worried. Maybe even downright panicked.

He still hasn't insisted I leave. And now he wants my input.

I reach out and take his hand, drawing his attention to me. Very deliberately, I brush a kiss along his knuckles. "Yes," I say softly.

He stares at our hands for several seconds, then his eyes flick up to me.

I don't thank him for being reasonable, but I know he can see my gratitude.

He nods, but his expression turns grim. "Very well."

He exits the car, holding the door open for me to follow. Almost immediately, a crew of men and women close in on us.

"Your Majesties," one of them says, crowding me and Montes, "we're so very happy to have you here. Please follow me. We have your wardrobes waiting for you in the dressing room."

Wardrobes?

I raise an eyebrow at the king, but he's too busy scowling at anyone that gets too close to me.

We're lead to a makeshift room, which is really not much more than four temporary walls.

Inside it, a stylized black uniform and a tuxedo wait for us.

I remove my outfit from the wall. The uniform looks half paramilitary and half high-fashion. I can't help but grimace when I notice the shoulder and upper arms of the fitted top glitter.

Whatever. At least it's not a dress.

I change, making sure to strap my new gun to my outfit. My father's gun is packed with my things, which are Lord knows where.

That unsettling feeling still lingers in the air. It stays with me even after the king and I are ushered from the room.

We stand together behind a red velvet curtain, the two of us waiting to be introduced to the world.

I glance over at him.

The devil never looked so good. He wears a suit, his hair swept back from his face. And his eyes—a person could lose their soul in their dark depths. He appears just as he did when he waited for me at the base of those steps in Geneva. The monster who'd come in and ruined my life. And now, a hundred years later, I stand at his side, determined to fix everything he's broken.

"Thirty seconds," someone calls out to us.

Montes turns to me. "Are you ready?" Today we're walking out together and facing the crowd as a unified front.

I nod.

He doesn't say anything, just takes me in, looking at me like I'm his own personal apparition before he bows his head and faces forward again.

The people around us begin counting down with their fingers, like this whole production must be executed down to the very second.

Their fingers run out, and then the king and I are walking onto the stage.

Large screens have been set up in between the buildings. I see our faces projected onto them as we step forward. For the first time, I realize that it's not just the king who appears inhuman.

I do too.

The ferocity of the scar that runs down my cheek, the tightness of my jaw, the look in my eye—I'm no natural thing. Murder and violence have made me this way. Loss and war have made me this way.

I look like a savage.

A savage queen. One who doesn't need a crown or even a weapon to appear powerful.

I see it now—this world's faith in me. It's not just that I am an anachronism; the harshness of my face speaks to these people who have only ever known war.

No wonder the West wants me gone.

A century has gone by, and yet even after all that time I am still something to fear.

CHAPTER 39

Serenity

OUR ENEMIES WAIT until the king and I are separated.

Until I'm vulnerable.

"I did not choose this fate willingly," I say, right in the heat of my speech.

My eyes briefly flick to the wings of the stage, where Montes watches me. He said his piece and then left me win the crowd over.

"Just as many of you did not choose yours," I continue. "But these lives are still ours, and they matter."

The people need to know that whatever dream they held tightly onto, it can happen. Dead queens can be resurrected. Peace can follow war. Good can vanquish evil.

The back of my neck prickles, and my voice wavers.

Something ... is amiss.

I swear I hear the quiet drone of an aircraft, but when I look up to the cloudless blue sky, it's utterly empty.

"I don't bleed for the West," I resume speaking. "And I don't bleed for the East. I have and always will bleed for freedom, and I will always fight those who seek to oppress you."

The crowd roars.

High above us, something glints, catching the light of the noonday sun. It jogs my memory. Hadn't I watched something like this back at the king's palace?

My breath catches.

Oh God.

Now I remember.

Optical camouflage, the material that made the enemy all but invisible.

I turn to the officers. Their fingers are at their earpieces. My own hand goes to my gun reflexively.

Then I hear it. The horrible whistling sound of a bomb being dropped.

It's already too late.

BOOM!

The first one explodes to my left, in the middle of our audience. Concrete and metal and flesh blast into the air in a hundred different directions as a rotted-out building is ripped apart. A hundred people die before my eyes, all in an instant. Just like my mother had years ago.

A second explosion follows the first, this to my right. The bomb unfurls like a strange and terrible flower, and the sound that accompanies it is so loud it seems to move through my bones. I can feel the hot breath of it already, though I'm far, far away.

As I watch, several armed soldiers begin rappelling from an aircraft that's still all but invisible.

My eyes find Montes's. He's fighting his guards trying to get to me.

A third explosion hits, just off to the side of the stage.

BOOM!

My gaze rips from the king as I'm thrown back, my hair whipping around my face as I tumble through the air. Fire and heat unfurl, and this time, for a split second, it feels as though I'm being boiled alive. And then my body slams into the ground and the intensity of the explosion retreats.

For several seconds I stay down, dizzy and disoriented. I can't seem to suck in enough air.

I push myself up. I can taste blood in my mouth where my teeth cut the inside of my cheek. I spit it out, then run my tongue over my lower lip.

The air is thick with smoke and debris. But even through the haze, I manage to see the king's guards now vehemently trying to force Montes off the stage. He's thrashing wildly against them, and I can't hear what he says, but he only has eyes for me.

I turn my attention to the crowd beyond the stage. Bombs are still being dropped, and I notice a sick symmetry to it. They're roughly outlining the perimeter of the amphitheater and arena, corralling us in. The enemy is now amongst the civilians. I see small flashes of light scattered throughout the crowd where the soldiers are now firing their weapons.

This isn't a battle. It's a massacre.

I spot the microphone I used not a minute ago; it lays on its side some distance away from me.

No one is dying today without working for it.

I stand just as the king's soldiers turn their attention to me.

Unholstering the firearm stashed at my side, I flick off the safety and run to the fallen microphone, swiping it from the floor.

The cameras have shifted their focus to the audience. If the sight wasn't already horrific enough, it's being projected around us. Their screams are a chorus in my ears, and thanks to the video footage, their agony is intimately on display.

"Citizens of the East!" I shout into the mike. The skeptic in me figured the sound systems would be down, but they're not—not yet, anyway. My voice echoes through the speakers, harmonizing with the roar of the fire.

At my words, I see the cameras pan to me. The whole thing is macabre, especially since several of the large screens projecting my face have caught fire. "If you're going to die today, let it be on your terms, not theirs." I raise the hand holding my gun. "And let it be at my side."

I drop the mike and run to the edge of the stage.

"*Serenity!*" the king shouts from far behind me.

I don't bother looking back, and I don't hesitate. I leap into the crowd of bodies.

Down here it's bedlam. Madness. People are screaming as bombs continue to drop. The ground quakes, each explosion like a drumbeat.

There are people on fire. People missing arms and legs. People getting crushed underfoot. People bleeding and dying.

I cut my way through the crowd, my eyes pinioned to the enemy soldiers rappelling down from seemingly nowhere, their aircraft invisible to the naked eye. They slide down their ropes and drop into the crowd.

I aim my weapon at one of them and fire.

Even at this distance, I can tell I clipped them on the shoulder by the way their body jerks. Their hold loosens on the cable, and then they're falling. As soon as they reach the ground, the crowd swallows them up.

My eye catches the large screens. It's a close up of me. My hair is wild, my lip bloody, and cold determination glints from my eyes.

Savage justice.

The footage pans out and I see the king's soldiers cutting their way through the crowd, trying to get to me.

I rip my gaze away to aim my weapon at another enemy soldier descending down the ropes. I pull the trigger again, and again I hit my target.

Say what you will about the future, their guns have improved.

I begin picking the enemy off one by one.

The crowd parts for me, and I get to see exactly what hope looks like on their faces.

Amongst the chaos, something shifts.

I sense him before I see him. And then he's up there on the screen, his dark, ageless face blown up for us all to see.

The king strides through the crowd, straight towards

me. I turn away from the screen, and look behind me just as his soldiers reach me.

As they surround me, I see Montes, in the flesh, a gun brandished in his hand.

I've never seen him like this, walking amongst chaos and danger like he's striding down the halls of the palace.

This is not the king I knew. This is not the ruler cloistered away in his ivory tower, nor is it the killer who fought at my side in South America.

He's something else. Something *more*.

The sounds of battle rush back in. I'm no longer feeling so irreverent about jumping into fray. Not now that the king is on the battlefield with me, prime for the plucking. There are no Sleepers nearby, nothing to save him if he gets mortally wounded.

He reaches me then. This close, I see the vein in his temple throbbing and the hard set of his features. "There is no winning this, Serenity."

I know. I knew it before I leaped off that stage. It's just not my nature to run from danger.

The king's eyes leave mine to focus on something over my shoulder. His whole demeanor changes.

I turn in time to see enemy soldiers rushing towards us. They shoot my guards. I hear a grunt of pain as a soldier to my left falls to his knees, clutching his chest.

Next to me Montes growls, and then he lifts his gun and begins shooting at the enemy. I follow his lead, shooting more soldiers converging on us.

"Men, cover the queen!" Montes yells. "Let's get our asses out of here!"

I don't have time to marvel over the king before his men surround us, clearing a path towards the stage.

It takes less than a minute for the enemy to gun down those soldiers covering mine and Montes's front. I don't have time to check their vitals now that the king is exposed.

He won't die.

Not here. Not now.

Turns out, however, that the king is pretty effective at defending himself.

Montes and I back up as we fire. Every target Montes shoots at goes down. His accuracy is even better than mine.

"You've gotten good!" I yell over the noise.

His lips draw back from his teeth as he fires off three more rounds, his arm barely jerking at the gun's kickback.

"I've had a hundred years to practice!" he shouts.

"Not taking a compliment?" I say, pulling the trigger twice more. "How unheard of."

"If we live through this," he says, "I'm spanking you for that."

I smile gruesomely. He's still good at battle-talk.

"If we live through this, I might just let you."

He grins.

Slowly, we make our way through the melee, our guards covering our flanks. When we get to the stage, we have to turn our backs to the fighting.

Gunfire lights up the ground around us. One of the soldiers ahead of me jerks as a bullet tears through his arm, but he doesn't slow. Whoever these soldiers are, they're made of *tough* stuff.

We cross behind the curtains, and the shots cease now that our enemies no longer have a visual on us.

Up ahead, our motorcade waits for us, and the soldiers guarding me and the king now hustle us to one of the vehicles. Montes and I are barely inside when the door slams behind us and the car skids out. Now we're moving targets. Any enemy in the sky could get a bead on us.

I wait for the next explosion to come. The one that will kill me and Montes.

It never happens. One second bleeds into the next, and the sounds of fighting gradually fade away.

"*Nire bihotza.*"

I swivel just as Montes gathers me to him. He holds me tightly in his arms, like I might evaporate.

"We made it," he murmurs into my hair, "We made it."

I let out a breath. Things are not processing, not the way they will once the high wears off. My brain moves sluggishly.

For several seconds we sit there in silence, our car careening down the streets.

"Are you all in one piece?" he asks.

"Yes," I whisper against him. "You?"

"Yeah." A beat of silence passes, and then, "Don't fucking do that again."

There is my cold, cruel husband.

I don't respond.

"Marco and your officers?" I ask instead.

He sighs, knowing I'm evading the topic. "They're already on their way to the aircraft."

I nod.

Montes leans his head back against the seat rest. "No more, Serenity. No more."

Speeches, he means. Speeches and visits.

I nod again.

I might be determined, but I'm not suicidal. We'll figure out another way to sway the people, one a little less deadly.

The drive to the airfield is more than a little eerie. No one shoots at us, no one even seems to notice us.

And that damn tingle skitters up and down my back again.

Not right. Not right. Not right.

This isn't unfolding as it should.

The airfield comes into view, as does the hangar where our aircraft waits. A minute later, our vehicle pulls up to it, the rest of the motorcade filing in around us.

Soldiers hop out, several jogging over to our car. They usher us out, and Montes and I, along with his officers and his men, head towards the taxying aircraft.

We never make it.

I see the pool of blood first, near one of the rear wheels of the aircraft. It doesn't draw attention to itself, but it's shiny, fresh.

My steps falter.

Ambush.

It barely has time to register before the men and women loitering about the hangar withdraw their weapons. The enemy has camouflaged itself to look just like us.

The king's enemies knew that we would fly out of here.

They begin to open fire, and Montes's men go down one after another.

I unholster my weapon for the second time and begin to fire. Two shots in, the chamber clicks empty.

And now I am a sitting duck, no better than a civilian.

Ahead of me, Montes is busy shooting the enemy, his movements fluid. Practiced. My mercenary king is a strange and glorious sight.

The guards that surround us—those that still live—are also firing. I can see some of them calling in for backup, but by the time anyone else arrives, the fight will be over.

None of us are leaving here until the enemy is gone.

Or we're dead.

The bullet takes me by surprise.

My body jerks back from the impact. I don't feel the pain. Not immediately. The itch and burn of the bullet's entrance and the sickening tug of its exit are merely uncomfortable.

I hear the king's shout amongst the barrage of bullets. How loud he must be yelling to cut through all that noise.

I swear seconds slow to a crawl as I stare out blindly at my surroundings. My hand falls to my stomach. I actually *feel* my insides as I press my palm against the wound.

I stagger, then drop to my knees.

Now I feel the pain. Oh God, now I feel it.

That agony is so acute I'm nauseous. The only thing that stops me from vomiting is that the pain closes up my throat. I can barely swallow in air.

I need to move.

I'm hurt and soldiers are still attacking.

I suck in a breath and then another. Sheer force of will has me crawling across the cement. Scattered around me are several bodies, both friend and foe. I hiss in a breath as I grab a gun lying a foot from one of them.

Gritting my teeth, I force myself back to my feet. An agonized cry slips out as the movement tugs at the injury.

My eyes search for Montes.

When I find him, he's mowing the enemy down with his gun, making his way towards me. He holds his bloody left arm close to his side, and I realize I'm not the only one injured.

That is enough to invigorate me.

Someone hurt my monster.

I begin to shoot the men attacking the king, baring my teeth as I do so. I welcome my bloodlust like an old friend.

Enemies go down, one right after the next.

Aim. Fire. Aim. Fire. I'm screaming as I shoot, from rage and from pain.

The gun clicks empty.

I'm breathing heavy. I'll have to bend down to grab another, and I really don't know if I'll make it back up.

I'll shoot from the ground.

I collapse more than kneel onto the cement, and I cry out as my entire body radiates pain.

At the sound of my shout, Montes's head snaps to me. He falters, his eyes burning, burning as he takes me in.

Lately I've seen the king wear many new faces. This is another I've never seen. His nostrils are flared, his mouth parted and his chest heaving.

His mouth moves. *Nire bihotza.*

Seeming to forget about the fight still raging around us, he staggers towards me.

I'm shaking my head.

I'm just grabbing another gun, I want to tell him.

He doesn't stop. One tear falls down his cheek, then another.

A dozen different gun blasts are going off every second, but Montes doesn't hear any of them. He's forgotten about the fight.

I lick my lips. "Mont—"

A bullet rips its way through the king's neck.

Tha-thump.

Tha-thump.

Tha-thump.

My heart palpitates in my ears. And I'm choking, choking.

I try to scream, but nothing comes out.

Montes reaches a hand to his throat. Instantly, his blood envelops it. The king sways on his feet, his gaze locked on mine, then his legs fold out from under him.

A hundred years of war, a hundred years of fighting and waiting, and it all comes to this—a messy death in a hangar.

Montes. I mouth his name.

He's still staring at me, even as his body jerks. Death throes. I've seen them often enough.

This is my last fear, and just like all the others, I have to live through it.

Pain and anguish and rage all gather below my sternum.

I'm falling, falling back into that abyss that I've tried for so long to crawl out of.

I welcome the darkness.

Now a brutal cry tears from my throat. I grab a gun from the nearest dead man, my lips curling back, and then I begin to fire. I kill the closest people in a matter seconds, smiling terribly as blood and bone explode out the back of their bodies.

Freedom or death. It's an apt slogan. I will either live by my own terms or die by them. And I'll take as many of these fuckers with me as I can.

Someone clips me in the arm. My torso jerks back, but it only takes a moment to recover. And then I'm pulling the trigger once more.

I can feel the pain screaming across my body; it harmonizes with the screams inside my head. And still I shoot.

The enemy falls, one after another.

My gun clicks empty, but now the ground is full of scattered bodies. I crawl to one of them, pausing to vomit from the pain.

Just as my hand reaches for another weapon, a booted foot kicks the gun away.

Lightheaded and cold from blood loss. I reach a hand down to brace myself against the ground.

I sense more than see the soldiers swarm around me.

Something heavy slams into my head, and the world goes dark.

CHAPTER 40

Serenity

THE SOUND OF beeping wakes me.

I come to in a narrow hospital bed.

For a girl that hates doctors, I end up in quite a few hospitals. Of course, that's assuming I'm in one at the moment.

It smells like a hospital—that antiseptic smell hasn't apparently changed in the last hundred years.

The moment I try to move, I hear the jangle of metal, and the sharp edge of handcuffs digs into my wrists.

I tug on them again and find each hand has been locked to the metal frame of the bed I lay on.

Imprisoned to a bed. This is going to make going to the bathroom interesting.

I sit up the best I can, ignoring how the metal rubs away skin.

My last memories come rushing back. The explosions, the shootout at the hangar. My stomach was torn open, and then ...

Montes.

I can't catch my breath.

Dead.

The grief is instant, unfurling within me. My heart is shattering, just the way I feared it would.

A tear slides out, and my throat works. I lock my jaw to fight back the anguished cry I want to let loose.

It's unfathomable. My monster can't die. My nightmare can't be over. Not when I was just beginning to enjoy it.

My body shakes as I fight to keep myself together. I know better than to fall apart now. Not now when I'm clearly my enemy's prisoner.

I *will* kill them all. Every single person.

The girl who hates games needs a game plan.

By the time they come for me, I have one.

A SINGLE MAN enters the room. He's some sort of ex-military, even though he wears civilian clothes.

I glare at him. I can't help it. I want to gut him and savor his screams. The killer in me begins to hunger.

Because Montes—

I cut the thought off.

The game plan, I remind myself.

"Your Majesty," the man murmurs, dipping his head.

I'm surprised by the show of reverence.

He closes the door behind him and approaches me.

"You treat all your prisoners this nicely?" I ask, jingling my cuffs as I speak.

"No." He pulls a chair up to the bed. "Just queens, I'm afraid. I'm Chief Officer Collins, head of the Western United Nation's Security Department."

"And you're here to interrogate me?"

Collins gives me a wan smile. "I'm here to talk with you.

"Pretty words," I say.

He leans forward, bracing his elbows on his thighs. "You've done this before," he states, settling himself in.

My eyes wander to the suit he wears. The pleats of it are crisp, but the material has a faded look. "How many items of clothing do you own?" I ask.

He follows my gaze and self-consciously smooths down the material before he returns to looking at me. "We're not here to talk about my wardrobe."

"I bet not many," I continue. "And I bet you're still better off than most of the WUN's citizens."

He gives me a bored look, like he's only listening because he must.

"It was not always like that," I say. I draw in a deep breath and look around at my surroundings. There's not even a window in this closet of a room. "Where am I?" I ask.

"You're in the West," he says carefully.

I figured that much.

"And when am I?" It's an odd question, but judging by

the lack of pain, I'm guessing I've recently been removed from a Sleeper.

He threads his fingers together. "You were injured a week ago."

I only lost a week this time.

"Injured by your people," I clarify.

Collins nods. "But you weren't killed."

"How benevolent of them. And where was their compassion when they bombed thousands of innocents that day?"

"Some sacrifices needed to be made—"

"Then *you* die." I snap. "If you think sacrificing any life is necessary, then I want to see you give yours up first."

Collins mouth tightens. "I didn't give the orders for the West to bomb a city block."

"But you're defending them."

I'm not sure why I'm even engaging in this conversation. This man doesn't care.

He leans back in his seat. "The representatives want to work with you."

"Of course they do," I say.

Wars are often based off of ideological differences, and I have become an ideology that can win the war. And I am one that both sides can look to. After all, I was an emissary of the West before I was Queen of the East. Never has such an easy solution just fallen into the laps of so many powerful people.

"Give me one good reason why I should work with them."

"The king is dead."

My nostrils flare and my muscles tense, but other than that, I don't react.

Collins cocks his head. "No words?"

He doesn't want words. He wants me to weep or cheer or give him something that he can take to his bosses to manipulate me with.

Instead, I say, "Montes has cheated death longer than anyone else. I'll need to see a body before I believe it."

"You think highly of him." It's not a question, and Collins doesn't state it as though it is, but I'm expected to answer nonetheless.

"Is there a point to this?" I say.

"From what I hear, he's the one that hid you from the world for all this time."

"And?" I say it like I don't give a damn about the betrayal.

"It seems like something unforgivable," Collins elaborates.

I've been in enough of these rooms and talked to enough of these men to know they are always trying to dig under your skin. I'm sure the tactic works when someone can be caught off-guard. But what could I possibly be surprised by at this point? I have lost everything I ever loved.

"And you're assuming I forgave him," I say.

He raises his eyebrows but inclines his head.

"That is not the worst thing the king has done to me." I tilt my head. "What are you trying to do, create dissension between me and the king? He's dead."

But then, as I stare at him, my heart begins to beat faster and faster. Because creating dissention appears to be exactly what he's doing. That would only be useful if ...

I feel my shock wash over me. "The king *is* alive."

CHAPTER 41

Serenity

COLLINS SHAKES HIS head. "I already told you, he's dead."

Now that I'm looking for it, I can see the WUN officer's uncertainty.

He doesn't *know*, which is good enough for me. If Montes could be alive, he likely is—one doesn't survive a century and a half by sheer luck alone.

A surge of hope moves through me.

"Serenity, I urge you to weigh my next words carefully," Collins says, settling into himself. "The representatives are willing to work with you. They want to end the war."

I reign in my excitement. My plan—I'll need to change it now that the king is likely alive.

"If you agree to it, I will take you to them straightaway,"

he continues.

I narrow my eyes. "And if I refuse?"

He hesitates. "If you refuse, you will be transferred from this military hospital to a work camp." His face softens and his voice lowers, "You don't want that. It's not a good way to go."

I never did well with ultimatums, and I don't want to go along with this one. I'm tired of bad men getting their way.

I'm tired of being used.

"From what I've seen," Collins says, "all you want is peace."

I lean forward, my arms pulled taut against the handcuffs. "Men like the representatives will never give you peace. They will only ever give you tyranny."

I lean back against the metal headboard. "But, you're right. What I most want is the war to end." I draw in a deep breath and try to recall all the tricks my father used as an emissary. I'm going to need them. "So long as what they ask of me is reasonable, I will work with them."

WHAT CAN ONLY be a handful of hours later, I'm being escorted out of the hospital room, my hands bound behind my back.

Collins is by my side, along with several guards that look like they'd have no problem killing me if I so much as moved wrong.

I'm escorted out of the building. The sky above us is a hazy white, like the air has been sapped of its vibrancy.

A swarm of people, most wearing dirty rags, press against the chain-link fence that runs around the perimeter of the property. The moment they see me, they begin to shout and reach for me. I can't tell if their excitement is borne from love or hate.

The guards posted on my side of the fence train their firearms on the civilians. One person out of the crowd, a young man, begins to climb the fence.

The soldiers shout at the civilian, but he's not listening. He's staring at me, yelling something. I never get the chance to find out what he's saying.

A gunshot goes off, and the man is blasted back.

My body jerks at the sight. Now people are screaming for an entirely different reason, and they look angry.

"Come, Serenity," Collins says, pressing me forward. I hadn't realized I stopped to begin with.

I let him lead me forward, tasting bile at the back of my throat.

An armored car waits for us. Collins shoves my head down and into the vehicle before following me inside.

I adjust myself, letting him strap me in, my eyes drifting back to the crowd. They are all so skinny, so malnourished.

God, how they are suffering.

I lean my head back against the seat rests. "The West has a problem on its hands," I say.

For all the king's terrible qualities—and there are many, even now—his people never looked that close to death.

I want to weep. Those are *my* people. They might be several generations removed, but they opened their eyes and drew their first breaths in the same land I did.

They deserve more than what they've been given.

"We do," Collins says, his eyes lingering on the people swarming the vehicle. "But you can help us fix it."

I fully intend to.

IT DOESN'T TAKE long to get away from the crowds. Once we do, the land opens up, stretching out for miles in every direction. Every so often, we pass relics of old cities. Judging by the size of the buildings, they were nothing grand to begin with. The West's biggest metropolises were leveled by the king long ago.

These are just remnants of the land this used to be.

Eventually, those too fall away, and then there's nothing left but long stretches of dead, wild grass.

"Where in the WUN are we?" I ask.

"Northern hemisphere. West Coast."

I can't decide if I'm relieved that we are far away from my hometown or disappointed. I want to see it again, desperately so, but I fear it would look nothing like what I remember. And then I'd have to face the reality that there really is no place for me in this new world.

We drive for a long time. Much longer than I expected. Long enough to leave the grasslands behind and enter a mountain range. As our elevation increases, scraggly brush gives way to trees.

As the car ride passes, I toy with the grand plan I settled on back in the military hospital, a plan I'd been forming even before then. I use the hours to alter it, now that the king likely lives. It puts me in a darker and darker mood.

What I must do might break me.

I forget about my macabre plan the moment the mountains part. The deep blue Pacific stretches across the horizon, and my eyelids flutter as I take it in. Nothing that men can do to one another will ever make this sight less beautiful.

Breathtaking as it is, the ocean captures my attention for only a moment.

Directly ahead of us is a gigantic wall made out of cement and stone. I can see nothing beyond it.

Our vehicle drives up to a heavily guarded gate—a checkpoint of sorts. We're waved through, and then I'm inside.

On the other side of the gates is a city like nothing I've ever seen.

Built into the mountainside overlooking the water, this place doesn't look like a city of the future. It looks like the city of the past. Each structure is made of stone and adobe and plaster—every one beautifully crafted, but all with a handmade look to them.

In spite of the wealth of information I learned since I woke, I never read about this place. I don't even know the name of it.

At the center of the walled city a giant glass dome rises above most other buildings, reminding me of the greenhouse Montes took me to a long time ago.

Even that small reminder of the king causes so many emotions to flood through me—grief, hope, *vengeance*.

Our vehicle makes its way towards the domed building. I'm not surprised when we pull up in front of the behemoth.

"This is where I'll be meeting the representatives?" I ask, looking up at it.

"We call it the Iudicium in the West," Collins says. He steps out of the car then offers a hand to help me out as well, cuffed as I am. "And yes, it is."

I ignore his hand, though as soon as I exit the car, he grips my upper arm anyway. A series of other guards surround us, keeping the crowd at bay.

I've done this before—been paraded through enemy territory. The Queen of the East. What an acquisition.

I spare another glance at the sprawling building before me.

So this is where the representatives work. Corrupt leaders love their palaces.

I only have a moment to take it in before I'm shuffled forward, away from the eyes of the crowd and inside the building.

The doors close behind us, the sound echoing through the chambers I now stand in. Despite the rich furnishings and ample marble that adorns the interior, the place is cold and dark.

I'm led to a set of double doors on the other end of the expansive entry hall. Two guards open them, and then I'm staring into a cavernous, circular room filled with twelve men.

The representatives.

Twelve of them. *Twelve*. I bet this is more than the king has ever heard of gathered in a single room. The only representative missing is the mysterious thirteenth one.

The rest of them sit at the far end, behind a wooden bench, and each wears a different expression when they catch sight of my face. Most appear bored or impassive. A couple seem curious. The rest of them look at me like I killed their sons.

I might've.

"Come in," one says.

Collins forces me forward, and I walk down the aisle, past rows and rows of empty seats. I've only stopped once I stand in front of the representatives.

I recognize each from their photo. Jeremy, the one who established the work camps; Alan, who's likely responsible for kidnapping the regional leaders; Gregory, who legalized human trafficking. On and on I name them, along with the atrocities they've sanctioned.

Some of these men are Montes's former advisors, men who plotted my death. Men that were involved in the death of my unborn child.

A quiet calmness settles over me. This is the place I go to when I kill.

They should never have met with me. They're now all marked. I won't let them live, not so long as I have life in me.

"Serenity Freeman Lazuli, Queen of the East," begins Alan. "Welcome to the West. I hear it was your home once."

"Once," I agree.

A drawn out silence follows that, until someone clears their throat.

"In the hundred years you've been gone, you have become quite a legend," Alan says.

My eyes flick to Montes's old advisors. Their frowns deepen.

The feeling's mutual.

"So I've heard," I say.

"Oh no," Alan says from where he's perched above me, "you've more than just heard. You've incited revolution. You are the world's rallying cry.

"And you've *acted*. Giving speeches, fighting the enemy," he says this with a wry twist of his lips. "It's all quite impressive.

"We talked to a certain paramilitary leader—Styx Garcia. He says you wanted to speak with us. So here you are."

I hide my surprise. He helped set this up?

The others watch me carefully.

"That was before you bombed a peaceful gathering."

This earns me a grim smile from Alan. "I would imagine a true rebel queen would be more eager, not less, to speak with the men that threaten *her people*." He says the last two words with disdain, like I'm a charlatan for supporting the citizens of the East rather than the West.

"And maybe this rebel queen feels she is beyond the point of civilly discussing *her people*," I shoot back.

"You don't have to be our prisoner," Jeremy interrupts. "The war has gone on for too long."

Begrudgingly, I incline my head. "It has," I agree. On this subject we have common ground. Ground I wish to exploit.

My eyes cut to one of the long, narrow windows that line the walls high above us. Through it I can see a sliver of the wall that encircles the city.

I feel the responsibility of this world, of my title, settle onto my shoulders. Today, I will be joining in the machinations of men.

It's time to finally set my terrible plan into motion.

The representatives watch me shrewdly.

"I know why I'm here," I say.

Diplomacy is a treacherous thing when neither party trusts the other but both want to work together. They need me, I need them, and we're all known for our ruthlessness.

"You want the war to end," I continue. "You want Montes dead, and you want me to be the one that kills him."

CHAPTER 42

Serenity

"WHAT MAKES YOU think Montes is dead?" Alan says.

"Don't take me for a fool," I say. "We would be having a different conversation if that were the case." One where they made demands rather than requests of me.

No one speaks, but in that silence I get affirmation that I am correct.

He lives. My husband *lives*.

Which means he will live long enough to see my deception.

"We want peace," Tito says, training his bulging eyes on me. "You and I know that will never happen while the king lives."

My jaw tightens. I know what these men want. I've been

preparing for it. *Planning* for it.

I take a deep breath. "I will kill Montes Lazuli for you," I say, carefully looking each of them in the eye.

My stomach churns sickeningly. I have become the traitor queen I was once accused of being.

The room goes dead silent. Around me, the representatives look surprised, suspicious even. I bet they didn't imagine the woman who's spoken out against them would state their terms then agree to them.

"How do we know your word is good?" Gregory lazily asks.

I can't stop the ironic twist of my lips. It's real rich of them to ask me that like they weren't trying to convince me to work for them only seconds ago.

"Your options are limited here," Gregory continues, "but as soon as you board a plane and see your pretty life again, what will stop you from going back on your word?"

What would my father do?

Convince.

I look around. "Do any of you know about my history?" The king's former advisors do. Way back when, they had to watch the king parade around the sullen girl from the West.

I take a step forward. "Let me tell you all a story." I let my eyes rove over them. "Once there was a girl who lived in a city that no longer exists. She had a mother and a father and friends. And then a strange king came and took each one away from her, one by one. But it wasn't enough. He forced her to marry him. And then, when she was planning on betraying him to his councilmembers, he found out."

The lie slips in easily enough.

I see Montes's old advisors sit up a little straighter. They betrayed the king a century ago. They still might remember the bloodbath that occurred in the conference room when the king learned of his councilmembers' disloyalty. I'm hoping they do.

"Yes," I say. "Why do you think you and your brethren were spared? There are things the Beast of the East and I plotted, things he never got the chance to tell you all. We gave Montes the wrong names that day the councilors were shot dead."

My father, bless his soul, would be proud of me in this moment. Lying is a terrible thing, but it is better than violence, and when it has the power to end a war, it can even be admirable.

"So the king found out his wife had betrayed him. But he couldn't kill her." My gaze moves over the representatives. "No, the evil king had fallen for his wife. So he kept her locked away in a machine, asleep indefinitely. And he never intended to wake her."

I go quiet, letting this alternate history sink in.

"Why would I help him?" I finally ask. "With every fiber of my being, I hate him." I glance down at my boots. "I always have," I say quietly.

The silence that follows this is pensive.

Finally, "We will deliberate," Ronaldo says. "Collins, take the queen to the prison quarters."

Collins hesitates, and it's plain to see that this decision shocks him. He'd been so sure the representatives would treat me well if only I agreed to their demands.

I don't bother telling Collins it's better this way. The king's silk sheets and his sweet words made me forget several times what he was.

There will be no forgetting this.

The King

My eyes blink open.

I stare at the ceiling and breathe in deeply. I've been in the Sleeper enough times to know that when I wake up in this manner, it's because I've come from one.

Several officers surround my bed.

Something's wrong.

I push myself up, my brows furrowing. I look for Serenity. She's not here.

I almost choke when I remember.

She took a bullet to the gut. She fell, and she never rose.

I saw her death upon her.

"*Tell me,*" I order my men.

If she's dead, I will not rest until every last Western leader is obliterated.

"The queen is alive," Heinrich says, his face grim. "The representatives have her."

Some things are worse than death—being a prisoner of the West is one of them.

I rise then, heedless of the fact that I'm essentially wearing thin cotton pants and nothing else. Worlds should end for all the anguish I feel.

My men hurriedly stand, trailing after me as I storm through the palace.

"Montes, you should rest," Marco says.

I overturn a nearby table and spin on him. "*Fuck* resting." He of all people should know. "Get the goddamn West on the phone. We're getting her back."

Serenity

APPARENTLY THE REPRESENTATIVES like to eat where they shit. That's the only explanation for why their prison sits directly below their domed building.

I can tell from the stairwell I'm dragged down that there are floors upon floors of cells down here. Between the West's decimated population and their work camps, I have no idea why they'd ever need so many.

Then again ... bad men have endless enemies.

We move so far below the surface of the earth, that I feel all memory of the sun has been erased from this place. I don't want to be underground so soon after I was released from the Sleeper. It's damp down here. And cold. The chill of the place worms its way into my bones in a matter of minutes.

"Are the East's regional leaders imprisoned here?" I ask Collins.

I don't expect him to answer, but several seconds after I ask, he grunts something like an affirmation.

"Are they okay?"

Again, the silence draws out. Then, "You should worry about yourself," he says gruffly. His answer leaves me more concerned for them, not less.

The cell I'm led to is nothing short of medieval. What isn't covered by bars is inset with stone. There's fetid puddles in several locations, and the entire area reeks of shit and piss and death. There's no bed, and a filthy bucket is the closest thing to a toilet I'm going to get.

You can tell a lot about a territory by the way they treat their prisoners. This doesn't speak well for the men who depend on my loyalty. And it's not endearing me to them.

"I'm sorry," Collins apologizes. He sounds genuine.

I turn to face him. "You shouldn't be." I don't elaborate.

His head dips, like he can't bear looking at me. "I'll be back later." He leaves quickly after that, taking most of the guards along with him.

I pace for a while.

Kill the king.

I've never been able to accomplish this one task. And that's exactly what the representatives want. What they've always wanted. All so that they can continue to torment the world without resistance.

Slavery, concentration camps, crippling poverty. What fearful lives Westerners must live.

All thirteen of those bastards need to die, even the one who wasn't present.

I will end the war, and I *will* kill them.

CHAPTER 43

Serenity

AFTER A WHILE, I force myself to sit. I lean my back against the wall and rest my forearms on my knees, bowing my head over them. A shiver runs through me. My eyes land on that bucket.

Fuck prisons.

I haven't heard a soul down here.

"*Hello?*" I shout, just to see if any other prisoners are down here.

Silence.

Not even the guards respond, if only to tell me to shut up.

I don't know how long I sit there before I can no longer beat back thoughts of the king. Now that I'm almost sure he's okay, I should feel relieved. That's the last thing I feel. I promised the West his *head.*

If only I could return my heart to the way it was before I met him. Duty and love are often opposing forces. Now is no different. And it doesn't matter what paths the king and I travel together. There is only one way this can end.

The only way it must.

I dread that ending more than I've dreaded anything in my entire life.

I'm dragged from my thoughts when I hear the whispers. Down the hall, up the corridor. Guards gossiping like the women of court.

I lift my head. That's when I notice it.

A storm's brewing.

There's a heaviness to the air, like my captors are bracing themselves for the worst.

A grim smile stretches across my face.

He's coming.

The devil is coming for me.

WHEN COLLINS RETURNS to my cell, I'm waiting, my back against the wall, my legs crossed at the ankles, and my arms folded across my chest.

"The representatives have come to a decision."

And here I was almost positive they'd leave me to molder for at least a day.

He watches me as the iron bars slide back and the cell door opens. The guards come in and spin me around roughly, pushing my chest against the wall. They jerk my hands behind my back then cuff my wrists together.

I'm dragged out of the cell and marched back to the circular room where the representatives wait. I'm cold, I smell like a latrine, and I'm not feeling very diplomatic at the moment.

Just angry. Really, really angry.

Twelve representatives wait for me.

"We would like to work with you," Tito says, his jowls shaking as he speaks. He says this as though they have the upper hand.

I might be in shackles, but the representatives are the ones with their hands tied. I die, the king wins. It's as simple as that.

Nothing brings people together like a martyr.

I pretend like I don't grasp this very obvious fact.

"You have thirty days to bring down the king," Tito continues. "We will be monitoring you regularly. In case you have any misgivings, you should be warned: we have moles everywhere. If you decide to go back on your word, we will find out. You won't like what becomes of you; traitors don't receive clean deaths in this land."

The irony of the king's old advisor telling me this isn't lost on me.

"Understood?" he adds.

I give a sharp nod.

"One of our men will seek you out. You will work directly with him.

I look down at my shackled hands.

"If I do this," I say, lifting my head, "it will be filmed and distributed. I want this on record."

For the first time since I met them, I see some of the representatives smile.

"It will be theatrical," I continue, "and it will require your assistance."

"You will have it," Alan says. He pauses before saying, "We will need proof of the kill."

A body. It's the currency of conquerors.

The men look hungry for the king's death.

"You'll get a body," I say, "but I want a peace agreement in return, one with equitable terms for my people."

"That goes without question," Rodrigo says.

Without question my ass. These men would rob an old lady blind if they could get away with it.

"If you agree," Tito continues, "we will release you immediately to the king."

This is happening.

Oh, God, it's really happening.

I nod. The weight of my task settles on my shoulders. "I agree to your terms."

I STAND IN the middle of the Western city's large central square, my hands still bound behind my back.

Still a queen held for ransom.

On all four corners, soldiers stand at the ready, loosely holding semi-automatic rifles in their arms. I can tell by the deadness in their eyes that these men have killed many people. I can also tell many people have died right where I stand by the brown bloodstains that stain the concrete at my feet.

The rendezvous area doubles as an executioner's square.

Around us, the citizens of this place watch impassively. I bet most of them had to cultivate that bored look, lest their trigger-happy leaders find fault in whatever real expression they wish to wear.

A single camera focuses on me and the representatives who sit at my back. Ahead of me, a large screen has been erected, much like the ones that were mounted at the speech I gave. Right now the screen is blank, save for an emblem of some sort that's projected onto it. I'm guessing it's the flag of the West. It looks nothing like the American flag I grew up with.

We all wait. The wind stirs my hair, the square eerily silent.

I don't understand any of this, the presentation of my handoff, the strategy of it all, and what role I play. For all I know, this is actually an elaborate execution. The stains on the ground seem to suggest that.

The screen flickers to life. A moment later, I see the king's face stretched across it.

I have to lock my knees to stay upright.

Alive. I hadn't fully believed it until now.

His jaw tightens, his dark eyes unreadable.

Now I really have no idea what's going on.

Behind me, one of the representatives begins to speak. "The thirteen representatives of the West do hereby release Her Majesty, Serenity Freeman Lazuli, to the Eastern Empire. We guarantee the queen safe passage home."

It's the king's turn to speak.

Montes's vein begins to throb. "I, Montes Lazuli, King

of the East, do hereby declare before gods and men that in exchange for Her Majesty Serenity Lazuli's safe return to the East, the territory known as Australia will be ceded to the representatives of the West."

Those words are strange, foreign things that should not be strung together in the same sentence.

An entire landmass in return for me.

I can't catch my breath.

An entire *landmass*. And it's now under the care of the creatures at my back.

I look over my shoulder, just to catch a glimpse of the representatives. Most of them wear grim smiles.

Just as I've played the representatives to keep up appearances, they've played me and the king.

Love is a weakness the king has discovered in himself. A weakness the representatives have exploited.

I face forward again and find Montes staring at me. I can feel unbidden tears welling in my eyes.

Now I've had two men in my life choose me over the welfare of a nation. First my father, and now my husband.

Never again will I underestimate this man's devotion. He will ruin countries for me.

Above us, a jet of sorts enters the airspace.

My hair whips about my face as it lowers itself to the ground ahead of me.

"As a sign of good faith, we have allowed one of your aircraft into our city," one of the representatives says.

Montes and I still stare at each other when Collins approaches me and begins to unlock my cuffs. "Stay safe, Serenity," he says quietly. "And be careful."

I don't acknowledge his words. It would probably be bad for him if I did.

I'm marched onto the aircraft. At the last minute I turn around and face the representatives. I catch Ronaldo's eye, and he nods to me.

The West is ruled by thirteen devils, the East, two.

And I am the worst one of them all.

CHAPTER 44

The King

IT TAKES NEARLY fifteen hours for the aircraft carrying Serenity to return to the East. This time, I wait for my queen just off to the side of the airstrip.

I have this unreasonable fear that something will be wrong. That my pilot is a traitor. That as soon as the video call ended, the representatives shot her in the back. That the West will ambush the aircraft before it lands.

My worries breed more worries, extrapolating into elaborate scenarios that I know cannot occur, but my heart won't be reasoned with.

Not until I watch her plane touch down.

My pulse gallops.

The aircraft rolls to a stop a short distance away from

me and the engines die down. Each minute I wait is an eternity. I managed to stay away from Serenity for over a century, yet I now find I can barely stand the time we're apart.

Finally the engine quiets. The staircase lowers.

A moment later, Serenity stands on the threshold. Her eyes find mine almost immediately. I know what she's thinking, what they're all thinking.

How could he?

How could I indeed? Australia is a territory I've ruled for a 113 years. A good territory.

A territory I'll get back. But I will do it with my queen at my side.

A landmass is not nearly so fragile as a human life. It'll be there tomorrow and the next day and the day after that.

I step away from the soldiers gathered around me, and they all give me plenty of space. This greeting is personal.

I begin to move towards Serenity, my strides quickening the closer I get. She storms down the steps, her eyes trained on mine.

The distance evaporates between us, and then I'm dragging her to me and forcing a kiss on her. I can't say it's all that gentle. I want her to fight back, I want to feel that brutal life force of hers come to life beneath my mouth and my hands.

It does.

She grabs the lapels of my suit, fisting the material in her hands. I feel her shake me roughly, like she can't decide whether she wants to pull me closer or push me away. I'm not going to give her the option.

"You are such an idiot," she whispers when our lips briefly part.

I smile into the kiss. "That is no way to talk to the man who just saved your life."

I allow her to pull away. "You gave them an entire continent."

"I did."

"You're going to lose the respect of your people."

I capture her hand.

Still alive. It's going to take several minutes to believe it.

"And you'll win it back for me."

Serenity

THE KING MIGHT very well be losing his mind, I think as we pull up to the palace. I'm still going over the last twenty-four hours in my head.

Never has he given up a kingdom for a single person. I doubt he's ever even given up a car for someone.

Not true, I correct. He gave up quite a few things in the past when my life was slipping through his fingers.

But this is unprecedented.

I exit the car with him, staring up at his enormous Mediterranean home. After spending time holed up in a plane, a dungeon, and a Sleeper, I can't bear the thought of a roof pressing down on me.

"Serenity."

My eyes move to the king.

He must be able to read all of my emotions because I

see panic in his own. I don't blame him for it. I'm here, but I'm also a million miles away.

I agreed to kill him.

My throat works. "I don't want to go inside. Not yet—please."

I'm so rarely polite, and I see Montes physically react to this.

The king might not be the only one losing their mind.

He gives me a subtle nod, then looks to one of his men. "Have someone get the boat ready, and make sure it's stocked with everything the queen and I might need."

As soon as the order leaves Montes's mouth, one of the guards begins to radio commands to his men.

I'm still stuck on the word *boat.*

I jog my memory, trying to remember if I've ever been aboard a boat. Nothing comes to mind.

A nervous thrill runs through me, chasing away my dark thoughts.

Pressing a hand to the small of my back, Montes steers me around the edge of the palace, towards the back gardens. I can tell he wants to touch me. More than touch. He wants to devour me alive. I can feel his hand trembling with the need.

He's not alone. But it's more than just his body I wish to explore. I want to see inside that twisted mind of his and understand what drove him to give up so much for me.

He gave away a territory for me. I intend to take his head.

A sick sensation courses through me, and I sway a little.

Montes notices. "Once we dock at the end of the day, you will get checked out by the royal physician."

I've passed through quite a few hospitals and seen quite a few doctors since I married the king. My prior phobia of them has only increased.

The king must see the fresh mutiny in my eyes. "That is not a suggestion, Serenity."

I know it's not. Even if I refused the king's order, he'd find a way to force me into a medical examination.

It doesn't mean I like it.

His eyes flick to my stomach, and oh God, I know where his mind drifted. What his motives are.

My hand drifts over my midsection. "I'm not pregnant," I say quietly.

"You don't know that." He looks concerned, but he sounds ... hopeful. Of course the greediest, loneliest man in the world would get a taste for companionship and want more.

And he's right. I don't know that I'm not pregnant, but it's doubtful. I took a bullet to the stomach, after all.

Regardless, I'm not having this conversation right now.

I squint off to the horizon, seeing the blue ocean stretch on and on.

"I've never been on a boat," I say.

I'm sure Montes doesn't miss the subject change.

I feel his gaze on me. "Then I hope you enjoy it."

CHAPTER 45

Serenity

I CLING TO the railing, another wave of nausea rolling over me. I've been on this blasted thing for not even ten minutes and already I feel like this was a grave mistake.

I'm pretty sure I fucking hate boats.

"When we get back, you're seeing the physician *straightaway*."

"I'm *not* pregnant," I growl.

He's trying to goad me. I can hear the smile in his voice.

"The waves are bad here," he says. "Once we get farther out, your—" *pregnant* pause, "*stomach* should settle."

He heads over to me, pulling my form away from the railing and forcing me to sit on one of the plush couches arranged on the deck.

"Keep your eyes on the horizon and rest. I'll be right back."

I sit a little straighter as he moves to the interior of the boat. I don't dare try to follow him out of fear that the close quarters will make the sickness worse.

Montes returns several minutes later with two items—a glass of something fizzy, and a bottle with a cream of some sort.

"For your stomach," he says, handing me the drink, "and to protect your skin," he says, holding up the bottle of salve.

I take it from his hand and read the label.

Sunscreen.

I have vague memories of using this when I was younger, before the world had gone crazy.

"You'll want to put that on your face. Otherwise your skin will burn."

Sunburns, now *that* was something I was familiar with.

I have time to neither try the drink or use the sunscreen before Montes takes my jaw and kisses me roughly. "I have to go man the helm. Remember—eyes on the horizon."

He leaves me there so that he can start up the engine.

He's doing all this because I asked him to. The sunscreen, the drink, the day out at sea. He just wants to see me happy.

Was this what love was like? Not just something to fight and die for, but something that didn't draw attention to itself unless you looked for it?

I think back to my conversation with the representatives. The agreement we made, the one I intend to see through to the bitter end.

My nausea only deepens, and I take a sip of the drink the king gave me.

I find the fluid does help settle my stomach, as does watching the horizon. And once the boat gets moving, the last of my seasickness dissipates completely, and I begin to enjoy myself.

My gaze drifts to Montes. He's shrugged off his suit jacket and rolled up his sleeves. He's also unbuttoned his shirt, so it blows behind him.

Those abs he sported when I met him are still there.

Glorious, wretched man.

Normally I'm taken by how otherworldly he appears, but that's not the case now. Now he seems startlingly human.

I force my attention back to the horizon, where sea meets sky. It's such a far cry from the dank dungeon I was in only a day ago.

The boat slows to a halt.

I glance over at the king just as he removes his shoes. Then his socks.

"What are you doing?" I ask, my eyebrows rising.

"Going for a swim. And my pregnant queen will be joining me."

My annoyance flares. A command given in the third person, and that insinuation again that I'm pregnant.

"I don't have a swimsuit."

Montes actually looks charmed by my words. "That didn't stop you the last time you swam in the ocean with me."

His hands move to his zipper of his slacks.

"*What are you doing?*"

The king sighs, dropping his pants and stepping out of them as he does so. "Remember what I said about inane questions? I'm not answering that."

I glance over my shoulder. The palace is fairly far away, but I don't doubt that there are eyes trained on our location.

Montes's hands go his boxer briefs. With one swift tug, he removes the last of his clothes.

The king has never had many qualms about being naked. That doesn't change as he approaches me.

He takes the drink out of my hand and sets it aside.

I lean back as he enters my personal space. He drops to his knees, his fingers going to the hem of my top.

I grab his wrists. "What are you doing?"

"Undressing you, in case that wasn't apparent," he says, his mouth curving up just a little.

He wants us to swim ... naked? My shock is tempered by a good dose of curiosity.

He must sense my interest, because he takes the opportunity to lift my shirt. I raise my arms passively.

"People do this?"

He tosses my shirt aside and squints at me, his head tilting. "My queen, have you never skinny-dipped?"

I don't even know what the term means, though by its context I figure it out real quick.

I'm sure my expression says enough.

"Another new experience," the king says. I can hear the wonder in his voice.

I let him undress me until we both stand together, naked from head to foot.

He spends a moment drinking me in. Then he grabs the sunscreen from its resting spot and squeezes it onto his hands.

I think he's going to put it on his own body, but then he begins to rub my shoulder, dragging his hand down my arm, massaging the sunscreen in to my skin.

I watch him for several seconds, utterly transfixed by him. Montes appears to be enjoying the excuse to touch me.

"What's the point?" I ask. He has pills and machines that can do far more than sunscreen can.

He doesn't look up as he responds, "You don't like doing things my way, so I'm trying to do them your way."

I stare at him in awe. He's a different being entirely from the one I married. One that compromises and works to be good even though it goes against his very nature.

Montes smooths more sunscreen onto me, his hands brushing across my ribs, over my bellybutton, beneath my breasts. I don't bother telling him this last spot probably won't capture the sun. I'm enjoying his hands on me far too much.

He touches me with familiarity, and I'm charmed despite myself. He's taking care of me. Aside from my parents, I've never had anyone take care of me. That's what happens when you're strong. No one thinks to.

"Done." He caps the bottle and, setting it aside, stands. "Now for the fun part."

Without warning, he scoops me up.

I think I know what's coming.

"Montes, put me down," I command. Even as I speak, I wrap my arms around his neck. I know better than to assume he'll listen to me. He just finished making one consolation. Two within such a short timespan would be pushing it.

He just smiles at me, those white, white teeth looking even brighter against his olive complexion. Out here, in the open sun, my skin pressed to his, I notice just how much his body dwarfs mine.

Once, that realization would've made me uneasy. Now it makes me feel safe in a very innate way.

That terrible sensation takes root in my stomach again, partly guilt, but partly something else. It tastes a lot like desperation. Like this man, who has outlived everyone else, will leave me soon.

My heart begins to race, and I wonder if, for the first time in my life, I could be a coward and back out of the promise I made to this world. He gave up a continent, I would give up the world. All for him.

But I can't. I *can't*. It's not in my nature, and unlike the king, I'm not sure I'm capable of really changing.

Montes carries me to the edge of the boat, completely unaware I'm having an existential crisis right now.

He pauses to stare down at me, his gaze latching onto my lips. Right when I think he's going to lean in, he steps off the edge.

For the merest moment, we're falling, and then together we hit the water.

It's cold enough that I almost gasp the ocean into my

lungs. And the sensation of liquid running all over my naked skin. It feels ... strange and exquisite. I kick away from Montes and come up for air.

The king surfaces a moment later, slicking his hair back. He flashes me a grin. "Welcome to the Aegean. You are now officially swimming in Homer's wine dark sea."

I give him a strange look. I know of Homer, but I don't get the reference.

His eyes soften just a smidge. "When the war is over, I will show you other things that you have missed."

When the war is over. Not *if*.

"You believe we can end it," I say, treading water. He's never admitted this before. I assumed he thought it was a lost cause, especially now that he traded away Australia.

"Let's not talk about war for one afternoon," he says.

I can respect that. He's given me the outdoors, I can give him this.

I move my hand through the water, watching light dance along it.

There's a fullness in my heart, like it might burst. With happiness, I realize. It's all so unbearably wonderful. The sea, the sun, the man staring intensely at me.

"I wish this could last forever," I say, tasting sea salt on my lips as I speak. It's far too wonderful, which means it won't.

I know it won't.

It can. Montes doesn't say it, but it's all there in his eyes.

He swims over and pulls me against him, cradling my body in his arms. And it isn't lewd, or sexy, or erotic.

It's romantic. Intimate.

I see the sunset in the king's eyes, those old eyes that look so young when they gaze at me.

My gaze drops to his neck. I touch the pulse point that throbs to the beat of his heart, trailing a finger over the dark skin there.

"Never have I been so afraid," I admit softly. I can still see the moment; it plays on repeat in my mind. The moment I nearly lost him.

I'm still so, so afraid.

Montes swallows, his face growing serious. "I know the feeling."

He did. Had the Sleeper not existed, the king and I wouldn't be in each other's arms; we'd be six feet under.

As the water laps at us, I shake off the morbid mood. "Sorry—I didn't mean to lead the conversation right back to war."

He presses his thumb against my mouth. "*Nire bihotza*, to hear you feared for my life ... I *want* to know that."

Slowly, I nod.

Montes's thumb begins stroking my lower lip, his brows still puckered.

The sun loves the king. It makes his dark eyes glow amber and his skin brighten. A lock of his wet hair slides over his eye.

This man is mine.

I brush the lock of hair away from his face, allowing my fingers to trail over his features. There's nothing out here but us, the sun, the sea, and the sky.

"This might be the happiest moment of my life," I admit. It isn't grand, and it shouldn't be particularly memorable—nudity aside—but ... but perhaps that's why I enjoy it so much.

It is beautifully normal.

Montes brushes the backs of his fingers against my cheekbone. "I'm certain it's mine."

I raise my eyebrows. "Out of all of them?"

"Out of all of them."

I play with another wet strand of his hair, and he closes his eyes for a second, like he just wants to revel in the feel of it.

"Why?" I ask.

He opens his eyes. "Because for once it's not a memory, and it has you in it."

CHAPTER 46

Serenity

DOCTORS HAVE BEEN and will be one of the things I hate most passionately. Especially royal ones.

I'm not very good at hiding my distaste. I know the royal physician can sense it as she inspects me for injury.

Back in the WUN, doctors often meant death. And when it comes to the king's medics, they've been known to turn traitor.

But it isn't all bad. The appointment is the perfect excuse to look into an issue that I've been meaning to for some time.

The king holds my hand from the chair he sits in, but make no mistake, this isn't some shining example of his devotion. The bastard is making sure I don't bolt for the door at the soonest possible moment.

The doctor straightens. “Your Majesty, everything looks good.”

I’m not surprised.

“The only thing that’s left,” the doctor continues, “is the blood work.”

The blood work Montes insisted on.

When it finally comes back in, she flips through it. “Not pregnant,” the physician says.

I give Montes a bored look. *See?*

“Hmmm,” he says in response, and I really don’t like the look in his eyes. Like he wants to rectify the situation immediately.

When the exam ends, the king leads me out.

Once we return to the main section of the palace, I halt. “Shit,” I say.

“What is it?”

I glance behind us. “I left my jacket behind.”

“Someone will return it to our rooms.” The king begins to steer me forward once more.

I dig my heels in. “I’m just going to grab it,” I say.

Montes gives me a peculiar look. He knows me far too well. To willingly suffer through more time in the medical wing is out of character.

“Alright,” he says carefully. “I’ll be in my office.” Giving me a final, poignant glance, we part ways.

I turn around and stride back towards the medical facilities.

Being sneaky is not a forte of mine. I tend to storm into situations guns a-blazing. Unfortunately for me, the king knows this. I just have to hope that other tasks keep him busy enough to ignore my inconsistent behavior.

When I run into the royal physician, she glances up from the paperwork she holds.

"Did you forget something?" she asks.

"My jacket," I say.

"Let's go get it for you," she says, dropping the file on the desk near her. I head back to the room with her.

Something has niggled at my mind for some time, something that I might be able to make use of.

"How many Sleepers does the king have?" I ask as we walk.

"Here?" she says, tucking a wispy strand of white hair behind her ear. "Seven I believe—of course, that's not including the one you were in. Globally, there are twenty-four, again, not including yours."

"And how many of them are occupied?" I ask.

The doctor glances over at me sharply. She doesn't appear all that enthusiastic to answer it.

"Three here, not including yours, and eight others worldwide. Many of the remaining Sleepers are periodically in use depending on the needs of the people."

"How many of those contain long-term occupants? Like me." I began the conversation casually enough, but now there's no masking the fact that I'm probing with a purpose.

She licks her lips. "Two."

"I want to see who's in them."

"Your Majesty, I don't see how this is—"

"You don't need to understand my motives," I interrupt her to say. "All you need to do is follow through with my request."

"You didn't come back for your jacket, did you?" she asks.

"I didn't," I confirm.

The doctor doesn't slow when we pass the room I had my checkup in.

"I'm only authorized to show you one," she cautions.

That makes me all the more eager to find out who's in the remaining Sleeper.

"Fine," I say. "Show me the one."

I STARE DOWN at the occupant of the king's Sleeper.

I was right.

"How long has he been here?" I ask, glancing up at the physician. I'm sure she has a busy schedule, and this is the last place she wants to be, but she is patient, acting as though she has all the time in the world to spend answering my questions.

Then again, if I served the queen, I might make time for her as well.

"For as long as I can remember. And for as long as the doctor before me can remember."

I have no doubt this man has been resting here for just as long as I had. Over a century.

The room he's housed in is not nearly as grand as the temple made for me, but time and lots of money have clearly gone into the richly painted frescos that adorn the walls around us. This is as beautiful a crypt as I've ever seen.

I frown as I return my attention to the man, visible through the Sleeper's porthole.

I'm not the only beloved person Montes kept alive. Marco rests inside the machine—the original one—his face expressionless.

I'd wondered for a while now how the king managed to clone Marco. Where he got the DNA. Now I know.

It just goes to show you how twisted my life has become that I pity the man trapped in this box, I pity him and his fate. Doomed to remain alive even though there is nothing sentient left in his body, not after the bullet he took to the brain all those years ago.

Death must come to all men. It is our due.

Marco hasn't been able to claim it, though his soul has long since left this place.

I still hate the man with a vengeance, and I haven't been kind to his doppelganger, but there are some dignities even my enemies deserve.

When the time is right, I will give this man the death he deserves.

CHAPTER 47

Serenity

THE NEXT DAY, when I walk into my office, an unassuming envelop sits on my keyboard along with a small packet of matches.

I pick up the envelope. *Serenity* is scrawled along the front of it.

I open it and pull out a sheaf of paper made from thick cardstock.

Rendezvous in your office at 02:00. Burn this message after reading.

Lowering the note, I look around. Someone slipped into my office to drop this off. My hackles rise at the violation of space.

My attention returns to the note.

The first communication from the representatives.

Grabbing one of the matches, I strike it against the desk and bring the flame to the note, watching it burn.

How absurd to think that we could meet in my office. There are cameras in here. I stare up at one of them pensively.

Unless ...

It takes me fifteen minutes to find the head of security, who's outside with some type of technician, discussing models and makes of camera equipment.

"Your Majesty," he and the technician bow when they see me, "it's an honor to finally meet you."

"Likewise," I say, trying not to sound too impatient.

"What can I do for you?"

"I would like to go over the last several hours' worth of footage taken from my office."

He appears baffled by the request. "Of course. Right this way."

He leads me to a small auxillary building a short distance away. Inside is a bank of monitors, all showing different images of the palace and the surrounding grounds. He pats the shoulders of the two men manning the desk. "Would you two mind handling Steve? He's on the northwest end of the palace."

They get up, startling when they see me behind their boss. Placing a fist to their chests, they bow and murmur, "Your Majesty." Quickly, they exit the room.

Once they leave, the head of security pulls one of the vacated chairs up and taps on a screen. "This is one of them, and—" he taps on several others, "these are the other three."

Pulling out a keyboard, he begins typing. "You said you wanted to see footage from the last hour?"

"The last several hours would be even better."

He pats the chair next to him. "Take a seat. We'll be here awhile."

IT'S DUMMY FOOTAGE. All three hours of it.

I never see who placed the envelope and matches on my desk, and I never see myself enter and retrieve the letter. Someone went in and tampered with the video feeds.

Even after all this time there are holes in the king's security.

Someone's betraying the king.

We come to the end of the footage.

"That's it," the man says, rubbing the gray scruff of his beard.

He gets up, prepared to leave.

I stand with him, my eyes still locked on the bank of screens. "I want to know the weaknesses in the palace's security, should there ever be an attack."

"Your Majesty," he seems startled, "I assure you, no such thing will—"

I cut him off. "I haven't survived based on luck alone. I want a thorough understanding of this place—how many officers are stationed around the grounds, their hours, tasks, the weaponry they carry, what sorts of emergency exit strategies the king and I have at our disposal. And today, I want to start with the rest of the security footage and audio for the entire palace."

"But your Majesty, the security footage alone will take hours, possibly even days, to go over."

"Then we better get started now."

The King

I RUB MY lower lip as I watch Serenity through the very cameras she's inspecting.

My vicious little wife has taken a keen interest in the palace's inner workings.

She's a strange creature; this could just be one more way she feels she has some control over her situation. But it could also be something else.

Something that could come back to bite me in the ass if I don't watch her.

Does she believe an attack is imminent?

Or does she have other reasons?

I already know she visited Marco's Sleeper yesterday when she'd claimed she needed to retrieve her jacket.

I squint at her image.

I steeple my fingers and press them to my mouth. I have to acknowledge what I've always known: I have made Serenity larger than myself. She's only rising to the role I've given her. Not just as queen, but as some sort of savior.

I call in Heinrich.

When he enters my office, I nod to my computer screen, where the footage of Serenity still plays. "Keep an eye on her, and give me updates on everything she does."

My grand marshal inclines his head.

"Is that all?" he asks.

"Yes."

I watch his back as he exits.

"Oh, and Heinrich?"

"If she begins to do suspicious things or breaks palace code, let her."

"Even if it involves your men?"

I nod. "Even if it involves *you*."

Serenity might be sneaky, and right now she might be secretive, but I have my men's loyalty.

I want to see what she's up to.

Serenity

I RUB MY eyes then pinch the bridge of my nose.

By the time 2:00 a.m. rolls around, my brain feels like it's about to explode with all the information I've gleaned today.

Blueprints of the palace and the surrounding grounds are spread out in front of me. Already I've begun circling areas where I know cameras are installed. Some of them will need to be rigged.

I roll up the blueprint and set it aside.

A few minutes later I hear a gentle knock on the door. My pulse speeds up in anticipation.

Time to meet one of the West's moles.

Withdrawing my gun from its holster, I approach the door. Whoever has been planted amongst us, I don't trust them any more than I would an enemy aiming a weapon at my head. Traitors are the worst sort of people.

I would know. I have become one myself.

I open the door. I can't hide my shock when I see who's on the other side.

"*You?*"

Marco.

He brushes past me, and I quickly shut the door behind him.

"I could ask you the same thing," he says.

The king's wife and his closest friend are conspiring against him. It makes me sad, and it makes me feel sorry for Montes, who is so desperate for companionship.

I force my feelings back so I can say, "The king's taken everything I've ever loved from me." It's the truth, and yet it feels like a lie when I say it now.

Marco takes in my office, then rotates to face me.

"What has he done to you?" I ask. The original Marco was many things, but he wasn't a traitor.

"Trinity," the man in front of me says, like her name is explanation enough. "He never loved her, not in any sense of the word."

There hasn't been enough time for me to understand intricate inner workings of the king's house. And when it comes to vendettas the devil is *always* in the details.

"When she died, Montes didn't mourn her. If anything, he was *relieved*," Marco says. "She looked *just* like you, but it never mattered to him. She was just a copy, a poor man's Serenity. I loved her, and he let her die. I can't forgive him for that."

Love and hate, they are so very interconnected.

"The disappearances," I say. "You're the insider that's been telling the WUN of our plans."

All those leaders that had disappeared. We couldn't figure out how the West had known we were going to meet with them.

I swear I see a flash of remorse in Marco's eyes, and then it's gone.

"I am," he admits.

I fight the urge to grab my gun. If it weren't for this man, countless people would still be alive and several regional leaders wouldn't be undergoing God knows what at the hands of the West.

This man is *worse* than the Marco I despised.

It takes me several seconds to get my emotions under control. "So you're going to help me kill the king?" I finally ask. Saying the words aloud makes it all the more real.

He nods.

I move father into the room. I'm getting that prickly sensation at the back of my neck, telling me that something about this situation isn't right.

"Why haven't you done so before now?" I probe.

"I've considered it, as have the representatives. But the king has many ways to sidestep death, and I don't have the clearance or the connections to make sure the king dies and stays dead."

But I do.

I run my tongue over my teeth.

"How do you intend to kill him?" he asks.

Now for the tricky part, the part I've been toying with

since I awoke. A plan I'd finalized on the flight back here.

The king is going to die with just as much panache as he lived.

"We're going to burn the palace to the ground."

CHAPTER 48

Serenity

"We need to call Styx," Marco says as our meeting winds down.

I pull my head back. "Why?"

All I want to do is to crawl into bed.

"He has access to many of the East's military warehouses."

Shit, does the king know this?

Of course he doesn't.

And now I hate deception because it ties my hands.

"We're going to use the East's weapons against them?" I ask skeptically.

"Would you rather use the West's?" Marco challenges.

It's a loaded question.

"The West has already promised me their firepower," I say, leaning against my desk.

"They are an ocean away. It will be easy for the king to defend the palace against them."

I begrudgingly agree with Marco's assessment.

He gestures to my computer. "May I?"

I work my jaw, then jerk my head *yes*.

Sitting down at my desk, he sets up the screen for a video call.

Within minutes Styx Garcia's face fills the screen.

I frown, my nostrils flaring at the sight of him and all his scars. This is the last thing I want to be doing, surrounding myself with these two men.

"My beautiful queen," Styx says by way of introduction, ignoring Marco altogether, "what an honor to speak with you again."

I feel my upper lip curl. I'd forgotten just how much I disliked this man.

"You answered quickly."

Styx's gaze finally moves to Marco. "I was expecting the call."

My neck prickles again. This shouldn't be how it plays out; I should be the one coordinating. Instead I feel like a lamb being led—led to slaughter.

"Did you enjoy your visit out West?" he asks. "The representatives were very eager to see you once I told them that you wanted to arrange a meeting."

"A videoconference would've sufficed," I say sharply.

"I am just the messenger," he reminds me.

He does have a point.

"Pretty woman, I hear you're going to be a widow soon," Styx says, smiling slyly.

I narrow my eyes at him. That only makes his smile grow.

"Marcus seems to think we need your help," I say.

"You *do* need my help. The moment you kill the king, your men are going to turn on you."

"And you have men willing to defend me?" I ask skeptically.

"Aye, every one of them would die for you," he says. He hasn't blinked since he picked up the call, and it's beginning to unnerve me.

"She also wants to burn the palace down," Marco adds.

The news brightens Styx's eyes. "Ah, my queen, I have explosives for days."

"Explosives that belong to my husband."

Styx cocks his head at my accusatory tone.

"Yes," he says carefully. "And my own." He leans forward. "Speaking of your husband, he's still trying to kill me."

"It's a good thing he doesn't know the extent of your depravity," I play with the strap of my holster, "otherwise he might put more effort into it."

"It's a good thing he doesn't know the extent of *yours*," Styx replies.

Another good point.

"My queen, I will lend assistance to you. And when that day comes, I'll be there to congratulate you in person."

I NEED TO scrub off the evil that shrouds me. I've never done something like this before. I wonder what my father would think. I bet he would be proud. I bet, if he were still alive, this would be the moment he'd think, *she has finally understood my lessons.*

I head back to my room, quietly tiptoeing back in. I shouldn't have bothered. The lights are on, the bed still made.

The king isn't here.

I'm alarmed and relieved and disappointed all at once. I want to see him, but I don't want him to see me. I can't hide nearly enough of myself from his penetrating eyes.

Rather than get into bed, I head out onto the balcony. It's become the place I go to when my heart is all twisted up and my mind is addled.

Immediately I hear the sound of the surf.

My father might be proud of me—if he were here—but I'm filled with self-loathing. I no longer hate the king nearly so much as I hate what I have become and what I must do.

I lean against the railing for who knows how long, letting the night air wash over me. Eventually my gaze drops from the sky to the gardens.

A figure sits on one of the stone benches, his broad back facing me.

Montes.

Has he been there the whole time? What could he possibly be musing about deep into the night?

I push away from the balcony and leave our room. My shoes click down the hallway.

I want to see him, my king. Even though I'm plotting against him, and even though he's bent and broken all wrong, I want to see him.

You see, I love him.

So much.

I can finally admit it to myself now, at the end of things. It's been there for a while. Quite a while. I was just always afraid of it.

I stride out the palace's back doors and head down one of the paths that winds through the garden. My steps slow when I catch sight of the king's form. He sits next to a bubbling fountain, his forearms on his thighs, his head bent.

I am not the only weary one here.

He tilts his head in my direction when he hears my boots click against the stone, but he doesn't turn around.

When I reach him, I touch his shoulder. "What are you doing out here?" I ask quietly.

His hand goes to my arm, like he wants to make sure I'm tethered to him. "My wife wasn't in my bed." He smiles wanly, his focus on the fountain ahead of us. "I'm discovering I can't sleep when you're not in my bed."

I move to sit down next to him, surprised when he doesn't try to pull me onto his lap.

"So you came out here?" I fill in.

"You're not the only one that gets tired of those walls pressing in."

There something frightening about the way he's talking. The way he's acting. I might finally understand why Montes panics when I pull away. I can feel the anxiety there, right beneath my sternum. He's the one whose life will soon end, and he's acting distant, and I'm pursuing him. He's the decent one, and I'm the great evil who will destroy every last thing he holds dear.

When did our roles reverse?

He finally looks at me, and God, the look—I could live and die in it.

"Stop it," I say quietly.

He cups my cheek. "Every time you say that, I know I'm doing something right."

I frown, even as my eyes well with some soft emotion.

"*Nire bihotza*, why are you sad?"

I should be asking him the same thing.

"There's a lot to be sad about."

He shakes his head. "I've had a hundred years to be sad. I don't want to be sad any longer. And I don't want my queen to be, either."

But that's impossible at this point. The two of us have spent too long drowning in horrors of our own making.

That's all we know—pain and bloodshed.

Montes threads his fingers through mine.

I glance down at our joined hands, and amend my earlier statement.

All we know is pain, bloodshed—and *this*.

And it's this last one that will kill us.

CHAPTER 49

Serenity

THERE'S ONE LAST person I need to speak with, and he will be the one to play the most pivotal role.

I find Heinrich in his office. The grand marshal is on the phone when I enter, his voice gruff. The moment he catches sight of me, he straightens in his chair, rushing the caller off the phone.

I take a seat in one of the guest chairs across from him.

"Your Majesty," he bows his head.

I'm struck all over again by how hardened this man is. He's seen his fair share of carnage. I can tell he respects me, but I bet he also thinks I'm a bit naïve and disillusioned. Me with my grand speeches and rosy ideals.

He doesn't speak, doesn't ask me why I'm here, or what

I need.

"How loyal are you to the king?" I finally ask.

He rubs his chin and speculates me from where he sets. "I would die for him. And for you, Your Majesty."

You can't trust people. Even the most decent ones can turn on you for the right price; I know that better than most. But I decide to trust this man because I'm out of options.

"What if I told you that I needed your help to end the war?"

He stares at me for several seconds before saying, "I would ask you what you need from me."

"I was hoping you'd say that."

And then I tell him exactly what I intend to do.

I'm not even finished speaking when he starts shaking his head.

"*No*," he barks out, "I know what I said before, but I won't do this."

"Then I will die, and the world will continue to be at war."

"It's too risky." He's arguing with me, which I take as a good sign. It means he's considering it on some level. "For you *and* for the king. I will be executed for treason," he says.

"How many people has this war already killed?" I say. "How many more people will it kill if we don't end it? You and I both know I can manage it."

"Listen, let's forget for one second that we're not equals. Let me put this plainly: I like you, Serenity. You have a good heart. But this is madness.

"I won't tell the king you came to me. Just forget about this whole plan."

I run my hands through my hair. I need this man backing me.

I try one last time. "When I was nineteen, the general of the Western United Nations, our leader at the time, asked me to marry the king, the man who had killed my family and countless numbers of my countrymen. That was the king's price—if the WUN handed me over, the war would end.

"I couldn't imagine a worse fate, but I agreed to it because I knew the world would be better off.

"I'm asking the same thing of you now," I beseech the grand marshal, "to rise above the ethics of it all to serve the greater good. I know that's not fair of me to ask, but I can't do this alone."

He runs a palm over his buzzed hair. He shifts his weight. Deliberating, deliberating. The entire time, those flinty eyes watch me.

Finally, his jaw tightens, and he blows out a breath. "You have my loyalty, Your Majesty. I will do what you ask."

I feel my muscles loosen. I didn't know how tense I was until he accepted.

"Then this is what I need you to do ..."

The King

SOMEONE RAPS AGAINST my closed door.

I drop the report I'm reading, and lean back in my seat. "Come in," I say.

My grand marshal enters the room.

"Your Majesty," Heinrich says, bowing, "I have something alarming to tell you. Something that concerns the queen."

I feel my muscles go tight. "What is it?"

And then he tells me.

The news is a hit to the gut—so much so that it takes me several seconds to get my emotions under control.

Once I do, I lean forward. "You're going to go along with her plan," I say.

"But, Your Majesty—"

"You're going to go along with her plan *and* mine."

THAT NIGHT, WHEN I see Serenity, Heinrich's words echo in my head. I had to go to the gym and beat the shit out of an inanimate object to work off everything I felt. And I felt so goddamn *much*. Neither Serenity nor I can escape what fate has always had in mind for us.

She sits across from me at the small, intimate table. Seeing that loose golden hair of hers framing her bittersweet face, it's a shock to the chest.

I can tell by the way her leg jiggles that she wants to kick her heels up to the edge of the table and slouch in her seat.

Instead she runs a hand over one of the flames. "Why are you looking at me like that?" she asks.

I almost hunted you down and confronted you. I almost threw your damn body in a Sleeper. I almost went on a warpath in this palace. Only a hundred years of wisdom and temperance stopped me.

She's oblivious.

There's a deep ache in my bones that I can't drive away.

Her hand stops over the flame. "Is everything alright?"

I move her hand out of the way. "It's been a long day." I lean forward to kiss her scarred knuckles.

This beloved, wild creature. She doesn't belong here, inside these gilded walls, sitting in front of an intricately carved wooden table set with delicate china.

It was foolish of me to think that she could ever be caged.

I've been running from everything she represents for so very long. And I'm tired of running.

It's time to stop being so afraid.

It's time to accept everything she is.

It's time to set her free.

CHAPTER 50

Serenity

THE DAYS TURN into weeks. Time bleeds away, stealing hours from me. And as the time slips by, so does the strange happiness that had grown in my heart.

I might never believe Montes is truly a good man, but I'm not sure I ever wanted good. He's complex, and terrible, and at the end of the day he's my monster.

And I have to slay him.

This is what remorse feels like. It's premature, which is almost worse. Because I have time to change the course of my actions, but I won't. I made a promise to the world, one I intend to keep.

Things appear to go back to normal. The king watches me, and I swear he sees everything. But if he does, he doesn't stop me.

I can't even ponder that possibility.

Each day is worse than the last because it brings me closer to the moment I've arranged to kill my husband. I talk with Marco most days, Marco and Heinrich. I plot and plan until every last detail is accounted far.

Tomorrow, at precisely 9:30 a.m., this place will burn, the king along with it.

It's the king's day of reckoning. And mine.

"Everything's in place?" the representatives ask on the other side of the screen. I'm acutely aware that their thirty day timeframe is nearly up.

I nod, and Marco, who sits at my side, says, "It is."

The two of us are holed up in my office, hopefully for the last time.

All those years ago I sat next to my father, and spoke to a different set of representatives.

This is the world gone wrong.

"Good. Our men will begin to move in at nine-twenty. A vessel will be waiting offshore. Marco, you'll radio our men the moment Serenity takes out the king."

I have to breathe through my nose to curb the nausea that rises at the prospect. I have killed countless people; this should be no different. But it's a world apart. The man I love, the monster who's found his conscience, the king who gave up a piece of his empire to hold me in his arms again. Who defied death to have me by his side.

I dread this more than anything I ever have.

"We'll pick you both up from there," the representatives continue. "We won't consider the deed done unless you bring the body."

They're looking at me, even though Marco is just as much a part of this as I am.

I pull myself together. "I'll get you your body."

"Good. Then we'll see you tomorrow. We have a peace agreement to negotiate in the coming days."

Pretty words for ugly intentions. Knowing these men, it won't be a peace agreement so much as terms of surrender. It doesn't matter. I won't be agreeing to anything.

"Get some sleep," one of the representatives says, rousing me from my thoughts. "You'll need it."

BATTLE FATIGUE. IT'S a very real thing. You've seen too much, done too much, and at the end of it all you are so, so weary.

I stare at myself in the bathroom mirror.

I thought I had lost everything.

And I had. I lost everything I loved, even things I didn't realize I could lose—my memory, the past, my hate.

I've become something I loathe, and I don't know how to get back to the girl I was, the one that easily divided the world into right and wrong.

And to be honest, I don't know if I even want to be her anymore. I'd rather be the girl who was never touched by war. Who knew nothing of sleeping with the enemy, who'd never seen what flesh looks like when it was blown open. I want to be a girl who woke with a clear conscience each morning, whose demons didn't plague her late at night.

But I can't have that. Not short of injecting myself with that memory loss serum, and that was no solution. Forgetting doesn't mean it never happened; it means not dealing with the consequences.

And oh, have the consequences stacked up.

I gaze into my reflection, my hands tightening around the edge of the counter.

I may have suffered, I may have changed, but I *know* who I am.

I am the girl from the WUN—the girl born a citizen of the United States of America. I am vengeance and I am salvation.

And tomorrow, the world will know it, once and for all.

NOT LONG AFTER my revelation, I hear Montes enter the bedroom, back from whatever business he was attending to. We've both been keeping late hours.

I hear his footsteps head directly for the bathroom. A moment later, Montes enters.

Our eyes meet in the mirror, and I see such bottomless sadness in his own.

He knows. He must.

He steps up behind me and wraps an arm around my middle. His other hand clasps my neck so that he has me shackled to his body.

My hands tighten along the rim of the counter, but I don't fight his grip.

"I've never known my vicious little queen to be vain," he says.

I pass him an annoyed glance through the mirror. We're both aware that's not what I was doing.

His lips brush the shell of my ear. "Come to bed," he says, his voice husky.

My throat works. "I don't want to fall asleep," I admit. The idea of what's to come tomorrow has my stomach twisted in knots.

"Who said anything about sleep?" he breathes.

I turn my head to face him, and that's all the opening he needs. He kisses me fervently, his hands moving so that I'm no longer his hostage. They cup either side of my jaw.

I'm gasping into the kiss, and I play it off like it's passion, when all I'm really doing is choking back sobs.

I push against him, forcing him to back up. All the while I rip away at his clothing. I've never been like this, violent with the need to be close to him.

Montes welcomes it with a wolfish smile. He always was just as fucked-up as me.

He helps me shrug off the remnants of his shirt, and then his slacks. And then his large, sculpted body is completely on display. The sight of all that coiled power nearly brings me to my knees.

When my hands reach for the edge of my shirt, he captures them in his own.

"Ah-ah," he says. He hooks his fingers around my shirt collar, and, pausing just long enough to make it dramatic, he rips the garment down the middle.

This is *wrong*. To pursue sex with the man I intend to kill. I know it is, and I wonder if Montes ever had thoughts like this before he took me—in the beginning. Because my plans aren't changing, yet I still want this desperately, and I *will* take it.

He jerks my pants to my ankles then tosses me onto the bed. Now, as I see him prowling towards me, I remember why I'm usually the more subdued of the two of us.

I'm not sure I can handle him in all his intensity. Not here, where all the pretty layers that usually make me hardened have been stripped away with my clothes.

Hell lives inside me, and it's been consuming me for the last several hours.

Montes will see all my ugly intentions the moment we're locked together.

He unlaces one of my boots and tugs it off, throwing it over his shoulder. He does the same to the other. The entire time he watches me, those eyes.

Carelessly, he removes my pants and lets them drop to the floor. My panties follow soon after. Then he's between my legs, looming over me, his chest brushing against my own.

Montes searches my face. "What's bothering you?" he asks.

I need to pull myself together.

Instead of answering, I draw him to me and kiss his lips. My hands find his hair and I take great pains to muss it up.

I hear his rumble of approval deep in his chest. I know he hasn't forgotten his question, and I know he's probably more suspicious now than he was before.

I need to make him forget, to make us both forget.

No sooner does the thought cross my mind than he

wraps an arm around my waist and rolls us so that I'm staring down at him.

He unsnaps my bra and throws it to the side of the bed.

"You're no longer shy," he says.

Belatedly I realize that I used to make a habit of covering myself. I don't do that now.

"Does that make you sad?" I ask. In the past, Montes took great pleasure in shocking me when it comes to things between a man and a woman.

He sits up slowly, his abs tightening as he does so, until our chests are pressed together.

"No," he says, touching my scar. "I liked your modesty, but I love this more."

"Why?" I ask.

"Because it means you've accepted me."

My expression is on the verge of collapsing.

Montes saves me from myself; he recaptures my mouth, and we're desperate for each other once more. It's not until he lifts me onto him and he slides into me inch by agonizing inch that our frantic movements slow.

I exhale out my breath once we're fully joined, my arms twined around his neck. I stare into his eyes as I begin to move, my fingers playing absently with his hair.

"Say it," he whispers.

Swallowing back my emotion, I shake my head.

We're wrapped up in each other, our limbs tangled, and now his arms tighten around me. "I know you want to. I see it in your eyes."

I know he can.

"You don't get to have all of me, Montes." I don't know

why I say it. Maybe to harken back to the very beginning, because I'm feeling sentimental. Maybe to protect my heart, even though it's too late. I don't know.

I expect his normal retort. He doesn't give me it.

He brushes my hair back from my face. "Alright, Serenity. Alright," he says. His eyes are sad again. "This is enough."

I lean my forehead against his shoulder to hide my expression.

His hand tips my chin back up. He frowns at what he glimpses on my face. "Don't hide from me."

He flips us so that I'm staring up at him.

My terrible, undying king.

Who knew at the beginning of things that it would all come to this?

He makes love to me slowly, drawing out each thrust. He stares at me the entire time.

"*Nire bihotza, nire emaztea, nire bizitza. Maite izango dut nire heriotzaren egun arte*," he says.[1]

"What are you saying?" I ask.

He cups my face. "Just a promise." His thumbs rub my cheeks as he moves in and out of me.

"Now," he thrusts harder, ratcheting up the sweet burn, "come for me, my queen. I want your cries in my ear."

As if on command, sensation builds. I fight it, wanting to stretch this out for as long as I can.

Montes has other thoughts.

He puts more power behind each stroke and he takes

1 Translation: My heart, my wife, my life. I will love you until the day I die.

the tip of one of my breasts into his mouth. I squirm against him, panting as I try to stave my climax off.

"Come—for—me." He punctuates each word with a thrust.

All at once, against my will, my orgasm rips through me. I clutch Montes, my back arching as each wave of it washes over me. I feel him swell as his release follows my own.

The two of lock eyes as our sweat-slicked bodies crash against each other. I want this moment to last. But then it ends.

Montes eventually slides out of me, dragging my body onto his.

He holds me to him, stroking my back.

I wrap my arms tightly around him. Our ragged breathing eventually evens.

I don't want this night to end. I never want it to end.

Running a hand over his chest, I ask, "Montes, do you think we could have ever been good people?"

"My queen is full of deep thoughts tonight."

I don't bother responding.

He tilts my head back to face his. "I think we still can be. I don't think it's too late to try."

I maintain eye contact with him, but it takes so much effort. I want to curl up into him and just let go. I think death, when it comes for me, will be a great release. Oblivion from this cruel world.

"Montes," I say, "I need you to promise me something."

"Why don't you tell me what it is first?" he says softly.

"Promise me you will always try to do good."

He flashes me a quizzical look. "Where is this all coming from?"

"Promise me."

He frowns. "I promise you, I will always try."

That's the most reassurance I'm going to get.

I settle back in his arms. And for the rest of the night, I hold my monster to me.

IT'S EARLY IN the morning, when I finally pull myself out of our bed. The king's breaths have long since evened. I, meanwhile, haven't slept a wink this entire night. Instead I spent the long hours savoring the feel of him.

One last time.

I drag on my fatigues and boots, careful to muffle my movements. I clip on my two guns and then I head out onto our balcony.

I stare up at the stars and let the past wash over me. I carry a terrible history inside myself, one full of loss, but it's the only one I know, so I cherish it.

Over a hundred years ago I stood in almost this exact place, a woman married to her enemy.

How the tides have turned.

I continue to stare up at the dark sky, where everyone I love now lives. Or perhaps they don't. Perhaps death really is the end.

I push away from the railing and leave the room, not allowing myself to give Montes a parting glance.

Today I'm going to have to be strong.

I make my way to my office. I need a place to hide out

until all hell breaks loose. Anyone who catches sight of me before then will see that I'm acting cagey as fuck.

Once I'm inside, I pace a little, sit behind my desk for a bit, flip through reports that I'll never get around to addressing.

Slowly the hours creep by.

I'm checking the magazine of my new gun for the thirteenth time when I hear a rumble. I slide it into place with a satisfying click and stand, my head turned towards the door.

I hear a hollow, hissing noise, then—

BOOM!

I stumble back as the earth rocks. The walls shake violently. Books rain down from the shelves that line the room and my monitor topples over, along with a lamp.

I grab the edge of the desk and straighten. Out my window I see bits of the palace arcing through the sky. A large slab of marble slams into the fountain the king and I sat at mere weeks ago.

The screams start up almost immediately.

So it's begun.

CHAPTER 51

Serenity

I STORM OUT of my office, gun clutched in my hand, my heart beating a mile a minute.

I head down the halls to the main entrance as the sound of gunfire joins the screams.

People run past me, and none seem to notice the queen is amongst them, so focused they are on their own self interests.

The second explosion hits the southwest wall of the palace, the shockwave making me stagger. The screams ratchet up.

I throw open the front doors. I get a clear view of the chaos outside the palace.

Trails of dust and debris arc outwards from the blast

sites. Both wings of the palace are enveloped in flame. I can already smell the smoke on the wind.

The West's aircraft are all invisible, as are their missiles. But I can hear them all.

I stand at the palace's threshold, my clothes and hair whipping about.

BOOM!

The explosion hits directly in front of the palace. I'm thrown through the air, across the entrance hall. My body slams into one of the great columns that line the space, the force of it knocking the wind out of my lungs and the gun out of my hand. I fall to the ground, landing hard on my hip.

Those haunting pictures that line the great entrance drop from their perches, smashing against the ground, becoming just one more piece of the growing rubble.

I glance towards my gun, the palms of my hands pressed against the ground.

"*Serenity!*"

I close my eyes and swallow. I knew he'd come for me.

I am a spider, and I've lured my husband into my web. I don't bother looking above me, where several of the king's cameras are recording this footage.

I push myself to my knees, my hand reaching for my father's gun, the one still strapped to my side.

This is it. The moment I've feared since I left the West.

This will not be some detached act. It has always been personal between Montes and me.

When I look up again, I finally catch sight of my husband through the haze.

The king covers his head, and even amongst the chaos in the room he's trying to make his way to me.

On either side of us, bombs detonate, one after the next after the next, down the entire length of the great hall. Just as planned.

The entire thing happens in slow motion.

The walls blast out, blowing plaster and stone across the room. There is a strange beauty to the synchrony of it all.

The columns that hold up the second story sway, but they don't give out.

I don't wait for the explosions to stop before I stand, drawing my gun. At some point, the blasts threw Montes to the ground. He's halfway to his feet when he catches sight of me, gun in hand.

I'm not running towards him like I should be. I'm not panicking either. My true intentions are finally on display.

This must look like a savage reckoning–the king's brutal queen covered in dust and ash, walking towards him amongst the flames.

Montes doesn't appear betrayed or confused like I thought he would. It's desolation that I see in his eyes.

He's worked so hard for so long to keep me alive. All because that wretched heart of his loved me.

I have to draw on all the worst parts of me to keep my feet moving forward and my arm steady.

Perhaps Montes isn't guilty of all the depravity I initially attributed to him. It doesn't matter. Somewhere along the way, he lost his humanity. Whether or not he flicked that first domino and set events in motion no longer matters. We both have done too many unforgivable things. The blood on his hands, the blood on mine ... It's time for us to pay.

He rises to his feet, his eyes moving from my father's gun to my face. He drinks in my expression, his eyes pained.

"I knew you hated me when we met, Serenity," he says. "I knew you even hated me when I married you. But I never knew it ran this deep."

The blackened lump of coal that is my heart breaks.

Another thunderous boom tears through the hall. The ground shakes and the fire flickers.

For a second, Montes turns his head to the side, listening to the sound of his palace going up in flames. Everything he spent lifetimes building is being torn down before his eyes.

The soldier in me who fought for the WUN, the one who lost her family and nation to this man, she revels in the retribution. The rest of me simply weeps.

Montes's attention returns to me.

Had I thought before that he was majestic? Otherworldly? Now, even when he knows his empire is collapsing right in front of him and his wife has turned traitor, he looks untouchable. His shoulders are straight, his eyes still deep with secrets. That timeless face dares me to finish what I've begun.

"Do it." Montes walks forward, lifting his chin in defiance. "I'm tired of fighting. If you think this is right, then do it."

I taste smoke on my tongue. All around us, the king's mansion burns.

There is no happy ending for people like us.

Cold resolve takes over.

I cock the gun and point it at the king.

All those years ago my father told me a story about my name, my birthright. I was named Serenity for the peace I brought my mother. Peace has been the very thing my life has lacked. And my father told me long ago that in order to find peace, I had to forgive.

In front of me is the one man who has always stood between me and that.

A tear slides down my cheek, and then another.

After all this time and all the awful things we've done to each other, I finally, *truly* understand my father's words.

Montes. The Undying King of the East. My nightmare, my beautiful monster, my enemy and my soul mate.

I forgive him.

My throat tightens up.

This is what happens when you love and hate something.

I know what I have to do. I've always known.

"I love you, Montes," I say.

His eyes widen at my admission.

And then I make good on my age old vendetta—

I pull the trigger and kill the undying king.

CHAPTER 52

Serenity

THERE ARE MANY types of death.

There's the literal one, the one I am most familiar with. You stab a man in the chest and watch him bleed out. If you do it right, you will see his life and his soul slip out with all that blood.

But then there are other types of death. No one ever talks about those. The death of your identity. The death of your dreams. The death of your innocence.

I know all of death's pseudonyms, because he and I are very good friends. He's been my shadow since I was a child.

And he's here in this room with me and the king.

In an instant, the bullet cuts through skin, bone, and

finally muscle. Not just any muscle either. The most important one.

The heart.

To kill the king, I had to kill a part of myself. A hundred years ago he took my heart and never gave it back. Montes might be the only person who would want that rotted organ of mine.

He clutches his chest, his eyes wide with shock. The king staggers, and my lips begin to tremble as I hold back all the emotion that's welling inside me.

I holster my weapon, and grab the gun that I dropped earlier, clipping it back into place as well. And then I approach the king.

I walk amidst the flames to get to him. The most terrible thing in the world might be fire. That's why hell is always imagined as an inferno.

But fire doesn't just burn, it *transforms*. And here in this blazing building, as Montes's palace and his life fall to ashes, it's not the end. Of him. Of us. Of our efforts.

If you can survive the flames, what becomes of you?

The two of us are about to find out.

I hook my arms under the king's shoulders. His eyes have slid shut. I begin to drag him, forcing my muscles to move faster than they ever have.

The clock is ticking, and time is not my friend.

From the wings of the entryway, Marco steps out.

He must've seen the entire thing. His eyes are red, though I can't say whether it's from remorse or the burning smoke that hangs thick throughout this place.

"Let me help you," he says.

I shake my head, not slowing down in the least.

Tick-tock, tick-tock.

"Call the men we're rendezvousing with, then clear a path for me outside. I'll be heading out the back main entrance."

He hesitates.

"Now!" I bark.

That's all the encouragement he needs. He leaves my side, racing back down the long hallway, his form disappearing in the haze.

I begin to move in earnest, straining all my muscles to drag the king as quickly as possible.

I head to the nearest room, a room I requested Heinrich disable the cameras in. Up until now, the representatives have been watching a live feed of the king and me vis-à-vis the palace's security cameras.

That's about to change.

To the representatives, it will appear that the explosions took the system out. But it was deliberate.

Inside the room, five soldiers wait, a gurney at their feet. As soon as the door closes, they rush to help me, loading Montes onto the stretcher.

Beyond them, the mirror at the back of the room has already been shot out. Beyond it, I see the shadowy hall of the king's no-longer-secret passageways. I grab an edge of the gurney alongside the other soldiers, and together we step into the passageway.

And then we run.

Everything down to the last detail of this day has been carefully crafted to look spontaneous. Believable.

But it's all a lie.

The entryway, this guest room—all of it was picked for a specific reason. These were the closest rooms to my crypt. Marco doesn't know that, but I do, and so does Heinrich.

Still, there's a good twenty-five yards between us and my Sleeper and only so long that the human body can return from death unharmed.

Tick-tock. Tick-tock.

"Hurry!" I shout.

We pass through the double doors that lead to the subterranean room, and then we trip down the marble steps in a mad rush to get the king into the Sleeper. As we descend, the moat, the walkway, and then, finally, the golden Sleeper all come into view.

This should work.

I'm betting that it does.

I've learned quite a few things from the king, and one of them is gambling. I doubt the king ever imagined I'd take this to heart, or that he'd pay for it with his life.

The six of us make it down the stairs, and then our footsteps are pounding against the marble floor. The roof above us shivers with each muffled explosion. From what I've learned, this room was designed to survive an earthquake. Or an attack.

Heinrich waits for us next to the Sleeper, a scowl on his face. As soon as we get to him, the soldier and I hoist the king's body into the very Sleeper I lay inside for a hundred years.

And then the victim becomes the villain, and the villain the victim. The king and I have utterly swapped roles.

I only have a moment to stare down at him.

I hope I'll be able to gaze at his face again. I hope, but I doubt it.

The king's men hoist the Sleeper's lid back into place, and the machine flares to life. The readout of this one is on the back of the machine, hidden from view by a removable golden panel.

I go to read it, but Heinrich catches my arm and gives me a warning look. "You don't have time for this."

"I need to know that he's okay."

The grand marshal gives me a look that's scarily similar to the ones General Kline used to give me. "Your Majesty, you have a job to finish. Be strong, so that the men that have died today will not have done so in vain."

If I could, I would stay rooted here until I was positive the king was completely healed, but Heinrich's right.

I draw in a deep breath and nod.

"The body?" I ask.

"It's waiting for you in the passageways, just as we discussed."

I place a hand on the Sleeper. The machine will save my husband. I have to believe that. "Montes stays inside this until I return, or until … the alternative." I can't have him foiling me this far in.

"I will see you tomorrow, my queen."

I stare at the officer in the eyes. I don't think either of us actually believes that, but I incline my head anyway.

"Be safe my queen," he says.

The last thing I'll be is safe.

CHAPTER 53

Serenity

THE BODY I drag out of the palace is burned past the point of recognition. The mutilation is intentional since the body is not that of the king.

It's Marco. The original one.

I gave him the death he deserved. As much as I hated the man, I know in my heart of hearts this is how he would want his final death to go. His life for his friend's.

I glance back down at the body. Heinrich's men were really liberal with the lighter fluid.

This isn't going to work.

It can't possibly.

Soon after I exit the palace, I catch sight of Marco—the living one. He jogs up to me, unwittingly grabbing his double's legs and helping me carry him down the back steps.

Around us the palace still burns, and I can hear the sound of gunfire as the king's men fight the ground troops the WUN brought in as a distraction.

So many men will die today. I hope this will be the last bits of death that this war will claim.

"What took you so long?" Marco asks as we cross the gardens, winding our way around the elaborate hedges, some of which are on fire.

I give him a look that plainly says, *Are you fucking kidding me?*

"I'm dragging a grown man," I say.

He grunts, like I have a point.

We make our way to the beach, where a small group waits. Heinrich's men have been ordered to avoid attacking us unless it would appear suspicious not to. But they are legitimately preoccupied at the moment, so the need doesn't arise. Now we just have to avoid getting hit by stray bullets.

When Marco and I arrive on the sand, the WUN men close in on us. Amongst them is Styx Garcia, his scars even more prominent in person.

He stares at me with wonder. "The mythical queen in the flesh." He bows his head, but he can't quite tear his eyes from me. "An honor."

Yeah, whatever.

Some of the soldiers take the body from Marco and me and began to load it into the boat.

"What are you doing here?" I ask Styx. He hasn't

stopped staring at me.

"Meeting you in person, as promised. I am escorting you and the king's former right-hand," he gestures to Marco without looking at him, "to the West."

My gaze cuts to Marco, who's openly scowling at Styx.

"Alright," I say with a shrug, brushing past him to board the boat. This is where my control in the situation begins to unravel. If the West thought this was a decent idea, then I'll go along with it. And if I happen to kill the leader of the First Free Men en route, that's on them.

One of the WUN soldiers steps in front of me. "I'm sorry, Your Majesty," one of them says, "but we can't let you bring your weapons onboard."

I glance back at Marco, who shrugs. "It's their policy," he says as he divests himself of his weapons. They hit the shallow water we stand in with a splash.

I've been here before. I'm not leaving my father's gun.

"You're not taking my weapons, and I don't give a shit if you think this flies in the face of diplomacy."

"Your Majesty," one of the soldiers says, "the representatives—"

Fuck the representatives.

"I can walk right back into the palace, douse the flames, and continue to war with the West as the Queen of the East," I say. "You and I both know I have the backing of the people. So I suggest you let me take my damn guns and we get on with it."

They don't look like they're going to get on with anything.

"Let the queen have her weapons," Styx says, crowding

in close and covering my hand, which is resting on my holster, with his own.

I tighten my jaw. Those mad eyes of his bore into me, and they contain no little amount of heat.

I can feel Marco stiffening at my side, and I swear I'd say he was acting protective. *He was in love with a woman who looked just like me.* Of course he's being protective.

I shoulder past both of them, stepping onto the boat, and no one else tries to stop me.

Once we're all boarded, the motorboat cuts through the water, moving out into open water. This time, I don't get seasick, though I'm not surprised. At the moment I'm too hopped up on adrenaline and desensitized from the earlier attack to notice something like nausea.

"It is a strange thing," Styx says, looking over at the body. "The king is very badly burned, and yet you appear unharmed."

I expected this.

I raise an eyebrow. "It wouldn't be so strange if you'd been there."

Styx cocks his head. "Perhaps. Or perhaps our sleeping queen is now a scheming queen."

I lean back in my seat and squint up at the sun, ignoring the stares. "I guess we'll just have to find out, won't we?"

The tension on the boat ratchets up at my words.

"We will."

AT SOME POINT we exchange boat for helicopter, then helicopter for aircraft.

I'm pensive as I stare out the window. These might be the last hours of my life. I should savor them. Instead, I spend that time letting my mind drift, unwilling to let my thoughts settle on any one thing.

Marco sits at my side. Every several minutes, he glances over like he wants to talk. Each time he does, I tense. What could we possibly have to say to one another? He betrayed his friend, and I know he thinks I did as well.

"Garcia has been staring at you since we boarded," he finally says.

"I know," I say, not bothering to look away from the window.

Marco's voice lowers. "He's not a good man."

"I know," I repeat. These aren't epiphanies or anything.

Marco grabs my chin and forces me to look at him. "He's been married twice," he says, his voice low. "Both women bore strong resemblances to you. Both died mysteriously."

"What do you want me to do about it, Marco?" I hiss. "Now take your goddamned hand off of me."

Reluctantly, he releases my chin. "I can't protect you once we're in WUN territory."

"I didn't ask you to." I'm insulted he thinks I need protecting, and I'm even more annoyed that he thinks I'm ignorant about Styx's perversions. If there ever was a man who I should be immediately wary of, Styx would be it.

"Just be careful. He's going to come for you at some point. I want you to be ready."

I stare at him for several seconds. My eyes flick up to

Styx, who is indeed still watching me, and I nod.

I can already tell Styx is not someone to underestimate.

NOT AN HOUR after our conversation, the aircraft begins its descent.

The walled city comes into view. It looks even more magnificent as we circle it, the bright blue water of the Pacific nicely framing the city nestled in the coastal cliffs.

We touch down shortly after that, bouncing in our seats as the aircraft's tires skid down the runway.

We're here.

As soon as the engines die down, I stand. Resolve steals over me.

I will be the king's Trojan horse.

That's the promise I made all those years ago. To make it past the gates and wreak destruction from the inside out. But unlike Troy, there are no heroes here. Just killers and corpses.

I head down the aisle, and as I pass Styx, his head swivels to follow my movements. I can sense his excitement. Just like the representatives, I'm sure he thinks of me as nothing more than a war prize.

I am exactly that, and I will lead to the downfall of this nation.

CHAPTER 54

Serenity

ONCE WE EXIT the plane, Marco and I are taken in one direction, the body in another.

Dozens of guards escort us from the airfield. No one from the West mentions what's going on or where they're taking us. Half of me is sure we're being led straight to an execution. But then Marco and I are loaded into armored cars and driven up to the Iudicium, the domed building I'd so recently been in.

On either side of the street people crowd the sidewalks, cheering. Ever since my father and I entered Geneva, I've been on the losing side of those cheers.

Our car pulls up to the Iudicium, and Marco and I are unloaded from the vehicle and led inside. Rather than entering the circular courtroom, our guards steer us to an elevator.

We arrive on the third floor and then we're shuffled down a wing of the building. In the short time I've been here, no one's tried to take my weapons. I wonder how long that will last.

Eventually, the group of us halt in front of a solid wood door. I still have no idea what's going on.

Marco stops alongside me.

"Not you," one of the soldier's barks. "That's the former queen's room."

Former queen. The WUN is already taking efforts to strip me of my titles.

"I'm still Queen of the East, soldier." I say to the guard that spoke. "Do yourself and your leaders a favor and don't piss me off until after we have a signed peace agreement."

The guard dips his head and manages to bite out, "Apologies, Your Majesty."

Marco leans in. "Be careful," he whispers. I don't have time to get a good look at his face before he's led farther down the hall.

Five guards remain at my side, and while one of them is busy unlocking the door, another says, "The representatives would like to give you a chance to sleep before you meet with them. They give you their regards and look forward to speaking with you in person tomorrow."

The door to my room opens, and a luxurious guest suite waits for me on the other side. I assess it like one would a trap.

"Please," one of the guards says, gesturing for me to

enter.

I eye him, just to let him know I am no fool. I'm aware that as soon as the door closes behind me, I'll be locked in.

Knowing this doesn't change the fact that I'm supposed to at least attempt to go along with the West's schemes. So I step inside.

"We'll be posted outside your doorway and along the halls for your protection." *So don't try anything.*

"Tomorrow at eight a.m.," the soldier continues, "we will escort you to the representatives."

The soldier doesn't wait for my response. The door closes behind me. Just for the hell of it, I try the doorknob.

It doesn't budge.

Short of shooting my way out of this room, I'm trapped.

I BATHE, WASHING off the smoke and dust that seems as though it's embedded itself into my skin.

After I finish, I shake out my old clothes and put them back on. Briefly I eye the platter of cheeses and cold cuts someone's left out for me, along with a pitcher of water and an uncorked bottle of wine.

If only I trusted the representatives not to poison me. Instead I drink water from the tap. Even if the WUN's water supply doesn't filter out radiation, I'd rather take my chances with it than with these men.

I unholster my guns, and once I make sure the safety's off on both of them, I place the weapons under the pillows of the large bed that dominates the room. Most people that enter this walled city don't come out alive. If they come for me, I'm not dying without a fight.

Pulling back the covers, I slide into bed, combat boots and all. Just to be ready.

Now that I'm in bed, my body at rest, my mind only wants to return to one thing.

The king.

My throat closes up at the thought of him. I should've forced Heinrich to let me see the Sleeper's readout, I should've stayed longer to make sure Montes lived through his wound. I can't bear the thought of that powerful body of his devoid of life. Life that I snuffed out.

My chest tightens. He survived the gunshot. I *have* to believe that.

I cover my eyes with my hand. I shouldn't be worrying about the king when I'm currently sleeping in the lion's den. The odds of me escaping this place aren't good.

I fall asleep without realizing it, and when I wake, it's dark out. I'm disoriented before I remember. The bombs, the king whom I fatally shot, the flight over.

And now this.

The king's reckoning came yesterday. Mine will come today.

Grabbing my guns, I get up and sit at the window that faces out onto the street below. The city is dark beyond. Every so often I see a light glimmer from somewhere far off in the distance.

Even here in the WUN's capital, the world is bleak. I'd hoped that a century would be long enough for my homeland to get back on its feet, but obviously it wasn't.

I lean my head against the window. I should get back to bed; I need the sleep. But I can already tell it won't happen anytime soon. I'm too wired, and even if I wasn't, the West has a habit of snatching people up in the night.

So I watch and I wait.

I'm comfortable with this. There's a lot about war that is simply waiting. Waiting to kill. Waiting to die. Waiting, waiting, waiting.

Hours pass before I hear footsteps moving down the hall, straight towards my room.

I pull out one of my guns but don't bother aiming it. Not yet.

Is it Marco? A representative? My executioner?

My money is on this last one.

The door that's been locked since I entered now creaks open.

I wait as a shadow enters the room. It's big enough for me to know it's a man, probably a soldier on active duty.

I wait, studying the individual while they cross the floor and head towards my bed. Their eyes clearly haven't adjusted, or else they'd know I was no longer in it.

Now I point the gun.

"Were you planning on killing me in my sleep?" I rise to my feet slowly as I speak, gun still trained on my target.

"My queen."

Styx.

He's going to come for you at some point.

I step away from the window, my aim trained on Styx's chest. "Or were you simply going to rape me?"

Styx isn't like Montes. He might want me just as the

king did all those years ago, but at least then the king had struggled with the morality of the situation. This man hasn't. I sense that if he gets the chance, he'll assault me and he'll enjoy it.

Just knowing that has me putting pressure on the trigger.

"I came to talk," he says. I see his silhouette lean against the wall next to my bed.

"And that's why you knocked." If I shot this man now, how would that affect my meeting with the representatives? It's very, very tempting.

"I still can't believe you're real," he says in a hushed tone. "That you have a personality behind that face. I've wondered what you would be like. I didn't imagine this."

He takes a step forward, out of the shadows. The moonlight catches the contours of his face. It brings out his scars. He looks more monster than man.

"That's the last step you get," I say. "Move towards me again, and you're going to bleed."

He lifts his hands in the air, like that'll appease me. "I wanted to speak privately with you."

"There's no such thing as privacy here, Garcia."

"I don't want to talk about politics," he says.

That leaves personal affairs. "We have nothing else to talk about."

"Come now, my queen, we will be working closely together in the coming days, and you need friends in this world." He's the worst type of predator. I'm amazed that after everything he's seen of me, and after that sneaky entrance of his, he still thinks he can convince me to let down my guard.

"You think I've never come across men like you? You think I haven't *killed* men like you?" I say. "There are cemeteries of them beneath this earth."

"Are you trying to scare me?" He hasn't dropped his jovial act.

"My first victims were exactly like you. Big men who thought that they could take advantage of a little girl. They picked the wrong girl."

Attached to Garcia's side I can see the handle of a wicked knife. It's the kind of weapon that you used to subdue someone. Place it right next to their jugular and you'll get a person to cooperate real well.

I have no doubt he was going to use that on me.

"I don't know who you think I am," Styx says, starting to sound aggravated, "but I came here to get to know you. Nothing more."

"I don't want to know anything about you," I say, "and I sure as hell don't want you know anything about me."

In the moonlight, I see his expression tighten. Any minute now he's going to get violent. Fortunately for me, a bullet moves faster than a full grown man.

"Now," I say, "get the fuck out of my room, or I will shoot your dick off." I'm tempted to anyway. I have an unhealthy amount of violence for predators.

The seconds tick by, and he doesn't move. Just when I'm about to pull the trigger, the corner of his mouth lifts. "You will be fun to tame." His voice—hell, his entire demeanor—changes.

Shoot him, shoot him, shoot him, my heart chants.

I can't. Not yet, anyway.

My upper lip curls. "Get. Out."

He inclines his head. Still keeping his hands in the air, he backs up, towards the door. The barrel of my gun follows him. I know enough about men to know that this one is obscenely dangerous. Not the same way Montes is. Styx is not terribly strategic or calculating.

He's just evil.

"I'll see you in a few hours," he says when he reaches for the knob. "Sleep well."

As soon as he leaves the room, I sag against the window.

That was far too close a call.

IT'S ONLY ONCE the sun peaks out from between the mountains that someone else comes for me.

These footfalls are not quiet, which is a relief. If Styx Garcia came for me again, I wouldn't give him the benefit of the doubt.

The door to my room opens, and I see a familiar face. Chief Officer Collins stands with a group of soldiers out in the hallway.

"It's good to see you again, Your Majesty," Collins says by way of greeting.

The feeling isn't mutual.

He and the soldiers march me to the Iudicium's main room, the same place where, only weeks ago, I agreed to kill the king.

Twelve representatives wait for me. I bite back my disappointment when I see that thirteenth seat once again unoccupied.

My plan hinged on having all thirteen representatives gathered in a single room.

When I'd plotted with Heinrich, I'd been so sure the cocky SOBs would finally unveil their elusive thirteenth representative.

I stare up at them, no longer in shackles like I was last time, but it doesn't take handcuffs to be someone's prisoner. How stupid they must think I am to get myself in this situation.

"You decided to come into the West armed." Tito is the first to speak, his bulging eyes staring at my firearms.

"And you decided to lock the Queen of the East in a guestroom," I say. I glance at the several guards that still surround me. "I was brought here under the assumption that we were going to discuss a peace treaty between our two hemispheres as allies would."

"Yes, we will discuss the treaty momentarily," Alan says. "Please," he gestures to the benches that face them, "be seated."

"I prefer to stand." My eyes move over the representatives. "What, exactly, is the hold up?"

"We're waiting for the bloodwork and dental records to come back," Alan says.

I stare stoically at him.

He leans forward. "You didn't think we were just going to assume the body you gave us was the king's, did you?"

I don't respond.

"Once it all checks out," Alan continues, "we will begin negotiations."

Not five minutes later, someone knocks on the double doors at my back.

"Ah," Alan says, "that should be the medical examiner. Let him in, let him in."

I can feel Ronaldo's eyes on me. "Troy," the traitor-turned-representative says to one of his soldiers, "keep a bead on the queen. If the results don't match the king, please shoot her where she stands."

A soldier to my right removes his gun from its holster, the barrel of it pointed at my temple.

My situation settles over my shoulders.

I'm not leaving here alive. And now all I can think about is my monstrous king.

He's going to wake up and I'm going to be dead, and I can't guarantee that the world will survive it.

A man in a lab coat strides down the aisle, stopping just a few feet away from me.

"The results?" one of representatives inquires.

The man's eyes slide to me, then back to the line of men sitting above us.

"It checks out. The body is that of Montes Lazuli."

CHAPTER 55

Serenity

IT TAKES A moment to register.

The DNA matches?

Impossible.

Is the man lying? That's the most obvious possibility.

The soldier to my right lowers his weapon.

"Do you swear before God and men that this is the truth?" Ronaldo asks the medical examiner. I can tell he's hoping it isn't.

"I do," the medical examiner says. "My technicians can verify it. The remains belong to the former king."

The representatives look almost disappointed.

The remains are the king's.

"It seems our suspicions were misplaced," one of them

says to me. "Our apologies. Surely you understand ..."

The king is ... dead?

I give no sign of it, but my fallen heart is falling apart. It fell for a fallen king amongst the ruins of this fallen world. And all of that has now fallen into the hands of these men.

No, I refuse to believe that. There was a mix up of some sort. The king can't be dead. Otherwise, these men win, and they don't get to win. That is not how this world ends.

The double doors swing open again.

I swivel to see who's entered this time.

Styx Garcia strides down the aisle behind us, his eyes devouring me.

I fight the urge to touch my gun.

What's he doing here?

This is not going according to plan.

"You're late," one of the representatives says.

"I couldn't fall asleep." He stares at me proprietarily. "Jet lag."

I watch him with narrowed eyes as he passes me and heads back behind the representatives, taking the final, empty seat.

I don't breathe.

Styx Garcia is the thirteenth representative.

"YOU'RE SURPRISED," STYX notes, scooting his chair in.

I don't bother denying it.

He leans forward. "How do you think I managed to find you in the first place?"

"The First Free Men?" Did the group even exist, or was it just an elaborate ruse meant to throw off the East?

"A real organization that I also run. Convenient when the West needs mercenaries to get a job done without any of the messy political ties."

Removing me from the Sleeper had been one of those jobs.

"My queen, I will admit, I didn't think you had it in you to kill the king," Styx says, changing the subject. "You're a more dangerous woman than even I gave you credit for."

I'm going to die. I can sense it.

"We are in a quandary, Serenity," Ronaldo interjects. "We could just kill you—that would be the easiest.

"But that still leaves the problem of swaying public opinion. It seems they like you.

"Fortunately, Styx here has a solution."

The representative in question leans back in his chair, his sick eyes on me.

You will be fun to tame.

He doesn't even have to say what the solution is.

We will be working closely together in the coming days.

My anger feasts on the indignity of their proposal. I've already been given once to a man. That will never happen again.

I'm done with the deception.

I let them see my empty, empty eyes. Killer's eyes.

In the distance, I hear a muffled sound. The ground shivers then resettles.

I am chaos. I am the undoing of man. And all the world will fall to my feet.

That's what this feels like. That's what everything since my awakening feels like. And today it ends.

CHAPTER 56

Serenity

I SEE THE first stirrings of unease. The representatives didn't really think it was going to be that easy did they?

How do you take down the West? You gather all thirteen representatives together. How do you gather thirteen representatives together?

You make them believe they've won.

More vibrations follow the first.

"I've been a thorn in a lot of men's sides for quite a while," I say. "You know the problem with my existence? I've always been just useful enough to keep alive."

Ronaldo stands. "Guards–"

"Your time is over." I speak over him. "Those pretty walls of yours are coming down."

"Seize her!"

I smile viciously as the adrenaline begins to move through me.

High above us, the glass dome explodes. That's my cue that the clock's begun. Heinrich is going to blow this place up, and if I don't escape in the next fifteen minutes, I'll get blown up along with it.

The representatives and guards shield their heads as shards of glass rain down on us. From beyond the opening, the king's soldiers begin to rappel down.

I use the distraction to unholster the gun.

And then I fire.

I go for the armed guards nearest me first. The gunshots echo throughout the room as my aim moves from one temple to the next. Troy doesn't even have time to react before my bullet lodges itself in his temple, his blood splattering against the bench directly in front of Ronaldo.

The traitorous former advisor now stares at the blood in shock. His eyes move from it to me. The barrel of my gun is trained on his forehead.

He was a marked man the moment he turned on the king.

I pull the trigger.

Ronaldo's head whips back as my bullet catches him between the eyes. His body collapses half-on, half-off his chair.

Outside, distant gunshots echo my own.

The Western soldiers around me are now recovering, but even as they reach for their weapons, the king's men are dropping to the ground and firing at the enemy soldiers and representatives.

Collins takes a bullet to the gut, as does the medical examiner. Alan's body seems to dance as he's pumped full of bullets.

Many of the other WUN commanders duck behind their desks. What big men they are now that they can't control their enemies.

I round the bench, gun aimed. It's like fish in a barrel; the representatives are all lined up, some of them reaching for weapons they've stashed near their seats.

I shoot Gregory and Jeremy in the head, the two men responsible for human trafficking and concentration camps, and they die where they stand.

At the end of the row, Styx stands, gun in hand, a dark look on his face as he stares out at the room.

I train my gun on his forehead. This is a kill I'm going to enjoy.

As if sensing my attention, he turns.

And smiles.

A split second later a large body rams into my backside, tackling me to the ground. I grunt as the soldier pins me down.

"Drop your weapon," the man on top of me says.

When I don't immediately comply, he grabs my hand and slams it repeatedly into the ground until I release the gun.

Styx heads down the bench, shooting soldiers as he moves. I see the king's men go down.

"*Get up!*" Styx shouts to some of the representatives he passes, kicking one as he goes.

A couple of the men do shakily stand. A few others remain crouched.

Amongst the madness, Styx levels his gaze on me.

He lifts his gun, the barrel focused somewhere between my chest and that of the guard pinning me down.

Styx and I stare at each other, and I can tell he's having an internal debate about what to do with me.

Before he comes to a decision, I hear the familiar clank of heavy metal right outside the doors.

I close my eyes and breathe out. Saved by a freaking grena—

BOOM!

The blast unbalances my captor and he releases my wrists to stabilize himself.

This might be the only opening I'll get.

I reach for my discarded gun. My fingers lock on the cold metal, and I point it at the guard's face. He only has time to widen his eyes before I pull the trigger.

His blood splatters down on me, his body collapsing on mine.

I grunt as I force his dead weight off of me. Styx slips between fighting men, heading for a side exit.

He's getting away!

I can't let that happen. All thirteen men must be either captured or killed, otherwise, today will have been for nothing.

I've barely gotten my feet under me when I stare down another gun.

Tito, Montes's traitorous former advisor, trains his weapon on my chest. Sweat dips down his ruddy face. His hand trembles just the slightest.

"You better aim for the head," I say, rising slowly. "You don't want me coming back."

But it's not my head that gets blown away.

One moment Tito's bulgy eyes are glaring at me. The next, they're gone, along with a good portion of his face.

I follow the bullet's trajectory back to its owner.

My knees almost give out.

Impossible.

Standing just inside the threshold of the room is the very man I shot through the heart.

The love of my fucked-up life.

Montes Lazuli, the truly undying king.

The King

SHE'S WAR AND peace and love and hate. She's my death and my salvation, and right now, standing amongst all these massacred bodies, she's staring at me like I'm the mythic one.

"Montes?" Her voice shakes. Uncertainty is an endearing emotion on my wife.

"You're shit at keeping secrets, my queen," I say.

Finally I can speak on this subject.

And finally I can breathe easy, knowing Serenity's alright.

Bloody, but alright.

Her mouth is slightly parted, and her brows are furrowed. I know my queen well enough to know she's trying to piece together what she feels is an impossible series of events.

One of the representatives nearest her moves, and she shoots him without question.

Deadly, savage woman.

I make my way towards her, shooting anyone I don't recognize. Already my men have taken out most of the enemy soldiers and representatives in here.

Now I just need to get to my wife. My scheming, violent wife who concocted this elaborate, *foolhardy* plan so that war could end and I could live.

Even after everything I put her through, she did this for me. It is without a doubt the single greatest show of love I've ever received.

Which makes me all the more frantic to keep her safe.

I feel Marco at my back, covering for me.

The three leaders left standing now balk at the two of us.

Marco never was the West's mole, he was a double agent working for me.

Serenity sees Marco as well, and she appears equally confused. But quickly her gaze returns to me, her eyes dropping to my heart.

In my peripherals, I see the last of the West's representatives and their royal guard go down. I breathe a little easier as I step up to Serenity.

"How?" she asks.

I whisper in her ear, "I surround myself with loyal men."

Loyal men, and loyal women.

All of my elaborate plans, all of my late nights, all of the details I worked hours on ironing out. Montes had known, and he'd kept it from me.

I want to be angry, but my heart's not letting me have my moment of indignation. It's far too happy that the king is alive. Alive and … not all that upset himself, considering that I shot him.

"How long have you known?" I ask. There had been nights where he gazed at me with such sad eyes, and I could've sworn he'd seen right through me.

He stays quiet.

"How long?" I repeat.

"Serenity, you are not that good at being subtle."

Goddamnit, had he known the whole time?

Around us, the gunfire has ceased, and the only ones left standing are the king's men.

"And you just let me go along with my plan?"

Montes's eyes are stormy. "It was … *difficult*. All the details were so very reckless. And I wasn't looking forward to getting shot. But yes."

My eyes dip to his heart. Tentatively, I place a hand on his chest. I feel the organ thump beneath my palm. "Your gunshot wound?" An injury like that should've left him in the Sleeper for a week.

He covers my hand with his own. "I wore a bullet proof vest."

I tilt my head up to him. "But there was blood."

"It isn't hard to rig a blood bag to my outfit. You yourself managed to get ahold of an entire body."

The wrong body.

His body. The second impossible detail about this situation. "The bloodwork, the dental records—they said it was you."

"It *was* me."

I furrow my brows.

"I didn't just clone you and Marco."

The full force of what he's saying hits me. That single Sleeper I wasn't authorized to view. It had housed his double.

"You killed your clone?"

Smoke curls around Montes. He looks for all the world like some terrible deity come to feast on the violence. Only, he's here to save me, to avenge me.

He gives me an indulgent look. "You've killed dozens and dozens of men and you're worried that I killed my twin? My queen, you are a strange creature. But to answer your question, the body was braindead to begin with. I didn't want to chance another version of me ever getting loose."

That was something we could agree upon.

He continues. "I'd planned on faking my death for some time—"

BOOM!

I'm nearly thrown off my feet as the explosion rocks the ground, the sound of it deafening. Montes grabs my arm, bracing me.

The roof above us groans sickeningly, and more glass

shards rain down on us.

I glance at the king.

"Is Heinrich still planning on bombing—?"

Montes nods sharply. "We need to go."

CHAPTER 57

Serenity

THE TWO OF us dash out to the front of the building, the hot breath of air from the blasts whipping my hair about. From here we have a panoramic view of the walled city.

There are fires everywhere, and people are running, panicking.

More bombs go off, one right after another. I see chunks of the seaside buildings blown out from the side of the mountain. A few of them are blasted so far out I see them hit the water.

As I watch, one of the walls circling the city goes down with a thunderous boom. A plume of dirt and debris billow up into the air.

Troy indeed.

I'm breathing heavily, all but ready to cease fighting, when I remember.

The regional leaders and their children. They might be in the dungeons below the building.

My pulse accelerates. Oh God, they're trapped.

I begin to back up.

Montes looks over at me, a warning in his eyes when he sees what I'm doing. "Serenity–"

"The prisoners–they're below the building." I can't even fathom how close I came to forgetting, swept up in the action as I had been.

"Call Heinrich, tell him to hold fire."

I don't wait for Montes to respond. I swivel on my heel, dashing back the way I came, drawn back to the dungeons below the building.

The king curses, and I hear *martyr* amongst the oaths.

I don't care what he thinks. There are children down there.

I head back through the main entryway, hopping over dead bodies. The king isn't at my back, so I take it he's getting ahold of Heinrich rather than chasing after me.

Ignoring the elevator, which could be out of commission, I storm down the stairs, descending deeper and deeper into the earth.

I ignore the prickly sensation that breaks out along my skin as I feel the walls press in on me. My boots echo as they slap against the ground.

When I see royal detention center stamped over one of the levels I descend to, I exit out the nearest doorway.

The light from the stairwell pours out onto the dungeon's floor. Beyond it, lightbulbs are spaced thirty feet apart.

I slow, my boots echoing. I try not to shiver as I head farther into the wet, subterranean chamber. This chill never gets any easier to bear.

I move down the first row of cells. There are at least three more rows, and several more floors. I'd better hope the king gets ahold of Heinrich soon, or else I'm a dead woman.

A pebble skitters in the distance.

I readjust my grip on my gun. "Hello?"

My voice echoes. I hear whispers in the distance, then silence.

"My name is Serenity Lazuli. I'm here to help."

"Serenity?" someone calls out weakly.

I jog towards the voice, which is one row over.

The family is in a cell at the far end of the row, where the shadows seem deepest. A man, a woman, and two children huddle in the corner of it.

The regional leader of Kabul and her family.

"Nadia, Malik?" I ask them.

Nadia nods her head jerkily.

"I'm going to get you all out of here." My eyes drop to the lock. It and the rest of the cage is made out of iron.

"Back up," I say, lifting my gun. This is no safe extraction, but I'm out of options.

I fire off two shots before the lock splits open.

For once, this feels like the right thing, saving instead of killing.

I swing open the cell door, and the family files out.

Malik clasps my hand in his. "Thank you, thank you." His whisper is hoarse. I don't want to imagine what these four have been through since they got here.

I nod to them. "Go to the end of this hall and up the stairs as quickly as you can. I have to get the rest of the prisoners out." I pause. "There are other missing regional leaders. Do you know anything about their whereabouts?"

"They're not on this floor," Nadia says. "We were it."

That's good to know.

We separate at the stairwell, Nadia and her family going up while I continue downwards.

I only just exit the stairwell when I hear sobs, coming from somewhere deep within.

"Hello?" I call out, striding down the first row.

The crying cuts off, but the prisoner doesn't respond.

I tense when I hear footfalls behind me.

"I knew I would find you here," a familiar voice says.

I turn.

Styx Garcia stands between me and the only exit out of here. He holds a gun, its barrel trained on my forehead.

I don't know why the terrible ones always fixate on me. I suppose they think I'm a challenge. But I'm not.

I'm just death.

I adjust the grip on my own weapon. I have no idea how many bullets—if any—I have left.

"You fool," I say. "You should've never come back for me."

"You know why I like you?" he says, his eyes unnaturally bright in the dim light. "Because even when you're cornered and held at gunpoint, you still have this confidence.

I'm sure if I stripped you, I'd find a pair of brass balls between those pretty little legs."

I begin to lift my weapon.

"Ah-ah," he says, cocking his gun. "Lift that thing any higher, and I will blow your face away."

I don't believe he'll shoot me in the head. I've seen too much of this man's fucked-up interest in me to think he'd give me the easy way out. He wants me alive.

At least, for a time.

"... And if you're dead, then who will free these prisoners?"

I lower my weapon back down.

"Good girl," he says, and it's so damn patronizing. "Now drop the weapon."

My jaw tightens, but I don't release the gun.

He takes a step forward, and my hand twitches. If he gets much closer, I will risk death to bury a bullet in that scarred flesh of his.

"Drop it," he repeats.

"You're a dead man, Styx," I say. "You'll never leave this place alive."

The corner of his mouth lifts.

The gunshot echoes down the cellblock.

I grunt and stagger back as the bullet hits my upper arm. I feel it enter, feel it rip through sinew, then exit out the other side. My gun arm.

My other hand goes to it just as the blood begins to pour out of the wound. I hiss out a breath at the pain.

"You should worry about your own life, my queen." He says my title like an endearment. Considering he just shot me, he's doing himself no favors.

Styx heads down the cellblock, towards me. "Ever since I was little, I heard about the great Serenity Freeman, a child of the West, sacrificed for the lusts of the East." His eyes are far too bright as he speaks. There's more than just a touch of madness in them. "I saw the footage of you bathed in blood. I saw your horror and your violence. I saw your sacrifice. It made me want to be a soldier.

"And that *scar*." He lifts his gun and drags the barrel of it down his cheek, tracing the phantom path of my scar as he stares at it.

I'm beginning to sweat from the pain, and the cold subterranean air is only getting colder with the blood loss. It drips between my fingers and down my wrist onto the dank ground.

"It was inspiring," he continues. "The strong carry scars."

I had imagined Garcia dangerous before, when I first saw his mutilated face. But now there's the extra knowledge that his scars might've been inspired by mine.

I begin to lift my injured arm again, the handle of my gun slick with blood.

"You aim that weapon and I will shoot you again."

"Fuck you," I say.

He closes the last of the space between us. "I won't kill you," he says softly, confirming my earlier thoughts. He studies me for a moment, and then his gaze drops to my injury.

He presses his gun into my wound. "But you might wish I had by the end of it all."

I stagger back, but now he grabs me with his other hand, keeping me rooted in place.

I try to jerk away from him as the barrel of his gun digs into the ragged flesh. My jaw clenches through the pain, and my nostrils flare.

"The representatives are gone, aren't they? All but me. That makes me the sole ruler of the West."

He presses harder, watching me the entire time. He's so busy keeping eye contact that he doesn't notice me lifting my gun. This evil, crazed man. He's so lost in my pain that he's not paying attention to things he should.

"How would you like to be my queen?"

The edges of my vision darken.

Aiming for his groin, I pull the trigger.

Click.

Fuck. Whatever ammunition I had, it's now gone.

The sound breaks Styx from his trance. He glances down at my gun, aimed at him. His grip tightens as he realizes I meant to kill him.

I pull my head back, then jerk it forward, head-butting him.

He releases his hold on me and staggers back, placing a hand to his forehead.

I follow him, reaching for my father's gun. This ends now.

My fingers barely skim the handle when Styx lifts his gun and shoots at my holster.

I jerk back in surprise as the bullet whizzes past my hand, only just missing it.

Styx storms forward, gun now trained on my chest, his

expression murderous. “And I thought we were finally coming to an understanding, my queen.”

He yanks my father’s gun from its holster and tosses it aside.

I know he’s about to hit me. I can see how badly he wants to pull his hand back and pistol whip me. My muscles tense.

But he doesn’t hit me, and I get a glimpse of how he’s managed to gain this much power. For a psycho, he has a good measure of control.

Instead, he presses the barrel against my temple. “Where were we?”

I stare unflinchingly back at him. I think he wants me to be scared, but he’s picked the wrong girl to try to frighten. I don’t fear men like him.

I hunt men like him.

“Ah, yes, I remember,” he says. “You could be my queen, but only–if–you–behave.” He punctuates the last words by tapping the barrel his gun against my temple.

I glare at him as the blood that still coats the end of his weapon now smears against my skin.

He drags the barrel down, further smearing my blood across my face. He draws it over my cheekbone and across my mouth.

Then he pauses.

He taps my teeth with his weapon. “Are you going to behave?”

“Fuck. You.”

He smiles. “Dear, sweet Serenity, let me rephrase: you will behave, or I’ll start giving you more scars.” He leans in close. "And I will make them very, very distincti–"

The gunshot takes us both by surprise.

Styx and I stare at each other, and I have no idea how I look, but the thirteenth representative appears shocked. He glances down between the two of us.

There's nothing. No bullet holes. No blood. No pain.

But then Styx staggers forward, his body slumping against mine. And I realize, there is blood, it's just not mine.

I disarm Styx easily enough, and then I'm holding both his upper body and his gun with my good arm. Behind him I see a man, who's nothing more than a shadow against the light spilling down into the prison from the stairwell.

But I know who it is. I would recognize that silhouette anywhere.

Montes prowls forward slowly.

"*No one* threatens my queen."

The king's voice is poison-laced wine. It's the same voice that asked me to dance in a gilded ballroom over a hundred years ago. It's the same voice that broke the world.

The voice that shattered my heart before he claimed it.

His shoes click against the cobblestone floor, his gun still smoking as he approaches us.

I release Styx, whose body slides out of my arms. The thirteenth representative groans as he hits the ground.

"For months I had to listen to you disrespect my queen."

Shit. It *had* been months.

He stops at Styx's feet. Using a booted foot, he forces

the injured man onto his back. A line of blood trickles out of Styx's mouth, and his breathing is labored.

Punctured lung. I've heard the sound enough times.

"And you thought you could just take her?" Montes continues. "From me?"

This is out of my hands. The king has few demons left, but the ones that survived his transformation–those, he's about to feed.

Montes steps up to me. His face goes grim when he sees my wound. "Are you okay?"

I run my tongue over my teeth, then nod.

He pulls me to him and kisses my forehead. He doesn't chastise me for running down here. I think Montes knows exactly how to fan the flames of my love.

When he lets me go, the atmosphere in the dungeon changes to something dark and violent.

The devil has come to feast.

Montes towers over Styx. "I was ready to torture you before, but now ..." He crouches down. "I could hurt you, then heal you, then hurt you some more. On and on until I die." He pauses. "I've lived for a century and a half. I could make you immortal, only so that you'd live lifetimes of torture."

What Montes is suggesting is beyond horrific.

Styx's gaze moves to me, and for once I actually see fear on his face. He never believed he was going to lose his power. And now he's facing a man and a fate that might be worse than death.

The king aims his weapon. "We could start now."

"Please–"

The gunshot cuts Styx's plea short.

The representative's body goes still, and I realize that sometimes Montes's empty threats are not just lobbed at me. The fresh bullet hole carved between the Styx's eyes is proof of that.

And that's how the thirteenth and final representative falls.

WE FREE THE rest of the prisoners, and then there's the gruesome task of carting Styx's body topside, where twelve others are already laid out.

Only then do the West's soldiers believe leadership has fallen. And only then does the military cease fire.

As soon as Montes and I are well out of range, Heinrich lights up the Iudicium.

Now, an hour later, the building the representatives reigned in is nothing more than a pile of stone and ash.

It probably wasn't necessary, but I'd insisted on it. I didn't want that monument, where so many evil men gathered, to remain standing.

I lean against one of the West's military vehicles that's long since been abandoned. Montes has fished out a first aid kit from inside it, and now he bends over my upper arm, bracing it with one hand and cleaning my wound with the other.

I keep jerking away from him every time he wipes the antiseptic over it.

"This would all be over with much sooner if you let a proper medic tend to you," the king says conversationally.

I refused any other type of medical care. The bullet had just skimmed my skin; it was nothing more than a flesh wound.

"I don't want a proper medic. I want you." I won't lie, I'm enjoying my husband taking care of me.

Montes dips his head back towards his work, but not before I catch the edge of a smile. I think he's enjoying taking care of me too.

"You know," he says, grabbing a roll of gauze, "it was all intentional."

I furrow my brows, not understanding.

"How and when you woke up," he clarifies.

Now he has my full attention.

"After Trinity died, Marco did want revenge."

My eyes move to the king's right-hand. He's busy discussing something with the cameramen who are setting up a stage and a screen.

"He spent decades gaining the West's trust, then decades more solidifying that trust. He leaked information approved by me. It benefitted me to have Marco feed them certain select pieces of classified information because in return, I learned of their plans.

"I created my double around that time," Montes says, "thinking that ultimately I'd need to fake my death. That was also when I began making plans to wake you.

"I didn't want to expose you to this world," he says.

My mouth tightens.

"I was afraid that after all that waiting, you'd still just be killed like Trinity," he continues. "I couldn't bear that possibility. But you needed to wake up and the war needed to end and those two things were appearing more and more mutually inclusive."

Montes finishes wrapping my wound, tying off the gauze.

"So eventually," he continues, "I let Marco pass along information on your resting place. And thus set in motion all that has happened."

He had woken me. It took him years to wait for the right moment, but that's exactly what he did.

You know the thing about strategy? he said all those years ago. *It takes knowing when to act and when to be patient.*

What he's saying reframes everything.

He'd been planning an end to war for a very long time. "How could you have possibly known what was to come?" I ask.

"I discovered what you did—that the key to winning the West was taking out the representatives. And only victory would do that.

"I never imagined sending you in—it was always going to be Marco—but then you made a deal with the representatives and I couldn't undo the situation—short of calling the whole thing off. Much as I wanted to do that, I had faith in you."

My throat works. There aren't any words that can convey everything I feel, so I wrap my hand around my monster's neck and kiss him instead.

He believed in me enough to put both our lives on the line. Enough to ignore his controlling nature and his obsessive need to shelter me. I can think of no greater show of love from this man.

ONCE I'M PATCHED up, the king and I gather at the city's central square, the same place I stood at only weeks ago. Like then, cameras hone in on me. A microphone rests in front of us.

I know I am a sight—bloodied, dirty, tired. The king, for all his unearthliness, looks little better.

My eyes move over the city.

Much of it lays in ruins, the buildings smoldering, the wall encircling it little more than rubble.

I wish I could say that everyone who stared back at me was happy, that this felt like some great milestone for them, but the truth is that this city was home to many people, and now there's nothing but destruction here.

There are many people beyond this city who won't be pleased, and there will be many more who won't know how to react.

But then there are the multitudes that will be freed from work camps and multitudes more living on the edge of survival who will now begin to receive aid. The neglected cities of the West might finally, finally know peace.

But beyond that, there is one thing that can bridge everyone that lives in this time.

I lean into the microphone. "Citizens of the world: the war is over."

CHAPTER 58

Serenity

My gunshot wound takes an agonizing month to heal. It's the first serious injury since I met the king that's healed without the aid of the Sleeper.

I insisted on it. He acquiesced.

I think we're finally getting somewhere.

He kisses it now, his lips running over the scar, his hands sliding up my sides.

The scar that cuts down my face I'd always thought of as a permanent tear for the lives this war took. I wear this latest one with pride, because it marks the day it ended. For good.

Even as the king and I sit out here in the sand yards away from one of his island homes, the surf crashing close to our toes, my mind is pulled to the future.

We only get one more day before we head off to the Western hemisphere and begin the toiling task of rebuilding this broken world.

I'm starting with medical relief and efforts to clean any remaining radiation from the earth and groundwater, the very things that a long time ago the king tried to deny my people. Then will come subsistence, much of it government-subsidized.

Montes is not too thrilled about this last one, but I still sleep with my gun, and he's a smart enough man.

True infrastructure will eventually be put back in place. Continents, regions, cities—they all need local leadership. The end of the war marks the beginning of the arduous task of rebuilding the governments the world lost long ago.

The king smooths my brow, tiny granules of sand sprinkling down my forehead and nose as he does so.

"I can tell you're going to be a bigger workaholic than I am," he says.

His face is cast in shades of blue from the moon above. I cup it, letting my thumb stroke the rough skin of his cheek.

Montes's gaze turns heated. "Say it."

The heart is such a vulnerable thing. Encased beneath skin and muscle and bone, you think it wouldn't be. But it is. Even ours.

I still have to grapple with the words; I drag them out kicking and screaming.

"I love you," I say.

Montes closes his eyes.

"Again," he says.

I'm not sure how many times he's heard these words in his lifetime. I imagine whatever the number, it's far smaller than the amount he needed to hear them.

We have plenty of time to rectify that.

"I love you," I say.

Plenty of time, but not forever.

I won't take the king's pills, and I've asked him stop taking them as well. I don't know if he has, but I haven't seen the pill bottles around.

People aren't meant to live as long as us. And people aren't meant to experience the horrors we have.

Bloodshed, death, hate—I used to wake every morning to this. It's actually quite odd not to. Perhaps that's why I've thrown myself into my work, so that I don't forget.

High overhead I catch a glimpse of the stars.

I'd always imagined the dead resided in the heavens, and here and now I feel both closer and farther from them than ever before.

My eyes search the night sky, looking for one constellation in particular. I smile when I find it.

The Pleiades, the wishing stars. I hear an echo of my mother's voice even now, pointing them out to me.

The king rolls onto his side, placing a hand on my abdomen. He follows my gaze up to the star cluster.

"Have you ever heard the story of the lost Pleiad?" Montes's fingers are gathering the material of my shirt, lifting it as he talks.

I narrow my gaze on him. "If you're about to lie to me

…"

Montes has developed a bad habit of teasing me. Apparently I'm gullible. Considering, however, I'm also violent, he never takes it too far.

He laughs. "*Nire bihotza*, I'm not. This is *true*. Apparently there are seven stars—Seven Sisters—but you can only see six of them in the night sky. The seventh is 'lost'."

We're both quiet for a moment while I ponder his words. The night air stirs my hair. Mine and the king's.

He leans in close to my ear. "It's because I caught her," he whispers.

My eyes return to the constellation.

"Make a wish," I whisper.

He stares at me for several seconds, then softly says, "I don't need to anymore."

Montes is no good man, and I am no good woman. We grapple day in and day out with our demons. Long ago, I married a monster, and the king's war made one out of me. And all our terrible edges fit together, and together we've become something else, something better.

The world is at peace, and for once, so am I.

After all this time, I finally found serenity.

EPILOGUE

5 years later

The King

I FLIP OVER and stare down at my queen. Often I wake early—a habit I've developed over the decades. I used to spend those early hours working, squeezing another hour in if I could. It used to fuel me when I needed a distraction from my lonely life.

Now I tend to use the time to marvel over the fact that this *is* my life. After all the turmoil, all the violence and poor decisions, somehow the wrongs were made right.

Serenity made them right.

I run a hand over the swollen slope of her stomach. This is something else to marvel over.

Only a few more weeks. It's just simply not possible to be this excited.

Or this petrified. Or this protective.

I'll be a father for the first time at the ripe age of 174. I can barely fathom it.

"Mmmm." Serenity stretches beneath my touch.

"*Nire bihotza*, today's a big day for you," I whisper.

Her eyes snap open. "Shit."

She sits up, her gaze moving to the windows. The sun is just rising. "What time is it? Did the alarm not go off?"

"Ssssh. It's still early. Go back to sleep." She hasn't gotten enough of it. I don't believe being eight months pregnant is particularly comfortable.

Instead of going back to sleep, her hand lazily combs through my hair. Then it freezes. She leans forward and peers at my hair more closely.

"You have a gray hair." She says this wondrously.

My grip on her tightens just a fraction as I nod. I'd noticed it a week ago. This is also something that petrifies me.

I know Serenity's wanted me to stop taking my pills for a while now. At first I couldn't—old habits die hard and all that. And then one day I woke up and realized that I wanted to get old with this woman. I wanted our skin to sag together and our faces to wear wrinkles together the same way Serenity currently wears her scars.

So I stopped.

"I'm surprised I haven't gotten any sooner," I say, "considering who I'm married to."

She swats me. "You should just be thankful I've stopped sleeping with my gun."

I roll over her. "Oh, I am."

And then I decide she doesn't need sleep nearly as much as she needs me.

Serenity

TODAY I WEAR my hated crown.

One final time.

Five hundred men and women gather in the room before me and the king, regional leaders from all over the world.

It took Montes nearly a hundred and fifty years to conquer the world. It took me only five to give it back.

"Today marks a turning point," I say to the group spread out before me in the auditorium.

From this day forward, our world won't be ruled by monarchs. The road ends here. With us.

I remove the crown from my head. Next to me, Montes mirrors my movements. I would've thought he'd fight this more, but the man is weary of ruling. At last.

I don't spare the headpiece more than a passing glance.

"Today we hand the world over to you."

There will be a single government made up of regional leaders appointed from each territory. All will work and vote together on issues that afflict the world.

Like every government that came before it, this one won't be perfect—it could even be a disaster. Only time will tell.

I look over at Montes. My beautiful monster.

I wasn't looking for redemption in this man—or from

him, for that matter. But that's what I got.

I return my attention to the hundreds gathered in this room.

There's a place for me here, in this future I never expected to be a part of. I no longer straddle two hemispheres and two time periods. Instead, I am the woman that loves both the West and the East, the woman that will always fight for the blighted and broken, the impoverished and the oppressed. I'm the woman that came from the past to help the future.

I'm no longer the loneliest girl the world, the woman who fits in nowhere.

Now I'm the woman who fits in everywhere, and I'm the woman that believes in freedom and justice, and above all–

Hope.

TO MY READERS

To say I am sad to leave this world and these characters is an epic understatement. I'm not sure I've enjoyed writing a series quite as much as this one. And the things it made me feel! I hope I'm not alone in that.

Everything about these characters and this world got under my skin, essentially from the start. When Montes first came to me, he was wholly wicked, and Serenity wholly good. They were never supposed to fall in love. It wasn't just Serenity who fought it, it was me. But, as you know by now, these characters did fall in love, and the story became something else entirely from what I'd planned.

I hope you enjoyed reading *The Fallen World* series. I'm sorry to say that I don't plan on revisiting this world again. However, I do have plans in the future to write a four book post-apocalyptic series, though only time will tell when I'll release those! Until then, I hope you'll consider joining my newsletter at laurathalassa.com so that we can share more stories together in the future.

Until then—

Hugs and happy reading,

Laura

Keep a lookout for this new paranormal romance series
by Laura Thalassa and Dan Rix

Blood and Sin

Coming July 15, 2016!

Other books by Laura Thalassa

The Unearthly Series:

The Unearthly
The Coveted
The Cursed
The Forsaken
The Damned

The Fallen World Series:

The Queen of All that Dies
The Queen of Traitors
The Queen of All That Lives

The Vanishing Girl Series:

The Vanishing Girl
The Decaying Empire

Novellas:

Reaping Angels

BORN AND RAISED in Fresno, California, Laura Thalassa spent her childhood reading and creating fantastic tales. She now spends her days penning everything from young adult paranormal romance to new-adult dystopian novels. Thalassa lives with her husband and partner in crime, Dan Rix, in Oakhurst, California. For more information, please visit laurathalassa.com.

Made in the USA
San Bernardino, CA
16 April 2018